OUT WEST

STORIES OF THE AMERICAN FRONTIER

Mark Huenemann

Proficient Consulting LLC
PEORIA ARIZONA

Mark Huenemann/Proficient Consulting LLC
14861 N 88th Lane
Peoria, AZ 85381

Publisher's Note: This is a work of fiction. Names (with some historical exceptions), characters, places, and incidents are a product of the author's imagination. Locales and public names are sometimes used for atmospheric purposes. Except as already noted, any resemblance to actual people, living or dead, or to businesses, companies, events, institutions, or locales is completely coincidental.

Book Layout ©2017 BookDesignTemplates.com

Ordering Information:
Quantity sales. Special discounts are available on quantity purchases by corporations, associations, and others. For details, contact the publisher at the address above.

Out West/ Mark Huenemann – 2nd ed.
ISBN 978-0-9996962-2-4

Contents

Acknowledgements

My most sincere appreciation to the numerous friends who reviewed draft manuscripts, and to my wife for allowing me to sequester myself in my office for far too many hours and for proofing the edited manuscripts. Remaining errors are solely mine.

For West is where we all plan to go some day. It is where you go when the land gives out and the old-field pines encroach. It is where you go when you get the letter saying: Flee, all is discovered. It is where you go when you look down at the blade in your hand and the blood on it. It is where you go when you are told that you are a bubble on the tide of empire. It is where you go when you hear that thar's gold in them-thar hills. It is where you go to grow up with the country. It is where you go to spend your old age. Or it is just where you go.

–ROBERT PENN WARREN

PREFACE

The American West is a region filled with rich and varied history often obscured by the limitations and distortions of memory, myth and imagination. Mention the western frontier and images of scenic grandeur, desperadoes and gun-toting heroes spring to mind. This was as true a century and a half ago as it is today. Articles and brochures produced by railroads, land speculators, and others who stood to profit from increased settlement exaggerated the attributes of the region while ignoring its many perils. Romanticized depictions of life in the West, filled with larger-than-life characters, appeared in magazines, dime novels, and later in Hollywood films.

But behind the facade of melodrama characteristic of such accounts of frontier life, there lies another type of story. Ordinary people, either attracted by dreams of independence and prosperity or repelled by their current circumstances, crossed the Mississippi, the Missouri, the Platte, and other rivers in hopes of making a fresh start in life. As the Midwest became populated, many moved on toward harsher areas, sometimes simply to preserve the solitude to which they had become accustomed. Individuals or families sometimes relocated three, four or more times, each time penetrating farther into areas of the country that were anything but hospitable.

To say life in the early West was not easy for most people is a colossal understatement. Day after day they faced obstacles ranging from topography and climate to disease, poverty and loneliness. Some did not remain, either leaving of their own accord or forced to do so by factors beyond their control. But most stayed, determined to overcome the immense challenges of frontier life, and many succeeded. The lives of each of these often unremarkable but strong-willed people contain stories worth telling and lessons worth learning. The stories in this book, though fiction, attempt to provide some insight into life on the western frontier.

1 THE BOUNTY HUNTER

Clay should have known better. He'd made this trip many times before. Dozens of times. And he'd never had any trouble. Now, one bad decision had put him in serious jeopardy, and might even cost him his life. He pushed himself onward, half stumbling through waist deep snow, his eyes on the crest of the hill ahead of him. He kept a firm grip on his horse's reins, pulling the animal along behind him, his hands burning from the cold. How could he have let himself get this close to freezing to death after all he'd been through?

He paused to rest just a moment, and to let his horse catch its breath. He thought back over the past couple of days, and then the past years. He had worked too hard, endured too much, to let his life end this way. Yet he knew the odds were against him. He would be a very lucky man, indeed, if he ever again stood next to the big, black stove in the center of his one-room house, feeling the warmth of its fire.

Clay was a survivor. He came from a poor family, his mother widowed at an early age. When he reached the age of 15, he felt himself a burden on the mother he had watched age before her time. So he left her, and his five brothers and sisters, and set out on his own. The day he arrived in town, the streets were abuzz with news of war. America had entered a contest with Spain, and a fever of patriotism was spreading through the country. Clay set out for the nearest army post to enlist. He could do his nation some good and probably set some money aside at the same time. When the war was over, he'd come back and pursue his dreams of becoming a cattle baron.

It had taken two days to reach the army post. Clay received a not unfriendly welcome from a young lieutenant he encountered near the gate. The lieutenant accompanied him to a nearby building with a sign that said "Office". Inside, he was greeted by a gruff speaking soldier with several stripes on his sleeve. "So," said the sergeant, "you want to sign up, do you?" He looked Clay up and down without a hint of interest. "How old are you?", the sergeant asked. "Seventeen," Clay answered, "I'll be eighteen in a few months." The sergeant scowled. "If you're seventeen, I'm a dance hall girl," he growled. The lieutenant smiled. The sergeant looked at Clay again, and after what seemed like several minutes, spoke. "Tell you what, kid," the sergeant said, "let's have a little test. If you pass the test, I'll let you join up." Clay looked hopeful. "What kind of test?" he asked. "A shootin' test," the sergeant said. "If you can outshoot me, you're in." The lieutenant chuckled softly. Clay said nothing.

"Well?" said the sergeant. "You just gonna stand there?" Clay was startled by the man's rough demeanor. He tried to reply politely, "No, sir. I mean, yes sir. I mean, where do we shoot, sir?" The lieutenant let out a belly laugh, then said to the sergeant, "OK, sarge, tell the kid, where does he shoot? He's the first one that hung around long enough to ask that question." For the first time, the sergeant looked at Clay as though he were interested. He was silent for a moment, then said, "Follow me." He walked out of the office, leaving the door ajar. He crossed the parade ground and headed toward the main gate, with Clay and the lieutenant in tow. The sergeant passed through the gate and turned toward the afternoon sun. They walked about a quarter mile to the post cemetery. Clay noticed a collection of empty whiskey bottles lying near the entrance.

The sergeant turned to the lieutenant. "Lieutenant," he said, "you throw five of them whiskey bottles high as you can, one at a time." He did not address the young officer with "sir", and the lieutenant did not remind him of this oversight. The lieutenant bent down and picked up the first bottle. He faced away from the sun, then did his best to heave the bottle high into the air. The sergeant had his gun ready. He fired, the sound of the shot echoing against the timber walls of the fort. The bottle shattered. "Again!" commanded the sergeant. A second bottle was tossed, and a shot fired, but the bottle came to the ground with a slight thud. The lieutenant looked surprised. "What are you waitin' for?" asked the sergeant. The younger soldier tossed three more bottles into the air. The sergeant hit two of the three. "OK, kid," he said, "three out of five. Let's see if you're lucky enough to hit any."

The lieutenant had a curious look on his face. He picked up another bottle, and turned toward the sun. Clay was surprised to hear himself speak. "Hey," he called to the lieutenant, "not into the sun." The lieutenant did not smile. "What's the matter," he sneered, "don't want good light on your shooting?" He threw the bottle up and away from the men, into the sunlight, without giving Clay a chance to first draw his pistol. Clay watched the bottle fall to earth without getting off a shot. Then, he drew his gun. "Four to go, kid," said the sergeant. The lieutenant reached down and picked up four bottles, holding two between the fingers of each hand. Then, without warning, he flung all four bottles into the air, twirling and glinting in the sunlight. Clay fired five bullets as quickly as he could. None of the bottles made it to the ground intact. Shattered pieces of glass lay strewn across the cemetery. For an inordinate length of time, nobody said anything. Finally, the lieutenant spoke, "You used an extra bullet, kid," he said, "guess you broke the rules, so you lose." Clay was shocked. He'd never witnessed such an unfair spectacle in his life. "Well," he thought to himself, "if this is the army they can have it."

The sergeant, with a look of determination on his face, stepped toward Clay until the two were less than a foot apart. "Now what?" thought Clay, remembering his pistol had only a single bullet remaining. The sergeant spoke in a moderate tone. "I never said nothin' about how many bullets," he said. Then he drew his head back slightly, and looked Clay in the eye. "I never had to do this before," he said, "but I'm a man of my word. If you want in this man's army, I'll sign you right up." The lieutenant was wide-eyed. Then he walked toward Clay and took his hand. He shook Clay's hand as if he were a long lost friend and congratulated him on his fine shooting. "If there's anything we need in this outfit," he said, "it's somebody who can hit what he's aiming at." Clay was astounded at the lieutenant's behavior, but accompanied the two men back to the office. There, he signed the enlistment papers and became a U.S. soldier.

"Gotta keep movin'," Clay prodded himself. He forced himself to take another few steps through the snow. His horse, a strong and dependable gelding, now appeared to be having as much trouble as Clay making its way through the drifts of snow. Ice had formed on the horse's nostrils, and each breath produced a cloud of frigid condensation. Clay noticed the horse was shivering. "Not a good sign," he mused to himself, and he took another step. "C'mon," he said aloud to the horse, "if we can just make it to the top of that ridge, we might see a house or campfire." Clay wasn't at all sure either would appear, but was intent on encouraging his horse to continue the battle.

Clay's army unit was sent to Cuba. They were given a send-off that included patriotic speeches, hugs and kisses for soldiers who had wives or girlfriends, and music by a high school band. Then, the troops boarded a train to begin what would be for most of them their first trip away from home, and their first encounter with the carnage of war. Many left home as boys filled with dreams of heroism and returned as men with worried faces and looks of hurt in their eyes. Clay adapted better than most. He hated the thought of killing another human being but believed that those on the wrong side of the law, or the wrong side of a war, somehow deserved to die. He served bravely and was offered a battlefield commission, which he declined by explaining that he did not see himself as someone willing to risk others' lives, no matter the cause involved. His superiors tried to convince him otherwise, but he insisted on carrying out his duty as an ordinary soldier.

When the war ended, the survivors of his unit were welcomed home with as much gusto as they had been sent off to fight. Many of his compatriots reveled in their newfound status as veterans. Some would regale their saloon companions with war stories, including a graphic description of the charge up San Juan Hill. Clay knew that some of the storytellers had not been on San Juan Hill. He also knew there had been no mounted charge on the famous hill. He and his fellow soldiers, most of whom were black-skinned, had fought their way up the side of the mountain on foot, with bullets whizzing by their heads and occasionally finding their mark. But Clay never corrected the men's false tales of heroism. He believed they would have to answer some day for their exaggerations, and if they wooed a fellow saloon patron into buying a round of whiskeys as a reward for their supposed bravado, more power to them.

It was after the war that Clay headed west to Wyoming, anxious to make his dream of becoming a cattle baron a reality.

He signed on as a ranch hand at the Double Bar, working for the father of one of his army friends. He was dependable, worked hard, and learned his trade quickly and well. He got along with his fellow hands and the trail boss, and the ranch's owner liked him from the start, which is no doubt the reason he was able to secure a special arrangement regarding his employment. Rather than taking his pay all in cash, as most of the ranch hands did, Clay took half in cash and the other half in spring calves. Each autumn, at the close of the fall roundup, the trail boss would gather the hands for a trip to town, where they would receive their annual pay. The ranch's owner had already made his own trip to town, where he authorized the trail boss's withdrawal of the total amount due to all the hands for the year's work.

When they rode into town, the Double Bar group would tie their horses near the saloon, then walk down the street toward the bank. The trail boss went into the bank alone and, after a few minutes, emerged with a large envelope full of cash. Standing on the boardwalk in front of the bank, the trail boss would grasp a fistful of bills in his rough, weathered hands, and carefully count out the amount owed each eager recipient. The drovers would stuff the bills into their front pockets, and head back toward the saloon, where a variety of entrepreneurs waited to relieve them of their hard-earned year's wages. Clay's portion was always half of the others', with the other half reserved for payment in the form of newborn calves the following spring. He stood next to the trail boss, feigning small talk until the other hands disappeared into the saloon. Then he placed a small amount of money in his pocket and entered the bank to deposit the rest.

The ranch owner, fond of Clay and appreciative of his dedication, agreed to let Clay's calves graze on the ranch along with the main herd. This was with the understanding that, someday, Clay hoped to separate his cattle from the herd and begin his own operation. This required that each spring, when the ranch owner gave Clay his annual allotment, the young calves had to be branded. Clay registered a brand and had the town blacksmith make two identical branding irons, in the belief that at some point he would need more than one. Each year several ranch hands offered help in branding Clay's new calves, which he gladly accepted. The first year, one of the hands questioned Clay regarding his brand. "What's it supposed to be,", the man asked, "it looks like two peaks and a snake?" The corners of Clay's mouth turned up just slightly. "The two peaks are the letter M," he replied, "and the snake is an S." The other man pondered this information. "What's the MS stand for?", he asked. Clay answered, "Mountain Shadows. It's what I'm going to call my ranch when I'm on my own." The other man teasingly replied, "Well, I hope it's near a mountain, or you're going to have to change that name." Clay turned toward the man without smiling. "That's the name," he said, ending the conversation.

It took nearly ten years for Clay to build his collection of calves and their descendants into a group of cattle that would pass for a small herd. Meanwhile, he continued to bank the cash portion of his payment until, one evening after sundown, he walked to the main house and told the ranch owner he had made a down payment on his own spread. Although Clay had expected the conversation to be awkward, the rancher seemed genuinely pleased that Clay had made enough progress to go out on his own. The next day Clay made the rounds of the ranch hands, thanking them for their friendship and wishing each of them well. Two men offered to help guide Clay's herd of cattle the three days drive from the Double Bar to his new ranch. Clay was grateful for their help and in an act of generosity he could scarcely afford gave each of them a single calf, hoping it would be their start down the road to becoming independent ranchers.

The land that Clay purchased was not ideal for ranching. A stranger visiting the area, which would have been a rarity, might have described the area as dry, dusty, and desolate. It was covered with scrub brush and low cactus, with scant rainfall and just two small creeks. But the creeks were fed by snowmelt from the nearby mountains, and when they were full the water ran clear and cold. To Clay, the ranch was a dream come true. He had purchased the eastern third of a large tract and had an option on the other two-thirds, including a portion of the foothills that butted up against the snow-covered mountains. He was determined to succeed in ranching and to own the entire tract as soon as he could raise and sell enough cattle to pay for it.

Halfway up the slope, Clay stopped to listen. He cupped his ear, straining in vain for any sound that could indicate the presence of another human. A voice, a neighing horse, the bellow of an orphaned calf, anything that called out of the cold to announce he was in the vicinity of other people. He heard nothing. He turned back toward his horse. He noticed a red stain in the snow. Earlier, he had dislodged a chunk of ice that had built up on the horse's nose, completely covering one nostril. Perhaps he had caused a small wound which would quickly clot, then heal over a few days' time. He hoped that was the case. But Clay also knew he had caused the horse to exert itself beyond reason. In a desperate bid to advance through the drifts, he had pushed the horse past its limits. It was possible the source of the blood was his mount's lungs. If so, the horse could make little more headway before it would collapse, facing almost certain death. Clay cursed silently, something he seldom did, blaming himself for the horse's predicament as well as his own.

The first winter on his ranch had been the worst. Clay stayed on as a hired hand until the spring roundup and branding were complete. It was a late spring, so he had not moved to his own spread, proudly named Mountain Shadows, until early summer. Along with tending his herd, he began to build a small barn and much smaller house. Both were of timber beam and log construction, a method that is more than challenging when attempted by a single individual. During mid-summer, when work on the Double Bar was light, some of Clay's former fellow hands volunteered their help at Mountain Shadows. By fall, framing of the walls of both buildings was completed and the rafters had been set in place. Clay was hopeful both buildings would be enclosed before cold weather set in. Then he could spend his first winter on his own ranch, in his own house, built with his own hands.

Winter came early that year. The first big squall came down out of the mountains in mid-November. It dropped two feet of snow on the foothills, and over a foot at Clay's ranch site. He shoveled the snow out of the partially built buildings and re-sumed construction. But it was not to be. A second snowstorm followed closely on the heels of the first, striking three days be-fore Thanksgiving. Clay's attention was of necessity focused on protecting his precious herd of cattle from the elements. He worked sunup to sundown, fighting his way through snow drifts to find and retrieve cows scattered in the storm. He managed to get them herded into sheltered areas close to the barn, or in the trees at the edge of the foothills. He did all he could to save them, knowing some would undoubtedly be lost before spring.

Year by year, Clay pushed himself to complete his homestead, improve his ranch, and build up his herd. He worked alone, content to be away from other people, with only his trusty horse and growing herd of cattle as companions. He was satisfied with the progress he made, But his was a story of one step forward, and then a step back. Each time he pro-gressed along his envisioned path toward becoming a wealthy cattle baron, an obstacle was thrown into his path that stopped his progress. Disease, hard winters, wolves, mountain lions, and the inevitable process of aging all took their toll on Clay. After several cycles of ups and downs, fortune and misfortune, he found himself struggling and carrying substantial debt. With little hope of being able to repay what he had borrowed, he was about to lose the ranch. One day soon he would receive a visit from the sheriff, who would have the unpleasant duty of telling Clay the bank had foreclosed on the ranch and he must leave his home.

It was a clear, cold day in early December when a neighboring rancher rode to Mountain Shadows to tell Clay about some excitement that had taken place in town. In a matter of fact manner, he told Clay about a bank robbery he had witnessed the prior day. According to the visitor, two men had robbed the local bank, making off with a considerable sum. As the thieves mounted their horses to make their escape, a bank employee gave chase on foot and a bystander, who suddenly realized what was happening, attempted to grasp the reins of one of the robbers' horses. The escaping robbers fired two shots, striking the bank employee and the bystander. The sound of shooting brought the sheriff, who quickly ordered some nearby men to carry the two wounded men to the doctor's office. According to the visitor, one of the citizens felt for a pulse on the wounded bystander and said, "There's no need to take this one to the doctor." Upon hearing news of the fatality, the bank manager promptly offered a sizeable reward for the capture of the criminals involved. As a crowd of townspeople gathered, the sheriff announced, "I'll witness the reward offer, to be paid to whoever brings in alive the men you just saw do the shooting."

Several citizens objected to the requirement that the lawbreakers be captured alive, preferring the reward be offered on the terms "dead or alive." The sheriff, however, insisted the men be captured alive. "We don't know which one did the shooting," he said. "We're going to hang him, but we're not going to put two men to death if only one is a murderer." The neighbor told this portion of the story with enthusiasm, as if the tale were one containing good news. When finished with his story, the visitor paused, then asked Clay, "Well, what do you think?" Clay shook his head. "I don't think anything except I guess the sheriff is right," he said. "But the sheriff is the one who asked me to come tell you," the visitor declared, excitement in his eyes. "They tracked that pair of outlaws to the north end of the foothills and then a ways up into the mountains and lost them in the snow. The sheriff is sure they're headed to the back side of the mountain, to hole up there. He says you're the only one who knows the area and is good enough with a gun to bring 'em in."

Clay leaned toward the man next to him. "The sheriff said that?" he asked. "Yup," the man responded, "just like I told you. There's a good reward on those fellows, and it might just be big enough to help you hang on to your ranch." This was unexpected and uninvited. Clay had enough of killing in the war. He addressed the visitor, "I'm not a bounty hunter," he said, "I don't hunt down people." The visitor responded, "I'm not saying you do, or that you should. Nobody's askin' you to hunt anybody down and kill 'em. They don't want these guys dead. Like I told you, they want 'em alive."

Clay thought for a moment. No question, whoever held up the bank had not only stolen, but murdered a man. They deserved to die. But that was up to a judge and jury. Could he even find them? And if he did, could he capture them? And if so, how could he get them back across the mountain? What if he got the drop on them but they refused to come along back? What option would he have? Shoot them? No, he wouldn't do that. The whole thing just didn't make sense. "Sorry," he told the visitor, "I'm not interested." The man looked disappointed. "Well," he said, "it's up to you. And it's your ranch." Clay thanked the man for making the trip to his ranch. They shook hands. The visitor mounted his horse, shook his head, and rode off.

The piercing cold brought Clay's mind back to the present. Never before had the possibility of his own death so confronted him. Not even during the war, with bullets passing within inches of him and striking people around him. This was different. This was a thing of his own doing, and it was impossible to deny. The colder and more exhausted Clay became, the more vivid were the images of the world around him. The crisp, clear air. The crunch of the snow under his feet. The labored breathing of his horse, and the piercing, numbing cold that made his hands refuse to obey his simple commands. He hurt, inside and out. But he was not going to give up. He was over three-fourths of the way up the ridge. He was not going to quit now.

Clay's horse slowed his progress, but he refused to abuse it anymore. He waited until the pitiful animal seemed willing to take another step, then gently pulled on the rein. When the horse moved, Clay moved. When the horse stopped, Clay stopped. He tried to encourage it. "C'mon! Giddup! Move!" He half ordered, half pleaded with the animal. If only the steed understood that the top of the ridge meant survival. From there, they could survey the surrounding countryside, search out signs of human activity, and set their course down the slope toward whoever lived on that side of the mountain. "C'mon! Take a step! You can do it!" Clay was talking aloud to the horse, and silently to himself.

The day Clay decided to go after the bank robbers had dawned crisp and clear. The weather was unpredictable on this side of the mountains, but the sun was shining, the air was clear, and only a few clouds could be seen near the horizon. Clay had a plan. He would ride to the cabin in the foothills, where he often stayed when he searched for strays that had wandered into the trees and toward the mountains. He would stay there overnight, then set out early the next day in order to reach the back side of the mountain while it was still good and light. There, he would hope to pick up a trail. Two horses, riding together, tracks just a couple days old. He would find their camp, take a position above it, and wait.

Clay was a patient man, and he intended to use that attribute to his advantage. He would wait as long as it took. Then, when the men were at ease, eating or napping or simply away from their rifles, he would call down to them and tell them he had them covered. If either of them made a move for a rifle, he was a good enough marksman to place a slug directly into the stock of the gun, sending splinters flying and showing his prey they were dealing with someone who could hit whatever he wished. If they surrendered, he would tie them, place them on their horses, and lead them back the way he had come. If they resisted, he would use his talent with a gun to convince them their only option was to give up. He would take them back to the cabin, make himself stay awake during the night to guard them, then lead them down out of the foothills to his homestead. There, he would securely hogtie them inside the barn, while he rode to a neighbor who would take word to town that the sheriff could come collect his prisoners. Clay thought about the reward money. He had forgotten about it until now. He reprimanded himself, "Don't think too much about the money. Keep your mind on the task at hand. There's plenty of time for the money later." It was time to act.

Clay's stay in the foothills cabin was uneventful. He arrived just at dusk. He tied his horse to a nearby tree, loosened the saddle, and removed it and the blanket underneath. He carried both in one hand, and his rifle in the other. He opened the cabin door and looked inside. It was just as he had left it the prior spring, only dustier. He walked inside, laid out his bedroll, and went back out to tend to his horse. He fed it, brought it water from the creek behind the cabin, and massaged its shoulders and neck. He treated the horse as if it were an old friend, which it was. He had gotten it as a foal, and broken and trained it himself. He and the horse understood each other, and they got along well. He ate a couple strips of pemmican, washed down with water from the creek, lay down in his clothes and fell asleep.

He was up before dawn the next morning. He felt in the darkness for his boots, pulled them on, and rolled his bedroll without needing to see it. He had placed the saddle and blanket just beside the door. He picked them both up and stepped out the door. The horse neighed slightly, recognizing the shadowy figure in the doorway. Clay saddled the horse, then checked his belongings. His rifle was in its scabbard on the left side of the saddle, in front of the left stirrup. His grub bag, a canvas bag that contained a tin of coffee, a small cooking pot, several packages of pemmican, and some dried fruit, hung from the right rear of the saddle. A canteen and a bag of ammunition hung from the saddle's right front corner. His pistol was in its holster, loaded and ready. He ate some pemmican and some fruit, waiting for dawn to break. When it did, he surveyed the sky. There were more clouds than the day before, considerably more. The wind had shifted to the northwest, and it looked like it might snow.

Clay turned the horse toward the north, into the wind. The horse neighed once, shook its head side to side, then acquiesced. Horse and rider moved north along a familiar trail. This was not the trail they used the last time they had been near the cabin. In the summer, Clay crossed the mountain using what he called the "up and over" trail. It was a rather steep trail, with a rocky surface and multiple switchbacks. The "up and over" trail was trying for a horse and required one that was strong and surefooted, which Clay's horse was. But the rocky surface became slippery when it rained or snowed, and it was no place to be in the winter. So, Clay followed the much longer trail that wound around the north end of the mountain, hugging the upper edge of the wooded foothills. The trail surface was hard dirt, and it climbed and descended only gradually as it led Clay safely around the north end of the mountain. He thought about what a fine animal his horse was, and how glad he was to have it. He smiled when he thought about how many horses he would not trust on the "up and over" trail. Clay nudged his horse into a trot, mindful of the distance he needed to travel before nightfall.

It was not until Clay rounded the north end of the mountain that he could get a full view of the sky. It had been hidden behind the peaks during his trek along the east side of the mountain, but now he had a clear picture. What he saw was not encouraging. Clay knew the signs of an impending snowstorm. The clouds, their color, their shape, the wind direction. All indications were that a storm was coming. The temperature had dropped and the wind had picked up. Now, as he turned his mount toward the west, the force of the wind struck them both fully in the face. He pulled his sheepskin coat up around his neck, pulled his hat firmly down, and rode into the weather.

An hour after they had turned west, Clay and his horse had passed the north end of the mountain and gradually began to turn south. The sting of the wind lessened somewhat, though the clouds appeared more threatening than they had earlier. The trail continued to follow the tree line at the top of the foothills, sometimes offering a view over the trees to the valley beyond, but for the most part was hidden from view. In another couple of hours, they would be entering the area where the lawbreakers were likely camped. Clay would have to be very alert and keep his horse quiet. If the men he was hunting sensed his presence, they would bolt down the mountain and head for the treeless land below the foothills. Once on the open range, it would be impossible for a single pursuer to apprehend them.

As he traversed the area above the creek on the west side of the mountain, the area where anyone hiding out would most likely be found, only once did Clay think he spotted something in the woods below. He was rounding a boulder that had fallen onto the trail when his horse suddenly went stiff, its nostrils flared. The horse seemed to sense that silence was imperative. The animal and its rider were motionless and quiet. Clay heard a noise to his right. He stealthily pulled his rifle from its holder and slowly turned to face the sound. It was a false alarm. Just a young mountain lion, barely old enough to be hunting on its own. Clay made a clicking sound with his tongue. The young lion, startled, looked toward the sound, then quickly turned and ran off through the trees. Clay patted his horse's neck and spoke soothingly to it. The duo continued on.

About a mile farther down the trail, Clay smelled smoke, the unmistakable odor of a recent campfire. His senses tingled, every part of him alert to any signs of nearby humans. He stopped his horse. He peered down through the trees, straining to see where the smell came from. Then he saw a dark, smoldering mound of firewood surrounded by a circle of rocks. The snow had been trampled, twigs were broken off trees, and a small tent was sitting next to the smoking fire remains. Clay dismounted. With his rifle in one hand and pistol in the other, he slowly began his way down the slope toward the campsite. Fifty yards away, then forty, then thirty. He stopped and listened. Nothing. He looked around to make sure it was not a trap. He barely breathed. He waited.

A moment later, Clay heard distant voices, far off to the west, away down the slope. Whether they had heard him approach or simply decided it was time to move on, he could not be sure. But of one thing he was certain. They were gone, and he had missed his chance. His thoughts turned to Mountain Shadows Ranch. How would he ever be able to keep it now? He should have started after the men the instant he heard about them. He was a fool to wait. He trudged back uphill toward his horse. "Well," he thought, "what's done is done." He replaced his rifle, put his left foot in the stirrup, and swung his right leg over the saddle. In a way, he felt relieved. He was not looking forward to confronting the men, or to a possible gunfight. He signaled his horse that it was time to move on.

Clay knew he was more than halfway along the west side of the mountain. That meant that turning around and retracing their steps back to the foothills cabin would take several hours, and it would be dark long before they could get back. He had never taken the trail around the south end of the mountain in winter, though he had often used it when searching for strays in the summer and fall. The south end trail followed the tree line at the top of the foothills, just as the north end trail did. At the south end of the mountain, it turned east until it passed around the end of the mountain. Then it turned back toward the north, eventually intersecting the north end trail. Between the two, the north and south end trails, they encircled the entire mountain. However, following the south end trail meant that, after passing around the mountain and heading north, Clay would have to cross the Realto River.

The Realto barely deserved to be called a river. It was a shallow channel, without water most of the year, but nearly 100 yards wide. Clay had ridden across it many times, either as a dry creek bed or a small stream fed by melting snow. In midwinter it was frozen solid, and the only risk of crossing it was slipping on the ice. But in late fall or early spring, it could be filled with ice cold water covered by a coating of ice. The thought of crossing the Realto this time of year was not inviting, but neither was the prospect of returning the longer way and riding the north trail after dark. Clay nudged his horse into a trot and continued south.

By maintaining a fast, steady trot, Clay managed to reach the south end of the mountain with more than an hour of daylight left. The temperature had dropped and snow had begun to fall. The saddle creaked in the cold, and the horse's breath raised clouds of steam as it carried Clay along the narrow trail. As they turned east to go around the end of the mountain, the rate of snowfall increased. After more than an hour traveling east, Clay followed the trail's turn to the north. The horse, sensing that home was in the direction ahead, picked up the pace a bit. Clay did not try to hold it back. He was as anxious to get home as the horse was. The stress of hunting for the bank robbers had taken its toll. When that stress was relieved, Clay felt dead tired. As he thought about the missed chance to save his beloved ranch, the horse carried him toward home.

Clay had drifted into a state of semi-sleep, with his sheepskin pulled well up over the lower part of his face, when he felt the need to be awake. He was suddenly aware that his horse was walking very slowly. As his head cleared, he realized they were crossing the river. Without any guidance from him, the horse had stepped onto the frozen surface of the Rialto and was gingerly picking its way toward the other side. They were near the midpoint of the river, as the horse carefully put one foot after another onto the slippery surface. Clay knew he could only sit still and trust his mount.

They were nearly three-fourths of the way across the Rialto when he heard the Crack! Crack! of the ice. Clay's horse was frightened by the sound and changed its gait from a very slow walk to a rapid one. "Easy, whoa," Clay whispered to the horse. Another Crack! This time the horse tried to break into a gallop. Clay pulled sharply on the reins. "WHOA! Easy now!" he pleaded. But the horse was determined to get off the unfamiliar, noisy surface. It made two more strides before crashing through the ice and falling on its right side. For an instant Clay feared he might be crushed, but he managed to pull his feet out of the stirrups and free himself from the saddle. His head went under water. The shock of its icy coldness caught him by surprise. He grasped for reins, but they were not within reach. He tried to swim, but his heavy coat and winter clothing pulled him down. He kicked and hit something solid. It was the river bottom. He put his foot down and pushed up. He stood. The water was only waist deep. "Hallelujah!" he thought, "I'm not going to drown!"

It was not easy to wade the final few yards to shore. Clay's clothes were soaked and his boots were filled with water that was rapidly turning to ice. When he pulled himself up on the bank, his horse was standing directly in front of him with a questioning look on its face. The saddle was still intact, but Clay's rifle and the grub bag were gone, under the ice in the Rialto. His pistol had stayed in its holster but was wet and temporarily useless. Both Clay and his horse were thoroughly soaked, standing in over two feet of snow, with more falling by the moment. The north wind was attacking with a vengeance. Clay knew he had only two options. Find warmth, a fire, a house, a camp, some kind of shelter. Or freeze to death just half a day's ride from home.

Clay climbed up on his horse, kicked it with his heels, and turned it east toward the valley. He knew he could not make it home. His only hope was to move fast enough to get to a ranch before he or his horse were too cold to function. Ahead, he saw a snow-covered ridge, the last barrier between him and the valley. Ah, the valley, someone lives there, someone with a warm house, with a fireplace, with hot coffee, and a warm bed. He became enamored by the thought of warmth.

Clay knew his life and that of his horse depended on riding rapidly to safety. He had never been one to raise his voice at an animal, but now he was yelling, screaming at his horse. "Faster, faster, go faster!" he shouted, "Run! Run! Run!" He was kicking the horse, slapping it with his frozen hands, frantically wanting it to gallop at full speed. It took a couple minutes for Clay to come to his senses. He noticed his hand was bleeding. The horse was snorting and shivering as it fought its way up the ridge. The snow here was chest deep on the horse, which was giving its all to carry its master to safety. But part way up the ridge, its desire to save Clay was no match for the snowdrifts through which it tried to carry him. The horse stopped, shuddered, and could go no more. Clay shivered also, constantly now, as he slid down off the horse and grasped the reins in one hand. He waded slowly ahead until he was in front of the horse, then pushed himself through the deep snow, forming a narrow trench in which the horse could follow. His feet were numb and felt like dead weights being drug through the snow. Thus they continued up the ridge. Clay was determined not only to save himself but to save the horse that had tried so valiantly to save him.

Clay was clear-headed now, although the cold was penetrating him to a degree that was certain to rob him of his senses before long. He tried to focus. The sun was setting. He knew that on this side of the mountain the light from the setting sun played tricks on the eyes. Many times, as he rode home while dusk approached, he was certain he saw a campfire blazing in the distance. He must have seen them a dozen times before he realized the campfires were mirages. Tricks on the eye, refractions or reflections from the colored rocks at the edge of the mountains. He wondered if his horse saw them, too. He was brought back to reality by a tug on the rein in his hand. The horse had stopped. Clay turned back toward the animal and retreated to its side. He gently patted the horse's neck with his frozen hands and spoke softly. "Come on, fella," he said, "just a few more steps. The top of the ridge, then everything will be OK."

Somehow, Clay managed to drag himself and his horse to the top of the ridge. As they stood there together, broken, bleeding, exhausted, shivering, they looked out over the valley. And then he saw it. A flickering light. A campfire on the horizon. There were people there. They would make it. They were saved. He sat down in the snow, just to catch his breath, so he could yell loud enough for them to hear him. They would come and rescue him, and his horse, and take both of them to the campfire. To the fire, to the warmth, to the hot coffee, and the warm, dry clothes. And then to the house, to the fireplace, to the warm bed. He leaned up against the warmth of his horse and closed his eyes. It all felt so good.

2 THE SHERIFF

Ben Jackson looked intently at the picture before him, trying to remember if he'd seen the face before. He didn't
think so. The picture, which was a bit fuzzy, showed the
rather boyish face of a man who was probably in his mid-
twenties. He appeared to have fair skin, a thin nose, small ears,
and thick, dark hair that was slightly wavy. His ears were small
but stood away from the sides of his head to a noticeable degree. A small scar, about three-quarters of an inch long, ran di-
agonally from the middle of his left cheek, toward his chin.
There were no other distinguishing marks.

Ben read the information printed below the picture, then
placed the poster on the left side of his desk and picked up another. This one showed an older man, perhaps fifty or fifty-five
years old. His skin was dark. His graying hair was long and disheveled, and he wore a thin beard and mustache. His face appeared deeply wrinkled, and his dark eyes were scowling. He
may have been Mexican; it was hard to tell from the picture. The
name printed above the picture was unfamiliar to Ben, as was

the man's face. Ben stared at the picture a full minute, committing it to memory. He placed the poster on top of the prior one.

Ben was reaching for a third poster when he heard footsteps on the sidewalk outside the office. He removed his glasses, opened the top left drawer of his desk, and carefully placed them in the drawer. The door opened and a short, gray-haired man entered the office. The man appeared to be past sixty years of age, but walked and moved quickly. He stopped in front of Ben's desk, removed his glasses, and began wiping them with a handkerchief pulled from the rear pocket of his pants.

Ben spoke first. "Good morning, Doc," he said, his eyes still trained on the poster he had been reading. "Morning, Ben," the doctor replied, "Reading up on the latest desperados?" Ben gave a half smile. "Part of the job," he said, "gotta recognize 'em if they come through town." Doc returned the smile, picked up the top poster, and quickly examined it. "They sure print their names big," he said, "That, and the reward amount. Guess that's a good thing, don't you think?"

Ben did not answer the doctor's question. He pushed his chair back, rose to his feet and walked to the window. He looked out at the street and, with his back to his visitor, said, "Nice, clear morning. Sun is shining, not much wind. Peaceful. Let's hope it stays that way." "Wish it would, too," the doctor replied, "but I wouldn't bet on it. Too many fools out there think they want to be somebody."

Doc did not elaborate and did not need to. Ben knew what he was referring to. Once a lawman established the reputation of being good with a gun, there was no shortage of people who wanted to be the one to outshoot him. Young hotheads, older men with no other hope of making their mark in the world, or ex-convicts with a grudge against the man who had helped put them in prison. Sometimes, a relative or friend determined to avenge the death of some unfortunate soul who had challenged Sheriff Jackson with a gun.

"Well," said Doc, "guess I'll get over to my office. Got a patient or two to see this morning. See you at the cafe for lunch?" "Guess so," said Ben, "not much to eat around here when we don't have any prisoners." The doctor opened the door, stepped onto the sidewalk, and walked toward the east end of town.

The sheriff's office, one of the newer buildings in town, was situated at the west end of the main street. Some civic leaders thought it should be built near the middle of town, but Sheriff Jackson wanted it at the west end of town. The office was far from the bank, the dry goods store, the saloon, and the livery stable, all of which were nearer the east end of town. But the Sheriff was insistent, and the others acquiesced. A place like Plainview was lucky to have a Sheriff with Ben Jackson's reputation, and the townspeople were inclined to let him have his way.

The back door to the sheriff's office opened, and Deputy Bill Carson walked past the empty cells and into the front room. "Good morning, Ben," he said. Without waiting for a reply, Carson continued, "Just came from the livery stable. One strange horse in there today. Came in about dusk yesterday, according to Pete. I asked about the fellow, but Pete hadn't noticed anything unusual about him. Pete did say the horse appears to have been ridden quite a while since it was tended to. One shoe loose and badly in need of grooming." Deputy Carson paused, and his eyes met Ben Jackson's. The Sheriff was listening closely.

Carson went on, "The guy's staying at Mrs. Sanders' rooming house and ate breakfast this morning at the cafe. Mrs. Sanders said the guy looked to be about twenty-five or so. He said he didn't have any relatives in town, that's why he's at the rooming house. Said he had a bedroll and a small pack, his clothes looked like he'd been riding quite a while, and he seemed a little nervous. And he's wearing a gun belt. Probably nothing, but thought you'd wanna know. I told Emmet and Sally over at the cafe to keep an eye on him too."

"OK, Bill," said the sheriff. " Keep tabs on him, and let me know of anything that seems out of the ordinary." Sheriff Jackson turned to look out the window, in the direction of the cafe. "Oh," he said, "and you better look through the new wanted posters. They're on the desk."

Deputy Carson walked to the desk and picked up the top poster. The deputy was a tall, slender man, with dark hair, a strong jaw, and a mildly pock-marked face. He was well liked in Plainview. He had a pleasant mannerism, spoke slowly and calmly, and was a competent, dependable lawman. He had come to Plainview several years earlier at the invitation of Ben Jackson. The two had known each other for years, and Carson had at one time served as a deputy under Jackson in another state. When Plainview needed a deputy, it had taken the sheriff only a couple of weeks to locate and hire Bill Carson.

"Think I'll clean the rifles and make sure they're loaded and ready, just in case," Carson commented. "Just in case what?" asked the sheriff. "Nothing in particular," replied Carson, "never hurts to be prepared."

Bill Carson took a rifle and a steel cleaning rod from the rack on the side wall of the office. He examined the weapon, a forty-four caliber Winchester repeater. He walked to the desk, opened the bottom left drawer and retrieved a piece of cloth and a small bottle of oil. He reached into his pocket, withdrew a folding knife and opened it. He cut a small piece off the cloth and inserted it into a slot in the end of the cleaning rod. He opened the bottle and dabbed a small amount of oil on the cloth. Holding the rifle vertically, he carefully pushed the rod down the rifle's barrel, then pulled it back out. He repeated this several times. When he was satisfied the Winchester's bore was clean, he put a small drop of oil on the trigger mechanism, then wiped the rest of the rifle with the remaining dry cloth. He took a box of cartridges from the bottom right drawer of the desk and began loading the Winchester.

Bill Carson's boss, Sheriff Jackson, had a long and storied career. After serving in the Army as a junior cavalry officer, he held the sheriff's position in several towns back East. In one of those towns, he met Bill Carson, who shortly became one of Jackson's deputies. Later, Jackson became a U.S. Marshall. The government moved him to a series of western jurisdictions. Tired of the frequent relocations, Jackson decided to quit his post as a marshall and find a town in which he could settle as the local sheriff, which is how he ended up in Plainview.

Ben Jackson viewed his profession in simple terms. It was his job to enforce the law, not to make it or bend it. Outlaws broke the law and deserved the punishment that befell them. He was known as a fair and honest man and a dedicated law officer. He took his work seriously but never became emotionally involved in it. When he pursued a criminal, he did so with dogged determination but without personal malice. Like other lawmen, Ben Jackson sometimes found himself in circumstances that required shooting another person, and he did so without hesitation or remorse. He did not like killing others, but it was their choice to run afoul of the law and, eventually, pay the price for what they had done.

Jackson was a skilled marksman who could draw from a holster with exceptional speed. As he gained experience and expertise as a lawman, he garnered a reputation as a no-nonsense person not to be trifled with. Early in his career, Ben had been involved in some dramatic shootings. These incidents, in which he had quickly ended the careers and the lives of several outlaws of renown, earned Ben a reputation as a gunman any sensible person would not want to come against. Long before he came to Plainview, people of the community had heard about Ben Jackson the gunman.

Unfortunately, Ben's performance as a sharpshooting lawman attracted the uninvited attention of two types of people. His success in apprehending numerous criminals resulted in a number of people who did not appreciate his role in sending their relatives or friends to prison or to a cemetery. In addition, an occasional misguided individual attempted to make a name for himself by challenging Ben Jackson to a shootout. The fact that Ben consistently defeated these fame seekers only enhanced his reputation and added to his unwanted notoriety. Try as he might, Ben Jackson did not escape his fame by settling in Plainview.

Emily Sanders had promised Deputy Bill Carson she would observe the new boarder at her rooming house and communicate anything unusual or noteworthy. This was not the first time such a request had come her way, and she willingly cooperated. Of course she did not want to experience a repeat of what had occurred with a similar boarder less than a year earlier. It was mid-summer, as she recalled, when a stranger had arrived in Plainview and taken a room in her house. The boarder was quiet, bordering on sullen, and kept to himself for several days. He seemed to be brooding about something, but Emily Sanders had no idea what it was.

One afternoon the boarder walked to the saloon, drank rapidly for about an hour, and became loud and boisterous. He then stumbled out of the saloon and began yelling for the sheriff, daring Ben Jackson to face him in the street. Sheriff Jackson came out of his office and attempted to talk the man into returning to the saloon, even offering to buy him a drink. But the stranger could not be dissuaded, and pulled a revolver, threatening the sheriff and others in the vicinity. The sheriff, seeing no alternative but to do what he had done many times before, drew his revolver and shot the man through the heart. It was later discovered that the man's only purpose in coming to Plainview had been to provoke a fight with Jackson, who had several years earlier tracked down and arrested the man's brother for murder.

The new boarder at Emily Sanders' house was not a sullen or quiet person. He was quite the opposite -- friendly, talkative, and generally cheerful. In fact, Mrs. Sanders thought him overly joyful. She did not understand what a man traveling alone, with few possessions, and staying in modest accommodations in a town full of strangers, had to be so happy about. A couple days after his arrival, as the young man was leaving her house for the cafe, Emily asked how long he intended to stay. "Just until my job here is done," he said, as he smiled at her and went cheerfully out the door. "Hmmm," thought Emily, "I wonder who he's working for, and doing what?" But, as long as he paid for his room, she guessed it was none of her business what his job was or when he planned to start working.

Several days later, Ben Jackson was sitting at his desk in the Sheriff's office. He had just poured a cup of hot coffee from the pot on the stove and was settling in to read the current week's edition of the Plainview Press. He leaned back in his chair, used one finger to push the brim of his hat upward, and adjusted his glasses. He sipped some coffee, put the cup down, and began reading. "Not much news this week," he thought, "same as usual." He got up from his desk, took a couple steps, and looked at the clock on the wall. Five-thirty. Almost time for supper. He sat down and resumed reading.

As Ben scanned the newspaper, his thoughts drifted back in time. Back to when he was perhaps the best known U.S. Marshall west of the Mississippi. When his name was frequently in the newspaper. When headlines like "U.S. Marshall Catches Desperate Killer," or "Marshall Jackson Outguns Notorious Outlaw," were followed by articles touting his status as an exemplary enforcer of the law and his prowess as a gunman.

Those days were gone now, except for instances like the fellow he had been forced to gun down a year or so ago. But Ben could never be sure they were gone forever. He was always aware that the unfortunate incident from a year ago might be repeated. There were plenty of people who might think they had reason to wish him harm. But things had been quiet in Plainview for many months and he hoped they would remain that way.

Ben was jarred from his daydreaming by a man's voice. Someone was calling, "Sheriff! Sheriff Jackson!" The sound of footsteps on the sidewalk told him someone was walking rapidly toward the sheriff's office. Ben put the paper down, removed his glasses, and quickly placed them in his desk drawer. An instant later, the front door of the sheriff's office flew open and Emmet Walker entered. Emmet, the owner of the town's only cafe, was a nice enough fellow, but rather excitable. "What's the rush, Emmet?" Ben asked. "I came right over to tell you," Emmet replied. "To tell me what?" asked Ben. "Well, Bill asked me several days ago to tell you if that new fella that's boarding over at Emily's place done anything unusual or strange, or such." Emmet was speaking rapidly, in a high pitched voice. "Well," he continued, "it's kinda strange, so I thought you should know."

Ben Jackson frowned at Emmet, wondering when he was going to get to the point, when the back door of the office opened. Bill Carson entered the office and strode casually to the front, where he stood next to Ben. Emmet took up where he had left off, "Like I was sayin', maybe it's not so strange, but …" Ben interrupted, "Emmet, for gosh sakes, what is so strange, or not so strange?" Emmet paused, then said, "Well, that new boarder of Emily's, he was in the cafe for lunch, and then when he was leaving he said he was going over to the saloon, and then when he was good and ready he was going to do the job he came here to do. Only thing is, I don't know that he has a job, nobody ever sees him work, and I don't …."

They all heard the shout that came from outside the office, from the middle of the street. It was the stranger. He was calling out Sheriff Jackson. "Come on out, you good for nothin' murderer." the stranger yelled. "Come out here so I can finish you off like you got comin'."

Bill Carson was the first to react. He walked slowly over to the gun rack on the side wall of the office, and picked up the Winchester. He turned to face Ben Jackson, and calmly said, "I'm going out to do a little target practice." Ben nodded. "Fine," he said, "I'm sure I can talk some sense to that young hothead out there." Emmet Walker looked incredulous. He stared at Bill. "I don't believe you just said that!" he said, in a near whisper. "There's a crazy young coot out there that wants to kill Ben, and you're going target shooting?" Bill smiled. "Don't worry about a thing, Emmet." he said, "Ben knows just how to handle this type of thing." And without another word, Bill walked to the back door and left the office.

Ben Jackson lifted his gun belt from the hook behind his chair. He strapped it on, and fastened the holster tie around his thigh. He opened the top right desk drawer, which held a revolver and a wooden box of thirty-eight caliber cartridges. He picked up the gun, opened the cylinder, extracted one cartridge and placed it in the box. Then he closed the drawer and stood up. The stranger in the street called out again, "Ben Jackson, I know you're in there. Come on out here. Yer a stinkin' killer, and now yer gonna git yers!" Ben opened the cylinder of his revolver and began to load it. One cartridge fell to the floor, and he bent to pick it up. He carefully inserted five cartridges, put the revolver in its holster, and pulled down his hat. "Emmet," he said, "you stay put here. I'll be back in a few minutes."

The Sheriff walked to the front door of his office and slowly opened it. He stepped out onto the sidewalk. He could see the stranger standing in the middle of the street. A small crowd had gathered on the other side of the street, but they were now taking cover behind the edges of the buildings that lined the street. The stranger sneered, and spoke, "So, you ain't chicken after all, eh? Well, you're going to git what's comin' to you now." Ben looked straight toward the stranger and took a step into the street. The stranger squinted as he looked toward Ben. "You don't have to do this, kid," Ben said. "I've waited years to do this," the stranger responded, "and I'm finally going to do to you what you did to my pa!" Ben sounded calm. "I don't know who your pa was," he said, "but if he died by my hand like you say, it was for one reason. He broke the law and paid the price." The stranger's voice was louder now. "I ain't listenin' to you," he shouted, "yer a killer and liar. A murderer. You murdered my pa!"

The stranger's right hand begin to move. That's all it took. A single shot rang out. Both men stared at each other. Ben held his revolver in his hand. The stranger dropped his and fell face forward on the ground. One man emerged from among a group standing at the edge of a building near where the stranger lay and walked into the street. It was Doc Watson. He walked over to the stranger, knelt down and felt the man's neck. "He's dead," he said. "You two men there, pick him up and take him to my office. Then go and tell the undertaker he can come by in an hour and take care of him."

Emmet Walker opened the door for Sheriff Jackson. The sheriff walked into the office, took off his gun belt and hung it on a hook behind his desk. He pushed back the brim of his hat and sat down in the chair. "I can't hardly believe it," gushed Emmet, "he had the drop on you and you still got him! Wait 'till I tell folks that ain't here what you did!" Ben Jackson looked at Emmet. "Now don't you add anything to the truth of what happened out there, Emmet," he said sternly. "You don't have to worry about that, "said Emmet, "the truth is exciting enough!" Emmet thought a bit, and asked, "Can I take a look at your gun?" Ben feigned surprise. "If you don't shoot me with it," he said with a grin. Emmet pulled the revolver from its holster and opened the cylinder. There was one empty chamber. Emmet smiled a big smile. He put the revolver back in the holster, went to the door, opened it and rushed out.

The back door of the office opened. Ben did not look around. Bill Carson walked slowly into the office, nodded at Ben, and placed the Winchester back in the gun rack. "Well," said Ben, "guess I got another one." Bill grinned. "Yep," he said, "and as soon as Doc removes that forty-four slug, no one will ever know." Ben looked up at Bill. "I owe you and Doc a lot," he said. Bill was quiet for a moment. Then he said, "No, you don't. We're just doin' it to protect Plainview." Ben thought a bit, then said, "Well, I sure hope this is the last one." "Yup," said Bill, "me, too." Ben stood up, glanced around the office, and took a couple steps toward the front door. "See you tomorrow," he said. Bill nodded, turned, and started walking. The two men left the office, the sheriff by the front door and the deputy by the back.

3 The Cowboy

During the Civil War, the Union blockaded all shipping to and from the South. As a result, easterners were short of beef while herds of cattle multiplied in the South. By the end of the war, hundreds of thousands of unclaimed longhorns roamed throughout Texas. All cattlemen needed to do was round them up and get them to market. However, this was not an easy task. Railroads did not reach cattle country until well after the war, and prime destinations like Kansas and Missouri had outlawed cattle from Texas because longhorns carried ticks infected with Spanish fever, which was fatal to the local shorthorn stock.

Large-scale cattle drives began after the war as demand for marketable cattle dramatically escalated. Easterners wanted more beef and, in addition, the federal government was obligated to supply food to three sizeable groups: Indians subjugated onto reservations and promised provisions, soldiers spread across vast areas in an attempt to restrain Indians and protect settlers, and laborers working to expand the railroads across the great expanses of the West. The imbalance between supply and demand for cattle was so great that cattle worth four dollars in Texas brought as much as thirty dollars when transported to a rail terminus for shipment north or east.

Two years after the war Kansas revised its laws to permit Texas cattle to enter the western part of the state. A railroad spur turned Abilene into a busy cattle-shipping town and a key point on the Chisholm Trail. But the frenetic activity of the Abilene cattle yards lasted just five years. In 1872, having exhausted their patience with the antics of the cowboys who were paid when their drives ended there, the citizens of Abilene banned cattle drives from their town.

The cattlemen had other options. A number of trails headed north out of Texas and other communities clamored for the railroad expansion required to support the cattle-shipping trade. The Great Western Trail, established in 1877, ran from the southern tip of Texas to Dodge City, Kansas, and beyond. The Great Western remained in use until 1892 and carried more cattle than any other trail.

Dawn was just breaking as the rider brought his horse to a halt, swung his right leg over the horse's rump and slid down out of the saddle. He was tired, sore, hungry and thirsty. His clothes were covered with dust and his exposed skin was dirty and sunburned. He had not had a real bath in over a month and it was hard to tell which smelled worse - his body or the horse he had been riding.

He loosened the saddle cinches and lifted the saddle and saddle blanket from the horses back. The heat of the day was yet to come but the horse was already wet with sweat. The man carried the saddle and blanket to a grassy area near the chuck wagon, where he lay the saddle upside down to dry. Despite his small stature, he handled the saddle easily. Though barely five foot four, he was wiry and tough, and hard work made him stronger than his appearance might suggest.

He led the horse to a small stream at the edge of the camp, where the exhausted animal took a deep drink of water. Then, horse in tow, he walked around behind the chuck wagon. A row of halters hung near the wagon. He grabbed one and, restraining the horse by looping one arm around the animal's neck, removed the horse's bridle and replaced it with the halter. He tied the horse to the picket line and hung the bridle where the halter had been. He then took a metal cup from atop a wooden barrel attached to the side of the wagon, lifted the lid of the barrel and filled the cup with water. As the warm water met his parched lips, he glanced toward the horse. A slight grin appeared on his face as he considered whether the horse appreciated the fact that, on the cattle trails, horses drank before their riders.

The horse was one of over eighty that belonged to the company conducting the cattle drive. To ensure availability of fresh horses around the clock the normal ratio of horses to men on a drive was no less than six to one. Mr. Maxwell, the owner of the company, did not believe in running short of dependable horses. Thus he had supplied the eleven men on the trail crew with an ample quantity of good quality mounts. Mr. Maxwell also insisted that members of his company were of high quality and were held to high standards. This was the fifth consecutive year he had funded a cattle drive and he was not about to deviate from the practices that made the previous four drives success-ful.

The cowboy who had unsaddled and watered the horse walked wearily around the chuck wagon. He removed his hat, then reached down and removed his spurs. He loosened the bandanna that was tied around his neck and squatted down, resting against the front wheel of the wagon. The cook, who was kneeling at a small fire tending something in a cast iron pan, looked up and greeted the cowboy. "Long night, huh Billy?" he asked, "You hungry?" "You bet I am," replied the cowboy, "I'm so hungry I'd eat your cookin'." The cook grinned slightly, picked up a metal plate, filled it with hotcakes and handed it to Billy.

The cook liked the young cowboy who crouched oppo-site him washing down the stack of pancakes with gulps of hot coffee from a metal cup. He had met Billy two years earlier, when the two men signed on for Mr. Maxwell's third cattle drive and their first. When Billy joined the company he gave his name as William Corman, Jr. and told the other men he preferred to be called William, not Billy. But scarcely a week later he earned a nickname and had not been called William since then.

Mr. Maxwell always accumulated a herd of good, dura-ble horses for his cattle drives, but the herds included a number of horses either not fully broken for trail work or not broken at all. As part of the preparation for the drive, the cowboys were expected to ensure every horse was sufficiently tamed to prove useful on the trail. Breaking the previously un-ridden horses brought out the competitive spirit among the cowboys, and they were quick to recognize those with proficiency in bronc riding. William Corman, Jr. demonstrated superior ability to remain astride horses seeking to unseat him, and by the end of the second day of horse breaking was given the moniker "Buckin' Billy." The Buckin' part was soon dropped but Billy stuck and he answered to it from that day forward.

Billy was one of eight cowboys in the company, five of whom had ridden for Mr. Maxwell before. Though they worked closely together for weeks, men on cattle drives did not generally divulge much personal information. They addressed each other by first names or nicknames and seldom used each other's surnames. The qualifications for acceptance as a cowboy, horse wrangler, or chuck wagon cook were the skill to do the job well and the grit to endure the weeks of hard, dirty work on the trail. Personal histories were not part of the hiring process, and more than a minimal inquiry regarding another man's past was considered bad manners.

The most experienced cowboy with Mr. Maxwell's company, and also the biggest, was John T. He did not offer to explain the "T" and the others did not ask. Standing just over six feet tall, his large frame carried two hundred pounds, nearly all muscle. John T and Adam, another seasoned member of the group, had been with Mr. Maxwell since his first drive. Adam was nearly as tall as John T but considerably lighter. He was sinewy and agile and could rope a steer and bring it to the ground quicker than most men could ready their lariat.

It was the second Maxwell drive for three of the cowboys. Lefty, who spoke with a slight drawl, seemed to have an innate knowledge of cattle. He was known to alert the trail boss hours in advance that the cattle would be restless during the night, or that extra effort would be required to get the herd moving the next morning. None of the other men, including the boss, had any idea how Lefty knew these things.

Colorado and Lucas were also on their second Maxwell drive. Colorado's real name was a mystery but the nickname seemed fitting. He and Lucas had ridden together on a ranch east of the Rocky Mountains before coming to Texas. Both were top-notch cowboys and Mr. Maxwell was pleased when they signed on for another drive. He also assigned them the responsibility to look out for and help train the two newcomers to the trail, Jesse and Cal.

Jesse was a muscular young man with a shock of reddish blond hair and skin covered with freckles. He wore a perpetual grin and often added levity to the evening gatherings around the campfire by telling stories about his adventures in Alaska, a place the others were quite sure he had never seen. Cal, the other new man, was quiet and observant. He was not easily excited and the others admired his ability to remain calm when things got tense on the trail. Though not a tall man, he was sturdily built and seemed to have almost unlimited stamina.

Three additional men completed Mr. Maxwell's company. The trail boss, who had been with Mr. Maxwell since his first cattle drive, was a no-nonsense middle-aged man named Matthew Prescott. His friends called him Matt, but the men on the cattle drive just called him The Boss, never Matt or even Mr. Prescott. The horse wrangler, Jake, was a bull of a man, the type one would expect was capable of keeping eighty head of horses shod, trimmed and fed. He had a solitary bent but was liked by the other men. Rudy, the cook, did his best to turn the provisions carried on the chuck wagon into edible fare. The men did not complain about the food he cooked over a campfire and dished up on metal plates. After twelve hours or more of hard work on the trail it was not difficult to appreciate even mediocre cooking.

None of the men, including Billy, talked much about where they came from or what they did prior to their time in Texas. Like many others, when Billy went west he exchanged one difficult set of circumstances for another. He was born in Indiana shortly before the war began to a very young mother and an alcoholic father. Before Billy's first birthday his father left to join the army and was never heard from again. When Billy was four years old his mother, unsure if she was a widow or not, married an older businessman. The man attempted to form a relationship with Billy, but without success.

Billy developed a strong dislike for his home life and his time in school. He was bright but found school uninteresting. When he was eleven years old he encountered two things that were to greatly affect his life. First, he befriended a boy two years older who lived in the country. He began to spend his spare time on the friend's family farm, where he learned to ride and take care of horses. Second, he chanced upon a book entitled *True Adventures in the West* by Zachary Adams.

Although he was not much of a reader, after the first few pages Billy was hooked. Unaware that the book was fiction, he was completely entranced by its tales of adventure and excitement. He read of wagon trains, Indian skirmishes, gold strikes, riverboats, and cowboys. The romanticized life of the cowboys described in the book captured his imagination, and from then on Billy knew he wanted to go west to become a cowboy.

Shortly after he turned fifteen, tired of school and a fractious home life, Billy decided it was time to act. Early one morning he filled a knapsack with clothing, a couple of sandwiches and some apples, and wrote his mother a brief goodbye note. He walked to the train station where he slipped unnoticed through the open door of one of the freight cars. Inside the train car, he hid behind a shipping crate and waited for the train to start moving. It soon did and Billy began his journey west.

It took nearly a year for Billy to make his way from Indiana to Independence, Missouri. In the towns along the way he worked odd jobs, doing anything that could provide room and board and a little cash. He worked hard and spent little. By the time he got to Independence he had saved enough to buy a train ticket to Abilene, Kansas, which was then the end of the line, plus enough to buy a saddle, bridle, and other essentials in Abilene. Billy did not need a horse. Cattlemen normally supplied their cowboys with horses, but the cowboy was expected to furnish his own tack.

It took Billy less than two days to find employment on a ranch south of Abilene. The rancher was favorably impressed with Billy's work ethic and horsemanship and anticipated keeping the young fellow in his employ. But Billy had other plans. Working so close to Abilene, he regularly encountered cowboys who had driven cattle north from Texas. The drives terminated in Abilene and it was there the cowboys were paid. The sight of eighty or ninety dollars in a cowboy's hands was all it took to convince Billy his future was in Texas.

Billy had been cured of his earlier romantic notions about cattle, cowboys, Indians and the West in general. But hard work in the outdoors suited him and it seemed he was truly meant for life on the southern plains. He gradually worked his way south from ranch to ranch, never staying more than a couple months in one place. Two years after he had left Indiana Billy arrived in Pleasanton, Texas. He visited the local newspaper office to inquire about potential employment. The editor recommended he ask about town regarding the whereabouts of a cattleman named Luke Maxwell.

Mr. Maxwell was reportedly preparing for a large cattle drive and needed capable cowboys. When he met Billy he doubted the young man was capable of meeting his requirements. But when he saw Billy on a horse amid a group of longhorns he recognized the determined young fellow would be an asset on the trail. He offered Billy the same terms as his other cowboys: one hundred dollars upon safe arrival of the herd in Dodge City, Kansas, plus a guarantee of good riding stock on the trail. Billy need only supply his own clothing and tack. The two shook hands and Billy became a member of Mr. Maxwell's company. Two years later Billy was on his third drive with the Maxwell outfit.

Rudy, the chuck wagon cook, was also on his third cattle drive. He greatly disliked the long days in the hot sun, riding slowly along behind the grazing cattle in a continuous cloud of dust. In addition to punishing conditions, there was always a risk of injury or even death. When he began his first drive, he expected danger only when going through Indian Territory. But he soon learned the company was more likely to suffer a serious incident as a result of a stampede, a rattlesnake encounter, a swollen river or even an unfriendly reception in one of the towns they passed on the trail.

Rudy signed on the cattle drive for two reasons. The primary one was money. For a two-and-a-half-month drive from south Texas to western Kansas, Mr. Maxwell paid the cowboys an even hundred dollars. But Rudy's varied duties brought him considerably more. He was solely responsible for feeding the other men, providing the minimal medical care available on the trail, and fixing whatever needed repair. Luke Maxwell paid his cook one hundred twenty-five dollars per drive. This seemed high to some cattlemen, but Mr. Maxwell believed in hiring the best and paying accordingly. The wrangler, Jake, accountable for the condition and readiness of the eighty horses used by the cowboys, received one hundred fifteen dollars per drive. The trail boss was paid more than the other men, which was only fair given his heavy responsibility. On the trail, the boss was accountable for the welfare of the entire herd, cattle and horses, and the men. He alone had to answer for delays, cattle lost and all expenses of the drive. And on the trail the boss's word, like that of a ship's captain, was law.

The second reason the cook had signed on for the drive was identical to that of the other men hired to move the herd along the trail. Cattle drives presented an opportunity for adventure, camaraderie and a sense of accomplishment. During two months or more of facing danger and hardship together on the trail the company developed a bond similar to that of the military. Men who signed on for the cattle drives also had a sense that they were participating in something that would not continue forever. Settlers were already plowing portions of the prairie and planting crops and would eventually encroach on the open country occupied by the vast herds of free-range cattle.

Mr. Maxwell had been among the first to use the Great Western Trail. He used the route for his first large drive in 1877 and followed it on each of his subsequent drives. Thus it was that after nearly six weeks on the trail, Mr. Maxwell's company of eleven men, eighty horses, and three thousand cattle found themselves camped along the trail in northern Texas. They had nearly reached the border of Indian Territory and were well over half way to their destination. So far they had seen no more than the usual trouble and the cowboys wondered how long their luck would hold.

Billy Corman and the other cowboys had begun the drive by rounding up wild cattle in the area surrounding Pleasanton, Texas. When a sufficient quantity of longhorns was accumulated the men began the process of preparing the animals for the long drive. This consisted primarily of two tasks. First, as Billy described it, the herd of horses used on the drive needed to be "gentrified" -- that is, accustomed to carrying a variety of riders and moving in and among the huge herd of longhorns. The second was getting the cattle used to the horses' presence and identifying some less rambunctious longhorns that could be "trail broke" quickly to serve as leaders for the herd.

As soon as the cattle and horses were accustomed to each other the company headed north. The pace was purposefully slow. By allowing the herd to amble along, grazing on the grass found along the way, cattlemen could expect the longhorns to gain as much as a hundred pounds on the trail. Mr. Maxwell's company, averaging nearly ten miles per day, passed near a series of towns, a number of which benefited from the company's need for supplies.

Moving slowly across the landscape, raising a huge cloud of dust, the herd passed by Pleasanton, San Antonio, Kerrville, Menard, Brady, and Coleman. Day by day it continued on to Abilene, Albany, and Fort Griffin. After forty-one days on the trail the company arrived at Vernon. The trail boss decided to camp there two nights rather than one, giving the men and livestock an opportunity to rest prior to the next portion of the long trek north.

The cowboys had all worked hard, long days to bring the herd this far safely. So far only a small number of the longhorns had been lost. No more than a dozen had died from disease or other natural causes. Lightning from a thunderstorm struck a small group of longhorns gathered under a tree but luckily killed only six of the cattle. A horse galloping after a runaway longhorn stepped in a prairie dog hole, throwing its rider and breaking its leg. The rider was knocked unconscious for a short time but soon recovered. There was no hope for the horse and the trail boss shot it where it lay. All in all the drive was going at least as well as could be expected.

One day's travel past Vernon would bring the company within sight of the well-known C.F. Doan and Company store, located near the point where they would ford the Red River and enter Indian Territory. The experienced members of the company knew they would leave the Territory with fewer cattle than they entered it. This was not due to unexpected mishaps, but because the resident Apaches, Comanches, and Kiowas demanded cattle in exchange for the privilege of grazing the huge herd across their grassland. The cattlemen accepted this practice both out of sympathy for the Indians' plight following decimation of the bison herds and a realization that crossing Indian Territory was the only practical route to Kansas.

After nearly six weeks on the trail the herd of longhorns had grown accustomed to reaching a new location every evening. When the company stayed two nights near Vernon the cattle became restless. The trail boss anticipated this and assigned two extra cowboys to watch the herd through the night. The men had already worked a full day but knew they must follow orders. Billy was not called to work the extra shift, so placed his bedroll beneath the chuck wagon and got several hours of much-needed sleep.

The next morning, as Billy was saddling a horse for the day, he noticed there was one fewer mount than usual tied to the hitching line. There were also one less saddle and bridle on the rack behind the chuck wagon. Not sure if something was amiss, he approached the horse wrangler. "Jake," he said, "I think we're missing a horse." The wrangler pursed his lips, frowned and said, "We're missing more than a horse. One of the cowboys is gone." "Which one?" "Jesse," the wrangler replied. "Where'd he go?" Billy asked. "I don't know," said the wrangler, "but he won't be back."

Billy was puzzled. "What do you mean, he won't be back?" he asked "Simple," the wrangler said. "Boss caught him dozin' while ridin' herd last night. Fell asleep in the saddle, I guess." Billy scowled. The wrangler continued, "The boss treated him fair, though. Gave him five dollars plus the horse for makin' it this far. The horse is worth a good fifty dollars. Told him he was sorry but Mr. Maxwell don't pay people to sleep on the job. "Too bad," said Billy, "I got along OK with Jesse. Never no trouble." Billy went back to finish saddling the horse, and the incident was never mentioned again.

By late afternoon the next day the herd was gathered near the south bank of the Red River. The trail boss and the cook visited Doan's store, where they acquired most of the provisions needed to cross Indian Territory. It had rained upriver and the boss was concerned about the rapid current of the river. He decided to test it. He walked toward the chuck wagon, where the off-duty cowboys were gathered. Some had rolled cigarettes and were smoking; others were just thinking about the trail ahead.

"Billy and Cal," the trail boss called to the cowboys, "got a job for you." Billy and Cal looked at each other, then walked toward the boss. "You two cut out about a half dozen head from the herd and move them to the riverbank," he said. "Then Cal, you drive 'em across the river. I want to make sure they can make it." The cowboys exchanged glances, then walked over to the hitching line to saddle a couple horses. Billy was surprised the boss asked Cal, the least experienced of the cowboys, to take on such an assignment.

When they were behind the chuck wagon, Billy said, "Cal, you better take the orneriest horse you can stay on. Maybe that tall roan." The other cowboy nodded. "OK, if you say so," he said, "Guess I might need one with some fight in 'im." The two men saddled their horses, and a short time later held six long-horns at the water's edge. There was a drop off of about three feet, as the bank stood higher than the water. "Looks pretty fast to me," Billy said. "Mebbe so," the other man replied. "One way to find out." Cal spurred his horse and let out a loud "whoop" as he rushed directly toward the group of longhorns. The startled cattle reacted by turning their backs on the horsemen and dashing directly off the bank, plunging into the river.

Cal and his mount dove into the river behind the cattle, the cowboy yelling and whooping in order to keep the longhorns moving away from the riverbank. The current was stronger than was evident from shore and the cattle were wide-eyed with panic. They swam as hard as they could while the current swept them downstream. Cal, realizing the river was more dangerous than expected, pulled on the reins to turn his horse back toward shore. Suddenly, its eyes dilated with fear, the horse was sucked under water. When it surfaced about twenty yards downstream its saddle was empty.

Not knowing Cal's whereabouts, Billy jumped off his horse, pulled off his boots and dove into the river. Despite being a strong swimmer, he struggled against the current, towed along in the same direction as Cal's horse. He saw Cal bob to the surface, then go under again. Billy dove under with his eyes open trying to spot the other cowboy. Suddenly he was face to face with Cal, who was struggling furiously against the current. Then Billy saw something behind Cal that looked like thick, wet rope. He grabbed Cal's belt with one hand and with the other reached forward and grabbed the rope. He hung on as tightly as he could, trying to keep from being kicked as the rope began to move toward shore. A minute later Cal's horse clawed its way up the river bank, pulling the two sputtering cowboys behind, Billy clinging desperately to the horse's tail.

The other cowboys, who had heard the commotion and rushed to the river's edge, brought Cal and Billy from the river to the campsite. Both men had swallowed some water but neither suffered any permanent damage. The trail boss had been alerted and stood looking down at the two cowboys, frowning and rubbing his chin. "What the hell happened?" he demanded. Cal and Billy looked at each other, then at the boss, but said nothing. "I hope you learned a lesson," the boss said. "When you're in charge someday don't let anybody try a fool thing like that."

Hearing the boss's reprimand, Cal's face flushed with anger. He started to get to his feet, determined to confront the trail boss. "Whoa, cowboy," said one of the other cowboys, placing his hand on Cal's shoulder. "You don't know it, but you just got a big compliment from the boss." "I did?" Cal asked. "Yup," said the cowboy, "you heard him say it -- when you're in charge." Cal looked questioningly at Billy. Billy nodded. "I'll be danged," Cal said. "I just about got drowned and now I'm supposed to think the boss givin' me hell is a compliment." Billy grinned. "Yup," he said, "You might make a cowboy yet."

The company remained at the campsite near Doan's store for two additional days waiting for the river to go down. By dawn of the third day the trail boss decided a safe crossing could be made and the cowboys began pushing the herd into the water. Three cowboys crossed at the head of the herd to guide the cattle across and prevent them from straying while the remainder of the herd crossed. Once the lead cows began swimming across the others began to follow. But only a short section of the river was calm enough to allow fording, and if the cattle entered en masse they might drown in the swift-flowing current. The cowboys on the Texas side of the river had the tricky task of holding the anxious animals back, limiting the number entering the water. The men did their job well and after about two and a half hours the herd had crossed the Red River into Indian Territory.

About ten miles north of the river crossing the company met a small party of Indians. As expected, the trail boss negotiated the number of cattle to be traded for permission to pass through the area and the company moved on. This process was repeated several times over the next couple of weeks as the herd passed peaceably through areas controlled by various tribes or clans. The company was well-provisioned when it entered Indian Territory but by the time they reached Fort Supply seventeen days later supplies of bacon and coffee were exhausted and the men were beginning to complain. Fortunately, the quartermaster at the fort had a good supply of both, as well as some other items of which the chuck wagon was running short.

Through most of Indian Territory the company traveled without seeing other white people. And they seldom saw the natives, except for the occasional parlay that determined the number of cattle paid for passing through the Territory. Some of the men disliked this degree of isolation, but Billy liked the idea of the small company of men alone on the vast prairie. Loneliness was not part of his makeup. He dreamed of owning a spread far enough west to live in solitude, away from towns or close neighbors. Intent on reaching this goal, Billy saved most of the pay received for the cattle drives, just as he had since the first time an employer had pressed a dime into his palm.

As on previous drives undertaken by Mr. Maxwell's company, proper preparation and good employees helped ensure problems encountered by competing companies were avoided. During the drive's forty-two days in Texas and twenty-one days crossing Indian Territory, only a few incidents occurred. Somewhere in northern Texas the wrangler, Jake, was kicked squarely in the thigh while shoeing a horse. The blow knocked him to the ground, left a nasty imprint on his leg, and caused him to limp severely for several days. But he carried on, accepting help from the cook only when moving heavy barrels of water to tend the horses.

On the third day in Indian Territory the company found that a large pond at which they expected to water the cattle and horses had gone dry. The boss sent three of the cowboys to search for water. Billy went northwest, Lefty went due north, and John T headed northeast. About an hour from where the herd was grazing Billy chanced upon a small stream and decided to follow it, hoping it led to some type of reservoir. Just a few miles downstream he came to a pond bordered by a small grove of trees. He rode into the shade of the trees, dismounted and walked toward the water, intending to determine whether it was fresh. If the water was alkaline or too brackish to drink he would have to continue his search.

When Billy neared the pond he knelt down in the tall, thick grass that grew along the water's edge. Then he heard an unmistakable sound. He froze. He tried to use his peripheral vision to spot the snake. He had encountered rattlers multiple times, but always either astride a horse or walking with his heavy, nearly knee-high boots affording protection against the reptiles. Now he was at their level. The snake rattled a second time and Billy knew it was just to his left. Very, very slowly and carefully he drew his revolver. He listened intently but all he heard was his own breathing. He gradually turned the barrel of the gun toward his left, then inch by inch turned his head in the same direction. The snake was coiled about three feet from him. It was big enough to strike that far, he thought. He cocked the hammer. The snake rattled again. "Sure wish I could bring this up to my eye and aim good," he thought. Then he pulled the trigger.

The sound of the gunshot echoed across the countryside but there was not another person close enough to hear it. The snake lay still, blood oozing from its head. Billy stood up, kicked the snake farther into the grass and finished the task of testing the water. It was good. He filled his canteen as a sample to take back to the trail boss. What he did not know was that he would drink nearly all the water in the canteen during his ride back to the herd. Later he realized he was thirsty because he perspired profusely immediately after his encounter with the rattler. He decided not to mention the incident to the other men except to caution them about the likelihood of snakes when they herded the cattle to the pond to drink.

Twenty-one days after crossing the Red River and entering Indian Territory the herd crossed the border into Kansas. They were less than a hundred miles from Dodge City. It had been sixty-three days since the company had left Pleasanton and the men had grown weary of life on the trail. After sundown, as they sat around the fire, some said they would not ever sign up for another trail drive. This brought a faint smile to the boss's face. He had heard this type of talk many times before, including from some of the same men who were saying it now. He knew how they felt. He felt the same way but he also knew he would probably continue to drive the vast herds of longhorns north as long as he was physically able, or until the railroad lines reached into Texas and cattle were shipped directly from there to the hungry mouths to the north and east.

It took the company just eight days to move the herd, now numbering twenty-nine hundred and fifty head, past Ashland and Englewood and then on to Dodge City. The last night on the trail they camped about a mile outside town while the boss went into Dodge to find a buyer for the cattle. Early the next morning two men approached the campsite in a buggy pulled by a sleek black horse. The two men rode slowly around the herd, never stepping out of the buggy, then stopped for a brief conversation with the boss. Billy thought one of the men was Mr. Maxwell. The driver of the buggy clicked his tongue and shook the reins, and the black horse started back toward town.

After the buggy was gone the boss said to the men gathered near the chuck wagon, "You've all done a good job," he said. "Didn't lose many, none of you hurt much, and seventy-one days start to finish." Some of the men looked surprised, but it was hard to tell if they thought they had been on the trail more or less than seventy-one days. The boss continued, "We'll drive the herd around to the east side of town, there are enough pens there for 'em. Two thousand will go out by rail; the rest are going back on the trail. Fellow that bought them has a contract for beef delivered to Ogallala, Nebraska." The cowboys' expressions suggested they were not envious of whoever was planning to drive a third of the herd another three hundred miles. "When the cattle are penned," the boss said, "meet at the bank on the south side of the street. That's where you get paid. And Mr. Maxwell said you'll each get an extra ten dollars. You brought the herd along in real good shape, and he sold 'em for twenty-eight dollars a head."

Nobody said much. The cowboys mounted up and began to move the herd to the northeast. Less than an hour later, the stockyards crew closed the gate on the pen holding the last of the herd. The cowboys swung down from the horses and led them into another pen. They loosened the cinches and removed their saddles, blankets, and bridles. They lifted their saddles and placed them on the wooden fence that surrounded the horse pen. They would retrieve their tack later. The horses would be sold later that day or early the next. The drive was over.

Billy and the others walked toward the bank and waited. Soon the boss came out onto the wooden sidewalk and handed each of the men an envelope. He offered to buy them each a beer at the saloon across the street. Without a word, the company walked directly to the saloon and gathered at the bar. The men looked around the saloon. They had not been inside a building for two and a half months. The bartender slid cold, frothy mugs of beer down the bar for each of the men. They thanked the boss and took their first sips carefully, as though they weren't sure what to expect. The limits of camaraderie with the boss had been reached, and he turned and left the saloon. The men remained in the saloon until after dark, then went their separate ways. There was no talk of seeing each other on next year's drive, though some most likely would. The drive was over and that was that.

Billy had a hundred and ten dollars in his pocket but spent little of it. He did allow himself two luxuries. After walking back to the horse corral to get his tack, he took a room and a hot bath at the Wright House. And he ordered a steak dinner. After herding thousand of steaks across the prairie while subsisting on flapjacks, coffee, a little dried meat and bacon of questionable quality, he wanted a share of one of those grass-fed longhorns. The next morning he slept until past sunup, then began to ponder the best way to get back to south Texas. He decided that moving from ranch to ranch, working a month or so at each, had panned out all right before. He would do it again. He asked the desk clerk at the hotel to watch his tack while he visited the newspaper office. The editor knew of a rancher who needed help, and in less than an hour Billy returned to the Wright House, collected his belongings and climbed into a buckboard headed south out of Dodge.

4 THE DOCTOR

The stagecoach reached the crest of the hill and gradually began the long descent toward Plainview. The driver looked toward the horizon, then glanced at the sun, which was slowly descending in the west. He turned to the man on his right. "A good hour of daylight left." the driver said. "Should make Plainview just fine." The guard, his shotgun resting in the crook of his arm, nodded but did not speak. The four horses pulling the stage recognized the terrain ahead and sensed that the end of their journey was near. The driver slackened the reins, and the horses increased their pace. A fine cloud of dust followed the stage as it wound its way down the hillside toward the plain below.

The stagecoach was lighter than normal, as it carried only three passengers. Two of them, a burly man with a bushy mustache and a perpetual squint, and a taller, darker man with a deeply creased face, looked like they belonged in the open spaces of the West. The third did not. He was younger than the other two, with a light complexion and sandy colored hair, and had an expectant air about him. He wore a light-colored shirt, with brown trousers that just reached the top of his recently acquired boots, and viewed the world through wire-rimmed spectacles.

The stagecoach rocked and bounced along the trail, causing its passengers to jostle against one other. They had long passed the point where apologies were offered or expected and rode in silence. Each had his own reasons for traveling to Plainview, but all looked forward to disembarking from the bone-jarring, dust-filled conveyance.

The bespectacled young man, who showed more interest in his surroundings than did the other two passengers, looked out the window of the stage and announced, "There's a town up ahead. I think it's Plainview." The burly man glanced in the direction of the town and nodded. The tall, dark man looked at the other two, then out the window, but said nothing. The horses slowed to a walk as they crossed the rocky bottom of a small stream, then resumed their prior pace.

When the stagecoach pulled to a stop in front of the Plainview livery stable, men and horses alike were eager for a respite. The driver climbed down from his perch and called toward the open barn door, "You in there, Pete? We're here with the Overland." A middle-aged man emerged through the door and, without conversation, began to unhitch the horses. The shotgun guard walked to the rear of the stage and loosened the leather straps that secured the canvas covering the cargo. The stable hand led the horses two-by-two into the barn and returned with two fresh teams.

The young man approached the driver and asked, "Where might I find the local sheriff's office?" "West end of the street," the driver replied, "sheriff's name is Jackson." "Much obliged, thank you," said the young man. He made a vain attempt to brush the dust from his clothing, retrieved a large black valise from the rear of the stage, and stepped into the street. He lowered his chin and, looking over the top of his spectacles, examined the main street of Plainview. He grinned slightly, shook his head side to side, and began walking toward the west end of town.

Sheriff Jackson was seated at his desk when the stranger approached the front door of the office. He heard footsteps on the wooden sidewalk, then a slight pause, then a rap on the door. "Come on in," he barked. And, to himself, wondered, "What kinda fool knocks on the door of a sheriff's office?" The door opened and a young man stepped in. "Might I be addressing Sheriff Jackson?" the young man asked. "That's me," the sheriff replied, "what can I do for ya?" As he eyed the young man, Ben Jackson thought, "He's gotta be a school teacher, a parson, or a newspaperman. He sure ain't a cowman."

"Permit me to introduce myself," the young man said. "I am Jedediah Smyth. That's Smyth with a Y. Doctor Jedediah Smyth actually, from Philadelphia. I'm wondering if you might tell me where I can find Doctor Watson's house?" The sheriff eyed the young man suspiciously and asked, "You wouldn't be Plainview's new doctor, would ya?" "Most certainly," replied the young man, "and might I say I am most pleased to be here. Now if you would be so kind as to direct me to Doctor Watson's house, I would like very much to begin getting settled in there."

The Sheriff explained the location of the Watson house to Jedediah Smyth and recommended he stop in the cafe for a meal before it closed for the day. Jedediah took Sheriff Jackson's advice and walked across the street to the cafe. Entering the cafe, he nearly collided with a slightly built, balding man who appeared to be in his mid-fifties. "Oh, excuse me," the man said. He spoke rapidly. "Come in, come in, I was just going over to the saloon for a quick nip. We'll be closing soon. Sally can help you. My name is Emmet, Emmet Walker, and that's my wife Sally." He gestured toward a slight, friendly-looking woman standing at the stove. She smiled and nodded.

Jedediah introduced himself, "I am Jedediah Smyth. That's Smyth with a Y. I am the new doctor in town. I just arrived on the stage." Jedediah extended his hand and Emmet Walker shook it warmly. "Well, well, welcome to Plainview," Emmet said. "You have a seat and let Sally get you a plate of food. I'll be right back." Jedediah sat at a table near the window, placed his valise on the floor next to it, and looked around the cafe. The furnishings were spartan. Six small tables covered with oilcloth tablecloths sat on a bare wood floor. It was getting dark, and Mrs. Walker lit the two oil lamps that provided scant light in the cafe. Then she placed a plate of roast beef, boiled potatoes, and wheat bread in front of Jedediah.

He was hungrier then he realized and was surprised at how quickly he ate. It had been several days since he had eaten a hot meal and he was appreciative. Sally Walker replaced the empty dinner plate with one holding a large serving of apple pie. Jedediah enjoyed this treat, and thanked Mrs. Walker profusely. Anxious to find the Watson house, Jedediah nearly left the cafe without paying. He stood, grabbed his valise and started toward the door, then remembered he had not yet paid. He blushed, commented again on the delicious meal, and handed Emily Walker a dollar coin. She rummaged in her apron pocket and handed him two quarters and a dime. He thanked her again and exited the cafe.

It was well past sunset when Jedediah reached the Watson house. Fortunately, the night was clear and the moon nearly full, and he located the house with little difficulty. He walked up the three steps to the front porch and approached the door. He tried the knob and the door opened. He smiled. "In

Philadelphia, this would be locked," he thought. He stepped into the house and felt in his pocket for the small tin of matches. He opened it, took out a match, and lit it. A kerosene lamp sat on a table near the front window. He removed the chimney, lit the wick, replaced the chimney and adjusted the wick. He picked up the lamp and went from room to room, inspecting the house.

The house was larger than he had expected, given that Doctor Watson was a bachelor. There were four rooms on the first floor, a sitting room, dining room, kitchen, and a large room that had served as Doctor Watson's office. Upstairs were three bedrooms and a storage room used for both household and medical supplies. The house had an open front porch and a small, enclosed rear porch. Behind the house, Jedediah found a garden, a woodpile, a small chicken coop, and a privy. The rear yard was fenced.

Jedediah had just finished his inspection of the house when he heard a knock on the front door. Lamp in hand, he went to the door and opened it. A tall man in a dark suit was standing on the porch. The man spoke first, "I am Reverend Daniel Fossbender," he said without a smile, "and who, may I ask, might you be?" "Pleased to make your acquaintance," Jedediah said. "I am Doctor Jedediah Smyth. That's Smyth with a Y. I am the new doctor in Plainview. And I am pleased to meet you, parson," Jedediah added. "Likewise," replied Reverend Fossbender. I was just passing by and saw the light. I thought I'd check and see who was in Doc Watson's house. I am glad to see it was you, and I welcome you to Plainview."

Introductions completed, Jedediah and Reverend Fossbender continued to converse for several minutes. The parson offered some helpful information regarding Plainview, and the two men agreed that, as some of the few professionals in town, they would undoubtedly have frequent contact. The parson was about to leave the house when Jedediah asked him about Doc Watson. "A fine man, Doctor Watson was," said Reverend Fossbender. "He helped a lot of people in Plainview and made a good living doing so, though he never turned anyone away for lack of funds. We were sad to see him go." The parson frowned, paused, then continued. "But he led a good life and was up in years. Sixty-eight, I think he was. I had his funeral, and nearly everyone in town attended. But that's not unusual in Plainview."

"Could I presume from your comments that this is a close-knit community?" asked Jedediah. "Oh, yes indeed," replied Reverend Fossbender. "Uniquely so I would say. And, I'm gratified to say, a community populated by remarkably good people." Jedediah was impressed by what he heard. Fossbender continued, "Well, it's getting late. I shall let you get settled." The preacher bid the doctor goodnight, nodded pleasantly, then went to the front door and let himself out.

Jedediah turned down the kerosene lamp and took a seat in a wooden rocking chair in the front room. It was quiet in the big house. Jedediah thought, "This could be a lonely house. I think I'll get a dog or cat to keep me company." He rocked slowly while he reflected on the events of the last few weeks, and how he had come to Plainview. His predecessor, Doc Watson, had realized many months ago that he was dying. Not wanting to leave the town without a doctor, Watson had written an old friend who was on the board of the medical college in Pennsylvania. Watson asked that the board select a young doctor who could take over his practice in Plainview. As an inducement, Doctor Watson offered his house and practice free of charge to the individual selected. Jedediah Smyth was one of the top students in his class and was chosen as the recipient of the doctor's generous offer. He had never been west, but looked forward to experiencing life in a real frontier town.

Jedediah spent the next several days getting acquainted with the leading townspeople. In addition to the sheriff and Reverend Daniel Fossbender, he soon knew the mayor, the school teacher and most of the merchants in town. The more people he met, the more impressed he was with his new community. The citizens of Plainview were, as Reverend Fossbender had suggested, a close-knit group. Unusual as it seemed, there simply did not appear to be anyone who was really disliked by others in the community. Jedediah found this remarkable and could not quite grasp the reason, but attributed it to some natural effect of the frontier. Visits with his new friends and neighbors confirmed that Doctor Watson had been very well thought of and was sorely missed by the citizens of Plainview. This did not, however, prevent them from offering a warm welcome to his successor.

A few weeks after Jedediah's arrival in Plainview, the Overland stage brought two trunks containing medical supplies. One trunk held various instruments and an examination table. The other was filled with carefully packed bottles of medicines and other chemicals. Jedediah was pleasantly surprised when Pete, the sole employee of the livery stable, offered to transport the trunks to Jedediah's house free of charge on the livery's buckboard. This was just one of many kindnesses shown to Jedediah. The Walkers issued an invitation to Jedediah to dine at their cafe Saturday evening "on the house." Mrs. Fossbender presented him with a fine, hand-knit scarf, sure to help him resist the cold of the coming winter. And the proprietor of the local rooming house, Emily Sanders, upon hearing the young doctor intended to obtain an animal as a house companion, gave him a fine young cat from a litter recently delivered by her tabby. After only a short while in Plainview, Jedediah Smyth was developing a genuine affection for his fellow residents.

Life was not easy for the citizens of Plainview or the ranchers of the surrounding countryside. Accidents with horses or livestock left people crippled, or even ended their lives. Influenza and other diseases struck the town, often proving fatal to children or the aged. When a new disease reached Plainview, its out-of-the-way location often meant that needed medicines arrived too late to stave off an epidemic. Yet, as Reverend Fossbender pointed out, "The good Lord watches over Plainview and its people, often in very special ways."

It was Emmet Walker, owner of the local cafe, who first told Jedediah that God sometimes "took the least desirable" members of the community while allowing others to continue living. "No doubt in my mind," Emmet told Jedediah, "God has been good to our town. He's taken the worst away one by one, by one sickness or another. No doubt in my mind." Jedediah was taken aback by this statement. "Well," he said to Emmet, "I suppose it seems that way sometimes." But Emmet was insistent. "Just wait," he said, "you're the doctor, you'll see. Just you watch which ones get well and which ones don't." Jedediah smiled broadly. "My dear Mister Walker," he said, "I will do just that. I will do my utmost to restore health to anyone who comes to me for treatment. And I will wait, and watch, and see."

Later, Jedediah pondered the conversation that had taken place with Emmet Walker. What Emmet suggested did not fit with Jedediah's understanding of how God operated in the world, nor did it give much credence to the benefits of modern medicine. Although others bore tales similar to those told by Emmet, Jedediah discounted them as the misguided conclusions of uneducated people. He concluded that coincidences involving illness, recovery, and death had been misinterpreted by the locals as special provision from on high. Nevertheless, Jedediah was troubled by the fact that the stories were confirmed by educated members of the community, including the schoolteacher and Reverend Fossbender.

It seemed nearly everyone in Plainview could cite instances in which "God had provided" by ensuring the recovery of well-liked, pleasant members of the community, while the minority of townspeople who were disliked or in some way a detriment to the town met their demise. Despite his education and reliance on scientific logic, Jedediah simply did not have an adequate explanation for people believing such imaginative tales. He decided to put them out of his mind and concentrate on establishing his practice, which he did. That is, until the day he made an unwitting discovery.

Jedediah had ordered a supply of new drugs from a pharmaceutical firm in Denver. When they arrived he found that, in order to make room for them, it was necessary to reorganize the medicines and chemicals kept in the upstairs storage room of the house. Because he was thorough, and perhaps a bit compulsive, he decided to remove all of the containers from the shelving, then reposition them in alphabetical order. While removing the containers of chemicals left by Doctor Watson, he came upon a large brown bottle labeled "Cinesra". It appeared to be empty, so was of little value, but the name on the bottle piqued Jedediah's curiosity. He was unfamiliar with the substance and decided to research it in the medicinal reference guide he had brought from Philadelphia. To his surprise, Cinesra was not listed in the manual. A less curious, or less determined individual might have simply placed the bottle alphabetically with the other "C" containers, or perhaps emptied the bottle's contents down the drain and discarded the container or used it for another purpose.

Jedediah, however, was not one to give up easily. He composed a letter describing the container of Cinesra and sent an inquiry to the office of the pharmaceutical firm in Denver. He was surprised and rather disappointed when, a couple of weeks later, he received a reply indicating the pharmaceutical firm's chemists had no knowledge of a chemical substance or medicinal compound named Cinesra. Since he appeared to have reached a dead end, Jedediah placed the container in the "C" section of the storage shelves, where it remained undisturbed for many months.

It was during the following winter, in the midst of a serious outbreak of influenza, that Jedediah stumbled upon the answer to the mysterious connection between Plainview citizens' positive or negative reputations and their tendency to survive or succumb to illness. He had received a small shipment of medicines and was putting them away in the upstairs storage room. He had ordered a large bottle of camphor oil and was putting it on the shelf in the "C" section of the storage area when he accidentally knocked the bottle labeled "Cinesra" off the shelf. The bottle hit the floor and shattered. Jedediah, believing the bottle was empty, did not notice the minuscule amount of liquid on the floor. He was about to pick up the broken glass when he heard a knock on the front door and went downstairs to answer it.

Two days later, Jedediah noticed the daily saucer of milk put out for his cat had not been touched. He called for the cat but got no response. "Just like a cat," he thought, "thoroughly independent." He walked from room to room, searching for it without result. He hoped some departing patient or visitor had not inadvertently let the cat escape out the front door. He decided to search the house from top to bottom.

It was during his search that he discovered the cat in the upstairs storage room. It was lying near the spot where the old brown bottle had landed and was unmistakably dead. Jedediah carefully examined the cat and the floor upon which it lay. He recalled breaking the bottle and remembered that he had been interrupted and had not cleaned up the broken pieces. He carefully picked up the largest piece, with the "Cinesra" label still intact. He studied the broken piece of glass and the label. He thought about the inquiry he had sent to the pharmaceutical company in Denver and the reply he had received. Suddenly, everything was clear.

Jedediah half ran, half stumbled down the stairs, and out the front door. He did not bother with his hat, coat, or scarf, but ran directly out into the cold winter air. He headed toward the west end of town, moving as quickly as he could through the snow until he came to an abrupt stop in front of the sheriff's office. He stood outside, mentally reviewing the steps that had led to his recent conclusion, wanting to be certain he was not mistaken. Then he opened the door and barged into the office. It was empty. "The sheriff can't have gone far." he thought. "I'll wait here and tell him as soon as he gets back. After all this time a few more minutes won't much matter."

Jedediah turned things over in his mind. How was he going to tell Sheriff Jackson that he had found the secret behind the Plainview enigma? How would he tell the sheriff that he knew why some townspeople survived illnesses and others did not, why those who seemed a detriment to the community succumbed to common diseases but those who were well thought of usually recovered? How would he tell the sheriff about the large bottle of poison Doc Watson had nearly emptied while he played God in Plainview? His mind was racing, completely absorbed by his recent discovery and the awfulness of it.

Jedediah, lost in thought, scarcely noticed when the door opened and Sheriff Jackson entered the office. "Howdy Doc," the sheriff bellowed, jarring him back to reality. Jedediah looked blankly at the Sheriff. "Somethin' wrong?" asked the Sheriff. "Where's your coat?" "Never mind that," said Jedediah, "I've got something really important to tell you." "Must be pretty dang important," Jackson shot back, "to risk catching your death of cold. Okay, what is it?"

Jedediah turned away from the Sheriff. He thought about Plainview, his newly adopted home. He thought about the townspeople, and about what a pleasant and closely knit community it really was. He thought about how people had looked up to Doc Watson, and how much even Reverend Fossbender had admired the physician. He thought about how so little discord existed in the town, and how people really believed that, in the midst of the trials and tribulations of living on the frontier, God had blessed Plainview in a special way.

"Well?" said Sheriff Jackson, "Cat got your tongue?" Jedediah turned to face the sheriff. He took a deep breath. His voice was strained, and his face reddened. "This might seem more than a bit odd," he began, a little too forcefully, "First, I very much appreciate the way the people of Plainview have welcomed and accepted me, and ..." Jedediah hesitated. "And?" the Sheriff asked, with obvious impatience. "And ..." Jedediah started and stopped again. Then he said, "And I hope to stay here for a long time." He was no longer looking at the Sheriff. His mind seemed to be focused on something far away.

Ben Jackson looked at the doctor, not sure what to think of this supposedly important pronouncement. "Hmm," the Sheriff muttered, "well that's, um, that's fine, just fine. I hope you do just that. Stay a long time." "Well I guess that's it then," said Jedediah. His expression was one of relief. Then he said, "It's Saturday, so I guess I'll see you at the cafe for supper." The sheriff nodded. The doctor looked as though he might say more, but just smiled weakly. He turned and walked out the door, closing it behind him. Sheriff Jackson stared at the closed door. He shook his head and muttered something unintelligible. He looked at the clock on the wall. "Half hour 'til supper," he said to himself. He opened his desk drawer, took out a flyer, and began to read.

5 The Merchants

Few people know the story of how the business partner-ship between Samuel Goodwin and Hiram Johnson started, or how it ended. Residents of Plainview were at one time well-acquainted with Goodwin and Johnson and their store on the main street. Nearby ranchers and farmers also frequented the G&J General Store and depended on its varied stock of goods. Even non-residents who passed through the town by stagecoach or train often frequented the establishment, whose owners were among the town's most prominent citizens.

The origin of the two men's partnership can be traced back to a chance meeting aboard a train headed west from St. Joseph, Missouri, in the spring of either 1871 or 1872. Each of the men had a history of business success, but both were convinced that greener pastures could be found in communities out West, where settlers in need of both the staples and niceties of life could be counted on to purchase such items in stores which were often local monopolies. Both Mr. Goodwin and Mr. Johnson had liquidated their eastern business interests and headed west in hopes of multiplying their hard-earned capital.

Samuel Goodwin had, during the Civil War, profited from the sale of supplies to the Union Army. He supplied blankets and other cloth goods, tents and their required hardware, and from time to time other items such as encampment cooking utensils, or saddles and other tack for the cavalry. He made a handsome margin on these goods, though his net income would have been larger had it not been for the considerable expense associated with securing the right to supply them. A small number of well-connected entrepreneurs controlled most of the government contracts for war materials. These men demanded a sizeable percentage of the value of goods supplied as their reward for selecting the suppliers. Still, Goodwin made the most of the opportunity, and before the war unfortunately came to a close had amassed a tidy sum. However, he had also developed a taste for an above-average lifestyle, so deemed it necessary to find a new source of funds.

Hiram Johnson's business experience was considerably different from that of Samuel Goodwin. Johnson had operated a dry goods store in a sizeable community in Illinois. He quickly learned the finer points of business, and within a relatively short time understood that having local competitors had an adverse effect on profits. Despite having an income that most would consider more than adequate, he had aspirations of increasing his earnings by moving to a location where he would be the exclusive supplier of his customers' needs. In addition, he had since his youth entertained thoughts of generating sufficient wealth to facilitate transition to a life of leisure at an early age. So it was that on a bright, sunny morning in May, Samuel Goodwin and Hiram Johnson rode on the same train, unbeknownst to each other, each intent on realizing their ambitions somewhere on the frontier.

As the train headed west across the prairie, the two men occupied themselves according to their dissimilar personalities.

Samuel Goodwin was a large, ruddy-faced man with a bushy mustache, a prominent midsection, and large, meaty hands. He was exceptionally outgoing, and a loud and sometimes profane conversationalist. No man was a stranger for long, but quickly became an acquaintance of Mr. Goodwin whether he desired to or not. Goodwin had once been married, but the relationship ended about the time his former wife's inheritance was depleted.

Hiram Johnson, in contrast to Samuel Goodwin, was a slightly built man of average height. He was rather pale and slightly balding, and wore wire rimmed spectacles. His voice was thin, and when he attempted to speak louder than normal, often cracked or made a sort of squeaking sound. He was, however, very skilled at keeping books and accounts, and genuinely enjoyed creating and examining records of such things. Mr. Johnson was a confirmed bachelor, partially due to his belief that wives and children were an unnecessary expense, and also as a natural result of his appearance and demeanor.

The two men met when the train made a brief stop to refill the water tank of the locomotive tender. Hiram Johnson had disembarked from the train in search of a newspaper, hoping to find one that contained a list of stock and bond prices. Unsuccessful in his search, he was returning to the train when he noticed a group of men surrounding a tall fellow who was evidently regaling the onlookers with an interesting tale of some sort. Deciding to learn what he could, he stood on the edge of the group, listening to the storyteller. To his disappointment, the tale being told was nothing more than an attempt at humor, and a ribald one at that. As the other men engaged in a vigorous round of laughter, he turned toward the train, intending to board his car.

Before Hiram could mount the steps of the railcar, he heard a booming voice call out, "Hey, you there!" Hiram turned to see the big man smiling broadly at him. The man extracted a pipe from the pocket of his jacket, and said, "Do you happen to have a match, my friend?" Hiram rather resented the inference of the man's addressing him as "my friend," but raised no objection. Instead, he simply shook his head, and replied, "I do not smoke. It is a complete waste of money and unpleasantly odorous." "Well, then," said the man, "guess I won't have to worry about you stealing my tobacco." At this, the man laughed uproariously, his large belly shaking repeatedly. His laughter was interrupted by the conductor's call, "Aboard. All aboard."

As the two men walked toward the train, the loud man introduced himself. "Samuel Goodwin," he said, "of the Chicago Goodwins." He extended an oversized hand toward his companion. "Hiram Johnson," came the reply, and the two men shook hands. "Always glad to make a new friend," said Goodwin. "Where are you sitting?" "Second car, at the back," said Hiram. "Really?" replied Goodwin. "Same car as me; I'm up front, probably didn't notice you back there." As they boarded the car, Goodwin suggested, "How about we sit together? Get to know each other a little." Hiram began to raise his hand to indicate refusal of Goodwin's invitation, but the big man interjected, "Grab your stuff, Johnson, and bring it to the front. Let's sit down before this thing lurches forward and seats us both in the aisle." At this remark, Goodwin again roared with laughter, as if he had said something extremely humorous. Hiram, somewhat nonplussed, retrieved his valise from above his seat and moved to the front of the car.

Contrary to his expectations, Hiram Johnson found conversation with Samuel Goodwin to be interesting and at least moderately entertaining, despite the man's tendency to treat his vague attempts at humor as the pinnacle of levity. Hiram paid special attention when Goodwin described the circumstances and means by which he had accrued his considerable savings. Goodwin was so enamored of his own story and his own voice that he readily shared many of the trade secrets that enabled his success. Hiram listened patiently, only interjecting an occasional question that encouraged Goodwin to delve even deeper into his methods and techniques. Hiram primed the pump, and Goodwin poured forth his secrets.

When the day's travel ended and the train was shunted onto a spur for the overnight stop, the two men agreed to share a room in the local hotel. They ate together that evening, and again in the morning. By the time they boarded the train for the next day's travel, both assumed they would be traveling companions for the duration of the trip. Gradually, Hiram Johnson told Samuel Goodwin a bit more about his background and aspirations. Goodwin was delighted to learn he was in the presence of a fellow businessman with ambitions similar to his own. Hiram Johnson saw in Samuel Goodwin an opportunity to leverage the latter's experience for their mutual benefit. By noon of the second day of travel, the two men were in serious discussion regarding a business partnership.

It did not come to light until the evening of their second day together that neither Goodwin nor Johnson had a specific destination in mind, but only a sense of the type of community in which they wished to conduct business. It must be a town of modest size, preferably not on the main rail line, to minimize the possibility of direct competition. But it must also be large enough to support a retail business and, most importantly, show good prospects for growth. The two men agreed that they would, during the remainder of the train ride, carefully question their fellow passengers and the crewmen of the train to discover a suitable location for their planned enterprise.

A traveling hard goods salesman from St. Louis first suggested Plainview as a potential site for the new partners' venture. The town met the criteria of size and relative isolation, and was reportedly growing as new settlers arrived in the area. After verifying the salesman's description of Plainview with the conductor, Goodwin and Johnson made their decision. The fine community of Plainview, as yet unknown to either of the men, would be the beneficiary of their business acumen and ambition. At the appropriate stop, the two men left the train, purchased tickets on the stage line that served Plainview, and embarked on their entrepreneurial adventure.

As Goodwin and Johnson had anticipated, their combined business knowledge enabled them to not only locate and purchase a prime lot on the main street of their newly adopted town, but also to negotiate a sizeable bank loan on favorable terms. With the funds provided by the bank, the men constructed what was undoubtedly the largest and finest, as well as the only, general and dry goods store within many miles of Plainview. The business approach adopted for the G&J General Store, as it was named, was to provide a wide variety of merchandise, helpful advice, and the friendliest of service. The store also offered sales on credit, especially to ranchers and farmers whose income was seasonal.

Within six months, the store was turning a profit, and within its first year provided a higher percentage return on the owners' investment than either partner had realized in their prior businesses. Over the next couple of year, the success of the G&J General Store continued unabated, providing sufficient income for both men to live as comfortably as was possible in Plainview. Mr. Goodwin married the widow of the local hotelier, significantly enhancing his holdings. The couple lived in a large, well-furnished home two blocks behind the general store. Johnson, true to his values, lived in a modest rented home on the other side of the main street. Most of his earnings were sent away and invested in the financial markets, the details of which he kept strictly to himself.

It was during the third year of the partnership that Mr. Goodwin came to the conclusion that the rewards of the business he operated with Hiram Johnson were not being shared fairly. The success of the G&J General Store was built on his magnanimous personality and the exceptional rapport he established with customers. He had no ill feelings toward Hiram but knew that his partner was not an equal contributor to the store's results. However, he understood that even his highly developed conversational skills would not be sufficient to convince Hiram to accept the reality of the situation. Goodwin went so far as to bring up the subject of his impact on customers with Hiram, but the other man just listened half-heartedly and returned to his usual activity, that of maintaining the financial records of the business.

Samuel Goodwin pondered the situation for several months before deciding on a solution. The store operated efficiently because of Hiram's skill in keeping accounts, ordering, and watching over the inventory. And each evening, after the store closed and Samuel went home to his wife, Hiram remained to restock the shelves and ensure the large wooden barrels held sufficient quantities of bulk goods for the next day's business. But Samuel knew that the impressive volume of goods sold in the store resulted totally from his own friendliness and sales expertise. Hiram was good with numbers, but Samuel was good with people, and sales were made to people. Without a doubt, the success of the store depending much more on his contribution than on Hiram's. Therefore, it was patently unfair for the store's revenue to be shared equally between the two partners. Once the principle was established, the mechanism for dividing the rewards of the business was actually quite simple.

Samuel Goodwin was constantly on the floor of the G&J General Store, waiting on customers and offering advice regarding the various goods available (which nearly always led to the purchase of a higher-priced item due to its superior quality or usefulness). Hiram Johnson remained in the back of the store, where he tended to ordering, stock control, and bookkeeping. Samuel was the one who completed the vast majority of transactions with the store's customers. This made it easy enough for him to effect an adjustment to the revenue division between the two partners.

Most of the store's goods were sold in bulk, including many top sellers. Foods such as coffee, tea, sugar, salt, flour, meal, beans, ground oats, nuts, and candy were stored in large wooden barrels situated throughout the store. Other wares, such as cloth goods, thread, hardware, rope, wire, nails, etc. were purchased in bulk and sold by the piece, the yard, or the pound. When customers paid cash, it was a simple matter for Samuel to receive payment for the amount sold but record a lesser amount in the sales ledger. If a customer paid cash to purchase, for example, five pounds of sugar, Samuel entered in the ledger a sale of only four pounds. He placed a sum reflecting a sale of four pounds in the cash register and pocketed the remainder of the cash. Thus, at the end of each month, the proceeds from the store were divided based on the falsified amounts Samuel had entered in the sales ledger. This system allowed him to skim much of the store's profit for himself while allowing Hiram to think it was divided equally between the two partners.

Samuel had no intention of using his method indefinitely. He knew that, given Hiram's meticulous record keeping, a discrepancy between quantities of goods sold and quantities needed to restock inventory would eventually be noticed. But he also knew from experience that if Hiram suspected an error in the firm's books, he would invest a great deal of time checking and rechecking his figures to be certain he accurately diagnosed the problem. This process could take weeks. Samuel had a plan to deal with this eventuality, one that could be put into action quickly. If Hiram began a detailed comparison of the records of sales and orders, Samuel would implement his plan before Hiram could complete his calculations.

Samuel's escape plan was basic but foolproof. He had already taken the action to place most of his assets in his wife's name. He kept only a small amount on deposit in the Bank of Plainfield, while most of his money resided in an account he kept in Chicago. The instant he sensed Hiram was on a trail of discovery that could uncover the falsified records, he would concoct a story about a close relative near death in St. Joseph and take the first train out of Plainview. He would then continue on to Chicago and, upon his arrival there, send for his wife. From the distant safety of Chicago, he would use a trusted lawyer as the go-between to dispose of the house and hotel he owned in Plainview. Hiram Johnson would be left as the sole owner of the S&J General Store, which was more than he deserved.

It was on a crisp Monday morning in late October that Hiram Johnson did not arrive on time for work. He had, to his partner's recollection, been late only once before in their years of business together. That was when he had contracted influenza, and even then he insisted on coming in each day and staying past closing to restock the store. Samuel was puzzled, but not worried. If Hiram did not appear by nine o'clock, he would send the young man who worked part-time cleaning the store to Hiram's house to make sure he was all right. The store was busy that morning, as customers had begun stocking up for the coming winter. It was past ten o'clock when Samuel remembered that Hiram might not have come to work.

Samuel momentarily excused himself from the customer he was waiting on, promising to return in just a minute or two. He went to the back of the store and through the doorway into the stock room, where Hiram's desk sat near the only window. The ledger books had not been opened, and there was no sign of Hiram. Samuel returned to the front of the store, where he summoned the part-time employee. Samuel had no great affection for his partner, yet felt a bit concerned as he gave instructions to the young man. "I want you to go over to Hiram's house," he said. "He didn't come in this morning, and I want you to go by just to make sure he is okay." Samuel was not speaking in his usual loud manner, and the perpetual smile had disappeared from his face. The young employee went out the front door of the store and crossed the street, headed toward Hiram's house.

Samuel was waiting on another customer when the young man returned from his errand. He had barely entered the store when he blurted out, "Mr. Goodwin, he ain't there!" "Well now, no need to get excited," said Samuel. "Maybe he had some business to take care of. Let's see, you should probably check over at the bank." The young man stood still. Then he said, "Mr. Goodwin, I think he's been kidnapped." "What," asked Samuel, "why would you think that?" "Because everything is gone, Mr. Goodwin." the youngster replied. "They took his good clothes and his best hat and his pictures and who knows what else. And I asked the lady next door if she knows where he went, and she said she ain't seen him since Saturday."

Samuel frowned deeply. For a moment, he felt as if he were in a fog. Where could Hiram be? What if someone, maybe a customer who owed the store money, had done him harm? Had he been kidnapped? It didn't make sense.

Just then the young man who had reported Hiram's absence saw someone pass by the store window. It wasn't Hiram, but the young fellow was in such an agitated state that he thought it was. He made a beeline for the window to confirm the sighting, and in his haste ran directly into a barrel containing coffee. The barrel, which should have been heavy enough to withstand the assault, tipped over and rolled partway down the aisle. A small quantity of coffee spilled onto the floor, along with a thin, round piece of wood that had been fastened inside the barrel about a foot from the top.

Samuel stared in disbelief. Then, to the total surprise of the others in the store, walked over to the sugar barrel and tipped it over. A small pile of sugar lay on the floor, along with another thin, round piece of wood. He moved quickly toward another barrel and gave it a shove. It fell over easily, disgorging its meager content of beans and yet another round piece of wood. A thin smile found its way onto Samuel's face. He spoke slowly, in a matter-of-fact tone, "The rat. The dirty, rotten, thieving rat. He's been robbing me blind, all the while I've been giving him more of the profit from this place than he had coming. And now he's skipped town, and there's no use going after him. He has a two-day head start. God knows where he sent all the money, but he'll find some out-of-the-way place. Then he'll send for the money, while I sit here like an honest sucker."

Samuel turned to the few remaining customers and said, "I'd appreciate it if you folks would come back another day." Perplexed, they began to leave the store, one by one. The young man spoke. "Do you want me to clean this all up, Mr. Goodwin?" he asked. Samuel laughed. His smile returned, as did the volume of his voice. "A mess like this can't be cleaned up," he said. "It's been a long time in the making, and it's too late now. You go on home." The young man shrugged his shoulders and slowly walked toward the front door. Samuel followed him. He reached toward the window and turned the sign from Open to Closed. He locked the front door and went out the back way, shaking his head in disbelief.

Meanwhile, in a town far from Plainview, Hiram Johnson stepped off a train and began walking toward the nearby hotel where he would spend the night. He had carefully surveyed the other passengers and found himself particularly interested in one of them. The party of interest was a short, overweight man, dressed in a grey suit and patterned tie, who was very outgoing and talkative. On the train, Hiram had overheard the man tell a fellow passenger he was an investor, hoping to make a huge return by backing some type of new business on the frontier.

At the hotel, Hiram made a few discreet inquiries at the desk. He then walked next door to the restaurant, where he spotted the man in the grey suit seated at a table. He walked by the man, nodding slightly as he passed. "Care to join me?" the man asked. "Always glad to make a new friend." Hiram shrugged and sat down. The man took a cigarette case from his suit pocket. "Happen to have a light?" he asked. "I don't smoke," Hiram replied. "It's a waste of money and smells bad. So you won't have to worry about me stealing your cigarettes." A broad smile spread across the fat man's cheeks, and he burst into loud laughter. Hiram smiled too.

6 THE DOG

Jason Cole sat erect in the saddle, his eyes scanning the woods around him for signs of life. The trail that ran along the top of the ridge was familiar territory to both him and his horse, and the animal followed it without any direction from its rider. The duo was accompanied by a rather nondescript brown dog, which alternated between loping and trotting to keep pace with the horse. The dog was first on one side of the horse and rider, then on the other, then slightly ahead of them on the trail. It never let a gap larger than about ten yards develop between itself and the horse, and when in the lead frequently turned and looked back, seeming to want reassurance the horse and its rider were close behind.

It was late fall, and Jason had gone up into the foothills to look for strays. A couple days earlier, with the help of some neighboring ranchers, he had moved his cattle down from the hills to the fenced pasture on the west side of the ranch where they would stay until spring. He had counted thirty-six cows but only thirty-two calves. That meant four of the cows either did not calve, or their calves had died, or the calves had been missed when the cattle were herded out of the hills. Young calves would not survive long alone in the hills, so the strays had to be found soon.

Early in the morning, Jason had saddled his best horse, fastened a lariat to the saddle, placed his forty-four caliber Winchester in the scabbard on the horse's right side, and hung a canteen of water from the saddle horn. His saddlebags held two wool blankets, useful if he found a calf suffering from exposure, and some hardtack and sandwiches his wife had prepared. As always, he wore a gun belt and Colt revolver. The revolver rarely left its holster, though earlier in the summer he had used it to shoot a rattlesnake sunning itself on the woodpile behind the house.

Tomorrow, hands from an adjacent ranch were coming to help brand the Coles' new crop of calves. That left only today to locate the strays and bring them back to the herd. It was just past sunup, brisk and clear, when the horse and rider left the ranch yard and started their trip up into the foothills. There was no guarantee that any calves would be found, but if there were one or more in the hills, Jason was determined to find them. If left alone, they were easy prey for cougars, wolves or bears. Raising cattle in this part of the country was not easy. No rancher could afford to lose any stock, let alone a struggling operation like the Coles'.

Jason had ridden toward the foothills for about thirty minutes when he looked back toward the ranch and saw an animal running toward him. He knew immediately what it was. Some months ago, he had gone to town to get some needed supplies and stopped to visit an old friend. The friend was not at all well and was, as is said, getting his house in order. He had few possessions, but was terribly fond of a dog he could ill afford to feed and convinced Jason to take the dog back to the ranch. The dog took a liking to Jason and began to exhibit the kind of loyalty dogs can show to their owners. The animal scarcely let Jason out of its sight and had to be restrained whenever Jason wanted to leave it behind.

Before Jason left the ranch yard that morning, he had brought the dog into the house and instructed his wife and children to keep it there until he was at least an hour away. But one of the youngsters, heading outside to do morning chores, exited the house without careful attention to the dog, which made a beeline out the door. The dog put its nose to the ground and trotted back and forth across the yard, sniffing as it went. It soon picked up the scent of the horse and rider and, sure it was on the trail of its master, ran to catch up.

Jason pulled the horse's reins, turned around to face the ranch, and waited for the dog. A short time later, it came bounding up to the horse, panting and wagging its tail as if expecting a warm welcome. Jason looked sternly at the dog and began to scold it. He pointed toward the ranch yard and commanded it to "go home." The dog looked up at Jason with a quizzical expression. "Don't play dumb," Jason said, "Go home!" The dog did not move, but continued wagging its tail. If he were to take the dog back, which he should do to teach the animal to stay in the yard, he would lose an hour's time. Finding the strays was more important than training a dog. Reluctantly, Jason addressed the dog. "All right, he said, " Come on. But you'd better keep up." He turned the horse and began to trot toward the hills. While he rode, he silently cursed the dog and berated himself for being so soft-hearted as to bring it home in the first place.

The trio of man, horse, and dog had ridden steadily across the pasture lands below the foothills, then followed a trail that took them to the ridge at the top of the first line of hills. It was late morning when Jason reached the wooded area where he expected to find any strays that might have been left in the hills. The woods were not overly thick and contained several small meadows that provided good grazing for the cattle. The sun was almost directly overhead now, and he felt its heat as he moved along the barren trail. A stream meandered down the west side of the slope, carrying clear water from the mountains above. He urged the horse off the trail and made his way to the stream, where horse, man, and dog drank deeply from its shimmering surface.

Jason returned to the trail and rode slowly, intensely searching for the lost calves. About a third of the way along the ridge, a group of boulders forced the trail to curve around them. Near the boulders, there was a thicket on one side of the trail. The thicket, which was several yards deep, contained a dense combination of sumac, wild berries, thistles, and small trees trying to establish themselves among the other plants. In previous years, he had seen calves run into a thicket like this and not be able to extricate themselves. If the mother cow or a ranch hand did not find them, they would remain until they died of exposure or starvation.

Jason had just reached the edge of the thicket when he heard the muted bawl of a calf. "Good," he thought, "At least I'll get one." He stopped the horse, swung down from the saddle, and wrapped the reins securely around the branch of a small pine tree. The dog was at his side. He looked intently at the dog and said, "Stay. Don't you dare move a muscle or you'll scare the calf and it'll try to run. Stay!" It seemed the dog was going to obey for a change, which pleased Jason. He walked several yards along the trail before spotting the little calf. It was standing in the midst of the thicket, completely bewildered as to how to extract itself from among the thick undergrowth. So as not to frighten the calf, Jason stepped slowly and quietly toward the thicket.

Out of the corner of his eye, Jason saw something move. He turned his head and was surprised to see a young bear cub, no doubt from the past spring's litter. Bears were rare, though not unheard of, in this part of the country and it had been several years since Jason had seen one. The young bear was on the edge of the thicket on the other side of the trail, its attention focused on a group of bushes heavily populated by thick, ripe berries. The thought that an adult bear might be nearby had just entered his mind when Jason heard a growl behind him. He turned and saw a fully-grown black bear facing directly toward him. The bear was between him and his horse, and he was between the bear and its cub, the worst possible situation. The horse shied and pulled its head back, but the reins held and it stood wide-eyed with fear.

Jason stood perfectly still, his mind racing. Running was pointless. The bear would chase him down in seconds. He could try to move slowly out of the bear's path, hoping to get behind a boulder and out of sight so the bear would turn her attention to her cub, but the movement might trigger an attack. His revolver was loaded and ready. Some shots in the air might temporarily frighten the bear. It would be foolish to shoot at the bear with a sidearm. These thoughts all passed through his consciousness in a couple of seconds, which was enough time to realize there were no good options. Just as he was forcing himself to choose a course of action, the bear raised itself onto its hind legs, bared its teeth, and let out a ferocious roar. Then, down on all fours, it started toward him.

The instant the bear began its charge, Jason heard a growling sound different from that made by the bear. Then he heard barking and knew the dog was very close. As the bear ran toward him, Jason drew his revolver, knowing it would be a futile defense. But, as he aimed at the oncoming bear, he saw the dog leap between them. Frantically barking and snapping its jaws, the dog rushed the bear, then veered to the side just out of reach of the bear's massive paws. It attacked again, circling the bear, dangerously close, causing the creature to whirl around as it tried to strike the dog. The dog repeated its perilous maneuvers, each time moving a bit farther up the trail. Then, with the bear in close pursuit, it dashed off the trail into a group of tall pine trees.

Jason saw his opportunity and raced toward the horse, flying around to its right side and quickly grabbing the rifle. He worked the lever action to place a round in the chamber and started after the dog and bear. At the edge of the pines, the dog resumed its risky pattern of attack and retreat. The contest was taking a toll on the dog, which was rapidly tiring. As Jason pointed his rifle in the direction of the bear, he could see the dog was bleeding from its left shoulder. The dog was now between him and the bear. Jason aimed carefully, training his sights on the bear's chest, hoping to strike the beast in its heart. Just as he squeezed the trigger, the bear lashed out at the dog with a mighty paw, its claws raking across the smaller animal's body.

The shot hit home. Jason quickly fed another cartridge into the chamber, but it was not needed. The bear tried to rise onto its hind legs, lumbered a couple steps toward Jason and collapsed. Blood gushed from the bear's wound, and it ceased breathing. The dog lay still, its fur matted with blood, and its eyes staring vacantly ahead. Jason knelt next to the dog, feeling for a heartbeat. There was none. He got up and walked to the horse.

There were two leather straps attached to the rear of the saddle, intended to hold a bedroll or rain slicker. He loosened them and walked back to the dog. He kneeled beside it, thinking about what had just transpired and wondering what would have happened if the dog had not followed him out of the ranch yard.

He scooped the dog up in his arms and carried it to the horse. He placed the limp animal across the horse behind the saddle and tightened the leather straps around it. Then, he walked back down the trail to where he had seen the calf. He waded into the thicket, freed the tiny calf from its prison, and hoisted it onto his shoulders. He carried it to the horse and placed it across the horse's front shoulders, just ahead of the saddle. He mounted the horse, pointed it toward home, and let it find its own way.

The ride back to the ranch was too long and too short. Too long because he wanted to get the calf back to its mother and safety. And too short because he didn't want to face his children and tell them about the dog. He knew he owed his life to the dog, which would make delivering the news of its death that much worse. He had never wanted the dog and had only taken it in at the request of his sick friend. He never asked for the critter to impose itself upon him and his family, and certainly had no intention of mourning the loss of an animal. He would tell his family, as briefly as possible, what had happened that day, with emphasis on the good fortune of finding the calf. They would bury the dog somewhere on the edge of the ranch yard, and that would be that.

The sun was setting by the time Jason reached home. As he rode into the ranch yard, he was firm in his decision to dispense with the business about the dog as quickly and as matter-of-factly as possible. Death was a regular occurrence on any ranch. Sooner or later his children had to understand that their ranch was not a place that tolerated sympathy for the loss of an animal, and this would be a good chance for them to learn. Life was tough in the West, and people had to be tougher. That's just the way it was.

Jason stopped his horse next to the pasture fence behind the barn. He got off the horse, then lifted the little calf and carried it to the fence. He dropped it gently into the pasture and watched as a cow approached the calf, smelling and licking it. The cow recognized her calf, and soon it was nursing from her. He led the horse into the barn, untied the leather straps, lifted the dog's body, and laid it beside the barn door. Then he unsaddled the horse, opened a stall, slapped it on the rump, and watched it walk toward the bunch of hay in the feed trough. He closed the stall door and started toward the house.

As soon as he set foot on the porch he smelled hot food and realized he had not eaten all day. The light inside the house was warm and inviting. As he opened the door and stepped into the house, the children came to meet him. His youngest daughter, who stood just waist high to her father, was the first to reach him. She looked up at Jason with a broad smile. Then a frown spread across her face, as she spoke, "Papa," she asked, "why are you crying?"

7 THE GAMBLER

It was either in the fall of '76 or '77, the year that odd thing occurred where Sam Goodwin and his partner, I think his name was Johnson, both up and left Plainview so unexpectedly, leaving the general store without anyone to run it. Anyway, whichever year that happened was the year that Louise Porter came to town. Some people said she was a friend of Sam Goodwin, and others said the two had never met, but nobody seemed to know for sure. The details are murky at best, but somehow Louise, who later decided to call herself Florence, ended up owning the hotel the Goodwins left behind when they abandoned Plainview.

Of course, owning the hotel also meant owning the saloon that shared the building. The saloon occupied the majority of the ground floor of the building, adjoined by a modest dining room, kitchen, and a small area containing the hotel desk. The hotel alone would hardly have provided an adequate income, even for a person with no family like Louise, but the two businesses combined generated a respectable sum. The saloon

was the first and last stop for most of the ranch hands who visited Plainview each time they were paid. It was not unusual for
the cowboys to leave most of their earnings there when they
returned to their respective ranches. Some drank up their wages, and others gambled them away, but few left with their hard-
earned wealth intact.

The hotel provided permanent housing for three
Plainview residents: Timothy Swanson, a boyish-looking young
man employed by the local bank; Alfred Miller, a lifelong bachelor who, when his small house burned a number of years earlier,
took temporary lodging at the hotel and simply never left; and
Miss Mildred Bauman, the local school teacher. Temporary
boarders included travelers on the stage line or the railroad who
required accommodations during overnight stops, such as traveling salesmen or others conducting business in the area. The
hotel provided lodging at a reasonable cost, and the saloon offered food, drink, and gambling.

Louise was a good businessperson. She hired depend-
able help, closely supervised the daily activities of both the hotel
and the saloon, and generally ran a reputable house. She kept
a keen eye on the accounts, insisted temporary lodgers pay
cash in advance, and never allowed saloon purchases on credit
to exceed two dollars per customer. Rules pertaining to those
who gambled in the saloon were prominently posted and strictly
enforced. All card players had a right to inspect the deck in use
at any time, side arms were to be removed and kept behind the
bar until the owner was ready to leave, and those who chewed
were to use spittoons at all times. Anyone who tried to grant
themselves an exception to the rules could expect a less than
cordial encounter with one of the local lawmen. Ben Jackson
and Bill Carson, the sheriff and his deputy, occasionally took
their meals in the saloon but were never expected to pay for
them. Rumors alleged that Louise was romantically involved

with one of the men, but the truth was that she simply considered it good business to be on friendly terms with the law.

Thanks to the careful attention Louise focused on her establishment, the hotel and saloon in Plainview operated with few problems. It maintained a reputation as a decent and welcoming place and generated a handsome profit. It was not long before Louise was not only the proprietor of the hotel and saloon but also owned a ranch a few miles outside of town. Whether due to her person or her possessions is anyone's guess, but more than one man attempted to interest Louise in a romantic relationship. But they did not succeed, and it became apparent she had no intention of marrying. Her explanation was simple, "I don't need a man to take care of me, and I don't need to take care of a man."

Louise and her business had been a prominent part of Plainview for over five years when, on a pleasant day in the middle of May, she received an unexpected visitor. She was behind the desk at the hotel, examining the registration list, when a rather large, red-haired woman entered the building and approached the desk. Louise was more than surprised to see her aunt standing in front of her. As far as Louise knew, the woman lived in Illinois, and the two had not communicated with each other since Louise had come to Plainview. She had no idea what brought her aunt so far west.

After a somewhat awkward exchange of greetings, Louise invited her aunt to her private quarters in the hotel, where the woman revealed the purpose of her visit. When the two returned to the lobby, the woman gave Louise a long hug, smiled at her, and left the hotel. Louise walked to the bar and sat down. The bartender noticed her face was flushed and expressed his concern. "Are you feeling all right?" he asked, "Can I get you something to drink?" "I'm fine," she replied, "just had an odd surprise. Nothing to worry about." The bartender had noticed the red-haired woman when she came into the building, as well as Louise's reaction when the two women met. But he accepted his boss's assurances, and the other woman was not seen at the hotel again.

Two days later, Louise decided that for the first time since coming to Plainview, she would embark on a trip east. Shortly after breakfast, she surprised her bartender by telling him she was leaving by train that morning for Kansas City. She had some business there, and he would be in charge while she was away. She would be back as soon as possible, but would not be gone more than four days. She gave him a sheet of paper on which she had written an address. "If anything goes seriously wrong," she told him, "send me a telegram at this address."

She left on the train with two large suitcases and a locked metal box. The bartender did not find it necessary to contact Louise, and no one else in town received any communication from her. Four days passed with no sign of Louise. Finally, a week after she had left, she stepped off the train in Plainview. Although she returned later than expected, she offered no explanation for the delay. The hotel and saloon had been well cared for in her absence, and everything seemed to be in order. Louise resumed her activities at the hotel and saloon and life continued as usual.

Since Louise never talked about her trip to Kansas City, local gossips filled the vacuum with theories of their own. The unidentified woman who visited Louise shortly before her Kansas City trip brought news that a wealthy relative had died, and Louise went to collect an inheritance. Or, the red-haired woman had given up Louise for adoption when just a baby, spent years searching and finally located her. But despite the inventiveness of those who created such rumors, the real reason behind Louise's visit to Kansas City remained a mystery.

Despite the enviable reputation enjoyed by Plainview's hotel and saloon, the establishment was not immune to problems. From time to time, a ranch hand or a drifter would stay too long in the saloon and, his alcohol-fogged brain overruling any sensible thought, would challenge another saloon patron to a fight. When this happened, the bartender usually dispatched the troublemaker with a swift blow from the wooden club he kept behind the bar. Sometimes, fortunately not often, the invitation to fight was accepted by the person the drunkard challenged. Then, as the fighters headed out the door to do battle, accompanied by a chorus of curious onlookers, Louise would send one of her employees out the back door with an urgent message for the sheriff. If all went well, the sheriff or his deputy would arrive before either fighter could inflict permanent damage on the other and place them both in jail until sobriety returned and tempers cooled.

Unlike those in some other western towns, the saloon in Plainview had rarely been the site of any serious incidents, and only once had seen actual gunplay. It kept its reputation as a place where a man could meet his old friends or find some new ones, enjoy some drinks together, maybe even get a little drunk, and bet some money on cards. And he could usually do so without worrying some fool might get liquored up and do something stupid to ruin the evening. Louise believed this aspect of her business's reputation was in large part responsible for the saloon's popularity and, in turn, her substantial income. She was determined that between her efforts and those of her employees, and close cooperation with the sheriff, the saloon's reputation would remain unmarred. And it did, at least until a certain stranger came to Plainview.

It was a warm spring afternoon, about a year after Louise's trip to Kansas City, when a train arrived in Plainview. As expected, the engineer blew the whistle twice, slowed the engine and brought the train to a stop beside the depot. The conductor stepped down from the lone passenger car, placed a stool on the ground and began helping passengers disembark from the train. Eight travelers got off the train. After receiving directions from the conductor and retrieving the luggage needed for an overnight stay, seven of the passengers began walking toward the hotel. The eighth passenger, a tall, thin man with a dark mustache, remained on the platform for several minutes, then followed the others.

The hotel clerk busied himself with assigning rooms and collecting money from the group of people in front of him. The guests, who had become acquainted with each other during their time on the train, chatted cordially with each other while waiting their turn to register. Each requested a room for just one night and indicated their intention to join the rest in the dining area for the evening meal. A casual observer might have mistaken them all for old friends rather than individuals who had only recently met. All, that is, except for the man with the dark mustache, who remained apart from the others. He was well groomed and richly dressed, stood facing the saloon, his eyes roaming across the room as though searching for something or someone.

When the other guests had made their way up the stairs to their respective rooms, the lone man approached the desk clerk and spoke softly. "I'd like a quiet room as far from the saloon as possible." he said, "I plan to be here a while." "I'll give you the end room on the left," the clerk replied. "I'm sure it will be to your satisfaction. How long did you say you'll be staying?" "I'm not certain," the man said, "maybe a couple of days, maybe more." The clerk pushed a piece of paper and a pen toward the man, and politely asked him to list his name and address. As the man wrote, the clerk retrieved a key from the board behind the desk and placed the key on the desk. "You have number eight, sir," he said "Upstairs, down the hall and on your left." The man nodded, took the key and climbed the stairs. The clerk turned the paper around, examined it, and frowned. The man's name was scrawled and hardly legible, and no address was listed.

Seven of the new hotel guests met in the dining room for their evening meal. The eighth walked the short distance to the cafe and ate alone. He was a fastidious eater, careful not to get anything on his clothing, and repeatedly wiped his mustache with a napkin. The cafe was nearly empty so Emmet Walker, the proprietor, decided to engage the stranger in conversation. At first, the man seemed rather aloof but was soon asking Emmet a number of details about the town and its citizens, and especially about the hotel and saloon. When Emmet asked what the man was doing in Plainview, he said something about eating before his food got cold and put a forkful of meat in his mouth, effectively ending their conversation.

The next day happened to be payday for most ranch hands in the area, and a good number of them came to town in the late afternoon. As usual, the men congregated in the saloon where they traded their newly acquired funds for drinks intended to clear their parched throats of a month's accumulation of dust. Some of the men moved to a table on the far side of the saloon and sat down. Louise signaled to the bartender, who retrieved a deck of cards from behind the bar. He walked over to the men and placed the cards on the table. A few words were exchanged, and the bartender went back to the bar, returning shortly with a bottle of whiskey and glasses. One of the men began to shuffle the cards, while another poured each man a drink of whiskey.

"Mind if I sit in?" The men looked up to see a stranger standing at their table. He was a tall, impeccably dressed man with a dark mustache. He was smiling slightly. The cowboys exchanged glances, then one of them said, "You new in town?" "Just here for a short visit," the stranger said. "First time, but I hear people here are real friendly." "We think so," another cowboy said, "where you from?" The tall man nodded toward the only empty chair at the table, and asked, "Do you mind?" "OK by me," said the first cowboy. The man eased his slender frame into the chair. "I sometimes enjoy a friendly game of poker," he said. He looked at each of the other men, and they looked at him, each sizing up the other. "Well," said the cowboy who had shuffled the cards, "I guess another dollar in the pot won't hurt nothing." He began to deal the cards.

After the first several hands of poker, the tall man had lost more than he had won, as had one of the cowboys. The other cowboys were enjoying a winning streak. The last round of whiskey was poured from the bottle. It had been emptied quickly as the cowboys satisfied the thirst that had built up over the past weeks. The tall man placed his cards face down on the table. "If you gentlemen will excuse me," he said, "I'll get us another bottle." Without waiting for a reply, he stood up and walked toward the bar. While waiting for the bartender, he noticed Louise standing at the end of the bar. He smiled and nodded. She stared briefly at him, then turned and left the room.

As soon as the tall man left the table, one of the cowboys said, "Well, I'll be danged. A slick lookin' fella like that, I was afraid he was a card shark or somethin'. But he's losin' right along. I'm likin' this. He's sure got a curious habit, though, keeps reachin' inside his coat like he's scratchin' or somethin'." Just then the tall man returned to the table, placed the fresh bottle in front of the man on his right, and sat down. He gestured toward the whiskey. "This is on me," he said, "drink up." The cowboys needed no encouragement, and the glasses were quickly refilled. Each man took a hardy swallow, except the tall man. Instead, he reached inside his coat, then withdrew his hand. He had, in fact, hardly touched his glass since they started playing. The others failed to notice, as they concentrated on taking more money from the impeccably dressed stranger.

As the evening wore on, the tall man's luck improved. He won more hands than he lost, and soon had more than recouped his losses. One of the cowboys was slightly ahead of break-even; the others were in the hole. The men at the table were on their third bottle of whiskey when one of the cowboys said, "I gotta go. I'll be right back." The tall man said, "I do, too." The two men stood up and left the table. One of the cowboys still at the table said, "I don't like what's goin' on here. How did he go from a losin' streak to a winnin' streak just like that?" He muttered something, cursed, and refilled his glass. "And another thing," he continued, "you notice the gal that runs this place, how she keeps lookin' over here at him. I think the two of 'em are in cahoots." The other cowboy frowned. "You mean Miss Louise?" he replied. "Oh, she's all right. She's probably watchin' him so he don't cheat us."

The tall man and the other cowboy returned to the table, and a new round was dealt. One of the cowboys, the one farthest behind in the game, was getting anxious to win back what he had lost. He looked at his cards and tried not to smile. "So," said another cowboy, "open?" The man in last place reached into his pocket, grasped something, and tossed a ten dollar gold piece onto the table. "Anyone wanna raise me?" the cowboy asked. He had begun to slur his words slightly. The others were silent. "I'm out," one said. "Me too," said another. The tall man looked across the room, trying to make eye contact with Louise, but she did not return his gaze. He looked at his cards and reached inside his coat. "You sure you want to do that, friend?"

he asked the cowboy with the gold piece. The cowboy sneered at the tall man and said, "What are you afraid of, mister?" The tall man slowly placed some coins on the table. "See you and raise you another ten," he said calmly.

Unnoticed by the poker players, who were intent on their game, a small crowd of spectators had gathered around their table. Up to this point, they had merely been interested, watching and making comments to each other about the game. But now no one spoke. All eyes were on the cowboy who was farthest behind. The cowboy glanced up and for the first time noticed the group of men that were watching. He looked at the tall man, and a deep frown formed on his face. He took a quick sip of whiskey, then put the glass down and reached into his pocket. He pulled out a gold pocket watch on a chain and carefully placed it on the table. "Anything wrong with that?" he asked, glaring at the tall man. "I'll trust that is worth ten dollars if you say it is," replied the tall man. "Worth more than that," said the cowboy, "but you ain't gonna have it anyway." He laid down his cards, face up. "A good hand," the tall man said. He placed his cards face down on the table, and slowly began to turn them face up, one at a time.

Everyone in the saloon was now gathered around the poker table, including the bartender. Louise was on the edge of the crowd, where she could see the tall man's face but not his cards. As each of the tall man's cards was turned up, the tension in the air grew more intense. Beads of perspiration covered the cowboy's brow. He unconsciously closed and opened his fists. The tall man noticed out of the corner of his eye that the bartender was carrying his club, in case there was any trouble. Finally, the tall man turned up his last card.

In the memory of most who were in the saloon that night, the next few seconds were a blur. The cowboy saw the tall man's card and leaped to his feet. "You dirty cheat," he yelled, "you got them cards from in your coat pocket. You been doin' it all night!" And in an instant, the cowboy reached inside his shirt, pulled out a small pistol, pushed it forward and pulled the trigger.

The bullet struck the tall man in the center of his chest, and he was dead by the time he hit the floor. He fell next to the poker table, and a small pool of blood formed next to his still warm body. The bartender and another man had grabbed the cowboy's gun as soon as he had fired, and held him in a grip so tight he could barely breathe. One of the young men employed by the saloon had already run to fetch the sheriff. He returned shortly and quietly informed the bartender the lawmen were in the country but were expected back shortly. The bartender nodded told the younger man, "We'll hold him here until they come back to town. Go on over and wait at the jail to make sure they git over here as soon as they're back."

The man who had done the shooting stopped struggling to free himself from the iron grip of the bartender. He looked at the other poker players, still seated at the table. "Tell 'em," he said, "tell 'em how he cheated. How he kept reachin' inside his coat for them cards." The other cowboys said nothing. One of them got up and stepped slowly over to where the tall man lay. He kneeled beside the body and opened the man's coat, revealing a single pocket. He reached into the pocket, felt a card-like piece of paper, and pulled it out. "What is it?" asked someone in the crowd. The cowboy looked intently at the object. "I'll be danged," he said. "It's a picture of a woman."

The crowd of witnesses mostly stood in stunned silence. Then one of the men said, "Killed in cold blood. And we don't even know his name." Another voice asked, "Does anybody have any idea who he was?" Silence. Then the cowboy holding the picture said, "I think somebody might. The picture has some writin' on it." One of the onlookers asked, "What does it say?" The cowboy replied, "It says 'Love always, Florence,' but ..." He paused for a second, then said, "But it's a picture of Miss Louise."

Louise saw every head turn in her direction and felt every eye staring at her. She felt as if a great weight was pressing down on her. She took a deep breath and slowly let it out. She looked down at the body lying on the floor, at the cowboy who had shot the man, and scanned the faces in the crowd. In a quiet and hollow voice, she said. "His name is Frank Carter. And he's my husband." Some in the crowd gasped audibly. Some exchanged confused glances. Louise half-smiled and said, "I'm not really Louise Porter. My name is Florence Carter. I guess I owe you folks an explanation." And she began to tell a tale that folks in Plainview will never forget.

Louise Porter, or to be accurate, Florence Carter, was originally from Chicago. When she was nineteen she met Frank Carter, who was six years her senior. She fell head over heels in love with him and, despite her having known him only a few weeks, married him over her parents' objections. At the time, she was employed by her uncle, Samuel Goodwin, who was teaching her the practical aspects of the retail business. She learned quickly, worked hard, and was rewarded with a salary considerably greater than that typically earned by even professional women of the time. When she married, her uncle granted her two weeks time off, and the newlyweds had a happy honeymoon.

Frank and Florence had been married only a handful of months when she realized marrying him had been a mistake. Although he was handsome and charming, he was unemployed and showed little interest in changing that aspect of his exist-ence. Not only did he not contribute to the couple's income, but spent many evenings apart from Florence, frequenting the saloons and gambling halls of the city. He would leave home with all the money the couple had on hand, often returning late, completely broke and reeking of alcohol. More than once, he took money from her handbag without her knowledge, leaving her without funds for household necessities. When Florence objected, his temper flared, and he became violent. When they argued, as they frequently did, she sometimes feared for her safety.

About two years into the marriage, Florence realized Frank was not going to change. He was a habitual drinker and gambler, and life with him offered only the prospect of continued misery and disappointment. His repeated promises to stop drinking and to stay away from the card games he consistently lost were just empty words. Sometimes, after he had dissipated whatever funds she managed to accumulate through hard work and thrift, he appeared to feel genuine remorse and for a time treated her somewhat better. But when money again became available, he returned to his pattern of drinking, gambling, and showing an interest in Florence only as a source of sympathy and ready cash. She finally admitted there was no hope for the two of them.

Having faced reality, Florence decided to leave her husband. She took the risk of sharing her decision with her uncle, Samuel Goodwin, who was sympathetic and promised to help her. He told her about the hotel and saloon he owned in Plainview, an aspect of her uncle's business interests of which Frank knew nothing. Uncle Samuel would help her get established as a hotelier and saloonkeeper, so long as she kept their arrangement completely confidential. Florence was grateful for the opportunity and support and made immediate plans to leave Frank and Chicago. And so it was that late one morning a couple of weeks later, Frank awoke from the previous night's drunken slumber to find Florence and her money absent. She had left a brief note, simply stating she was going far away and he would never see her again.

When Florence left Chicago on the long trip west, she decided she would have a better chance of making a fresh start if she kept her past a secret. She wondered if Frank would try to follow her, though only her uncle Samuel knew where she was headed and he was pledged to secrecy. Still, she wondered how she could be certain that if Frank ever tried to find her he would be unable to do so. Then she hit upon the idea of changing her name. If from the moment she reached her destination she went by a new name, any inquiry regarding a Florence Carter would receive a negative reply. By the time she arrived in Plainview, Florence had given herself a new name. She chose Louise as her given name, after her favorite aunt, her uncle Samuel's wife. She considered the surname Goodwin, after her aunt and uncle, but decided it would be unwise. Instead, after noticing the nametag worn by one of the railroad employees, she settled on the name Porter.

It had taken a long time, but she had gotten over Frank. She felt neither love nor hate for the man, merely a lingering sense of regret at having ever met him. She was grateful for her new life and almost never thought about the man she had left behind in Chicago. She was content in Plainview, and her life was the best it had ever been. That is, until about a month ago, when her favorite aunt made an unexpected appearance in Plainfield. Her aunt carried a message, and a plea that she found both disturbing and compelling.

Florence's aunt, unlike her uncle, had not cut off contact with Florence's wayward husband. Like other women, she found him charming and, although she was well aware of his reputation, enjoyed the attention and flattery he directed toward her. Over a period of many months, Frank convinced Mrs. Goodwin that he was not the same man that Florence had left years earlier. He told her he understood why Florence had left him and he had long since forgiven her for doing so. He said his wife's sudden departure had driven him to face the hard truth about himself and to truly reform. He had quit drinking, overcome the temptation to gamble, and found honest work. He had accepted a very responsible position in Kansas City and would be leaving Chicago within days. He asked Florence's aunt to find a way to communicate all this to her niece, and to plead with her to forgive him and give him another chance.

Florence's aunt succumbed to Frank's charms and agreed to help him. Frank wrote a long letter to Florence, pleading his case, and gave it to Mrs. Goodwin. Although Mr. Goodwin refused his wife's repeated requests for information regarding Florence's whereabouts, he agreed to send Frank's letter to Florence. To guard against her past ever being uncovered, Florence had told her uncle she had taken a new name but had not revealed it to him. Therefore, when the letter from Frank arrived in Plainview it was simply addressed to "Hotel Manager, Plainview." The letter upset Florence, though she tried hard not to show it. She destroyed the letter without responding, hoping her silence would end Frank's efforts to reconnect.

When three months passed without a second attempt by Frank to contact her Louise was confident her silence had been effective. She had nearly erased the letter from her mind and rarely thought about Frank or the ugliness of the life she had shared with him. And she certainly had no regrets about refusing to respond to his attempt to reenter her life. Her business continued to prosper and as she looked toward the future all she wanted or foresaw was a continuation of the life she enjoyed in Plainview.

However, while Florence, or Louise, continued her new life in the town she had adopted, her aunt from Chicago busied herself on behalf of her niece. Through persistent cajoling, alternated with complaining and pouting, she wore down her husband's resistance until he finally broke the promise he had made to his niece. Before telling his wife where Florence could be found, he made her promise not to tell anyone else, especially Frank, and not to attempt to contact her niece.

It was less than a fortnight later that Florence's favorite aunt, after a stopover to visit Frank in Kansas City, arrived in Plainview for a surprise visit with her niece. She had undertaken a mission to rebuild the failed marriage. She was certain that Frank deserved an opportunity to appeal to Florence in person and had taken it upon herself to help her niece understand that he had changed. It was the aunt's intention to convince her niece that there was little to lose by allowing Frank a personal visit. Because Florence's husband was just getting established in a new city he was temporarily short of funds. Therefore, Mrs. Goodwin had taken the liberty of purchasing for him a train ticket from Kansas City to Plainview for the following week. It was this news that prompted Louise Porter to pack her bags, place the saloon in the care of the bartender, and travel to Kansas City. She wanted to know whether Frank was telling the truth about his reformed life. If he was not telling the truth, she wanted to find out in Kansas City, not in Plainview.

Once in Kansas City, it was not difficult for Florence to locate Frank. Her aunt had hinted at the general area in which he was staying, and Florence was sure he would already have made a number of acquaintances in the city. The train had arrived in Kansas City about an hour before sunset. After making several inquiries at the train station, Louise learned that a man fitting Frank's description was boarding on Third Street, just a few blocks from the river. She hired a buggy to carry her to the address she had been given. A short time later, she stepped out of the buggy in front of a white two-story house surrounded by a wrought iron fence. She asked the buggy driver to wait. Leaving her belongings in the rear of the buggy, she opened the gate and walked toward the house. As she did so, she heard voices and laughter coming from inside. She walked up the steps, crossed the porch and knocked on the door.

Florence was shocked when Frank opened the door. He looked disheveled and was holding a glass of whiskey in one hand. Louise could see into the front room of the house. Sitting on a sofa was a woman, considerably younger than Florence, who also had a whiskey glass in hand. She called to Frank, her speech slightly slurred, "Who is it, sweetheart? Tell 'em to go away, they'll spoil our spoonin'." The woman laughed as though she had said something funny. Florence felt a knot form in her stomach. Frank looked sheepish. "She's just joking," he said, "Come on in and let me introduce you." Florence turned and walked away from the door and down the steps. When she reached the gate, she turned toward the house and said, "I'll be back day after tomorrow. I'll have some papers for you to sign." Frank looked puzzled. "Papers," he said, "what kind of papers? And why would I sign them?" "Because," Florence replied, "I'm also going to bring some money." Her voice filled with sarcasm, she added, "That is what you always wanted from me, isn't it?" She climbed into the buggy and directed the driver to take her to her hotel.

Florence had hoped against hope that Frank had really changed. But she was also nobody's fool and realized his recent messages were simply an attempt to use her as he had in the past. She had prepared for this eventuality before she left

Plainview for Kansas City. In addition to the suitcases filled with clothes and other items normally needed when traveling, she carried a locked metal box. The box contained an amount of cash Florence believed was sufficient to motivate even a man as selfish and wanton as Frank. The next morning she made an appointment with an attorney. She told the man she wanted him to put in legal form an agreement she had already drafted in her mind.

A couple days later, when Florence arrived at the house on Third Street, the woman she had seen previously was not there. Frank came to the door and invited her to take a seat in the front room. He began what was no doubt intended as an explanation or apology for what Florence had witnessed earlier, but she interrupted him. "Frank," she said, "I really have no interest in what you have to say since your actions speak so loudly." He started to say something but thought better of it. Florence opened a satchel, took out some papers, and continued, "This paper is your agreement that, after today, you will never ever again attempt to contact me in any way." Frank frowned and looked directly at his wife. He sneered at her as he asked, "And just why would I sign such a thing?" he asked. "Because," said Florence, "as soon as you do, I will give you this box, in which you will find five thousand dollars in cash."

Frank sucked in his breath. He shook his head, and let out a long, slow whistle. "Guess you really do hate me," he said, without any emotion in his voice. "I don't care one way or the other about you," Florence said. "I just want you to leave me alone, and I'm willing to pay you far more than you are worth to do just that." Frank took the paper from Florence and said, "I'll need a few days to read this over and think about it." "That's not how it's going to work," she replied. "You're going to sign it right now, or I and the money are leaving. And if I ever see you again, I'll be inclined to invest the money with someone who is in the business of making sure people like you don't bother people like me." Frank's eyes widened. "Was that a threat?" he asked, surprised at the aggressive tone of Florence's voice. "Take it any way you wish," she said, "are you signing or not?"

Frank got up from his chair and walked over to a small desk in the corner of the room. He retrieved a pen, a bottle of ink, and a blotter from the top right-hand drawer. He opened the bottle, dipped the tip of the pen in the ink, and scrawled his signature on the paper. He put the materials back in the drawer and without saying a word handed the paper back to Florence. She reached down beside her chair, lifted the metal box and handed it to Frank. Then, without either of them saying another word, she left the house. Frank stood at the door and watched until her buggy was out of sight. Florence did not look back.

The next morning, Florence boarded the westbound train out of Kansas City. She was glad the ordeal was over. She would never again have to see Frank. At some point, she might have a lawyer in Chicago file divorce papers. Not to open the way toward marrying again, but just as a means of making their parting permanent. During her time in Kansas City, she had not fully realized the stress she was under. Only when the train had crossed the Missouri and was rolling through the vast prairie lands of Nebraska was she able to release the tension that had built during her confrontation with Frank. The trip back home was very different from the first time she had headed west to Plainview.

It was during the train trip home that the possibility occurred to Florence that her husband might, in the same way he failed to respect her and her right to a decent life, ignore the provisions of the document he had signed. If he ever did try to follow her and got as far as Plainview, he would most likely inquire at the sheriff's office, since he was the one person whose business it was to know everyone in town. Depending on Frank's description of her, the sheriff might acknowledge her presence in town. She considered the possibility of asking the sheriff not to tell anyone she lived there, at least without her approval. But he would want to know why, and she wanted no one to know about her past, and especially about Frank, so she dropped the idea. The possibility of her no-good husband someday showing up in Plainview was highly unlikely, but it was a risk she would have to take.

It took some time for Florence to tell the whole story, but none of her audience lost interest. At times it seemed to them that it could not be true. They had never heard of anything like it. But Florence Carter, or Louise Porter, as they had all known her, stood before them describing everything that had happened between her and her husband. And Frank Carter lay dead on the floor of the saloon. It was real, all right, no matter how strange it sounded.

While Florence was telling her story, the sheriff had arrived at the saloon. He quickly assessed the situation and decided both the man on the floor and whoever had shot him could wait until the woman was finished. When Florence concluded her tale, the sheriff walked through the crowd and stood next to the bartender, who had relaxed his grip on the cowboy. "Well," said the sheriff, "what happened here? And who is the guy on the floor?" The group of men looked at each other, but no one spoke. Then one of the onlookers said, "Crooked card game. That fella in the fancy suit had some cards up his sleeve and he got caught. Served him right, I say." The sheriff looked at the body of the tall man and surveyed the crowd. "That the way it was?" he asked. Several men nodded in agreement.

The bartender had now let go of the cowboy entirely. One of the other cowboys spoke up, "He was provoked. The stranger was dealin' crooked, and he kept reachin' in his coat like he had a gun hidden under there." The sheriff thought a moment. Then he addressed the shooter, "I'm gonna let you go back to your ranch for now. I'll get word to you the next time the circuit judge comes to town. You'll have to come in for a trial." He turned to the crowd and said, "You men that spoke will have to repeat what you said when the judge is here. Nothin' to worry about. This fella will probably get off if it happened like you all said."

The sheriff turned and left the saloon. Nobody said much. The cowboys filed out the front door, mounted their horses and rode quietly out of town. The bartender recruited two men to carry the dead man's body to the undertaker. Florence stood motionless, as if trying to take in everything that had happened. The bartender approached her and asked, "Are you all right, Louise?" "I will be," she replied with a wry smile. "It's been quite a day. Thanks for all you've done. Oh, and from now on you can call me Florence."

8 THE BANKER

Familiar sounds filled the ranch yard as the owner of the ranch prepared to ride out the gate and head toward town. In the corral beside the barn, a horse neighed and stomped its feet, raising a small cloud of dust. A meadowlark on a nearby barbed wire fence chirped its high-pitched tune. Near the house, a chicken cackled as it scratched in the dirt for bugs. The pine trees behind the house sang their characteristic wind song as a steady breeze passed through their branches.

But the rancher paid no attention to the sounds heard in the yard that morning, including those made by his own actions. He scarcely heard the rusty pump handle squeal in protest as he moved it steadily up and down, or the gurgle of the water as it filled his canteen for the ride ahead. His mind was on other things. He walked slowly to his already saddled horse, put his left foot in the stirrup, and swung himself up and onto its back. The leather creaked as he settled into the saddle, pulled the brim of his hat down slightly in front, and gave a last look around the yard to ensure nothing was amiss.

The screen door of the house squeaked as it was pushed open, then slammed as it closed. He turned to see his daughter standing on the porch. "Good luck in town," she called, "I have a feeling it will be OK." "I hope you're right," he replied. He clucked his tongue twice, gently nudged the horse with his heel, and headed toward town. They had gotten an early start, and the sun was still low in the sky. Later in the day, as the sun stared down from overhead, the earth would bake in the mid-summer heat.

The rancher, a wiry, deeply tanned, taller than average man named Pete Wegner, had been on the Flying W ranch for over twenty years. As a young man he worked as a hand for other ranchers, including several years as a wrangler on cattle drives to Dodge City. He spent little and saved what he could. He had invested all his savings and taken a mortgage to acquire the ranch, which consisted of several hundred acres of wind-swept prairie and some gently rolling hills with a stand of ponderosa pines. With the help of his wife, and later their son and daughter, he had turned the modest spread into a workable ranch that provided at least a meager income.

Pete had built the few buildings on the place -- a modest single-story house, a lean-to barn with an adjoining corral, and a small chicken coop. He went up into the foothills to cut young trees and fashion them into fence posts, dug the postholes, and strung barbed wire to keep the cattle from wandering. A neighbor helped dig the well and erect a windmill. Like other ranchers in the area, he fought drought, blizzards, and livestock sickness to squeeze a living from the patch of earth he named the Flying W.

Life was not easy for the Wegners. Their oldest child, a son, was fifteen when he joined his father and a crew of other wranglers for his first cattle drive. About halfway to Dodge City, the Wegner boy was riding at the front of the herd when a stampede began. The boy was keeping pace with the older men as they tried to stop the panicky cattle when his horse shied and took a sudden, unexpected turn. He lost his balance, fell from his horse, and was trampled under hundreds of hooves before anyone could reach him. It was one of the few times Pete Wegner found himself unable to do what he felt he should. Another rancher brought the boy's body back to the Flying W and told Mrs. Wegner what had happened. Pete came home later, awash in grief and largely silent for weeks afterward.

Their daughter Clara was a bright spot in the Wegner's lives. She was a cheerful child, always willing to help her mother and anxious to learn the many household skills needed to make the ranch house a pleasant home. By the time she was thirteen, Clara was a more than adequate seamstress, launderer, gardener, and a cook who could butcher a chicken and roast it to near perfection. Her father sometimes joked that she was adopted, since no one so pretty and bright could be his descendant.

Little did the Wegners know how soon Pete would depend exclusively on young Clara's skills as a homemaker. The winter Clara turned fourteen, her mother contracted a severe case of influenza from which she did not recover. The funeral, attended by Pete, Clara, three neighboring ranch families, and the parson from town, was held at the ranch. Afterward, Pete buried his wife next to their son in a small fenced plot behind the house.

Pete Wegner and his daughter Clara were not the sort of people who questioned the good or bad things that happened in their lives or despaired in the face of adversity. Life was not meant to be easy, and complaining only made things worse. They did not deny the hardships they endured but faced trials straight on, determined to do what they could and trust that the lowest of times would be followed by something better. People lacking their determination might have left the Flying W, perhaps gleaning a small profit by selling the ranch. But Pete and Clara stuck it out year after year, never abandoning their loyalty to the ranch or to each other.

The ensuing years at the Flying W were especially hard. A three-year drought covering nearly all of five states left the ranch critically short of water. With limited feed and water, Pete and other ranchers found it necessary cull their herds, driving surplus cattle to Dodge City. This produced an oversupply of beef, and the market price of cattle plummeted. The following year, tick fever spread through the countryside, with some herds almost totally decimated. Although the Flying W was not affected as badly as many ranches in the area, Pete and Clara could ill afford the loss of the seven cows and calves that fell to the disease.

As a result of these problems, Pete found himself lacking the funds required to meet his annual mortgage obligation. Much as he dreaded the thought, it was necessary to visit the bank that held the mortgage and explain that he simply could not make this year's payment. Today was the day Pete had chosen to ride into town to face the banker. He knew full well that by the end of the day he would probably be returning home to tell Clara they were losing the ranch.

It took nearly three hours of steady riding to reach town. It was Pete's first visit in months, which was fine by him. He wished he could pick up some much-needed supplies from the general store, but that was out of the question. After he met with the banker it was unlikely he would need any more supplies for the ranch. He stopped his horse next to a building with a sign above the door that read "Walker's Cafe." Pete dismounted and tied his horse to the hitching post. Next to the cafe was a building with a large sign that proclaimed "Bank of Plainview." He looked up at the sign, exhaled, and walked resolutely into the building.

Pete walked directly to the teller's window and said quietly, "I'm here to see Mr. McGill." "He's expecting you, Pete," the teller replied, "You can go on back to his office." Pete thanked the man and walked around the end of the teller cage toward the rear of the bank. Entrance to the bank president's office was through a large door with a frosted glass window on which was painted in gold lettering, "President," and below that "J.B. McGill." Pete knocked on the door and a voice said, "Come in." He opened the door, swallowed hard, and walked into the office.

Mr. McGill was seated behind a large oak desk, an unlit cigar clamped between his teeth, writing something in a ledger book. Pete recalled that the banker carried a cigar in his mouth nearly all the time, but he had never seen one lit. A bank employee had once mentioned that McGill only actually smoked a cigar on "special occasions." A brass lamp with a green glass shade sat on the desk, along with a round cup-shaped container holding several pens, an inkwell and a small wooden humidor. A single window, largely covered by dark green draperies, allowed limited light to enter the room. To a person accustomed to the outdoors, the banker's office seemed gloomy and depressing. Pete found himself wishing he could visit with the banker at his own kitchen table, with light streaming in the windows and fresh air coming through the screen door.

"Well," said the banker, "I haven't seen you in quite a while, Pete. Have a seat." Pete sat in the large, round-backed wooden chair and began fiddling with his hat. The banker continued, "I noticed it is time for your mortgage payment, but you could do that with the teller. Something else you want to see me about?" Pete took a deep breath, then exhaled slowly. "No, Mr. McGill," he began, "Nothing else. Just the mortgage." The banker put his pen down and frowned. "What about the mortgage?" he asked. "Well, sir," Pete said, "you know it hasn't been easy on us ranchers the past couple of years. In fact, most all of us are havin' considerable trouble just keepin' our heads above water. Not that there is much water, mind you, just an expression." Pete immediately felt foolish over his comment about water.

"I understand that this isn't the best of times," said the banker. "Ranching is a risky business, and a man should know that before he gets into it." Pete nodded. "I suppose that's true," he said, "and it's been a bad risk lately. But we've both been around long enough to know that hard times are usually followed by better times." Pete hoped he hadn't sounded argumentative. The banker looked directly at Pete and asked, "So, what's this leading up to? Are you or are you not able to make your mortgage payment?" Pete looked at the floor, turned his hat over in his hands, and replied, "No sir, Mr. McGill, I simply don't have enough money."

The banker's frown deepened. He pushed his chair back from his desk and stood up. "I'm sorry to hear that, Pete," he said. "I was hoping it was something else." Pete looked up at the banker. "I'm sorry, "he said, "it's not from want of workin' hard. It's just the times. You know, the drought, the cattle sickness, the drop in beef prices. It's hit us all." "That may be so," said the banker; "in fact, it is so. Every ranch in the country seems to be in trouble. And that makes your situation worse." Now it was Pete's turn to frown. He wasn't sure what the banker meant. McGill continued, "I can't, that is the bank can't afford to bail out every rancher that owes us money. We have a business to run here. If we let one rancher's payment slide, what will we do with all the others? I'd like to help you, Pete, but it wouldn't be fair to the bank, and it wouldn't be fair to the other ranchers."

Pete felt as if a dark cloud had settled on the room, making it even more gloomy. "Mr. McGill," he said, his throat dry and his voice becoming hoarse, "I've made my mortgage payment in full every year until now, despite everything. And it's not like I can't pay anything. I have sixty-eight dollars saved up. That leaves me just forty-two dollars short. All I'm asking is some time on the forty-two dollars." The banker was silent. He frowned again, turned the cigar over in his mouth, and reached in his vest pocket to withdraw a gold pocket watch. "You're asking a lot," he said, "especially considering the others." "I know," said Pete, "but I'm not just asking for myself. I'm asking for Clara, too. The ranch is all she's ever known, and all either of us has."

The banker stared at his watch. "I'm going home for dinner," he said matter-of-factly, "You go over to the cafe and have something to eat. Come back here this afternoon and we'll finish talking this over." He was not being overly pleasant. "I carried some hardtack and bread," Pete said, "but I'll sit in the cafe a while. And I'll be back at one." McGill exited the office, with Pete trailing behind. The banker walked out the door, turned to the right, and headed toward the large, three-story house at the end of the street. Pete turned left toward his horse and retrieved a small sack from his saddlebag. He entered the cafe, ordered a cup of coffee, removed the contents of the sack and began to eat. He hardly tasted the food or drink, and nearly forgot to pay for the coffee, concentrating instead on the clock that hung on the wall of the cafe.

At precisely one o'clock Pete re-entered the bank building. He started toward McGill's office, but the teller stopped him. "He's not back yet," the teller said. "You can wait over there."

The teller gestured toward some straight-backed chairs along one wall of the bank, next to the potbellied stove that warmed the building in winter. Pete shrugged and took one of the chairs. His thoughts turned to the ranch, and to Clara. What would the two of them do when McGill threw them off the ranch? He was still a capable hand, with a good reputation, and could find work on any ranch that needed help. But what about Clara? Most women her age were married and had children. But Clara had chosen to stay on the Flying W and had given her all to care for it and for him. It seemed terribly unfair to her, though there was little more he could do. He had made his case to Mr. McGill the best he knew how, and that was that.

McGill did not return to the bank until nearly two o'clock. When he entered, the teller nodded toward Pete, as if reminding the banker that he had left his client waiting. The banker did not acknowledge Pete. Instead, he entered the teller's cage and began a hushed conversation with an older man who occupied a small, plain desk at the rear of the cage. The man assumed a quizzical expression, looked over at Pete, and said something inaudible to McGill. McGill nodded, handed the man a small envelope, and headed to his office. The teller motioned to Pete to follow the banker. Once inside the office, Pete resumed his seat in the round-backed chair, holding his hat in his hand.

For a few moments, neither man spoke. The banker drummed his fingers on his desk, retrieved a new cigar, which he placed in his mouth without lighting it, and appeared deep in thought. A soft rap on the door broke the silence. "Come in," said McGill. The man who had been at the desk in the teller's cage entered, and placed a long sheet of paper on the banker's desk. "I think it's all drawn up just as you asked," the man said. Then, smiling slightly at Pete, he left the room. Pete wasn't sure what type of paper people had to sign when they were fore-closed upon, but he assumed he was about to find out. He wondered how much time he and Clara would have left on the ranch. He realized he should have asked McGill whether they could stay through the year if he gave the bank the sixty-eight dollars he had saved. But it was too late for that. The papers were done, and so was his life on the Flying W.

Pete's train of thought was interrupted by the banker. "Pete," said McGill, "I want you to listen very carefully to what I'm going to say." Pete did not need much encouragement. He was certain this was a conversation he would remember the rest of his life. "As I told you this morning," said the banker, "this bank cannot afford to let people's debts go unpaid, no matter how unfortunate that may be." Pete felt a knot form in his stomach, just like he felt when he lost his son, just like he felt when his wife died. He wanted to bolt out of the room, but knew he mustn't. He began to perspire, and gripped his hat tighter.

The banker continued, "Now, despite the bank's position, I'm pleased to tell you I have been contacted by an anonymous investor who is willing to help." McGill's remark took Pete by surprise. He wasn't sure what the other man meant. "I have a paper here for you to sign," the banker said. "It contains three things. First is an agreement between you and the bank, allowing the bank to transfer your mortgage to the anonymous investor. Your future payments will be made through the bank, but will go the unnamed party." Pete was confused. He was sure McGill mentioned future payments. Did that mean even though he was losing the ranch he would still owe the balance of the mortgage? That couldn't be right, could it?

McGill went on. "The second is your acknowledgment that the anonymous investor is deferring this year's mortgage payment and adding it to the last year of the mortgage. And the third is your promise that you will retain no less than fifty dollars of the sixty-eight you currently hold for future purchases of supplies you will need for the ranch." Pete's head was swimming. Had he heard right? Was this really happening? Would he and Clara be able to keep the Flying W?

The banker's voice broke into Pete's thoughts. "Well, Pete," McGill said, "any questions?" Pete looked at the banker. "Ah, no sir, I guess not," he managed to say. "Good," said McGill. "Then sign right here." He pushed the paper across the desk toward Pete and handed him a pen. Pete took the pen and had just begun to scratch his name on the paper when the banker, with a slight grin, said, "Better dip it in the ink first." "Oh, yeah," said Pete, "kinda forgot." He dipped the pen in the inkwell and, shaking slightly, scrawled his name at the bottom of the paper. He handed the pen back to McGill, who refreshed the pen's ink, then signed his name neatly below Pete's.

Pete sat motionless in the chair. He felt a combination of relief, amazement, and disbelief. "Now don't forget," said the banker, "you still have a mortgage, and next year at this time you will be expected to make a payment to the investor through the Bank of Plainfield." "Oh, yes sir," Pete said, "I won't forget. In fact, I won't forget anything you said today for a long, long time." "Well then," the banker said, "unless there's something else …" "Oh," replied Pete, "I guess just. Well, this doesn't near cover it, but I just want to say thank you. Thank you for me and for Clara, and for all the Flying W means to both of us." "Don't thank me," said the banker, "You just be thankful that the anonymous investor was able to help out this time."

Pete grasped the banker's hand and shook vigorously, then felt silly for doing. His step was light as he left the office and walked past the teller's cage. As he opened the door to leave the bank, a man was about to enter. Pete held the door open, motioned for the man to enter, and with a huge smile, bowed to him also. The man came through the doorway with a questioning look on his face and thanked Pete for his courtesy. Pete walked to his horse, untied it and patted it on the neck. He put his foot in the stirrup and lifted himself into the saddle. As he turned the horse toward home, he began telling the animal what had happened in the bank that day. He recited every detail and then, since he was less than halfway home, began again and repeated the whole story. The horse seemed to take it in stride, perhaps realizing it was good practice for when Pete would tell the same story to Clara.

After Pete left the bank, Mr. McGill entered the tellers' cage and took the signed paper to the desk of the man who had prepared the document. "Well done," said the banker to the man, "Mr. Wegner is indeed a happy man. And someday, I hope, will be a prosperous one as well." The man replied, "Not likely. But at least with friends like you, he can continue on." The banker looked sternly at the man. "I'm a banker," he said; "bankers can't afford to become friends with borrowers." The man smiled broadly. "Right," he said, "that's why sometimes they have to be anonymous." McGill looked at the man but said nothing. He walked directly to his office, closed the door, and lit his cigar.

9 The Outlaw

The sun was low in the west when a lone rider rounded the hill on which the Plainview Cemetery was located and rode at full gallop through the main street, raising a cloud of dust behind him. He pulled his horse to a stop in front of the sheriff's office, dropped the reins, and slipped out of the saddle. The horse, trained to stay in place if its rider let the reins fall, stood next to the hitching rail, soaked in lather and breathing heavily. The rider bounded onto the boardwalk and burst through the office door.

Sheriff Jackson was seated behind his desk, leaning back in his chair, with his boots resting on a partially opened desk drawer. The rider didn't wait for an invitation to speak. "Sheriff," he said, "I just came from the Flying W ranch. You won't believe what I saw!" Sheriff Jackson removed his boots from his desk, leaned forward, and looked at the rider. "Well," he said, "supposin' you just tell me what you saw, and then I'll decide whether to believe it." "Oh, you'll believe it, all right," said the rider, "but ya might wish it weren't for real."

Sheriff Jackson was not a man who was easily excited. "OK," he said, "what's goin' on at the Flying W?" The rider took a deep breath, and let it out slowly. "Well," he said, looking intently at the sheriff, "I was out lookin' for strays, and had just rode up over the ridge on the north side of the place, so I had a clear view of the barn and the house. Miss Wegner was standin' on the front porch, facin' toward the barn. She looked up in my direction, so I waved. Instead of wavin' back, she shot a glance at the barn, and then real quick like turned and went into the house." "So," the sheriff said, "you rode your horse half to death to come tell me that Miss Wegner wouldn't wave back to you? That's somethin'."

The rider frowned, pushed his hat back on his head, and moved closer to the sheriff. "No, dang it," he said, "that's not it." "Well," replied the sheriff, "what is it then?" The rider clenched his jaw, glanced around the office, then said, "It seemed like she was actin' funny, 'specially the way she looked at the barn like that. So I eased my way down the hill behind the barn, just to where I could see into it through the big door on the north side." "And what did you see?" asked the sheriff. "A man," said the rider, "hidin' in the barn. Someone you and every lawman around has been wantin' to catch up and put away for a long time. I'm tellin' you, sheriff, the Kansas Kid is in that barn. Seen him with my own eyes."

"Are you sure?" asked the sheriff. "Course I'm sure," said the rider, "it ain't the first I've seen him. I was in North Branch the day he robbed the bank there. Saw him and his pardner get on their horses and ride out of town. I wasn't twenty feet away. Besides, the guy in the barn is the spittin' image of the picture on the Kid's wanted poster." "OK," said the sheriff, "you go over to the cafe and the saloon and the boarding house and tell everybody we're gettin' a posse. No need to say what for. Just tell 'em to get their horses and guns and meet here in twenty minutes." The rider nodded but said nothing. He strode out of the office and walked rapidly across the street to the cafe.

A short time later a group of eleven men stood in front of the sheriff's office. All had tied their horses nearby and waited impatiently for Sheriff Jackson to emerge from his office. They already knew the reason they had been recruited for posse duty. The man who had ridden into town with such exciting news seemed compelled to share it with the men he summoned for duty. Each member of the hastily assembled group was armed. Most carried rifles and all had pistols, with one exception. Standing amidst the other posse members was an unarmed and unexpected volunteer, Reverend James Rhodes.

The sheriff came out onto the boardwalk, looked over the group of volunteers, and spoke. "Men," he said, "I'm afraid this is going to be a tough task. We're goin' out after a fella with a real bad reputation. And unless I miss my guess, he ain't likely to come along peaceably. So, if any of you want to stay behind, you feel free to do so." Nobody moved, and nobody mentioned they already knew the identity of the intended quarry. The sheriff looked at Reverend Rhodes. "Parson," he said, "that includes you." The preacher pursed his lips, tilted his head slightly, and replied, "Sheriff, just because I'm a reverend doesn't mean I won't do my civic duty. I may not carry weapons, but I'm as willing to help apprehend a criminal as any man here." The sheriff looked knowingly at the preacher. "All right," he said, "let's mount up."

The group of men, with the sheriff in the lead, trotted through town with their eyes straight ahead. At the edge of town, they urged their horses to a canter. They did not want to tire the horses but knew the importance of reaching the Flying W before sundown. Each had his own thoughts, and each was aware that the possible outcomes of their expedition ranged from the satisfaction of catching a notorious criminal to being wounded or worse in the attempt to do so. They wanted the Kansas Kid caught and punished, all right, but they also wanted to make it back to town safely. None of the posse members saw any sense in giving their lives in exchange for that of an outlaw.

Deputy Carson rode next to Reverend Rhodes. "So, parson," the deputy said, "I'm a little surprised to see you joinin' this party." The preacher looked at the deputy with little expression. "It's my duty," he replied. "You surely wouldn't know this, but my father was a preacher in Wichita. And when I was just a youngster, I vividly remember his participating in posse work whenever there was a need." The deputy considered the preacher's comment, then nodded his head. The two rode in silence for a few minutes. Then the deputy asked, "Did your father carry a gun?" "Yes," said the preacher, "but I don't. I believe in saving life rather than taking it." "That's fine by me," replied the deputy, "too bad the fella we're after don't feel the same way."

The sun was just above the horizon when the posse reached the Flying W. Sheriff Jackson divided the men into two groups. One group was to circle around behind the ridge, then approach the barn from the rear. The other group was to make their way behind the house, putting them in position to block any escape from the front of the barn. Sheriff Jackson stayed with the men approaching the barn from the rear, while his deputy led the other men around behind the house. The deputy's group was to take no action unless the Kid tried to exit the barn from the front.

The sheriff and the men accompanying him reached a spot just over the ridge, directly behind the barn. There they dismounted, checked their firearms to ensure all was ready, and carefully began to approach the rear of the barn. They split into two groups, each headed toward one of the rear corners of the structure. They listened intently but heard nothing other than the normal sounds emanating from several horses, a cow, and a number of chickens kept in the building. When they reached the corners of the barn, the sheriff motioned for both groups to move toward the open door at the center rear of the building. Tension built as they neared the opening, expecting that at any second the Kid might spot them and open fire.

The sheriff was the first one to step into the barn. If he was afraid, he didn't show it. Gun drawn, he moved quickly to one side of the door, waiting for his eyes to adjust to the dim interior. Then the others joined him. Two men silently climbed the ladder into the haymow. Cautiously, the men on the ground began to make their way along the rows of stalls on either side of the barn. One at a time, they looked into each stall, wanting to spot the Kid, and yet hoping not to come face to face with him. A horse reacted to the unfamiliar presence in the barn by neighing loudly. Emmet Walker, the posse member closest to the horse, gasped in fright, then silently scolded himself for doing so. He hoped nobody else noticed.

The sheriff reached the front of the barn. He looked around at the men behind him, then looked up and scanned the floor above. One of the men in the haymow peered over the edge and shook his head. The sheriff frowned, then spoke softly. "He ain't in here," he said. It took a little while for the truth of what he said to sink in. "Well," said one of the posse members, "maybe he never was."

Just then a shot rang out. Wood splintered from the doorframe in the front of the barn. A man's voice came from the front of the house. "Don't shoot," it commanded, "I got Miss Wegner in here. If you shoot you'll hit her first." "Damn!" exclaimed the sheriff, "he's here all right." A posse member whispered, "What are we gonna do?" "Gotta think a minute," the sheriff replied. A second shot came from the house, striking the side of the barn. "Sheriff Jackson," the voice from the house called, "you out there?" "I'm here," said the sheriff, "and a whole bunch of other fellas are too. Your goose is cooked, Kid. Better give it up."

A third shot hit the barn, this one penetrating the plank wall uncomfortably close to one of the men. The earlier question from the posse member was repeated. "What are we gonna do?" The sheriff didn't answer. Instead, he climbed the ladder into the haymow and made his way to the small door at the front of the barn. He undid the latch and carefully opened the door just enough to get a good view of the house. He was not prepared for what he saw.

Reverend Rhodes was standing at the end of the front porch of the house. As the sheriff watched, the preacher began to move closer to the door. He had taken several quiet steps along the porch when the man inside the house saw him and called out, "Stay away, parson. I ain't got cause with you." "I'm trying to help you," said the reverend, "You're surrounded. You can't get out. If you give up peacefully, I'll speak for you at your trial." "Ain't gonna be no trial," the Kid answered. "I'm gettin' out of here. I got the lady in here with me. Anybody try to take me she'll never see another day."

The preacher took another step toward the door. "Stay back, I said!" the Kid yelled. The preacher stood still. He could see the muzzle of a gun aimed in his direction. He spoke calmly to the man on the other side of the screen door. "You know you haven't a chance, Kid," he said. "If you harm that woman, or if you make a break for it, they'll shoot you. The only way out is to let the lady come out and give yourself up. You'll get a fair trial. I guarantee it." The voice from inside the house sounded shaky.

"I said, ain't gonna be no trial," the Kid said, "I know what they'll do. They'll send me up the river. And I ain't never goin' to prison again. Never, ya hear? I'll die first! And so will she!"

The men watched with rapt attention as the preacher, to their amazement, took another step toward the door. Then, in a steady voice, he spoke, "Think about what you're saying. I wouldn't lie to you. You hurt that lady, you'll die for sure. You let her come out and give yourself up, you might go to prison. But you'll get out someday. Alive. You're young. You'll have years to make a better life for yourself." The house was silent. The preacher continued, "Listen, Kid. Whatever you've done, I know you didn't intend it to turn out this way. Think back to when you were just a boy. Think about your parents. How would they feel if they knew you were threatening to hurt Miss Wegner? What would they want you to do now?"

Emmet Walker was next to the sheriff, close enough to hear what was going on at the house. "What's he talking like that for?" he asked. "Is he crazy? Talking to the Kansas Kid about when he was a boy? He's gonna get himself shot for sure." "Maybe," said the sheriff, "You got a better idea?" "Yeah," said Emmet, "rush him. He can't shoot all of us at once." "No, he can't," the sheriff replied, "but he can shoot that woman in there, and he might just shoot you." The sheriff's comment ended their brief conversation, and the two men resumed their attention to the activity at the front of the house. They heard the preacher say, "You still have some hope. Don't give it up. Let the woman go. These men won't wait out here forever. I promise I'll speak up for you when the time comes."

No reply came from the house for what seemed to the onlookers like a long time, but was in reality just a couple minutes. Then the front door of the house opened and Miss Wegner walked slowly and carefully through it and onto the porch. The preacher beckoned to her, and she walked past him and to the end of the porch. Emmet Walker urged the sheriff, "Now! He's in there alone. All of us together. This is our chance to get him." "Wait a minute," the sheriff replied, "not yet."

Miss Wegner was now safely off the porch, being helped to the rear of the house by one of the posse. The preacher remained on the porch. He faced the barn and called across to the men waiting there. "I promised him a safe surrender," he said. "You men have got to honor that." While the men were waiting for Sheriff Jackson to reply, they were startled by a single gunshot. The preacher was at the door instantly, then inside the house. The deputy ran across the porch and entered behind the preacher. The Kid lay on the floor, gasping his last breath, as a red stain spread across his chest. Beside him lay his revolver, a small wisp of smoke drifting from the barrel. Other men entered the room and stared at the body on the floor. "Well," said the sheriff, "he said he wasn't goin' back to prison." The preacher said nothing.

Later, as the posse road back toward town, the men were mostly silent. The preacher rode near the rear of the group, next to Emmet Walker. Emmet didn't talk the whole way to town, but just looked down toward the ground. Part way back to town, the deputy guided his horse next to Sheriff Jackson's. He looked over at the sheriff, then back toward the preacher. He turned toward the sheriff again, and said quietly, "I don't understand. Why did the parson take a chance like that? What made him think the Kid wouldn't just up and shoot him? And that stuff he said about when the Kid was just a boy, and his parents and all that. He musta been just makin' that up."

The deputy noticed a wry grin on the sheriff's face. The sheriff looked at the deputy, then back toward the preacher, then straight ahead. "Oh, he wasn't makin' it up," said the sheriff. "Everything he said was right as rain. Somehow it got the Kid thinking, and that's how we all got through this thing without anyone else gettin' hurt." "Well, how do you know the parson wasn't just talkin' through his hat?" asked the deputy. "Because," said the sheriff, "he knows exactly what the Kid was like as a youngster." The deputy's voice showed exasperation. "How in tarnation would he know that?" he asked. "Simple," the sheriff said, "They had the same parents."

10 THE REPORTER

The engine, as if protesting the resumption of its journey, hissed clouds of steam along the rails and belched black smoke into the air. The cars lurched and shuddered, the couplers banging against each other until the slack between them was taken up. The train gradually began to gather speed and the last car passed the end of the station platform. The cacophony of sounds emitted as the train got underway was soon replaced by the rhythmic click-clack of the rails as the train followed the black thread of track across the prairie.

The passenger cars were in the fourth and fifth positions behind the engine, behind the tender, a baggage car and a freight car, and ahead of a second freight car, two empty cattle cars, and the caboose. Placing the passenger cars mid-train afforded passengers some protection from the smoke, soot and embers emitted by the locomotive. It also lessened passengers' risk of harm should the train encounter unfriendly Indians. Skirmishes between renegade bands of disgruntled natives and the trains invading their homelands usually focused on the engine, as the Indians attempted to gain control of it to stop the train.

Fortunately for those aboard, the hostiles were most often re-pelled by rifle fire from the locomotive and, when necessary, from the caboose.

Seated in the fourth row of the first passenger car, on the right side of the aisle, Franklin B. Underhill shifted slightly and turned toward the open window. He removed his wire rim glasses, extracted a handkerchief from his inside coat pocket and began to carefully wipe the dust from the lenses. He re-placed his glasses but noticed a slight smudge near the bottom of the left lens. He repeated the cleaning procedure, this time carefully examining the glasses to verify their spotless condition before refitting them. Satisfied, he again turned to the window and gazed at the scene before him.

During the recent stop at the Great Bend depot, during which the train took on a fresh supply of water and offloaded two freight shipments and one passenger, Mr. Underhill, in his usual efficient manner, had tended to three tasks. He sent a short telegram informing the editor of the *Saint Joseph Morning Herald* of his progress thus far, made a brief visit to the local saloon and cafe, where he obtained a cold beef sandwich and a jar of water, and made a perfunctory visit to the local newspaper office, where he purchased a copy of the town's weekly. Thus equipped, he returned to his place on the train precisely two minutes prior to the conductor's "all aboard" and the train's de-parture.

Underhill had positioned himself on the right side of the passenger car to avoid the harsh sun. Thus his view from the train window was toward the north-northwest. He was quite un-aware that he was facing in the direction of the original home-lands of many Indian groups that had been displaced to Kansas and other states. Although Underhill had for years held a deep interest in the West, most of his knowledge of the area was gleaned from imaginative accounts of the frontier published as newspaper serials or from dime novels filled with thrilling tales of western adventure.

Franklin B. Underhill was a reader. He had learned the alphabet at his mother's knee and read above his grade level throughout grammar school. By the time he was midway through secondary school he decided to pursue an English degree at a major university. It was during his college years that he tried his hand at creative writing. Despite receiving mediocre grades and scant encouragement from his professors, Underhill soon envisioned a career as a creative writer. And although he recognized it might be necessary to temporarily support himself through other endeavors, his dream was to become a successful author of Western literature.

It was Underhill's fascination with the West that led him to leave New York for St. Louis. He had, through the recommendation of a professor who happened to be acquainted with the publisher, obtained a position as a reporter for the Saint Louis Dispatch. His expectation was that he would advance rapidly due to his education and writing skills and soon enjoy an income that would facilitate pursuit of his writing career. Unfortunately, the rather shortsighted editor of the Dispatch failed to fully recognize Underhill's talents. Thus it was that, after slightly less than two years in St. Louis, he again moved west, taking a senior reporter position with the *Saint Joseph Morning Herald.*

The editor of the *Morning Herald*, Theodore Watts, under whom Underhill now worked, was a rather bookish but congenial and generally positive individual. He admired the confidence and work ethic Underhill readily displayed and took a liking to the young reporter. Within a short time a friendship developed between the two men, despite the fact that Watts was Underhill's supervisor and, in his late forties, some twenty years older than Underhill. Praised for the quality of his reporting and encouraged by his friendship with Watts, Franklin Underhill had little difficulty imagining a time in the not too distant future when he might become the editor or perhaps even the publisher of his own newspaper. This would provide the financial means to launch his career as a Western author.

After little more than a year at the Morning Herald, Franklin Underhill received some surprisingly welcome news from the editor. Near the end of the workday, the two men were discussing the layout of the next issue of the paper when Watts asked Underhill, "Franklin, how would you like to take a trip out west to Kansas?" Underhill reacted with surprise and enthusiasm. "Well, I would surely find that very appealing," he said, "though I don't know how and when I might have such an opportunity." His curiosity was growing by the second. "Well, here's the thing," said Watts, "it is no secret that a capable young man like you can go far in the newspaper business, and there is no reason why you can't advance here at the Morning Herald. In fact I have suggested to Mr. Carson, the publisher, that he consider naming you assistant editor."

This flattering bit of information, though of course wholly appropriate and deserved, startled Underhill. "I had no idea," he said. "It's wonderful, and I assure you, Theodore, that I am certainly more than appreciative. Can you tell me when will this happen?" Watts smiled. "Now Franklin," he said, "don't count your chickens before they hatch. I only said I suggested that Mr. Carson *consider* a promotion. He has not agreed to it." Franklin's face fell. "Oh yes, of course, how unlike me to make such an assumption," he said. "It's just that I do so want to advance and I know I could be a very good editor, that is, assistant editor. But if Mr. Carson is not ready for that, I understand."

"It is not Mr. Carson's feeling that he is not ready," said Watts. "Actually, it is his belief that you are not quite ready." "And how is that?" asked Franklin. "Quite simple, really," Watts said. "When I suggested you as assistant editor, Mr. Carson reminded me that a good deal of our newspaper content deals with the frontier, with what's happening as settlement progresses westward. He also reminded me that you have never been west of the Missouri River." Franklin was ready to interject some defense, but Watts continued, "Mr. Carson made a strong point, but after some discussion agreed to a condition for your appointment as assistant editor." Franklin looked puzzled. "A condition?" he asked. "Yes," Watts said, "just one simple thing You are to make a trip west and bring back a bona fide newsworthy story that our readers will enjoy and remember. Do that and the position is yours "

Franklin Underhill, unusual as it was for him, was uncertain of how to react. A real opportunity for which he hungered stood in front of him. Yet he could not help but feel that a sizable, perhaps insurmountable, barrier did as well. He was without a doubt a first-rate reporter and talented writer. Presented with the right circumstances he could do as a fine job as any man in creating written descriptions of noteworthy and exciting events that would be interesting and memorable. But he could hardly conjure up such events, and the condition that Mr. Carson had put on his imminent promotion seemed to require just that. His thoughts were interrupted by Theodore Watts.

"Now, I suppose you're wondering how you are going to travel across the Missouri, witness some interesting if not astounding occurrences, write about them and thus fulfill Mr. Carson's wishes," Watts said. "Well, Franklin, let me present to you the answer to that dilemma." Franklin B. Underhill listened intently as Watts went on. "As luck would have it, the telegraph operator told me just this morning that he received news of the impending surrender to the cavalry of the renowned Indian chief Lone Wolf. You could not ask for a better story than that. Lone Wolf. He is the last great chief of the Kiowa, the one who stood fast and refused to sign the Medicine Lodge Treaty in '67. He's the one who traveled to Washington D.C. to argue his people's case to the Great White Father. But he did not reach an agreement with the government. He came back and led ferocious raids from Kansas all the way into Oklahoma and Texas. The most feared Indian in all of Kansas is going to surrender, and you my friend can be there to see it."

Franklin's mood brightened considerably. "I must confess," he said, "I'm not familiar with the fellow, but if this Chief Wolf is what you say he is there is no doubt that his surrender will provide precisely the type of story Mr. Carson has demanded. It cannot fail." "Exactly," Watts agreed. "My only question, then," said Franklin, "is what do I need to do?" "Everything has been organized," Watts said with obvious pleasure. "I have arranged for your train travel to Fort Dodge departing tomorrow morning. This will ensure your arrival a full day prior to the scheduled surrender ceremony and allow sufficient time to acquaint yourself with the fort and the key personnel involved in the ceremony. Fortunately, an acquaintance of mine, a former cavalry officer, has been able to secure permission for your stay at the fort and your observance of the actual surrender ceremony. We are even hopeful that you may, through an interpreter of course, be permitted to interview the chief."

Theodore Watts was smiling broadly. Franklin Underhill was unusually taciturn. "Nothing to say?" Watts asked. "Oh," said Franklin, "I was going over in my mind exactly what I need to take along and how best to pack it. I suppose I'll have to take a trunk." "That's doubtful," said Watts, "all you will need are your reporter's gear, a change of clothes and the train ticket I've already purchased. You'll only be at the fort a couple of days, then on the train back. Mr. Carson expects you back here with the story in under a week's time." "Very well," said Franklin, "he shall have me back, together with the finest story the Morning Herald has ever put to print." "I have no doubt of it," said Watts, as he extended his hand to the younger man, "none at all." The two shook hands firmly. "Thank you," Franklin said. "Thank you very much." He turned, walked confidently to the door, and exited the newspaper building.

The following morning Franklin Underhill boarded the train carrying a valise and a portable writing desk. The valise contained a clean shirt, underwear, stockings, a shaving kit, a paper bag containing a sausage sandwich and two apples, and two western-themed dime novels. The writing desk had a single drawer which held a folder of blank paper, two pens, and a carefully wrapped bottle of black ink. On his person, Underhill carried an eyeglass case, a pocket watch and chain, a handkerchief, and a small pocketbook containing twelve dollars cash.

The train left the St. Joseph station promptly at 9:20 am and headed west. At Atchison, it crossed the Missouri River, after which the rail line curved southwest toward Topeka, where a brief stop allowed two passengers to leave the train. The route then passed through several small towns, including Carbondale and Burlingame, each separated by miles of hills and woods broken only by an occasional meadow or clearing. The train stayed close to schedule, each hour of exertion by the toiling engine resulting in a distance traveled of some twenty-five miles. It stopped only in towns where the stationmaster had raised a signal flag indicating either a passenger or a freight shipment awaited, or where the conductor's freight list indicated a shipment was to be offloaded.

Steadily emitting clouds of smoke and steam, the locomotive drew the train farther and farther across the gently rolling countryside. Franklin, having found his view along the route in most places limited by the terrain, contented himself by reading his dime novels. There were other passengers in the same car but it was doubtful they were capable of erudite conversation he would have found satisfactory. The train traveled through an expanse of unsettled country, passed Osage and Reading without a stop, and finally made its end of day arrival at Emporia. The engineer moved the engine and the appendages attached to it onto a sidetrack, where the steaming behemoth would rest for the night.

The passengers found it was a short walk to the Emporia House, where Franklin took a room for one dollar and twenty-five cents including meals, prepaid. Following a dinner of roast beef, potatoes, bread, and apple pie, the other passengers moved to the parlor to enjoy further conversation and, for some, a glass of whiskey or beer. Franklin, however, retired to his room. He intended to make notes of the day's journey, but the effect of the hours of travel and buffeting country air overcame him and he soon gave way to a sound sleep.

The next morning the passengers, having taken breakfast at the Emporia House, rejoined the train for an early departure. The route taken was nearly straight west now, passing through sparsely populated countryside and through towns like Cottonwood, Florence, Peabody, and Newton. The topography, unlike that witnessed during much of the prior day, was now much flatter and almost totally devoid of trees. Great expanses of tall grasses filled this country, waving in the nearly constant wind like waves of a great ocean. As far as the eye could see, mile after mile of open prairie beckoned the settler to try his hand at breaking the rich sod that lay beneath the grass.

In order to accommodate the settlers, the government felt compelled to remove the people who occupied these lands. By the time Franklin Underhill made his first trip west most Indians had been forced to comply with requests to vacate the areas destined for white settlement. But some had chosen to defend their rights through raids against settlers or wagon trains or through battles with the U.S. Cavalry or Texas Rangers. It was these conflicts, and the resultant fear on the part of settlers, that solidified Chief Lone Wolf's reputation. And it was Lone Wolf's impending surrender that created the opportunity for Franklin Underhill to enhance his reputation as a journalist and potentially a future author of Western literature.

Following the stop at Great Bend, where the tender's water tank was refilled and two freight parcels and one passenger were offloaded, the train continued west across the seemingly endless prairie. Franklin marveled at the immensity of the great plain that spread in every direction from the train. He hoped to see "buffalo", as the herds of bison scattered across the western prairies were called, but had thus far been denied the experience. He gazed out the window of the passenger car, ruminating on the events which brought him to his current circumstance. He felt a burst of pride as he recalled the conversation, now two days past, in which Theodore Watts had as much as promised him an assistant editorship. He liked the editor and looked forward to the mutual compliments the two men would bestow upon each other when Franklin's article about the chief's surrender appeared in the *Saint Joseph Morning Herald*.

The train rolled across the countryside, passing through Larned and Nettleton, and later through Petersburg and Spear. Well into the afternoon the conductor, walking slowly along the aisle from the front to the rear of the car, called out, "Next stop, Fort Dodge. Passengers leaving the train at Fort Dodge gather your belongings and be prepared to promptly disembark. Those continuing to Dodge City will have a thirty-minute stop at the depot there." Franklin opened his valise, assured himself nothing was amiss and closed it again. He checked his portable writing desk, found all in order, and withdrew from his coat pocket a slip of paper with a single name written in large letters: Corporal William Stagel. This was, per the arrangement made by Theodore Watts' army contact, the person expected to host Franklin at Fort Dodge.

As the train slowed, the conductor stationed himself at the rear of the first passenger car. Franklin again rechecked his belongings and prepared to get off the train. When the train had slowed to a walking pace the conductor moved to the platform at the rear of the car, fastened the car door open with a hook attached to the platform railing, and disconnected one end of the safety chain blocking access to the steps of the car. The train had barely stopped when the conductor, with a surprising lack of civility, commanded Franklin, "Get off quickly, young man. We don't tarry here." Franklin made his way through the door and down the narrow steps and stepped onto the wooden platform of the Fort Dodge rail stop. No sooner had he done so than the conductor called out, "Aboard" and the engine resumed the smoking and hissing required to again get the train underway.

Franklin surveyed his surroundings. The Fort Dodge train stop was just that, a stop. There was no depot, only a wooden platform about six feet wide and fifteen feet long, a hitching post, a signal post, a lone elm tree, and an outhouse. The stop was used only to let passengers destined for Fort Dodge off the train, those coming from the fort to get on the train, and to unload infrequent freight shipments addressed to the Fort Dodge supply sergeant. Franklin was disappointed, as he had expected to disembark at a depot more like those found at Emporia or Great Bend. He had hoped to find some type of accommodation that would permit him to make himself more presentable before meeting his host, Corporal Stagel.

As he was reflecting on the primitive condition of the Fort Dodge train stop a voice interrupted his thoughts. "Sir," the voice said, "might you be Mr. Underhill from St. Joseph, Missouri?" Franklin turned toward the voice and beheld a large man of above average height, with deeply tanned skin, a rather unkempt black mustache, and a face of dark stubble that gave evidence the man had neglected to shave for several days. He was dressed in a faded, dust-covered cavalry uniform, including boots sorely in need of dressing, and a sweat-stained blue hat. A short distance behind the man, a team of horses hitched to an open wagon stood tied to the hitching rail.

"I am the man you seek," said Franklin, offering neither his hand nor a smile. "Well, you got here all right," the man replied. "I'm glad to see that." The man smiled broadly, showing less than a full set of teeth, and thrust a large, rough hand toward Franklin as he introduced himself. "My name is Stagel. Corporal William Stagel to this man's army, but I don't much favor that title. My friends call me Big Bill, as may you if you're so inclined." Franklin reluctantly shook the man's hand, and said, "I appreciate your meeting me, Corporal Stagel." Looking past the Corporal toward the team and wagon, he asked, "May I presume that is our transportation to Fort Dodge?" "Yes, sir," the corporal answered, "you throw your things in the back there and climb up on the right side of that wagon and we'll be on our way."

With that, the corporal turned and walked to the wagon and untied the team. He placed a heavy boot on a wooden spoke of the left front wheel and hoisted himself up onto the plank seat of the wagon. Franklin was about to suggest the corporal remove himself from the wagon and assist his visitor with the two pieces of baggage, as any polite host would do, but for some reason thought better of it. He carried his belongings to the wagon, placed them carefully in the rear, and climbed up to the uncomfortable seat. Corporal Stagel grasped both sets of reins in his thick hands, spoke a sharp "giddap," and with a quick up-and-down motion slapped the horses with the reins. The horses responded, the wagon jerking slightly as it began to move. The corporal turned the team to the north, following a well-worn path through the tall grass.

They were scarcely a hundred yards from the train stop when the corporal turned toward Franklin. "You know how to use a .30-.30?" the corporal asked, pointing to a rifle that hung from two pegs on the rear of the seatback. "If you mean have I experience with firearms and their fundamental operation the answer is yes," said Franklin. Big Bill Stagel threw his head back and emitted an uproarious laugh. "Well, ain't you got a way with words!" he exclaimed, "They said you was a newspaperman and now I believe 'em, for sure." Franklin was nonplussed. He knew he should dislike the man and probably offer a strenuous verbal objection to these uncouth comments. But he said nothing. More notably he realized that, against his own better judgment, he actually felt an affinity for the poor fellow.

Big Bill continued the conversation. "You ain't answered my question," he said. "Do you know how to use that Winchester?" Franklin tried to answer by as simple means as possible. "I have not fired a weapon of that exact type," he said, "although I have shown considerable skill with other types of rifles." He paused for an instant, then added, "That is, I'm a good shot with some other guns." Big Bill nodded. "Glad to hear that," he said, "cause if we meet any unfriendlies betwixt here and the fort, I'm countin' on you to hold 'em off with the Winchester. I'll be kinda busy high-tailin' them horses." Franklin's face showed obvious concern. "Do you mean there are hostile Indians in this area who attack people such as us?" he asked. Big Bill shrugged his shoulders, and replied, "Not most days. You just be ready in case."

The ride to Fort Dodge proved uneventful. The fort was a bit less than ten miles "as the crow flies" from the rail stop but closer to twelve miles on the route the wagon followed. The trail went generally north but meandered a half mile east to avoid a slough, then nearly a mile west toward a suitable place to ford the small river that crossed the prairie between the fort and the railroad. The horses needed little guidance to stay on the trail, and Big Bill concentrated instead on scanning the horizon for possible trouble. But there was none that day, a circumstance for which both men were grateful.

Franklin, in an attempt to show courtesy to his host, asked Big Bill questions about the fort, the territory surrounding it, and the corporal's military career. Bill provided a willing, if somewhat disappointing, description of the fort and its environs. His description made the fort sound more like a temporary encampment than a permanent military installation, but Franklin decided to make his own assessment when they arrived at Fort Dodge. Bill was more reticent regarding his own history. To say his answer to Franklin's query regarding his background and experience in the army was brief would be an understatement. He recited the year of his enlistment, the year he had been assigned to the cavalry, the names of the forts at which he had served, and very little more.

Franklin pondered the fact that Big Bill had summed up a twenty-plus-year career in the army in perhaps no more than fifty or sixty words. He wondered if Bill's entry into the military might have resulted from such pressing circumstances as a run-in with the law or perhaps avoidance of a shotgun wedding. He also wondered if Bill's being a corporal after so many years meant he had been demoted due to some type of misbehavior. Franklin briefly considered these possibilities, then silently scolded himself for having such thoughts. He told himself he had no evidence for such speculation and determined he would not unjustly judge the man seated beside him even if he was uneducated, unrefined and, though Franklin did not intend it as criticism, for too long a time unwashed.

Franklin was concluding his ruminations regarding Big Bill Stagel when the wagon reached the top of a rise. In the near distance, he noticed the outline of a collection of buildings occupying a small knoll. He surmised it might be a settler's homestead, though there seemed to be too many buildings for a farm place. Perhaps a new town has been platted, he thought, and the handful of buildings were constructed to establish its presence. His curiosity piqued, he turned to Bill and asked, "What is that place?" Bill frowned. "What do you mean, what is that place?" he said. "That's Fort Dodge."

In all of Franklin's reading about the West, he had never imagined a place like Fort Dodge. There was no stockade surrounding the fort, which occupied a surprisingly small area. There were no guard towers, no parade grounds, and no signage identifying the place as a site occupied by the U.S. Cavalry. Instead, he saw a ramshackle assortment of small single-story buildings, a rail corral holding perhaps twenty horses, a small barn, and a short flagpole crafted from a felled sapling. The only substantial structure, which Franklin presumed to be the fort's headquarters, was a two-story building measuring not more than twenty by thirty feet. Several chickens roamed the grounds, accompanied by two mangy black dogs. A modest rail fence surrounded the property.

Big Bill stopped the wagon next to the barn, climbed down from the plank seat and began unhitching the horses. Franklin, uncertain as to the protocol for visiting a U.S. Army fort, remained on the wagon. "You ain't gonna ride much farther than this," said Bill, grinning at his passenger, "May as well fetch yer goods and go on in." Franklin climbed down from the wagon, retrieved his luggage and was about to ask Bill where he was to make his lodging when he heard someone call out, "Corporal Stagel, report to headquarters, and bring your charge." Big Bill looked at Franklin and nodded in the direction of the two-story building. "Time to meet the captain," he said. "He'll have someone get you situated."

As the two men entered the building a soldier was exiting it. He nodded at Big Bill, gave Franklin a precursory examination, and walked away grinning. Franklin was not sure what to make of the man's untoward demeanor but decided to make allowances for the fact that he was probably adversely affected by the isolation and conditions of his post. The room that Big Bill and Franklin entered, which measured no more than eight by ten feet and had only one small window, was sparsely furnished. Two wooden chairs sat against one wall. Directly across the room were a roughhewn desk and another wooden chair. On the third wall were a potbellied stove, a stand holding a U.S. flag attached to a thin wooden pole, and a picture of a bearded soldier. Franklin did not recognize the man in the picture.

A soldier with a long row of hash marks on his sleeve entered the room. Corporal Stagel managed a casual salute, but the other soldier motioned with his hand as if to wave away the salute. The corporal provided an introduction. "Franklin, this here is Master Sergeant Adam O'Toole," he said, "and this here is Franklin Underhill the reporter." The sergeant was, like Big Bill, a large man. He grinned and extended his hand. "Glad to have you here, Underhill," he said. "You'll have the run of the place. I'm told you're pretty durn read up on this part of the country." "Well, sir," Franklin replied, "I must confess much of my knowledge of the West has been gleaned from books, though popular ones. I certainly appreciate your hospitality and I hope my presence is not found by the men of the fort to be overly distracting."

Normally, Franklin would have ended his comments at that, but for reasons he did not himself fully understand he ventured a bit more, "To be perfectly honest, sir, I think I might have what I understand to be termed tender feet." The sergeant's expression went, all in less than two seconds, from a blank look to one of puzzlement, then enlightenment, as he grasped what the young reporter intended to convey. "So, you're a tenderfoot, are you lad?" he asked. "Well, no mind," he said, "anyone who can survive more than an hour alone with Stagel here can survive durn near anything this country can throw at you." Upon hearing this, Big Bill burst into prolonged, raucous laughter, in which he was joined by the master sergeant. It was evident that the two men were of similar nature and probably had a long-standing friendship.

As the men's laughter reached its apex the rear door to the room opened and another soldier entered. Ignoring Big Bill and the Sergeant Major, who were facing in the other direction, he stepped briskly to the desk but did not sit down. He was of average height, slender but muscular, with a shock of brown hair and matching mustache. His uniform was considerably cleaner than those of the other two men. On his shoulders were two silver bars. Franklin judged him to be about forty years old. When Big Bill and the Sergeant Major noticed the man at the desk their laughter immediately ceased and they brought themselves to attention and saluted. "At ease," said the man at the desk. "Corporal Stagel, " he continued, "may I presume this is the man we have been expecting?" "Yes sir, Cap'n sir," said Big

Bill, "this here is Mr. Underhill, sir." "Very well," said the captain, "thank you for transporting him here. That will be all, men." Big Bill and the sergeant again came to attention, saluted and left the room.

Franklin approached the desk. "Sir," he said, "I am Franklin B. Underhill, of the *Saint Joseph Morning Herald*. I am pleased to make your acquaintance, and I am certainly more than appreciative of your hospitality." The captain reached to shake hands and said, "Captain Percy Phillips, and likewise." He motioned for Franklin to take a seat. "I apologize that your accommodations here will be far from luxurious and perhaps less than comfortable. But none of us are here to enjoy ourselves." "I understand perfectly," "said Franklin, "and the mere fact that you have allowed my presence makes any apology unnecessary. I greatly respect the resolve it must take to do one's duty in a cavalry outpost such as this, and I, like you, am not here for my own enjoyment but to witness and report on what will most surely be a historic occasion."

Franklin suddenly realized that for reasons he did not fathom he felt a bit nervous in the captain's presence and had as a result become overly talkative. He hoped the captain did not take offense. "It's good you weren't delayed," said Captain Phillips. "The surrender you have come to see should take place day after tomorrow, that is if the Indians decide to keep their promise." "Do you mean the ceremony may be put off?" asked Franklin. "I hope not," said the captain, "Lord knows we've been after these holdouts more than long enough, playing hide and seek all over the dang country, trying to get them to come in and join the rest of their kind that are staying put where they are supposed to." Franklin began to feel apprehensive. "Do you expect it is possible they may not surrender after all?" he asked. "Oh, they'll surrender all right," said the captain. "They might make one last move to make their people think they still have a chance at resisting, but if they do it will all be for show. They're done for and they know it."

Franklin wanted to ask more about the Indians and how the cavalry had managed to convince them to finally surrender, but decided to wait until a more appropriate time. He feared he had already exhibited excessive verbosity and did not want to jeopardize his welcome at the fort. "Sir," he said, "I'm sure you have duties to attend to and I do not want to impinge upon your time. Again, I appreciate your hospitality and look forward to portraying Fort Dodge in a favorable light when recording the auspicious event we are both anticipating." "Let's just hope it goes off as planned," said Captain Phillips. The captain looked as though he were going to say more, but instead nodded to Franklin and turned his attention to the papers on his desk. Franklin, still carrying his valise and portable writing desk, left the building intending to rejoin Corporal Stagel.

Outside, the mid-day sun felt close and hot. Franklin squinted as he looked into the bright light, searching the dusty grounds for Big Bill, who was not to be seen. He decided to walk to the nearest building, hoping to find someone who could direct him to his lodging. He approached the building, a low, wide sod structure with a row of windows on one side. A short door stood slightly ajar. He was about to knock on the door when a voice boomed behind him. "There you are, lad," said the voice, "I was lookin' for you. Gonna show you to the barracks, but I see you found it." The voice belonged to Master Sergeant O'Toole. "Go on in," said O'Toole. "This is where we sleep. Well, us enlisted men. The officers bunk upstairs in the headquarters building. Nothin' fancy here but it keeps out the sun and most of the rain."

Franklin pushed the door open and peered inside. Two rows of posts, which supported the roof, ran parallel to the sidewalls. Two rows of canvas cots were crammed into the building, their heads against the sidewalls, with barely two feet between them. At the foot of each cot stood a wooden box twenty-eight inches long, sixteen inches wide, and twelve inches deep. The boxes left just enough space for a man to walk between the rows of cots. Franklin surmised that the soldiers' clothing and other personal goods were stored in the boxes. Master Sergeant O'Toole spoke. "An empty box means that bunk is free. Pick one and it's yours. Then let's head for mess. It's time to eat." About two-thirds of the way down the left-hand wall, Franklin spotted a box with its lid standing open. He made his way between the rows of cots, awkwardly maneuvering down the aisle with his valise in one hand and his portable writing desk in the other. He verified that the wooden box was empty, placed his luggage on the cot, and followed O'Toole out of the barracks.

Later, when Franklin was back home in St. Joseph, he described the meals served at Fort Dodge in a most uncomplimentary manner. However, given the relative scarcity of provisions and his hunger during his time at Fort Dodge, Franklin consumed everything on his plate at each meal. Though he looked askance at some of the items prepared by the mess cook, such as cornbread that was black on the bottom and spongy on top, or coffee that seemed to contain nearly as much grounds as liquid, he did not complain. In fact, he accepted that the food, the lodging and the stark environment of the fort were all part of the West as it really was rather than as he had imagined it would be. Franklin was determined to make the best of this trying situation. Being the sole civilian witness to the upcoming Indian surrender would undoubtedly prove worth the inconvenience and discomfort he was enduring at the fort.

The remaining day and a half awaiting the event for which Franklin had traveled west passed surprisingly quickly. He engaged the men of the fort in conversation, and despite their limited vocabularies and atrocious grammar found their stories of military service and skirmishes with the Indians fascinating. Some of the men had served in the war that had pitted the North against the South and told harrowing tales of that conflict. Franklin listened intently to their narrations and supplemented his recall through notes he made using his portable writing desk. Certainly, some of what he learned from these men would form the basis for the western literature he planned to eventually author. The day Franklin had boarded the train in St. Joseph he could not have anticipated his rapport with the cavalry soldiers of Fort Dodge, nor his proclivity to spend more time with sergeants and other enlisted men than with the officers. But a skilled reporter like Franklin had a talent for gathering information from those who knew, and in the Army of the West that meant those who lived the life of the common soldier.

When the day of the much-anticipated surrender arrived, Franklin could not have been more ready. He dressed in the cleanest clothes he had, though all his clothes were now dusty and somewhat soiled. He carefully cleaned his glasses, attempted to buff his shoes by rubbing them on the back of his trousers, and put a fresh nib on his pen. He intended to be fully prepared to record the events of the day while they were fresh in his memory. He walked to the headquarters building, where a private ushered him into the room where he had first met Captain Phillips. The captain was in dress uniform with boots that, though far from glistening, showed an appearance closer to a shine than any Franklin had seen since his arrival at the fort. The Captain acknowledged him with a nod but did not speak. "If you don't mind, sir," said Franklin, "I would much appreciate some foreknowledge of the particulars of the ceremony, which will aid me in most efficiently observing it and thus ensuring the subsequent written record is as accurate and complete as possible." Captain Phillips thought a bit, then said, "I'm not sure exactly what you are expecting. Presuming the Indians actually show up today as promised, they will come to the fort and their leader will sign a document confirming the surrender, though he probably won't be able to read it. They'll camp here at the fort for a day or two, and then I'll send a squad of men to escort them to their assigned area on the reservation. That's about it."

Franklin frowned. He wondered why the captain had not described in detail the actual surrender ceremony, though he was glad to have foreknowledge regarding the surrender document and the planned relocation to reservation ground. He decided it was best not to press the captain and to trust his reporter's instincts to glean all he could from the event. "Just one more thing," said Franklin, "and I trust I'm not imposing. What time do you expect the surrender to occur?" The Captain, who had taken his chair behind the desk and begun to read what appeared to be a piece of official correspondence, threw Franklin a sideways glance and said, "When the sentry tells me they're here." He turned back to his reading and Franklin, feeling embarrassed, left the room.

It was nearing sunset when the call went up from the sentry keeping watch toward the north. "Wagons comin'! Look like Indians," was all he said. This news did not result in a flurry of activity on the part of the soldiers. Some began walking slowly toward the north edge of the fort to gain a view of the approaching Indians, while others went to the barracks to retrieve their rifles. The remainder simply continued as they were. Franklin saw Captain Phillips emerge from the headquarters building and decided to join him. He approached and said, "I trust you don't mind if I accompany you." "Not at all," said the officer, "suit yourself." The Captain did not walk to the north side of the fort or request any additional information from the sentry or the other men who had gone to observe the approaching Indians. Instead, he stood silently in front of the headquarters building. In light of the nature of the impending event, Franklin could not fathom the man's seeming disinterest.

A whorl of dust entered the fort from the north and within the dust were, as documented the next morning by the reporter present, twenty-six Indian braves on horseback, fifty-nine women and children, three small wagons, each pulled by a single horse, and an additional forty horses, some carrying pack loads and the remainder barebacked. The Indians wore solemn expressions and many displayed obvious dislike for the bluecoats as they approached. The procession stopped next to Captain Phillips. The officer motioned and a soldier came to his side. "Ask them which one is their leader," he said. The soldier approached the first wagon and, in a tongue distinctly foreign to Franklin, directed the question to the man driving the wagon. The driver responded with a surprisingly long statement delivered with unexpected emotion and dramatic hand gestures. The soldier returned to the Captain. "He said he is not their chief, but was chosen to speak for the chief, who is very ill and is in the back of his wagon. He said his people are starving, many are sick, and their hearts are broken. They long for a time before the white man came, when the buffalo were as many as the blades of grass. They have prayed to the Great Spirit to return them to their home in the North but he has not heard them. It is a sad day that will be remembered forever."

Upon hearing this, the Captain strode briskly to the wagon and peered over the sideboard. On a bed of blankets, an old man lay with his eyes closed. His grey hair was pulled back from his bronze-colored face, which was crisscrossed with countless crevices. His sunken cheeks and thin, sinewy arms verified the spokesperson's assertion that the Indians were in dire need of food. The man in the wagon opened his eyes, trying to focus on the face that looked down at him. He slowly lifted one arm and tried unsuccessfully to raise his head from the blanket. He spoke in a barely audible voice. The captain summoned his interpreter, who leaned over the side of the wagon and listened intently to the old man. The interpreter turned to the captain and said, "He said he is sorry he cannot lead his people anymore, even to surrender to the white man. He says he will soon die but that is better than what will happen to his people."

The Captain called for Master Sergeant O'Toole. "O'Toole," he said, "I want you to get these people situated and make them as comfortable as you can. Have the mess cook start at once to prepare as much food as is necessary for all of them to eat their fill. I don't care if he has to use next week's rations. And when they set up their tents, if they are too weak or tired to do it tell the men to help them." The Master Sergeant was obviously surprised but responded as expected. "Yes, sir," he said, "right away, sir." He offered a hasty salute, turned on his heel and walked quickly away. Franklin, standing just behind the captain, was astounded. Almost nothing about this encounter resembled what he had expected. The Indians, far from ferocious warriors, were a sick and suffering group. The chief appeared to be near death and was too weak to sign the surrender document. The captain, rather than completing the formal surrender, focused instead on getting the Indians fed and lodged for the night.

All Franklin could do was observe the sudden flurry of activity within the perimeters of the fort. The Indians, assisted by the soldiers, unpacked their horses and wagons, erected their tents and were herded to the mess area for what was evidently their first full meal in a long time. The language barrier resulted in some confusion, especially as the Indians tried to communicate to the soldiers the proper way to erect their lodging. In other circumstances the soldiers' consternation might have been considered humorous, but there was no laughter among the men. It amazed Franklin that some of the soldiers placed their rifles against the side of the mess shack while they ate, clearly within reach of the Indians. In the dime novels with which he was familiar the natives would surely have sprung for the guns, wounding or killing as many soldiers as possible before they were overrun and killed by the rest of the troops. Instead, Indians and soldiers sat amidst each other, concentrating on devouring their heaping plates.

It was soon dark. The captain had left the scene, apparently choosing to go to his quarters early. The Indians were getting settled in their tents and the soldiers made their way one by one to the barracks. Franklin, following the soldiers, entered the barracks, threaded his way among the cots until he found his place. He sat down next to his valise and pondered the thoroughly unexpected events he had just witnessed. He wondered why the Indians were in such terrible condition. He wondered why the captain had not completed the surrender and why, after giving Franklin the impression he did not at all care for Indians, he had treated them so hospitably. Franklin, puzzled, looked forward to the next morning, when he would depend on the captain for the answers to his questions. Resigned to waiting, he lay on his cot, closed his eyes and drifted off to sleep.

The next morning Franklin arose at sun-up, packed his valise, checked the contents of his portable writing desk, and headed toward the mess shack. He was one of the first in line for breakfast. This was his last day at the fort, and he wanted his questions answered before Corporal Stagel took him to the train stop to catch the noon eastbound. He noticed a private carrying a plate of food toward the headquarters building and intercepted the young soldier. "Is that for the captain?" Franklin asked. "Sure is," the private replied. "I'm going to meet with him now, so I'll save you the bother," said Franklin, taking the metal plate from the private. "Well, thank you, sir," the private said and turned back toward the mess area. Franklin walked directly to the headquarters building, entered, and knocked on the door of the captain's office.

"Come in," said the captain. "Mmm, that smells good." He did not look up from his desk. "Just put it there on the edge of the desk," he said. Franklin did so and said brightly, "Yes, sir!" At this, the captain looked up and said, "Oh, it's you. Aren't you supposed to be on your way to meet the train?" "Not just yet, sir," Franklin said, "but soon. If you don't mind, would you grant me a few minutes to address some pressing questions related to yesterday's events?" "Well, sir," said the captain, "I'm not sure I can answer your questions. But since you came all this way, I'll surely try." "Thank you," Franklin said and launched into the questions that had been at the forefront of his mind since the prior evening. "First," he said, "why are the Indians sick and so very hungry?" "That's simple," replied the captain, "the strategy to force them to give up their wanderings and raids is to cut off their food supply. Unfortunately, when we do that they become more susceptible to illness." Before he could catch himself, Franklin blurted, "But that's inhuman, to starve people on purpose!" The captain remained calm. "The alternative," he said, "is to use military force, in which case many Indians and a number of cavalrymen would lose their lives. This way, I don't lose any men and the Indians only lose a few here and there."

Franklin was taken aback. He was learning the realities of the West and rather wishing he weren't. "What else?" asked the captain. "Last evening," Franklin responded, "you demonstrated true Christian charity to the Indians, which I found surprising." "It has nothing to do with charity," said the captain. "I am a man of my word. When we cut off the lines of supply to this band and ran off the buffalo in the area, I sent word to their chief. The message was that when they surrendered I would honor their cooperation by holding a feast in the chief's honor.

Unfortunately, he was not able to participate." Franklin continued his questions. "About the chief," he said, "how did an infa-
mous warrior like Lone Wolf, who certainly must have the
support of many other Indians in this part of the country, come
to circumstances in which he was forced to surrender in a manner which surely will bring shame upon his memory?" The captain looked at Franklin, and a look of incredulity spread across
his face. "Who did you say the old chief was?" he asked. "Why,
Lone Wolf," said Franklin, "the last great chief of the Kiowa."

The captain leaned back in his chair and stared at
Franklin. "Mr. Underhill," he said, emphasizing "mister," "I understand you are not experienced in Indian country and I don't
know where you got your information. But dang, you could tell at
first glance when those renegades rode in yesterday that they
weren't Kiowa. And the old chief sure isn't Lone Wolf. He surrendered in Oklahoma last December and was sentenced to
prison in Florida." Franklin felt weak. "Not Kiowa?" he mumbled,
"not Lone Wolf?" "No sir," said the Captain, "Sorry to disappoint
you, but this raggedy bunch are holdouts that split off from the
main body of Cheyenne a couple of years ago. Dang, man, I'm
not even certain of the old chief's name."

Franklin sat stunned while the captain's revelation sank
in. He was lost in thought, recalling the promised promotion, the
condition under which it would be awarded, and all he had endured on his inaugural trip west. A sharp rap on the door
brought him back to the present. "Come in," said the captain.
Corporal Stagel entered. "Got the team hitched and ready to
go," he said, "I put your gear in the wagon. It's near time to
leave." The captain stood and extended his hand. Franklin
stood, grasped the captain's hand lightly and managed a weak
grin. "Captain Phillips," he said, "despite this unanticipated turn
of events, I remain appreciative of your hospitality. And I wish
you and your men well." Suddenly feeling magnanimous, Frank-

lin added, "And I hope the Indians continue to be well-treated." "Have a safe trip back," the Captain said, "and when you get your story published I'd appreciate a copy, if possible." "You shall surely have it," Franklin replied. The corporal opened the door and he and Franklin headed toward the wagon.

Little was said during the return trip to the rail stop south of Fort Dodge. Big Bill knew something was amiss but did not want to pry into the younger man's affairs. The sky was a beautiful blue color with wisps of airy clouds, and the sun beamed down from overhead. Clouds of dust followed the wagon and an occasional breeze from the north enveloped horses, wagon, and passengers in the gritty material. As they were nearing the rail stop Big Bill, not wanting to see his new friend depart under such strained circumstances, cleared his throat and said, "Franklin, I know this didn't go the way you wanted. But there's lots of things in life like that. You're a smart feller and you'll figure out a way to make this turn out for the best. Yes sir, I believe you will." "It won't be easy," said Franklin. He did not offer to share any details. "But I thank you, and I am certainly …" "I know," Big Bill interrupted, "you're very appreciative of my hospitality." Big Bill laughed at his own comment and Franklin could not resist smiling.

A short time later the two men arrived at the rail stop. Big Bill climbed down and tied the horses to the hitching rail. Franklin went to the rear of the wagon and retrieved his valise and portable writing desk. Big Bill waited under the elm tree with Franklin, searching the horizon for an oncoming train. It soon came into view and the two men walked to the wooden platform beside the tracks. The engine passed by spewing cinders and sparks, and both men turned their backs to the train to avoid the unwelcome shower. When the train came to a halt Franklin offered his hand to Big Bill, who gave it a vigorous shake. Franklin climbed up the narrow steps at the rear of the car, entered it and made his way to an empty seat. The train slowly pulled away from the platform. Big Bill watched until it was nearly out of sight. Then he untied the horses, climbed on the wagon and started back to the fort.

As the train belched and steamed its way eastward across the prairie, Franklin B. Underhill pondered his fate. He had watched a great career opportunity slip through his fingers and had seen his image of the West shattered by the reality in which he had been immersed. His friend Theodore Watts would be immensely surprised and, due to the closeness of the two men, would share in Franklin's feelings of disappointment. He thought about how he would break the news to Mr. Carson, the *Morning Herald*'s publisher. Franklin harbored no resentment toward either of the newspapermen. The conditions of Franklin's anticipated appointment as assistant editor had been made crystal clear, and Theodore Watts had both proposed the promotion to Mr. Carson and gone out of his way to make arrangements for Franklin's trip west.

As the train moved steadily across the vast grasslands, Franklin had ample time to think. He carefully weighed his options, trying not to miss any feasible way to salvage the situation. He decided to outline the possibilities in writing. He opened his portable writing desk and took out a sheet of paper. He retrieved a pen and carefully unwrapped the bottle of black ink. Then he stopped. He stared out the train window for a long time, watching mile after mile of tall grass, isolated homesteads, and the occasional clump of trees or small creek pass by. His mind was fully occupied by his own thoughts, though he gave no sign of what they might be. Then he put his pen to paper and began to write:

"The sun had scarcely risen over the horizon when fresh sentries relieved those who had kept watch in the guard

towers through much of the night. The fort's occupants, a well-disciplined company of experienced and highly skilled soldiers, had anxiously waited for this day to arrive. For on this day, at this fort, one of the most feared and notorious Indians in the entire West, Chief Lone Wolf, was to lay down his arms and lead his people in surrendering to the U.S. Cavalry. After a series of bloody raids carried out against defenseless wagon trains and countless skirmishes with both the U.S. Cavalry and the Texas Rangers, the last great chief of the Kiowa had finally admitted defeat."

Franklin turned the sheet of paper over and continued:

"This was not a defeat in armed battle, though Lone Wolf's tribe had lost many men to the repeating rifles of the white soldiers. It was a defeat that came through the realization that progress marched forward as surely and steadily as a company of infantrymen. The Kiowa knew that the white man's arms and resources were superior, buffalo would never again roam free across vast parts of the West, and they could not return to a prior time. Faced with almost certain annihilation if they continued fighting, Chief Lone Wolf and his council had reluctantly faced reality and, for the sake of his people, agreed to the terms of surrender dictated by the army. Lone Wolf had held out for a few provisions related to food supply and a process for permission to leave the reservation to hunt game, but the Kiowa held few bargaining chips, and the agreement to be signed decidedly favored the U.S. Government."

The narration continued on a second sheet of paper:

"At mid-morning, a sentry raised the alarm. "I see a column of riders," he said, "They appear to be Kiowa." The

men of the fort sprung into action. They retrieved their weapons, checking and double-checking the readiness of rifles and pistols. Every gun was loaded by soldiers who hoped they would not need to fire them, but knew the Indians might break their word and attempt an attack on the fort. The officer in charge, Major Phillips, emerged from his tidy office wearing a freshly pressed uniform, shiny black boots, and calfskin gloves. At his appearance, the officer of the day, Lieutenant O'Toole, called the men to formation. The soldiers stood at attention in straight rows and with all arms in hand. The Captain quickly reviewed the troops and concluded all was ready.

About twenty minutes later, the huge gates of the stockade fence that surrounded the fort swung slowly open and a colorful procession of Indians started through the gates. At the head of the long column of Kiowa, astride a magnificent stallion, rode Chief Lone Wolf. He was a tall man, muscularly built, with piercing eyes and a demeanor like that of royalty. Despite the circumstances of the Indians' entry into the fort he carried himself proudly, looking straight ahead as if the dozens of soldiers on either side of the Indians did not exist. This was the chief most feared by whites throughout Kiowa territory, the man who had led his people to victory after victory, and who ..."

Franklin put his pen down and read what he had written. He was pleased. There would be ample time to complete the narrative before his arrival back in St. Joseph.

11 THE DROUGHT

The woman stood atop a small knoll at the edge of the farmyard. She was slender, taller than average, and somewhat stooped at the shoulders. Her face was darkly tanned and bore the deep lines and skin texture of someone exposed to countless hours in the prairie sun. She stood gazing toward the west, her hands on her hips, watching the gathering clouds darken the sky.

The breeze that had blown from the southwest all day had turned to the east and become much stronger. The wind kicked up clouds of dust and drove tumbleweeds across the bare fields, threatening to dislodge the bonnet from the woman's head. She tightened the strings under her chin and turned to the south, facing the small barn at the edge of the yard. Just past the barn, a dry creek bed ran toward the east. The creek had once fed a pond frequented by wild ducks, a variety of small critters, and the occasional wolf or coyote. But when the rains ceased, the stream and pond dried up and most of the animals vanished.

Inside the barn, the woman's husband carefully placed a bucket of water into the wooden trough from which the couple's single cow and her calf ate and drank. Despite the shortage of feed and his concern that the shallow well on the farm might at any time go dry, he kept the animals well fed and watered. The couple depended on the cow for milk and hoped in the coming autumn to have it bred to a neighbor's bull to gain another calf. The man reached deep into a sack of wheat, extracted a handful of the precious grain, and held it out toward the cow. The animal's raspy tongue tickled the man's palm as it ate from his hand. The calf, jealous of the treat offered to its mother, pawed the ground, raising a small cloud of fine dust. "Sorry," the man said, "none for you today." He shook his head, carefully tied a length of twine around the top of the grain sack to prevent the cow or calf from eating more than their allotted ration, and turned to leave the barn.

As the man walked toward the house he saw his wife standing in the open yard. She was watching the weather and did not notice him. Dark clouds were building in the west, blotting out the sun. Thunderheads crowned the massive clouds, rising high into the sky, rolling and churning as they rose. Green streaks in the clouds signaled the likely presence of hail, but with the year's crops nearly lost to drought the possibility of a hailstorm was of little concern. In fact, even hail might be a welcome bit of moisture. The man looked intently at the sky and thought of the many times he had witnessed a similar buildup of clouds and wind, only to have a storm front pass through without so much as a drop of rain.

As he approached the house, the man's eyes fell on the small row of zinnias his wife had planted near the door. The corners of his mouth turned up slightly as he looked at the flowers. Their meager display of color stood in sharp contrast to the surrounding dirt and the unpainted wall of the house. His wife had always loved flowers, and when he made the annual spring trip into town to purchase supplies, he had included in the limited provisions they could afford a single pack of flower seeds.

She had planted the seeds with care, protected them from bugs and wild critters, and nourished them through the long, hot summer. It seemed to him that she gave them the love she might have given the children they did not have. And, even though she kept the flowers alive by using well water essential to the couple and their livestock, he never suggested she stop watering them. In a very real sense, they were a visible symbol of the couple's determination to stand firm against the trials of the frontier, including the years of drought.

The woman stood with her back to the wind, deep in her own thoughts. Her mind went back to a time over two decades earlier when she had become the bride of a young man determined to seek his fortune in the West. "Sarah Carson," she slowly murmured to herself, "do you take Lucas Barnes to be your lawful wedded husband?" She smiled slightly. "Of course I did," she thought, "I was so in love, and he was so handsome. I wanted to go anywhere Luke wanted to go, and he longed to seek his fortune in the West."

Sarah and Luke did go west. They settled in Ohio, where they worked long and hard to clear a small acreage of wooded ground and turn it into a farmstead. They worked side by side, and often in concert with other nearby settlers, felling trees, dragging them out by mule or oxen, and constructing log houses and outbuildings. But after a handful of years, as the area around them was cleared and settled, Luke began to complain that Ohio was getting too crowded. They sold their land, packed their belongings, and trekked west to Missouri. There they started over, clearing new land, seeding new crops, and raising a new set of buildings. Sarah liked Missouri, and became friends with the two neighbor women who lived within walking distance of their little farm.

Then the couple repeated their Ohio experience. As the area around them became populated, Luke began to talk of moving farther west. Sarah at first resisted the idea. But when the couple learned that under the recently enacted Homestead Act they could receive 160 acres by paying an eighteen-dollar fee, improving their property, and living on it for five years, she agreed to move once again. Together with their meager household belongings, they traveled by train to central Kansas. There, they purchased a wagon, two cows, a plow, and other supplies, and set out for their homestead site.

Turning virgin land into farm ground proved much easier in Kansas than in Ohio or Missouri. Trees were few, and all that was required to begin cropping was to plow the soil and plant the seed. The first winter Sarah and Luke lived in a sod house built partially into the ground, which enhanced its protection from the blizzards that buried the prairie under a heavy blanket of white. A small barn was constructed the next summer, and by their second winter in Kansas the couple was ensconced in a two-room cabin they called a house. One room served as the kitchen, larder and sitting room, and the other as a bedroom. Each spring they broke more ground, and were rewarded with annually increasing harvests.

Then the drought hit. Within a few short months, Sarah and Luke realized why some maps of the period referred to the entire midsection of the country as the Great American Desert. They had experienced times in Ohio and Missouri when rains were delayed, causing them to worry about the condition of their crops. But the rain always returned and they never had an actual crop failure. Kansas was different. The rain did not taper off; it stopped. Clouds formed, storms approached, but no rain fell for months on end. Time after time, the couple watched in desperation as lines of thunderstorms moved in from the west, only to pass over without releasing a single drop of moisture.

The first drought year, Sarah and Luke endured the pain of watching green fields turn brown, and they lost their crops. Because they had managed to accumulate a relatively large store of grain, the couple had enough seed to weather the first year's crop failure without going into debt. But for many others, as the drought continued for a second year, failure to pay off bank loans led to foreclosures. As they watched heartbroken neighbors leave their homesteads, often following a sheriff's sale of their belongings, Sarah and Luke considered themselves fortunate.

The second dry year was even worse than the first. The seed planted by Sarah and Luke barely had enough ground moisture to sprout. Week after week, the couple watched as the sky periodically filled with clouds and storm fronts massed on the horizon, only to dissipate without yielding the much-needed rain. The crop grew only a few inches, turned brown, and died. The small amount of grain remaining in the barn was barely enough to feed one cow through the winter. The other was butchered and the meat dried, the only way to avoid letting the animal starve to death.

The next spring, though he strongly resisted doing so, Luke found it necessary to borrow money to buy seed, counting on a crop big enough to retain seed for the following year and pay off bank loans by selling the surplus. This placed the couple in a dire predicament. They were in their fifth year on the homestead and had to remain through the year in order to prove their claim and receive title to the land. If unable to repay the bank loan, they would be forced to leave and the land would revert to government ownership. All their effort would be lost, and they would have no place to go. Fully aware of their circumstances, the couple forged ahead, placing the precious seed in the ground. Hopefully, when the drought broke and the rains came it would return to them all they needed to repay their debt and start another year.

But the rains had not come. Day after day, as the hot winds blew across the prairie, Sarah and Luke watched as the grain stalks stopped growing. Then the deep green color of the stems began to fade to light green. They knew time was running out. The fragile plants had to have rain soon or die. There was nothing they could do but stare at the sky, hoping against hope, and wishing for the miracle they so desperately needed.

Sarah was still lost in her daydream remembrance of their early years together when Luke walked up beside her. They both stood looking at the long line of clouds, at the towering thunderheads, and at the lightning flashes in the distance. They felt the wind at their backs grow stronger, nearly pushing them off balance. It was strong enough to raise huge dust clouds, and the dust was already covering their clothes and getting in their ears, and eyes, and noses. They knew that when the front had passed everything in the house would be covered with a layer of fine dust. The couple could have taken refuge in the house or the barn, but without saying a word they somehow agreed to stay and face the storm.

Sarah glanced around at her flowers. They were bent over in the wind, half covered with dirt, but still offering a splash of color against their bleak surroundings. She hoped they would survive the storm. Then she heard a sound, a sort of dull thud. It was barely perceptible amid the noise of the wind, and she wasn't sure what it was. She looked across the yard and saw a puff of dust spring up from the ground just a few feet away. What was it? She saw another puff of dust, and another, and another. Soon the rest of the farmyard was erupting in little explosions of dust.

Then, something struck Sarah's face. She touched her cheek, and turned toward Luke. Streaks of dirt streamed down his face. It looked like he was crying, but then why was he grinning? He was smiling ear to ear, as the drops ran down his cheeks. Then she realized what was happening. His face was streaked with raindrops. She felt her own face; it was becoming wet. Her hair was getting wet. Her clothes were getting wet. She looked up at the sky, and raindrops fell into her eyes.

Then the rain began in earnest. Great sheets of water fell from the sky, rain so heavy they could hardly see the barn. Luke grabbed Sarah around the waist and began to swing her around in a circle. Neither spoke. They swung round and round, smiling and crying and laughing, and splashing each other full of mud. Black, wet, dirty, filthy mud. It was beautiful.

12 THE JAILBREAK

The ranch hand stood near the door with his hat in his hand. He shuffled his feet nervously. Sheriff Jackson leaned back in his chair and stared intently at the young man. "Anything else you want to tell us?" the sheriff asked. "Told you all I know," the cowboy replied. "I wouldn't a said nothin' if they had treated me fair," he continued, his voice rising slightly. "Cuttin' me loose I could take, but they shorted my pay, and that just ain't right." The sheriff stood and shook the young man's hand. "You did good comin' in," he said. "Don't tell nobody else and the McGreedys will never know." The young man nodded, put on his hat and left the office.

Ben Jackson turned to the other man in the office. "Well," he asked, " what do you think?" Bill Carson, the sheriff's deputy, frowned and thought a moment before he spoke. "I'm not sure," he said. "He might be for real, or the McGreedys might have sent him here to throw us off. I s'pose I can ask around town to find out if he was really fired or if he's lyin'." The sheriff shook his head. "Won't help," he said. "If the McGreedys did send him packin' he might a told folks he quit just to save face. And if he's still with 'em, he'll say whatever they told him to say." The deputy frowned again. "So what do we do?" he asked. The sheriff rubbed his chin and looked at the clock on the wall. "Stage is due in less than an hour, Bill," he said. "Can't hurt to have a good look at what it brings." The deputy nodded and without speaking opened the door and left the office.

The young ranch hand who had told the sheriff and his deputy about being fired by the McGreedys also told them something of much greater interest. As everyone in town knew, Rory McGreedy was being held in the local jail awaiting transfer to the territorial prison. After a night of drinking and gambling, he had gotten into an argument with a man over a game of cards. Others broke up the confrontation and Rory stormed out of the saloon but waited in the shadows beside the building. When the other man left the saloon, Rory attacked him from behind, knocked him to the ground and beat him senseless. Several men heard the commotion, rushed to the street in front of the saloon and witnessed the event. They immediately seized Rory and dragged him to the sheriff's office, where he was put in a cell.

The McGreedys had a reputation for dishonesty and occasional violence, and the incident solidified the townspeople's dislike of the family. Shortly after the incident a local jury heard the testimony of the eyewitnesses and found Rory McGreedy guilty of attempted manslaughter. Based on the jury's verdict, the circuit judge sentenced him to five years in prison. Those who knew Seth McGreedy, Rory's father and the patriarch of the McGreedy clan, were certain he would take action to keep his son out of prison. Fully aware of the McGreedys reputation and concerned that they might attempt to prevent the transfer, Sheriff Jackson arranged for Rory to be moved to the prison on a train that was transporting a group of army soldiers to a nearby fort. Their presence guaranteed the McGreedys would not be able to rescue Rory after he was placed on the train. Any attempt to snatch him away from the law must be done while he remained in local custody.

The ranch hand who came to see Sheriff Jackson claimed he had overheard Seth McGreedy and two of his sons discussing their plans to retrieve Rory. Because the family was both well-known and uniformly disliked in town they knew an attempt to break Rory out of the jail would be met by an armed force of local citizens. A better approach, they reasoned, was to pay a gunman unknown in the area to rescue Rory. It would be a simple matter for an experienced mercenary to enter the sheriff's office and, using the element of surprise, free Rory from his cell and leave the sheriff bound and gagged in his own jail.

Other than the train that was to take Rory McGreedy to the territorial prison, the only commercial means of transportation in the area was a stagecoach that came to town once a week. It may have been a coincidence that the stage was due to arrive so soon after the sheriff and his deputy had been alerted to the McGreedys plan, but it troubled Sheriff Jackson. "I don't like it," the sheriff said to himself. "The guy spills the beans just before the stage is due and doesn't know a dang thing about who's been hired to do the job." He glanced at the clock on the wall. "Well," he mused, "Bill's a good deputy. He'll get a read on whoever comes in on the stage. Prob'ly spot the hired gun if there is one."

Deputy Carson stood on the boardwalk across from the livery stable, leaning against a post that supported the walkway's cover. He saw the stage come to a halt in front of the livery stable and watched as the driver looped the reins around the brake lever and climbed down from his perch atop the conveyance. A man came out of the stable and approached the horses. "Here you go, Pete," the driver said to the man. "These are done for the day. Hitch me up six fresh ones and we'll move on. Don't want to get behind schedule." The man did not reply but quickly set about releasing the horses from the tongue of the stagecoach. Within a few minutes, the harnesses of three new teams were attached to the tongue, ready to hurry their load to its next scheduled stop.

The driver opened the door of the stage, and as the deputy watched three passengers emerged from the coach. The first to exit was a short, stocky man with a ruddy face, a reddish mustache, and spectacles. He wore a brown suit and a bowler hat and carried a brown valise. He set the valise down next to the front wheel of the stage and turned to accept a large black bag handed out by the next passenger. The second passenger, a tall thin man with a small black mustache, leaned out of the stage and looked up and down the street before stepping down. He quickly retrieved the black bag from the shorter man, again glanced toward each end of the street, and stepped into the shadow of the livery barn. As he did so the final passenger disembarked from the stage. He wore a black suit, a black hat and a white collar which the deputy surmised identified him a member of the clergy. He carried two black bags and, in the crook of his arm, a large black Bible.

The driver said something to the passengers and pointed up the street. The man in the brown suit picked up his valise, brushed the dust off and began walking up the street. The other two men followed. At the corner just past the general store, the three men turned onto a side street and, after walking another block and a half arrived at a large white clapboard house. A hand-lettered sign attached to a porch post announced: "Rooms to Let." The men climbed the steps and crossed the porch. The first man opened the door, to which a small bell was attached, and the three entered the house. The ring of the bell brought the proprietor, who greeted the men with a broad smile. "Welcome, friends, welcome," she said, "I'm Emily Sanders and I am blessed to have the opportunity to offer sustenance and lodging to you, my guests." The men exchanged quizzical glances. After an awkward silence, the man in the brown suit said, "I think we'd each like a room."

Mrs. Sanders smiled and said, "Well, of course! Gladly. The rate is one and a half dollars per day, including breakfast and supper." She looked at each of the men as if trying to recognize them. Then she said, "The rooms are right up the stairs and to your right." She glanced at the two black bags belonging to the man wearing the white collar. "And I'll have my husband bring those up for you," she said, turning to call for assistance. "No," said the man in the collar, "I mean that won't be necessary. They aren't heavy. As the good book says, God helps those who help themselves." Mrs. Sanders smiled, stepped aside, and let the men pass to ascend the stairs. She called after them, "Parson, would you perhaps do us the favor of saying grace for our meal this evening?" The man in the collar looked back toward his hostess and said, "Certainly madam, if that is your desire." "Wonderful," she replied. "We will gather at six o'clock."

Deputy Carson returned to the office to tell the sheriff about the three men who had arrived on the stage. The sheriff seemed disappointed in the report. "So," he said, "other than the fellow who surveyed the street before they walked to the boarding house, there wasn't nothing else the least bit unusual?" The deputy shook his head. "Nope," he said, "not much luggage, but I asked the driver about that and he said none of the men intend to stay in town more than a night or two. Didn't know where any of 'em were from or which way they're headed from here." The sheriff's eyes narrowed and he drummed his fingertips on the desk. "Well, if that fella that was in here today was tellin' the truth it has to be one of 'em. Did you talk to Emily Sanders?"

"Sure did," replied the deputy. "She'll let us know if she sees anything out of the ordinary." The sheriff took a step toward the door. "Think I'll just stroll through town and look around a little," he said. "Keep a sharp eye when the prisoner's supper shows up. Someone might see it as an opportunity." The sheriff left the office and the deputy settled into the big chair behind the desk.

It did not take long for the sheriff to encounter one of the men who had arrived on the stage. As he entered the saloon he noticed four men playing poker at a table in one corner of the room. He recognized three of the card players. The fourth was a tall, slender man with a thin mustache. Arrayed on the table was an unusually large number of chips, about half of which lay in front of the stranger. "Well," the sheriff thought, "if he's a hired gunman he's got two ways to make money. Looks to be a pretty good gambler." The man with the mustache had noticed the man wearing a badge and tipped his hat. "Howdy," he said as he nodded slightly. "I presume you are the law in town. Might you wish to join our friendly poker game?" Sheriff Jackson looked directly at the man. "I'll pass," he said. "My only interest in gambling is to make sure it's honest." The stranger smiled. "Couldn't agree more," he said. "Nothing better than a good honest poker game, and nothing worse than a crooked one. I've seen both." The sheriff surveyed the remainder of the saloon, nodded to the bartender and went out into the street.

The other men who had arrived on the stagecoach spent the evening in the boarding house along with two other boarders. The evening meal was tasty and portions were ample. The diners ate heartily and a number of compliments were awarded their hostess. The men all seemed to enjoy the mealtime conversation, though as was the norm among strangers little was asked or volunteered about each other's history or future plans. After the meal, Mrs. Sanders invited the men to move to the drawing room to continue socializing. "I do find all of your company most enjoyable," she said, "but I hope you will excuse me as there are tasks I must attend to." The men nodded politely and the man in the brown suit said, "No doubt you are busy indeed maintaining an excellent establishment like this." The hostess smiled warmly. "Thank you, sir," she said, "it does occupy one's time." She turned toward the man with the white collar and said, "But as the good book says, idle hands are the devil's workshop. Isn't that right, parson?" The man in the collar grinned slightly and replied, "Absolutely, my dear lady." Mrs. Sanders smiled once more and stepped out of the room.

The next morning, after the prisoner was fed, Deputy Carson left the office and began walking up and down the main street. He hoped to learn more about the men who had arrived in town the prior afternoon. At the west end of the street, he stopped in front of the stable and chatted with the liveryman. He then headed east on the south side of the street, pausing for brief conversations with proprietors of the café, the bank, the dry goods store and the saloon. As he left the saloon he was surprised to see Mrs. Sanders suddenly appear at his side. She did not greet him with her usual warm smile. Instead, she looked furtively about, placed a folded piece of paper in his hand and said, "Give this to the sheriff." Then she turned and walked quickly back toward the boarding house.

The deputy continued his rounds along the north side of the street, stopping to talk with the owners of the blacksmith shop, doctor's office, and newspaper office. He passed the schoolhouse and returned to the office, where Sheriff Jackson was waiting. The two men sat together, the sheriff in the large chair behind the desk and the deputy in the chair next to the gun case. The sheriff spoke first. "The train is due in at one o'clock," he said. "If there's goin' to be a ruckus, it'll be before noon." The deputy nodded his agreement. "Yup," he said, "closer to the time the train comes the more they'll think we're on guard." The sheriff cocked his head to one side. "Learn anything this mornin'?" he asked. "Yup," replied the deputy, "I sure did."

The sheriff listened intently as the deputy described his activities of the morning, beginning with the livery stable. "So while I'm standin' there talkin' to Pete," the deputy said, "the tall guy with the skinny mustache - the one you said was playin' poker in the saloon last night - he was there lookin' over some horses when that young fella who told us he'd been fired by the McGreedys showed up." The sheriff leaned forward in his chair as the deputy continued. "The ranch hand said to the other fella, 'I've been lookin' for you," and then the two of 'em went back behind the horses. I couldn't hear what was said but I saw the young fella hand some money to the other man. It coulda been a payoff and the tall thin one might be the McGreedys' hired gun."

"Might be," said the sheriff, "or maybe not. The young fella that came to see us yesterday was in a poker game in the saloon last evening and he was losin' to the fella with the mustache." The deputy stroked his chin. "So you think he was maybe just payin' what he lost last night?" he asked. "Maybe," the sheriff replied, "or maybe you're right and he is our man." The deputy thought a bit, then reached in his pocket. "Nearly forgot," he said, "Emily Sanders said to give you this." He handed the note to the sheriff, who reached into the desk drawer for his spectacles, propped them on his nose, unfolded the note and carefully read it. He raised his eyes and looked at the deputy over the top of his glasses. He handed the note to his deputy, "Here's our answer," he said.

Just after eleven o'clock, there was a knock on the door of the sheriff's office. The door swung open and the man with the white collar stood in the doorway holding his large black Bible. He smiled at the sheriff. "Good morning," the man said, "I hear you have a convict here. I know nothing of him, but I awoke this morning feeling I should offer the man some Bible reading and prayer." The sheriff smiled back at the man. "C'mon in," he said, "I'll get the keys." The sheriff pushed his chair back and the man stepped through the doorway. As the sheriff stood up, the man with the white collar saw that the lawman held a revolver that had been hidden under the desktop. The sheriff pointed the revolver directly at the other man and said, "Parson, you don't move a muscle or I'll drop you right there. My deputy is right behind you and another fella just behind the jail door has a gun aimed at your heart. Now drop that Bible on the floor."

The man with the white collar looked at the sheriff in disbelief. "But sir," he protested, "I'm here to do the Lord's bidding and ..." The sheriff interrupted. "You do my bidding right now and drop that Bible or you're gonna meet the Lord and I doubt you're ready." The blood began to drain from the man's face. He slowly relaxed his grip on the Bible and let it fall to the floor. As it did so it opened, revealing a small pistol hidden in the hollowed out book. "Like I told you," the sheriff said, "I'll get the keys." He motioned the man with the white collar toward the jail door. The parson stepped forward and found himself face to face with a man holding a shotgun. The man with the gun pointed toward an empty cell and the man with the white collar entered it. Then he turned around and addressed the other three men, each of whom was holding a gun pointed directly at him. "How did you know?" he asked. "How in tarnation could you possibly know?"

The sheriff didn't reply. Instead, he glanced toward the deputy and nodded. The deputy looked straight at the man in the cell, a slight grin on his face. "It's simple," he said, "Emily Sanders knows all about what's in that book you been carryin' around." The man in the white collar looked puzzled. "But she couldn't," he insisted, "I never let it out of my sight. She couldn't have known what was in there." The deputy shook his head.

"Not the gun," he said, "but she knows full well what's written in the Bible." The man's expression was one of total confusion. The deputy continued, "A real parson would know that them things you said were from the good book - about the Lord helping those who help themselves, and idle hands being the devil's workshop - they ain't even in it."

The man in the white collar slowly sat down, his head in his hands. Then he noticed another man in the adjoining cell. The man in the other cell was standing with his hands on the bars looking at the man with the white collar, an angry look on his face. "So the old man done hired himself a idiot, did he?" he said in a loud voice. The man in the white collar looked at the other prisoner and in a steady tone of voice said, "You must be Rory McGreedy. I expect we'll be seeing each other a bit more than either of us want." The lawmen left the jail room and closed the door. "Well fellas," the sheriff said, "you two may as well go get somethin' to eat. The train ain't due for another couple hours." The deputy nodded, and he and the other man walked out into the street and turned toward the cafe. The sheriff settled into the big chair behind the desk. "Well," he thought, "I guess the good Lord does work in mysterious ways." Then he smiled and asked aloud, "I wonder if that's in the good book?"

13 THE COLONEL

Colonel Forsythe was frustrated and angry. Four of the last ten gold shipments sent east from San Francisco had not made it to St. Louis. The stagecoaches carrying the shipments had been set upon by gangs of outlaws who stole the gold they carried and robbed the passengers. Two guards had been shot and one died. If these unfortunate incidents continued people would soon lose faith in Wells Fargo and Company as a trustworthy transporter of both freight and people. And to make matters worse for the colonel, the recent robberies had occurred on the Overland Express portion of the stage route, the section for which he was directly responsible.

Colonel Forsythe had recently learned that some mining companies in California were considering sending their gold to the east coast by ship as they had in years past, preferring the much longer transit time to the risk of losing a shipment to thieves. If this happened, the colonel would assuredly be replaced as head of the Overland Express. At best he would be demoted and at worst he would be fired. Neither prospect had much appeal, especially to a man who would soon celebrate his fifth year with Wells Fargo.

William Forsythe was a native of Indiana. He came from a prominent and well-respected family. His father owned a prosperous company and those who knew the Forsythes assumed William would follow his father as head of the business. However, Mr. Forsythe encouraged his son to broaden his knowledge by first gaining a college education and then working elsewhere before returning to run the family firm. William attended a private boarding school in the East and then an Ivy League university, where he studied economics and business. Upon graduating from college he accepted a position in a company owned by Richard Holladay, a close friend of William's father. Thus, shortly after his twenty-first birthday William began his employment with the Holladay Freight Company.

Mr. Holladay was immediately impressed with William's industry and leadership traits and within just a few months was telling friends and family members about the bright young man he had hired. He went so far as to speculate about ways he might convince William to remain with his company rather than return to the Forsythe family firm. However, neither the plan agreed upon by William and his father nor that envisioned by Richard Holladay was to come to fruition. William had been with the Holladay Freight Company less than two years when, following unsuccessful attempts to heal the breach between northern and southern states, war broke out between them. William Forsythe, like many of his friends, left his employment to enlist in the Union Army.

The ambition and leadership qualities Mr. Holladay had noticed in William Forsythe surfaced during the young man's time in uniform. William served with distinction, earning a battlefield commission and several subsequent promotions. By the time he was in the army just over three years he had risen to the rank of major and was in command of three companies totaling four hundred soldiers. By the end of the war, William's confidence in his own abilities had grown dramatically, as had his ego. He had been in charge of a large number of men, operating under intense pressure in a very dangerous environment. A man of his caliber could hardly be expected to return to a family business in Indiana; he needed a position with greater authority and adventure. The army offered him the rank of colonel as an inducement to make the military his career, but William saw little opportunity in peacetime service. He chose not to reenlist but appropriated the rank of colonel when he left the army.

William returned to the family home in Indiana a different person from the one who had left just a few years earlier. His siblings and parents initially found it amusing when William referred to himself as Colonel Forsythe but at his insistence gradually accepted the title. His friends were impressed by his rank and experience, as were the young ladies of the community. He often entertained them with stories of his adventures during the war. They had no reason to think the accounts of his daring exploits were exaggerated, and over time the line between truth and fiction blurred in William's mind.

William, or Colonel Forsythe, had been home just a short time when he announced to his father his intention not to rejoin the family business. He explained that his military experience made him overqualified to run the company and he would not find it sufficiently challenging. William's father, who among other attributes possessed a good deal of patience and a strong sense of reality, did not argue with his son's decision. Though disappointed, Mr. Forsythe offered to contact his acquaintances and business associates, of which he had many, in hopes of finding a position that might match his son's lofty expectations.

He kept any misgivings about William's excessive self-confidence and overbearing manner to himself.

It was during a discussion with his longtime friend Richard Holladay that Mr. Forsythe learned of an opportunity that might appeal to William. Mr. Holladay had recently received a letter from his brother Benjamin, who years earlier had left Indiana and the Holladay Freight Company to seek his fortune on the frontier. After several false starts, Ben Holladay had managed to use the knowledge he had acquired while working in his family's firm to establish a successful freight company in the West. Ben's company, known as the Overland Express, transported mail and passengers between St. Louis and Salt Lake City by stagecoach. His line connected with the Overland Mail Company, owned by Wells Fargo, which ran from Salt Lake City to Virginia City, Nevada. From there, stagecoaches of the Pioneer Stage Line, another Wells Fargo subsidiary, continued on to San Francisco.

Just after the Civil War ended Ben Holladay sold the Overland Express to Wells Fargo, ensuring for himself a life of wealth and leisure. The sale included an agreement that he stay on to run the Overland Express, but after serious disagreements regarding its management he resigned his position. This left Wells Fargo with no one in charge of a sizeable stagecoach operation between Salt Lake City and Saint Louis. Despite the rift between Ben Holladay and Wells Fargo, John Butterfield, president of Wells Fargo, asked Ben to help find someone to manage the Overland Express stage line. This was the subject of the letter Ben's brother Richard shared with William Forsythe's father. Mr. Forsythe immediately nominated his recently discharged son William as a candidate for the open position. Richard Holladay's remembrance of the younger Forsythe was based on the short period of time William worked for the Holladay Freight Company. He responded positively to his friend's suggestion and dashed off a letter to his brother Ben enthusiastically recommending young Colonel Forsythe for the job. A short time later Colonel William Forsythe headed west to assume command of the Overland Express.

Once in charge of the Overland Express and its chain of stations that dotted the route from St. Louis to Salt Lake City, Colonel Forsythe quickly established a reputation as a force to be reckoned with. He treated those working under him just as he had treated lower ranking men in the army, as inferiors from whom he demanded absolute, unquestioning obedience. He expected all-out effort and flawless work and refused to tolerate excuses for delays, late shipments, or other negative results. By relentlessly driving the people under him, Colonel Forsythe improved the results of the Overland Express and prided himself on doing so.

Colonel Forsythe's approach to running the Overland Express produced a profit, but at high human cost. Opinions and ideas of older and more experienced but lower ranking employees were dismissed out of hand. Seasoned veterans of the company, whose expertise regarding the problems and perils involved in crossing the Great Plains by stagecoach was potentially of immense value to the operation, soon learned to keep their ideas to themselves. By the time the colonel had been at the helm of the Overland Express for a year most experienced employees had left the company. Few of their replacements stayed long, but a flood of returning veterans provided a ready pool of new employees. Shipments and profits increased and Colonel Forsythe continued to be viewed favorably by his superiors. That is, until the recent spate of gold shipment robberies.

William Forsythe did not possess in-depth knowledge of the transportation business or the specifics of operating an overland stagecoach route. But he did understand that a continuation of the losses that recently occurred between Salt Lake City and St. Louis would mean his certain replacement. This possibility disturbed him a great deal for two reasons. First, losing his position would hurt his finances and his reputation. If he were dismissed by Wells Fargo word would spread rapidly, making it difficult to find another position that suited his exceptional talents. Second, his termination would be a source of pleasure to the incompetent and disrespectful former employees he inherited when he took over. He was not sure which bothered him more but was determined to retain control of the Overland Express. And the only way to do that was to end the string of stagecoach robberies that plagued the line.

Protecting gold shipments during the trip east from Salt Lake City was no small task. The stagecoaches, pulled by six-horse teams replaced at each Overland Express station along the route, crossed high deserts, mountains, rivers, woodlands, and desolate prairies to reach St. Louis. Along the way, stage drivers might encounter dust storms, rockslides, floods, hostile Indians, or thieves. In summer the searing heat of the sun beat down on the plains, punishing both horses and men. In winter, blizzards roared down out of the mountains and across the prairie, burying everything in their path under thick blankets of ice-cold snow. Just carrying passengers and mail safely over the fourteen hundred mile route was a formidable challenge, without facing the additional hazard of determined gangs of outlaws.

The recent attacks on the Overland Express followed a similar pattern, and Colonel Forsythe was certain the robberies were perpetrated by a single gang. Their method was deceptively simple, and the fact that his stagecoach drivers fell prey to it made the colonel furious. First, the gang located a section of the trail narrow enough to prevent the stagecoach from turning around. Then, some type of barrier was put in place to partially block the trail, such as a fallen tree trunk, a wagon with a broken wheel, or a pile of rocks. When the stage driver slowed the horses to maneuver around the obstacle, a couple men appeared on the trail, guns drawn, and ordered the driver to stop. The rest of the gang, reportedly four or five additional men, approached from behind and ordered everyone off the stage. The men in front of the stage removed the strong box while the others robbed the passengers. The outlaws then cut the horses loose from the stage and drove them off before riding away with the gold and other valuables. Two attempts by guards to defend the stage were unsuccessful, one fatally so.

Colonel Forsythe paced back and forth across his office ruminating on the bad luck that allowed the gold robberies to occur on the Overland Express. Why not on the first leg of the journey from California, the Pioneer Stage Line that ran from San Francisco to Virginia City? Or the Overland Mail Company route from Virginia City to Salt Lake City? He cursed the outlaws for picking this section of the Wells Fargo for their robberies. He had met the fellow who ran the Overland Mail Company and immediately noticed the man's dullness and lack of ambition. Though he had not met the person in charge of the Pioneer Stage Line, it was likely he was also a weak manager or perhaps even a complete dolt. Why the outlaw gang had made the obviously unfair decision to rob his stages was beyond knowing.

While Colonel Forsythe was alone in his office his assistant in the anteroom next door received an envelope containing a telegram addressed to "W. Forsythe, Overland Express." The aide opened the telegram and read it. His eyes opened widely as he did so, then his face formed a slight smile. He placed the envelope in the trash basket, carefully folded the telegram and knocked on the door to the colonel's office. "Come," the colonel said. The aide opened the door and without speaking handed the telegram to his superior. "Go," commanded the colonel. When the office door closed, Colonel Forsythe unfolded the telegram and read it. He frowned deeply, sat down and read it again. The message said, "Next shipment large. Counting on you. One more robbery will be your last." It was signed simply "J.B." There was no doubt the message was from Mr. John Butterfield, president of Wells Fargo and Company.

Colonel Forsythe stood up, cursed and walked briskly across his office. He began to examine a large map on which was plotted the entire route of the Overland Express. He squinted at the map, pursed his lips and slightly cocked his head. For several minutes he stood silent and motionless. Then he said aloud, "That's it. That's what we need to do." He strode quickly to the office door, opened it and commanded his aide. "Get Mitchell and Harper in here right away," he snapped. "Yes sir," the aide replied and started on his errand. The aide hated calling the colonel sir, both because he disliked the military atmosphere in the office and greatly disliked the man who had imposed it. But it was easier to address the colonel as sir than endure the unpleasantness sure to result from disobeying the man.

Clyde Mitchell and Frederick Harper were by title assistant general managers of the Overland Express. Ostensibly, Mitchell was in charge of the company's accounting, scheduling, and routing, while day-to-day operation of the stagecoaches and route stations was supposedly managed by Harper. In reality, however, all significant decisions within either of these areas were made by Colonel Forsythe. The colonel insisted on being involved in the details of both men's departments and was not above reminding them that his involvement was necessitated by their own incompetence. Both men strongly disliked their boss and looked forward to the day when the colonel's abrasive nature and unwillingness to learn from others would lead to mistakes serious enough to end his career with the Overland Express. In the meantime, they had as little direct contact as possible with the colonel and tried to shield the people under them from the man's criticism.

When Clyde Mitchell and Frederick Harper arrived at Colonel Forsythe's office they could hear him talking to someone so they waited in the anteroom. The aide soon appeared, looked questioningly at the two men, and said, "Better get in there. He's waiting for you." Hearing the colonel's voice, the aide added, "There's nobody in there." Mitchell slowly opened the door, and he and Harper entered the office. The Colonel was standing in front of the Overland Express route map, completely absorbed in his own thoughts. "Yes, " the colonel said, "it will work. They have fooled us too often, and now we will fool them. If they think for one minute they can do what the whole Confederate Army couldn't do, they've got another ..." Clyde Mitchell cleared his throat, and the colonel noticed the two men's presence in his office. "About time you got here," he barked. "Pay attention and I'll tell you what we're going to do." Mitchell and Harper exchanged a sidelong glance and awaited with trepidation the explanation that was to come.

"Here's the plan," the colonel announced to the two men standing before him. "The gang that's been robbing the stages knows our route and knows our station locations. They're smart enough to attack about midway between two stations, so after they've driven our horses off they have time to go some distance before the driver can get word to anyone. They know the guards are spineless cowards who wouldn't lift a finger to save their own mothers." Mitchell and Harper looked at each other. Frederick Harper spoke. "So," he said, "do you plan to add more guards? That might mean less room for passengers." The colonel glared at Harper. "Did I say more guards?" he snapped. "No, sir," Harper replied. Mitchell spoke next. "What about making sure the passengers are well-armed and ready whenever the stage goes through areas like the ones where they've blocked the trail?" The colonel responded quickly, "Do you really think we can count on passengers? If you weren't such an idiot, you'd realize not a single passenger was of any use during any of the robberies. Maybe if you listen instead of wagging your tongue you just might learn something." Mitchell bristled and was tempted to reply, but simply thought to himself, "You arrogant fool. Your time is coming, and sooner than you think." With the men's silence ensured, the colonel began to reveal his plan for defeating the outlaws.

"The key to warfare," the colonel began, "is the element of surprise. That means either striking the enemy before he is ready or using an unexpected strategy that gives you the advantage. We are going to do something totally unexpected." Clyde Mitchell raised his eyebrows and Frederick Harper listened with greater attention. The colonel continued. "We're going to take a different route;" he said, "we won't stop at any of the stations, and the gang will have absolutely no idea where we are." Mitchell and Harper were stunned. After a few seconds' silence, Mitchell asked, "Not use the stations? What is the route? And what about fresh horses, feed, water?" The colonel did not appreciate the question. "Do you think I haven't thought of that?" he said, then shook his head and continued. "The robberies have all been between Fort Bridger and Fort Laramie, We'll leave the Overland Express route at Fort Bridger and follow the old Buffalo Trail, as it's called, until just west of Fort Laramie, then rejoin the normal route. We'll take five extra men, a dozen extra horses, and all the supplies we need. We will not only deliver the gold shipment safely and on time but will leave those ignorant outlaws hopelessly confused."

Clyde Mitchell and Frederick Harper had many questions but knew better than to interrupt. The colonel surprised them by asking, "Well, got it?" Clyde said nothing, but Frederick broke the silence. "If you don't mind my asking," he said, "how do you plan to provide for the horses?" "Simple," said the colonel, "with no passengers we fill the inside and the top of the stage with food for horses and men. And we'll add platforms around the rear to hold enough water barrels to sustain men and horses while on the Old Buffalo trail." Clyde nodded, and asked, "No passengers, how about freight?" "Just one strong box," replied the colonel, "with more gold inside than we've ever carried." "And will the guards know that?" asked Clyde. "They won't need to," said the colonel. "they won't be on the stage this time." Clyde and Frederick looked puzzled. "I contacted some of the best riflemen in my old army outfit;" the colonel said. "four of them are due into Salt Lake City tomorrow. They'll ride some of the extra horses and guard the stage until it gets to Fort Laramie."

It was clear to Clyde and Frederick that the colonel had actually thought through his plan. They also realized the plan depended on a number of assumptions, none of which the colonel would appreciate having questioned. Hopefully, the presence of at least eighteen horses accompanying a small group of white men would not prove too tempting a target for Indians in the area. The old Buffalo Trail, unused for years, must still be passable by a Concord stagecoach with a six-horse hitch. And, should the outlaw gang happen to discover the ruse and pursue the stage, the colonel's former army associates must prove superior in any conflict that ensued. There was also the issue of which driver or drivers would be selected to guide the stagecoach and its entourage along the unfamiliar path of the Old Buffalo Trail. That question was answered by the colonel's next statement.

"This is the most important shipment the Overland Express has ever carried," the colonel said. Clyde and Frederick suspected its importance had less to do with the reputation of Wells Fargo and Company than with William Forsythe's continued employment by the firm. "Because of this," the colonel continued, "I will personally select two drivers who will alternate at the reins." He paused to let the significance of his next pronouncement sink in. "And in order to guarantee a successful trip," he said, "I will personally be in command of the stage until it reaches Fort Laramie. It is high time someone shows these criminals they cannot win against the Overland Express and Colonel William Forsythe." As he spoke the colonel stood as if at attention, his jaw set in an attitude of uncompromising certainty.

Upon receiving detailed instructions from Colonel Forsythe, the Overland Express crew in Salt Lake City worked even harder than usual to prepare for the upcoming trip. They procured all the supplies prescribed by the colonel, including twelve strong and energetic horses. They also modified a standard Concord stagecoach to carry a full load inside plus six large water barrels attached to the rear of the stage. While the workmen prepared the stage and loaded it with food, feed, and water, the colonel schooled the two drivers and four sharpshooter guards on the route and details of the expedition. Then he sent the guards and extra horses ahead to Fort Bridger, where they and the stage would depart from the normal Overland Express route. By the time of the scheduled departure from Salt Lake City all was ready. The colonel, riding in front of the heavily loaded Concord on a tall buckskin horse, gave a command and the stage started rolling east.

The route selected by Colonel Forsythe followed the Overland Express trail from Salt Lake City to Wahsatch, a small settlement on the eastern edge of Utah, a distance of about seventy-five miles. It then continued another forty-five miles to Fort Bridger. From Fort Bridger, the route the colonel laid out left the Overland Express trail, turning south toward Lone Tree. There it intersected with the Old Buffalo trail and followed it eastward to the Green River. Once across the river, the colonel's route remained on the Old Buffalo Trail as it meandered two hundred and fifty miles along the southern edge of Wyoming. Then it left the old trail, heading northeast on the final thirty miles to Fort Laramie. Once safely at Fort Laramie, the stage would rejoin the usual Overland Express trail through Denver to St. Louis.

To take full advantage of the long summer days, the stagecoach left just after sun-up. The colonel's schedule called for the stagecoach to reach Fort Bridger, some seventy-five miles from Salt Lake City, after the first day's travel. However, recent rainfall in the area slowed travel, and the overloaded Concord did not reach the Wells Fargo station at Wahsatch until late afternoon. After a brief stop at the station, the colonel announced it was time to resume the trek toward Fort Bridger, about forty-five miles farther on. The stationmaster, whose isolated position had not allowed him the opportunity to become familiar with Colonel Forsythe's personality or reputation, told Forsythe in plain terms that only a fool would consider leaving for Fort Bridger so late in the day. "You'll never make it by dark." the man told the colonel. "It's wild country between here and there. Get caught out overnight, and if the Indians don't getcha, the bears will." The colonel decided to remain at Wahsatch overnight in order to rest the horses and get a fresh start in the morning.

By noon of the second day the stage reached Fort Bridger, where the sharpshooter guards and the extra dozen horses were waiting. With fresh teams hitched to the stagecoach, and the guards and additional horses in the rear, the procession departed from the Overland Express trail and headed south. Despite having no established trail to follow, the party made good progress. At four o'clock in the afternoon Colonel Forsythe signaled the stage driver to stop. He consulted his hand-drawn map, studied the terrain around him, and declared they had found the Old Buffalo Trail and would follow it toward the east. Some of the men had their doubts but obeyed the orders they were given.

The colonel's directions proved surprisingly accurate when, shortly before sundown of the second day, the party found themselves atop a hill overlooking the Green River. "A good place to camp," the colonel announced, "We'll cross in the morning." The other men set about tending the horses, gathering driftwood for a fire, and setting up their tents. After a scant meal of beans, hardtack and coffee the men bedded down for the night.

Nothing more threatening than mosquitoes bothered the travelers during the night, and they were up at dawn. By the time the sun started its climb up the eastern sky the party was on its way. The rush of waters from the spring snowmelt had long since subsided, and the river was a wide, lazy stream of slow-moving current. Fording it was not difficult, thanks to the foresight of one of the drivers who suggested hitching some spare horses on the front of the stage before crossing. If the heavy Concord had relied on only its six-horse hitch to pull it across the sandy bottom of the river, they might well have been unable to do so. Once during the crossing the horses stopped and the wheels of the stagecoach began to sink into the soft river bottom. But by applying his whip and an impressive vocabulary of foul language, the driver got the team moving and completed the crossing without further incident.

When the party reached the eastern bank of the Green River the colonel decided to reorganize the procession under his command. He gathered the small cadre of travelers around the stagecoach and explained the new arrangement. "Men," he began, "we are at this point far enough from the usual trail to have little concern about the gang that has been preying upon the Overland Express. I expect they are planning to intercept us on the main route about forty miles north of this trail. The task ahead of us is simply to continue on the Old Buffalo Trail toward Fort Laramie."

The colonel continued, exuding confidence as he spoke. "The stationmaster at the fort informed me that there are, to his knowledge, no settlements between here and there," he said, "a distance I estimate at approximately two hundred and ninety miles. I have received no report of hostiles on the trail ahead. However, to be certain we are prepared for any eventuality, from here on the guards will ride at the head of the column. The spare horses will be put in teams and tied in a string behind the stage. The off-duty driver and I will ride beside the stage keeping close watch for any threats originating from either side of the trail."

As the men listened to the colonel's monologue two pieces of information caught their attention. First, they were nearly three hundred miles from their destination, and second there was in all likelihood not a single settlement along the entire way. One of the guards voiced the question others had in their minds. "How long do think it will take to get to the fort?" he asked. The colonel looked squarely at the guard and said, "Allowing for the terrain in this region and the indirect route taken by the Old Buffalo Trail, we should arrive at Fort Laramie precisely five days from today. We have no doubt outmaneuvered the outlaw gang and have only to progress steadily through the country ahead to complete our mission." Presuming his answer had satisfied the men, the colonel ordered the group to mount up and move out. With the guards now in the lead, the party proceeded eastward along the Old Buffalo Trail.

Although the members of Colonel Forsythe's expedition had no sure way to calculate the distance traveled they knew long before dusk that they would not cover the desired sixty miles that day. The area was more undulating than expected and the Old Buffalo Trail was even more crooked than anticipated. When they finally stopped to make camp for the night, the colonel estimated they had traveled between forty-five and fifty miles. In reality, they were barely thirty miles east of their starting point that morning. "We'll make it up tomorrow," the colonel assured the men, "flatter terrain and a more direct route." The men wondered about the accuracy of this prediction but chose not to question the colonel.

The next day, the fourth since the men had left Salt Lake City, turned out to be considerably more productive. The men had no idea whether the colonel's optimistic forecast of the previous evening was fact-based or speculative, but they were glad to be traveling a more direct and level route on which they made considerably better time. They were in good spirits and remained on the trail from early morning until sunset. By the colonel's reckoning the day's travel totaled a good fifty miles. At this rate they might make up enough time to reach Fort Laramie on the scheduled day. The men made camp and, exhausted, quickly drifted off to sleep.

The travelers got a very early start the next morning. Anxious to be underway, the men were striking their tents and hitching the horses at first light, and before the sun was fully visible the campsite was empty. Everyone in the party shared the colonel's determination to reach Fort Laramie on time, though not all of them for the same reason as the colonel. Most of the men simply wanted to get through the experience and collect their pay, but their obvious commitment to maximizing each day's distance pleased the colonel. He was now completely confident that his scheme would result in restoration of the Overland Express's reputation as well as his own.

The morning went well despite having to cross two small rivers swollen from rain that had fallen in the high country above them. The colonel recalled the previously successful fording by using extra teams of horses on the front of the stage's six-horse hitch and ordered the technique repeated. The stagecoach was thus hauled across both rivers with minimal difficulty and the party continued on its way. The Concord groaned under the weight of the supplies aboard but was sturdily built and, at least thus far, gave the men no reason to doubt its capability to complete the journey intact. When they had crossed the second river the extra horses were unhitched from the stage and the water barrels refilled. The colonel informed his companions of an important detail. "According to my information," he said, "that's the last water between here and Fort Laramie. So be meticulous in parsing it out to the horses and yourselves. The water in those barrels must last until Fort Laramie." The men took this admonition seriously.

By noon the party had covered another twenty-five miles of the trail. Morale was high and even the horses seemed to sense that things were going well. The colonel told the men that according to information from the stationmaster at the fort the Old Buffalo Trail would soon lead them into less hospitable terrain. The trail would cross an area of forested foothills before emerging onto another expanse of flat prairie. Fortunately, the portion of the trail that climbed through the foothills was only a few miles long. Once through this segment of the trail the party could expect to resume their previous pace.

By mid-afternoon the guards were leading the stagecoach and the dozen horses behind it up a steep, rocky section of the trail that taxed the capability of the horses pulling the stage. The driver did everything within his power to keep up with the guards, who were some distance ahead of the stage and holding their horses to a slow walk, but the six horses could only do so much. Beyond the top of the hill the trail would emerge from the trees and become a long, smooth path that ran steadily downhill for over a mile. Once they reached the hillcrest the stage and its accompanying horses and riders could greatly increase their speed. But first the stage had to make it up the hill. The colonel, riding at the right side of the stage, was becoming impatient.

The colonel's thoughts were focused on the six horses hitched to the stage, pulling with all their might but moving too slowly. He wondered whether it was feasible to replace them with fresh horses at this point on the trail, or perhaps add additional horses in front as had been done earlier to ford the rivers. If the colonel had known what was transpiring in the rocky hills that adjoined the trail, he would have realized he faced a much more serious issue than the slowness with which the stagecoach was crawling up the rocky trail. Immediately north of the trail, on the left side of the stage and about seventy-five feet above it, three men were watching the activity on the trail below. When the stage neared the crest of the trail, one of the men above it signaled to a second group similarly situated above the stage on the south side of the trail. At the signal, the men on both sides of the trail opened fire.

The volley of gunfire that rained down on the trail was so totally unexpected it took the colonel's men a second or two to recognize the sound. Bullets whizzed past their leader's head as he tried to make sense of what was happening. Some lead struck the stagecoach, sending splinters flying in every direction. The guards on the trail ahead jerked their horses' reins, wheeled about, and raced back down the hill to defend the stagecoach. They stopped beside the six-horse hitch, jumped

ity to confirm the schedule he had been sent a week
ould not have been the first time he had received an
chedule, so he was not certain the stage was sup-
rive at the Fort on the day he expected it. By the time
ply verifying that the schedule was correct, the stage
days late. The stationmaster then wired the office in
City for instructions. Another day passed before in-
were received to request assistance from the army
Fort Laramie. So it was that five days after Colonel
was due to arrive there, a squad of soldiers left Fort
n search of the colonel and his party. Five of the
re on horseback, the other man drove a small buck-
gon carrying tents, shovels, two barrels of water, and
plies. Having been made aware of the unusual route
by the Forsythe party, the searchers headed southwest
e Old Buffalo Trail.

he search party reached the Old Buffalo Trail by mid-
followed it west until nightfall. They camped under the
got an early start the next morning. It was a hot sum-
and the sun beat down upon the soldiers as they rode.
d been riding less than half a day when they crossed
f a small ridge. In the distance they saw what appeared
group of animals resting in the grass. As they got closer
f the scene came into focus. The bodies of eight horses
he ground. They were already beginning to decay and
ch filled the air. Near the horses were the bodies of four
o leaning against each other, and the others lying a few
part. Some of the horses had died naturally, others had
hot and their jugular veins cut as the dead men tried to
their thirst by any means possible. The sergeant in
of the search party, a large man with a grizzled, sun-
face, surveyed the spectacle. He shook his head, then

off their mounts and began shooting toward the source of the gunfire as bullets continued to strike the stagecoach. The trees and rocks hid the attackers from sight, and all the guards could do was aim for the puff of smoke that accompanied each shot. The stage driver, apparently enjoying either a spurt of bravery or a failure to think clearly, remained at the reins encouraging the horses to move the stage the remaining few yards to the top of the hill. The gunfire frightened the horses into one last effort and suddenly the stagecoach crested the top and headed down the other side.

The assailants continued firing after the stage while the driver struggled to control the now panicky horses, racing down the long hill at breakneck speed. The colonel, in a state of shock, had remained alongside the six-horse hitch and now found himself kicking and slapping his horse to keep up with the runaway stage. The guards, realizing attempts to hit any of the attackers were futile, mounted their horses and galloped after the stage. Thus the party left the scene of the attack, each man fleeing for his life in a desperate race toward safety. They had gone nearly halfway down the hill when it dawned on them that no one was in pursuit. The gunfire had ceased and they heard no sound of horses behind them. The colonel chanced a glance to the rear and saw nothing but the cloud of dust raised by his own party.

The stage driver recognized the danger had passed and now tried as hard to slow the horses in front of the stage as he had tried to keep them moving just a few moments earlier. After another quarter mile the horses' adrenalin was depleted and the driver was finally able to bring the stagecoach to a halt. The horses stood panting, coated with lather and foam dripping from their mouths. They had been exhausted before they crested the hill, and the mad dash downward had taxed them to the limit a horse could be expected to survive. The driver noticed blood dripping from the nostrils of some of the horses. "Not a good sign," he thought, "we'll probably lose these three." He was grateful the expedition included twelve spare horses.

When the guards reached the stagecoach the colonel realized one of them was missing. "Where's your other man?" he demanded. In unison, the guards looked back toward the scene of the attack. "He got hit," one of them said, "fell off his horse. Had to leave him." The colonel stared at the guards. "So who's going back for him?" he asked. The guards looked at each other but remained silent. Finally one of them spoke up. "It'd be suicide to ride back down there between those hills." The colonel rubbed his chin and frowned. The other men expected an unwelcome order to go to the aid of their comrade. Instead, the colonel asked, "And the other horses?" It suddenly occurred to the others in the party that the spare horses had not emerged from the hills. They looked back toward the hill, searching for a sign of the horses but seeing none. The stage driver said, "I reckon they're either shot dead or run off back down the hill in the other direction." The colonel swore. As much as he hated to admit it, the driver was no doubt right.

The guards dismounted from their horses and the driver climbed down from the stage. The men gathered around the colonel, who remained atop his buckskin. "All right," said the colonel, "we have the horses on the stage, plus the ones the five of us are riding. That makes eleven. The stage has some damage but is still serviceable. And we still have most all the supplies. I think we can assume whoever was back there has no idea what's in the strongbox. They also had no way of knowing about our special guards. Having faced you once, they no doubt appreciate your sharpshooting ability and have decided it's not worth coming after us. If they thought otherwise they would have done so immediately." The men, in various stages of regaining their composure, seemed to accept the colonel's

reasoning. One of them n⟨
sounds right." Their thoughts ⟨
called to them from behind t⟨
bunch," he said, "and they plar⟨
this."

The colonel got down⟨
walked to the rear of the stage.⟨
conclusion about the men who l⟨
glected to take a careful asses⟨
now clear why so many of the⟨
stagecoach. They were not prim⟨
the coach itself but at the water⟨
the coach. The barrels were pepp⟨
watched in stunned silence as the⟨
the dry ground.

The colonel took a deep br⟨
did not have to tell the men what⟨
water for the horses, let along the⟨
They could not make it to Fort Larai⟨
going back through the hills they wo⟨
to reach Fort Bridger. Their only hope⟨
help while the others remained with⟨
would take whatever canteens still c⟨
who stayed would do without. Finally⟨
surprise of the other men he did not⟨
anyone else for what had happened. H⟨
responsibility. I'll go." The men whose⟨
water handed them to the colonel wh⟨
ment, mounted the big buckskin and ⟨
east.

The Overland Express stage wa⟨
Fort Laramie when the stationmaster th⟨

Salt Lake C⟨
earlier. It w⟨
incorrect s⟨
posed to a⟨
he got a re⟨
was three⟨
Salt Lake⟨
structions⟨
garrison a⟨
Forsythe⟨
Laramie⟨
troops we⟨
board wa⟨
other sup⟨
followed⟨
toward th⟨

T⟨
day and⟨
stars an⟨
mer day⟨
They ha⟨
the top⟨
to be a⟨
details⟨
lay on⟨
the ste⟨
men, t⟨
yards⟨
been s⟨
satisfy⟨
charge⟨
baked⟨

off their mounts and began shooting toward the source of the gunfire as bullets continued to strike the stagecoach. The trees and rocks hid the attackers from sight, and all the guards could do was aim for the puff of smoke that accompanied each shot. The stage driver, apparently enjoying either a spurt of bravery or a failure to think clearly, remained at the reins encouraging the horses to move the stage the remaining few yards to the top of the hill. The gunfire frightened the horses into one last effort and suddenly the stagecoach crested the top and headed down the other side.

The assailants continued firing after the stage while the driver struggled to control the now panicky horses, racing down the long hill at breakneck speed. The colonel, in a state of shock, had remained alongside the six-horse hitch and now found himself kicking and slapping his horse to keep up with the runaway stage. The guards, realizing attempts to hit any of the attackers were futile, mounted their horses and galloped after the stage. Thus the party left the scene of the attack, each man fleeing for his life in a desperate race toward safety. They had gone nearly halfway down the hill when it dawned on them that no one was in pursuit. The gunfire had ceased and they heard no sound of horses behind them. The colonel chanced a glance to the rear and saw nothing but the cloud of dust raised by his own party.

The stage driver recognized the danger had passed and now tried as hard to slow the horses in front of the stage as he had tried to keep them moving just a few moments earlier. After another quarter mile the horses' adrenalin was depleted and the driver was finally able to bring the stagecoach to a halt. The horses stood panting, coated with lather and foam dripping from their mouths. They had been exhausted before they crested the hill, and the mad dash downward had taxed them to the limit a horse could be expected to survive. The driver noticed blood dripping from the nostrils of some of the horses. "Not a good sign," he thought, "we'll probably lose these three." He was grateful the expedition included twelve spare horses.

When the guards reached the stagecoach the colonel realized one of them was missing. "Where's your other man?" he demanded. In unison, the guards looked back toward the scene of the attack. "He got hit," one of them said, "fell off his horse. Had to leave him." The colonel stared at the guards. "So who's going back for him?" he asked. The guards looked at each other but remained silent. Finally one of them spoke up. "It'd be suicide to ride back down there between those hills." The colonel rubbed his chin and frowned. The other men expected an unwelcome order to go to the aid of their comrade. Instead, the colonel asked, "And the other horses?" It suddenly occurred to the others in the party that the spare horses had not emerged from the hills. They looked back toward the hill, searching for a sign of the horses but seeing none. The stage driver said, "I reckon they're either shot dead or run off back down the hill in the other direction." The colonel swore. As much as he hated to admit it, the driver was no doubt right.

The guards dismounted from their horses and the driver climbed down from the stage. The men gathered around the colonel, who remained atop his buckskin. "All right," said the colonel, "we have the horses on the stage, plus the ones the five of us are riding. That makes eleven. The stage has some damage but is still serviceable. And we still have most all the supplies. I think we can assume whoever was back there has no idea what's in the strongbox. They also had no way of knowing about our special guards. Having faced you once, they no doubt appreciate your sharpshooting ability and have decided it's not worth coming after us. If they thought otherwise they would have done so immediately." The men, in various stages of regaining their composure, seemed to accept the colonel's reasoning. One of them nodded, and another said, "That sounds right." Their thoughts were interrupted by the driver, who called to them from behind the stage. "Unless it's one smart bunch," he said, "and they plan to just wait us out. Come look at this."

The colonel got down from his horse and the men walked to the rear of the stage. In their haste to come to some conclusion about the men who had attacked them they had neglected to take a careful assessment of the damages. It was now clear why so many of the attackers' bullets had hit the stagecoach. They were not primarily aiming at the men or for the coach itself but at the water barrels attached to the rear of the coach. The barrels were peppered with holes, and the men watched in stunned silence as the last bit of water dripped onto the dry ground.

The colonel took a deep breath and slowly let it out. He did not have to tell the men what this meant. Without enough water for the horses, let along the men, they were doomed. They could not make it to Fort Laramie, and even if they risked going back through the hills they would not survive long enough to reach Fort Bridger. Their only hope was for one man to go for help while the others remained with the stage. Whoever went would take whatever canteens still contained water and those who stayed would do without. Finally the colonel spoke. To the surprise of the other men he did not swear, nor did he blame anyone else for what had happened. He simply said, "You're my responsibility. I'll go." The men whose canteens still contained water handed them to the colonel who, without further comment, mounted the big buckskin and began to follow the trail east.

The Overland Express stage was two days overdue at Fort Laramie when the stationmaster there sent a telegram to

Salt Lake City to confirm the schedule he had been sent a week earlier. It would not have been the first time he had received an incorrect schedule, so he was not certain the stage was supposed to arrive at the Fort on the day he expected it. By the time he got a reply verifying that the schedule was correct, the stage was three days late. The stationmaster then wired the office in Salt Lake City for instructions. Another day passed before instructions were received to request assistance from the army garrison at Fort Laramie. So it was that five days after Colonel Forsythe was due to arrive there, a squad of soldiers left Fort Laramie in search of the colonel and his party. Five of the troops were on horseback, the other man drove a small buckboard wagon carrying tents, shovels, two barrels of water, and other supplies. Having been made aware of the unusual route followed by the Forsythe party, the searchers headed southwest toward the Old Buffalo Trail.

The search party reached the Old Buffalo Trail by midday and followed it west until nightfall. They camped under the stars and got an early start the next morning. It was a hot summer day and the sun beat down upon the soldiers as they rode. They had been riding less than half a day when they crossed the top of a small ridge. In the distance they saw what appeared to be a group of animals resting in the grass. As they got closer details of the scene came into focus. The bodies of eight horses lay on the ground. They were already beginning to decay and the stench filled the air. Near the horses were the bodies of four men, two leaning against each other, and the others lying a few yards apart. Some of the horses had died naturally, others had been shot and their jugular veins cut as the dead men tried to satisfy their thirst by any means possible. The sergeant in charge of the search party, a large man with a grizzled, sunbaked face, surveyed the spectacle. He shook his head, then told the others, "Find identification if you can, then start diggin' and bury 'em. Let me know if you find the colonel."

The soldiers completed the unpleasant task of burying the men and the search party continued west on the Old Buffalo Trail. They found nothing more that day and camped overnight at the edge of a large expanse of grassland. The next morning the small cadre of searchers was again underway at sunup. Before they left the campsite the sergeant told the men, "We'll go west until noon, and if we don't find nothing, we'll turn around and camp back here tonight. I'd like to find 'em, but I ain't gonna risk running out of water in this god-forsaken country." The image of the bodies they had buried the day before was fresh in his mind and he was not about to endanger the lives of the soldiers riding with him to find the other missing men, who were almost certainly dead.

Shortly before noon, the troops had started up a long, grassy slope that led to some wooded foothills when one of the men called out, "Sergeant," he said, "looks like somethin' up ahead." The sergeant had also seen the object, which in the distance resembled a small building. A few more minutes of riding revealed the object to be a stagecoach sitting motionless along the trail. None of the men looked forward to what they were likely to find, and as they neared the stage their apprehensions proved accurate. The bodies of two more men lay on the shady side of the stage. Three horses lay dead, still hitched to the stage, which bore evidence of a serious gun battle.

The sergeant scratched his neck and said, "Here's how I figure it. The poor devils must have been attacked a ways up the trail. Don't know if it was Indians or whites. They made a run for it and ran three of the horses to death. Then they split up. The ones we found yesterday took all the good horses and made for the fort and these two stayed with the stage." Some of the soldiers nodded and a couple murmured their agreement with the sergeant's assessment. "Well," the sergeant said, "let's get these two buried. Any valuables on the stage put on the buckboard to take back." The soldiers collected the guns lying nearby and put them on the wagon, then buried the two men. The only things of value on the stage were boxes of ammunition, which were divided among the soldiers.

As they retraced the route back to Fort Laramie the soldiers continued to search for the colonel but found no sign of the man or his horse. This puzzled the sergeant. The only sensible action for a group of men stranded in the wilderness would be for one or two of them to ride for help. Since the colonel was not with the others he must have been the one that first tried to reach the fort. When no help came, the men they had buried the previous day decided to strike out on their own. Maybe the colonel got lost, or maybe a bear or mountain lion got him and the horse just wandered off across the prairie. Anybody's guess whether it was still alive, but the sergeant would have bet a dollar to a nickel the colonel was not. The sergeant shook his head. "Guess no one will ever know," he thought, "and he was some big war hero, too."

Although the sergeant's search party and the men who worked under Colonel Forsythe would never learn what happened to him, it was not true that no one knew. The colonel had not reached Fort Laramie because he had not continued in that direction. As he rode along the Old Buffalo Trail toward the fort, he reviewed in his mind the events of the day. He replayed the sounds and images of the attack, the narrow escape, and the discovery that one of his men had been shot, the spare horses killed or run off, and their water supply destroyed. He thought about the gang of worthless men whose greed led them to steal and to kill without mercy. He became enraged at the injustice of it all and could scarcely bear the thought of the outlaws getting away with what they had done that day. The colonel soon became obsessed with idea that the despicable criminals who left his men to die must not escape. And then, as if struck by a revelation, he knew what he must do.

The colonel left the trail to Fort Laramie and headed back toward the area where his party had been attacked. The gang of outlaws was probably camped close by, waiting for his men to die so they could take whatever they wanted from the stagecoach. Well, they weren't going to get that opportunity, he would see to that. He rode in a circular path, avoiding the place where the stagecoach sat, and headed toward the wooded area above the section of the trail where the attack had taken place. It was dusk when he reached the woods. He stopped his horse and listened, peering into the growing darkness. Then he saw the faint glimmer of a small fire and knew he had found the gang. He tied his horse to a branch and crept quietly through the woods. As he stepped carefully around the edge of a boulder, he saw seven men seated around a campfire. There they were, just sitting there, as if nothing out of the ordinary had happened that day. Just sitting there while the colonel's men were out there without a drop of water, waiting to die. He couldn't stand it.

The colonel drew his revolver, cocked it, and ran directly toward the fire. As he ran he screamed curses at the men and began shooting. He hit one man in the leg and another in the shoulder. As he turned to aim at a third man, a bullet struck him squarely in the chest. He fell dead at the edge of the fire. Even in the dim light the outlaws recognized the colonel. They were not strangers to the man they had driven to distraction by their lawless deeds. In fact, they all knew him. They had served under him in the Union Army. As the fire flickered against the darkness one of the outlaws spoke. "Well," he said, "that's the end of the colonel. A couple more days and we'll pick up our last strong box and this whole thing will be over." One of the other men stirred the coals with a stick, and the fire brightened. "Yeah, I reckon," he said, "it's taken a long time."

14 THE OUTSIDER

Plainview was not the first community whose citizens viewed Jake Turner with an attitude of uncertainty and suspicion. Jake and his wife Stella, like others possessed by the wanderlust common on the frontier, had repeatedly moved from place to place. Each time Jake and Stella established a small but viable ranching operation, the surrounding ranchers suddenly found they had lost a neighbor when the Turners left for some unknown place farther west. Yet no matter how far or how abruptly the couple moved they were accompanied by an atmosphere of rumor and mistrust.

Jake Turner was a large, sturdily built man with muscular shoulders, thick, dark unkempt hair, and a deep scar on his left cheek. He was the type of man people tend to feel negative about, not due to his actions but rather to his personality and mannerisms. Jake was a hard worker who viewed trips to town or visits to neighboring ranches as a frivolous waste of time. He preferred to spend his energy improving his own ranch and saw little value in interacting with others. As a result, most neighbors and townspeople thought of Jake as anti-social, unfriendly or even hostile. Infrequent visitors to the Turner ranch were met with a polite greeting followed by terse conversation and hints that time spent talking could better be used working. After an attempt or two at establishing friendship, most people simply left the Turners alone.

Stella Turner was a thin, wiry woman with plain features, straight brown hair, and large hands. She was slightly more outgoing than her husband but shared his focus on building their ranch. On the few occasions when neighboring couples attempted a social call she seemed ill at ease and impatient for them to leave, though she was never outright rude or impolite. The fact that they were childless also made them unusual in a time and place where children were seen as a blessing and large families were commonplace. Over time virtually everyone in the area came to the conclusion the Turners were an unusual and unlikeable couple.

Although the majority of people in the Plainview area decided to simply leave the Turners alone, there were two exceptions. The first was C.T. Barrett, who owned a large ranch that adjoined the Turners' property on the north. When Barrett made occasional trips to Plainview for supplies he passed directly by the Turner ranch. He often stopped to ask Jake Turner if he needed anything and brought back whatever was requested. This kindness penetrated, to a degree, the barrier Jake usually presented to others, and the two men formed a peculiar sort of friendship. The other person who succeeded in forming a relationship with Jake was the only preacher in Plainview. Reverend Rhodes called on Jake and Stella shortly after their arrival in the area and received the same reception as other visitors. But undeterred, the parson returned periodically for brief visits, and after repeated invitations Stella began attending church services. She would arrive in town just prior to the start of the service, slip in one of the back pews and return home as soon as the service ended. Parson Rhodes sometimes exchanged a few words with Stella as she departed the church building, but she seldom spoke to anyone else. Her husband did not accompany her on these excursions.

About half a year after the Turners arrived in Plainview rumors about them began to circulate among the townspeople. One involved the couple's purchase of their small ranch north of town. A traveler who passed through town told a local storekeeper of an unsolved robbery that had taken place near the community where the Turners had reportedly lived prior to coming to Plainview. The amount taken was close to the amount Jake had paid for the ranch, and the description of one of the robbers included a scar on one cheek. Although few who heard the story reached a firm conclusion regarding any connection between Jake and the robbery, most thought the possibility plausible.

A few months later news reached Plainview that a stagecoach had been held up while traversing a pass about twenty miles north of the town. The driver and guard were taken totally by surprise and surrendered the lockbox without resisting. But an armed passenger attempted to foil the robbery and was shot and severely wounded. The stage driver described the bandits as a big man with a gruff voice who appeared to be in charge and a smaller, slender man who remained speechless during the holdup. The larger of the two had a scar on one cheek. After disarming the passengers and turning the coach's horses loose, the thieves had ridden south.

A number of Plainview residents had theories regarding the identity of the stagecoach robbers and shared their ideas with the local sheriff, Ben Jackson. They were disappointed when, rather than pursuing the matter, Sheriff Jackson responded only with curt comments about lack of evidence and people jumping to conclusions. However, their suspicions were heightened a few weeks later when Jake Turner made a rare appearance in town. His only stop was at the livery stable, where he purchased a buckboard wagon. According to the livery owner payment was in cash, and the origin of the money became a popular topic of conversation among Plainview residents.

Sheriff Jackson found the rumors about the Turners bothersome and somewhat worrisome. He knew the townspeople were engaging in pure speculation, but his years of experience in law enforcement told him that such things could be dangerous. He was uncertain whether the Turners were aware of the rumors swirling about town, so decided to pay them a visit. He rode north to their ranch intending to make sure they understood what was being said in town and to discuss how the rumors might be quelled. While at their ranch he also planned to look for possible evidence of sudden wealth.

Jake Turner spotted Sheriff Jackson as the lawman turned from the main road into his ranch and walked toward the road to meet him. As they met, the sheriff dismounted and held out his hand toward Jake, who did not return the gesture. "Mr. Turner," the sheriff said, "I rode out here for one purpose and that is to help you." Jake frowned and said simply, "With?" The sheriff pursed his lips. "Well," he said, "people in town are talking about you and the recent robberies." Jake's frown deepened. "And you think?" he asked. "I won't beat around the bush," the sheriff said. "People don't like you, prob'ly 'cause they don't know you, so they're ready to believe the worst. My job is to make sure what they choose to believe don't cause trouble you don't deserve."

Jake Turner looked directly at the sheriff, who thought he detected a hint of respect in the man's expression. "Seems you have some sense," Jake said, then slowly shook his head. "I don't know what's wrong with people," he continued. "I never caused nobody no trouble, and yet ...." He did not finish the sentence. Sheriff Jackson pushed his hat up off his forehead. "Maybe if they knew you better ..." he began. Jake interrupted, "Waste of time. Same every place. Mind my own business, get run off anyhow. Or worse." For a full minute neither man spoke. Then the sheriff nodded, put his foot in a stirrup and swung his leg up over the saddle. Looking down at the rancher, he said, "If they give you any trouble you know where I am. I intend to keep the law." He touched the brim of his hat and turned his horse toward town.

Less than a month later the Bank of Plainview was robbed. Two men broke open a side door before dawn, hid in a back office and waited for the banker to arrive. The president of the bank and a teller arrived together, opened the bank and unlocked the vault. Before either man had a chance to turn the sign in the front window from Closed to Open the thieves ordered the two men to transfer cash from the vault into canvas bags. When the banker tried to make a break for the front door, the larger of the two robbers dealt him a severe blow to the head with a pistol. The banker fell to the floor, blood flowing from the wound. The other bank employee did as directed, then was bound, gagged and left in the rear of the building. The thieves exited the side door of the bank, mounted their horses and rode north out of town. The first customer of the day found the bank president lying dead near the front door and the teller tied up in the back office. The teller gave a description of the two robbers, the larger of whom had a scar on one cheek.

Sheriff Jackson did not need to recruit a posse to pursue the bank robbers. Within twenty minutes after the robbery was discovered, a group of men had gathered in front of the sheriff's office. They were armed, angry and certain of their objective.

Although few words were spoken, they quickly agreed that Jake Turner was one of the robbers, who had no doubt taken refuge at the Turner ranch. There they no doubt planned to obtain fresh mounts, so the posse must act quickly to prevent their escape. As the group of men was agreeing on their course of action Sheriff Jackson emerged from his office. He stood on the wooden sidewalk and faced the men, a stern look on his face.

"I don't have to ask what you're plannin' to do," he said. "I'm just tellin' you you're not goin' to do it." One of the men spoke up, "We know who done it and we know where they are," he said, "and we have a good rope. Now you gonna join us?" The sheriff stepped off the sidewalk and walked directly toward the man who had spoken, stopping with inches between them. The sheriff turned his head and spit in the street. As the other man's eyes turned to see the spittle land the sheriff swung, firmly planting his fist on the man's jaw and knocking him to the ground. The man did not get up. "Now," the sheriff said, "I'm going to ride out to Turner's place and bring him in here and question him. Any of you so much as show your face on the street and I'll put you …."

Just then a rider came galloping wildly into town from the north. The men turned toward the horseman, whom they recognized as Clyde Barrett, the oldest son of the rancher who lived north of the Turners. The rider pulled his horse to a stop and called out, "Somebody get Doc Smyth, quick!" As he dismounted, Clyde said, "It's Jake Turner, he's been shot!" Sheriff Jackson ordered the man nearest him, "Go get the doc." Then he turned toward the young man who had brought the news. "What happened, Clyde?" he demanded. Clyde shook his head and said, "I don't rightly know. My pa and I were ridin' past Jake's ranch when Mrs. Turner came running out of the barn. She was yellin', 'He's shot, he's shot!' We went to the barn and Jake was layin' there all bloody. Pa stayed with him while I came for the doc."

As Clyde Barrett was describing what he had seen and heard at the Turners' ranch, a second rider approached rapidly from the north. As the horseman entered town he slowed, and the men in front of the sheriff's office recognized C.T., the young Barrett's father. The senior Barrett reined his horse to a stop near the crowd of men. He spoke directly to his son. "No rush for the doc, son," he said, "Jake is gone." Clyde Barrett scowled. "You sure?" he asked. "He was gone before we got there," C.T. replied. "Put a gun in his mouth and pulled the trigger. Mrs. Turner said he just couldn't stand everybody talkin' about him no more." The group of men stood in silence. No one made eye contact with anyone else. One by one they left the sheriff's office and headed toward their homes.

Sheriff Jackson turned toward Clyde Barrett and asked, "You old enough to drink?" The boy looked at his father with a quizzical expression. "With what you witnessed today," C.T. Barrett said, "I'd say you are." "C'mon," said the sheriff, "I'm buyin'." The three men walked toward the saloon. As they walked, Clyde asked, "What's next then?" "Well," said the sheriff, "Doc will send Hiram Gibson the undertaker out to get Jake. We'll have a funeral and a burial. Don't know where, that's up to Mrs. Turner." The younger man thought a moment, then asked, "What about the bank robbery? Do you think it was him?" "Nah," the sheriff said, " It wasn't him. But we'll find 'em and when we do they'll hang." The men entered the saloon, which they found completely empty of customers.

Two days later Reverend Rhodes held a funeral sermon for Jake Turner. The service was sparsely attended but the parson preached a good sermon. Sheriff Jackson, who never attended regular services, sat in the front row along with the pallbearers he had hand-picked. After the funeral, the pallbear-ers, six of the most vocal of the mob that recently intended to hang Jake Turner, carried the casket to the local cemetery. Since Jake was a large man the casket was a burden to the pallbearers both literally and figuratively. At the cemetery, Parson Rhodes made a few more remarks, including a reference to the scriptural admonition against judging others. The pallbear-ers let the casket down and shoveled the grave full of dirt. The sheriff concluded the event by saying, "Well boys, I hope you learned your lesson. And if you did I'll buy you a drink." With that, the small group of mourners made their way to the saloon.

Stella Turner sold her ranch to C.T. Barrett for a good price, as Mr. Barrett had been looking for a place for his son Clyde to begin his own operation. Clyde bought the Turners' horses and Stella sold the tools, supplies, and other goods at public auction. Sheriff Jackson made certain the men of Plainview were present and participating at the auction and the sale brought a good sum of money for Jake Turner's widow. Curiously, the buckboard wagon Jake had purchased from the Plainview livery stable was not on the sale. After the sale, Stella Turner said farewell to a very small number of acquaintances and told them she planned to return to Ohio where her family resided. About a week later she boarded a train out of Plainview. Most members of the community were relieved when Stella left. They did not relish any reminders of what had taken place.

It was on a morning about six weeks later that Sheriff Jackson, who was seldom seen in either the house of God or that of the local parson, paid a call on Reverend Rhodes. The parson welcomed the sheriff into the rectory and offered him a cup of coffee. The two men sat across from each other at the kitchen table. After a couple sips of the steaming liquid the sheriff said, "Parson, I won't beat around the bush. There are a couple questions in my mind and I think you know the answers." The preacher nodded but said nothing. The sheriff continued, "I was down at the depot yesterday and the stationmaster told me he received a shipment of boxes for your church marked "Hymnals and Bibles" with a net weight of two hundred and twenty pounds." Reverend Rhodes interjected, "Oh, they have arrived. That is good news indeed!"

The sheriff did not share the parson's enthusiasm. He frowned deeply and said, "Them boxes of books at the depot got me to thinkin'. Sundays I take a walk through the town and when I pass by your church I hear either singin' or preachin'. And when you're preachin' if the windows are open I see folks followin' along in Bibles. Now I was in your church for Jake's funeral and there was no singin' and I don't remember seein' any hymnals or Bibles in the whole place. Now the first thing I want to know is, what happened to those books?"

The preacher looked up at a corner of the room as if trying to remember the answer to the sheriff's question. The sheriff continued, his eyes focused intently on the man of God. "The second thing I learned from the stationmaster is that Stella Turner bought a train ticket all right, but she wasn't headed to Ohio. She went west, not east." Reverend Rhodes tilted his head as if to say, "Who knows?" but did not reply. The sheriff raised one eyebrow and in a demanding voice, said, "OK then, just tell me this. Where is Jake Turner?" The parson smiled and nodded. "God only knows. A long ways west of here, probably."

15 THE CEMETERY

The hill on which the cemetery lay was only about thirty feet higher than the surrounding countryside. But due to the extremely flat topography of the area, on a clear day it afforded a broad view in any direction. Although it would have been a good location for a house, perhaps for a wealthy banker or merchant, the town's founders had set aside the parcel of land on top of the hill for a church and cemetery. As the town's population increased, the congregation outgrew the church on the hill and a larger building was constructed on a lot closer to the town's center. The original church fell into disrepair and was torn down and the lumber reused. This left only the cemetery to occupy the knoll that stood just beyond the western edge of the town.

The cemetery was of modest size, just over an acre, and was surrounded by an iron fence four feet in height. A single strand of barbed wire was affixed along the top of the fence, and the double-hinged gate was kept closed to keep wild animals from desecrating the graves. A lone tree stood in the middle of the cemetery, its branches home to an assortment of small birds. The edge of the hill upon which the cemetery sat was about two hundred yards from the buildings at the edge of town. It rose gradually from the flat plain around it, and the path from the town to the cemetery went directly up the east side of the hill.

Most townspeople seldom frequented the cemetery, climbing the hill only to witness a burial following a funeral or to participate in the annual memorial service honoring the handful of Civil War and Spanish-American War veterans who resided in the town. There were a few exceptions - parents, spouses or others who visited gravesites on the hill with some regularity. Some would leave a small bundle of flowers on a grave, or simply stand in front of a grave marker for a short while, then retrace their steps down the hill toward town.

The most faithful visitor to the cemetery was the widow of a Mr. James Stafford. Mr. Stafford had died of influenza the fourth winter after his family had come to town, and in the year and a half since his death Mrs. Stafford had come to the cemetery each week to visit her husband's grave. Every Sunday afternoon Mrs. Caroline Stafford and her four children climbed the hill west of town, entered the cemetery and paid a solemn visit to Mr. Stafford's gravesite. Warm or cold, rain or shine, the widow Stafford and her children made their weekly pilgrimage to the cemetery.

The Stafford gravesite was on the north side of the tree. The five family members would stand under the tree, in summer within its sheltering shade, often for an hour or more. Townspeople who saw them there reported that Mrs. Stafford was often heard speaking to her husband's grave marker. They initially thought this odd, but had become accustomed to her doing so, and ascribed the one-way conversations to her devotion to the late Mr. Stafford. No one knew how the Stafford children felt about these Sunday visits, nor did they ask. The citizens of Lyman, whether relatively well-to-do or poor like the Staffords, respected each others' privacy.

The Staffords had not always been counted among the poorer citizens of the town. Like many other residents, they had come west to better their lot in life. They came from Ohio, where Mrs. Stafford had given up her position as a school teacher to marry Mr. Stafford, at the time a somewhat prosperous land agent. Lured by tales of the lush environment and bountiful crops of the Pacific Northwest, the Staffords decided to join the thousands of others who saw the frontier as a place ripe with opportunity.

Despite protestations from Mrs. Stafford's parents, the couple sold most of their possessions, bid friends and family goodbye, and traveled by train to Saint Louis. Shortly after arriving in the bustling young city, they signed on with a wagon train headed to Oregon. They then spent several months preparing for the journey. They acquired a wagon, a team of oxen, and other items required for a trek across the western half of the country. When spring arrived, they and their fellow pioneers, filled with optimism and high expectations, left eastern Missouri, following the Oregon Trail west. It was to be a grand adventure, culminating in their arrival in a "land of milk and honey." However, as often happened, the wagon company's trip west did not go smoothly. In fact, it was fraught with challenges.

The Staffords' wagon company was not the only group of potential homesteaders to encounter difficulties along the route west. As the largely wooded and populated areas of Missouri gave way to the plains of Nebraska, the travelers experienced a sense of isolation many had never known. The primitive but easily followed roads of Missouri were replaced by long stretches of open prairie, filled with wild grasses that often stood taller than a man. In some places, particularly where the route west of necessity passed through a narrow gap or mountain pass, or converged at a landing that facilitated crossing a river, the Oregon Trail was a clearly recognizable route. But especially in its early years, it was more a collection of divergent paths across the prairie than a single, definable trail.

Navigation across this vast, open country involved a combination of "dead reckoning" based on the sun's position, crude maps supplied by the outfitters in Saint Louis, and a few well-known landmarks. Occasionally, settlers enjoyed the happy circumstance of encountering and then following a visible path created by a prior group of wagons, but these did not always follow the best or most direct route. Like other companies en route to Oregon or California, the Stafford's party found it difficult to stay on course, and several times veered far enough from the intended route to add one or more days to the length of the trek. When the party arrived at Scottsbluff, they were more than a week behind schedule and had consumed more food and other supplies than planned.

By the time the wagon train reached the western edge of Nebraska, several families in the party were losing confidence in the group's ability to reach Oregon prior to winter. Members of the company expected the captain of the wagon train to display confidence and offer reassurance that the trip could still be completed on schedule, or nearly so. Instead, he called a meeting of the men of the party and told them it was doubtful they could make it through the mountains that lay ahead before winter's snow overtook them. Though the members of the company were shocked and disappointed, the captain maintained it was in their best interest to go no further than an army fort located several days travel to the north, and resume traveling when spring came.

It was this disconcerting turn of events that led Mr. Stafford and several other men to rethink their commitment to Oregon as a final destination, and instead consider settling upon the plains east of the Rockies. They could do so either as homesteaders or as newcomers to one of the frontier towns being established along the trail. Mrs. Stafford had heard stories of people caught in the mountains in winter, tales of death by starvation or exposure, and of searchers finding the remains of people literally frozen solid inside their wagons. She informed her husband that she was not inclined to enter the mountains in late fall, and did not relish the thought of facing such desperate circumstances as might well be encountered if the wagon train decided to press on so late in the season.

After a short period of discussion and deliberation, the men of the company realized they would not reach a consensus on the issue of delaying departure until spring versus continuing on as soon as possible. Therefore, they concluded it was best to disband the company and let each family in the party decide for themselves the course of action they thought best. Thus it was that Mr. and Mrs. Stafford, neither of whom had an appetite for risking a winter mountain crossing, chose to temporarily forego the promised bounties of Oregon and take up temporary residence in the nearest suitable town, which happened to be Lyman.

The Staffords were not ones to dwell on their disappointment, but set about finding their place in Lyman. Mr. Stafford was not only a capable land agent, an occupation that could no doubt be quite lucrative when the area was more fully settled, but also an able horse trainer and farrier. Soon after arriving in Lyman he found work at the local livery stable, while his wife tended to their growing family. The Staffords attended weekly church services and frequented local merchants' establishments to the extent their limited income permitted. As the months passed and new friendships were formed, the Staffords' conversations about continuing on to Oregon became fewer and much less assured. The dream of life in the Northwest, which had carried them from Ohio to Saint Louis to Nebraska and beyond, gradually faded from their minds.

The Stafford family found contentment in the community fate had chosen for them. They were well-liked by most townspeople, and the children seemed especially popular. The older children were looking forward to starting school, and the teacher, a young woman who had only recently arrived in Lyman, had visited the Stafford home and established an immediate rapport with her future students. Mr. Stafford gained a reputation as an honest man and a hard worker, and both the townspeople and the rural settlers in the surrounding area admired his skill with horses, animals on which they were heavily dependent.

In addition to his work at the livery stable, Mr. Stafford established a small trade in horses, buying and selling them to local residents or to others passing through the area. His knowledge of horses and people ensured that the venture was profitable, and the supplemental income was more than welcome in the home of the growing Stafford family. It was apparent the Staffords had turned a disappointing set of circumstances to their advantage, and those who knew their story admired them for it.

No one knows for certain how influenza was brought to Lyman. Perhaps it was carried by one of the westward-bound families who had strayed from their own wagon train or decided the trek across Nebraska Territory had been challenge enough, and it was time to find a place to settle east of the Rockies. It may have arrived with the soldiers who passed through town with supply wagons bound for one of the forts in the region. Whatever its origin, the disease spread quickly through Lyman.

In a matter of weeks, it had taken the lives of several infants and children, as well as that of an elderly man who was, as it happened, one of the three people who founded the town.

Mr. Stafford acquired influenza, along with a number of other adults, and felt badly about having to remain at rest when there was work to be done at the livery stable. Mrs. Stafford cared for him according to the doctor's instructions, and all assumed that a man of his age and healthy physique would recover quickly. But instead of leaving him, the disease lingered, refusing to give up in its attempt to further weaken the man. The doctor was puzzled and the townspeople concerned, but all were confident of an eventual recovery. One can imagine their surprise when, after lying ill for some twelve days, Mr. Stafford succumbed to the disease and breathed his last.

His death deprived Mr. Stafford's family of not only a husband and father but also its means of support. Caroline Stafford, like most women of the time, was ill-prepared to support a family of five without a male breadwinner. She did what she could, which was barely adequate. Mrs. Stafford took in some washing and whatever seamstress work was available, the combination of which was just enough to keep her family together. By the time Mr. Stafford had been gone a year and a half, it would have been an understatement to say there was little extra in the Stafford household.

Mrs. Stafford was, indeed, in a hard circumstance. But, as was often the case among frontier people, she spent little time in self-pity or worry. She simply went on with the life and work at hand, dedicating herself to providing and caring for her offspring. She was wholly committed to her children, and was raising them to be responsible, thrifty, generous, and devoted. Both from necessity and a belief that it helped prepare them for life, she fully included them in daily household tasks, gardening

and canning, church services and daily devotions, the few decisions to be made about money matters, and the weekly visit to
her husband's grave.

Thus it was that on a Sunday afternoon, Caroline Stafford and her four children walked as usual from their modest
home in Lyman to the west edge of town and slowly ascended
the path to the top of the knoll. One of the older children opened
the gate, and the five of them entered the cemetery, gathering
in a small circle under the tree. As they had done so many times
before, the children listened as their mother faced the wooden
marker on their father's grave and began to speak. She gave a
detailed account of the family's week, including the older children's eager anticipation of the new school term. She spoke as
though addressing a trusted friend, her face sometimes exhibit-
ing a small frown or a gentle smile.

Caroline Stafford drew her monologue to a close, turned
toward her children, and nodded toward the gate. Like every
other Sunday afternoon, this was her indication it was time to
leave the cemetery. The children led the way, expecting their
mother to follow them out of the cemetery and secure the gate.
But for the first time ever, she stopped short of the cemetery
exit. "Children," she said, "you go on home. I'll be along shortly."
With questions in their minds, but not voiced, the Stafford children obediently started down the path toward town. Their mother watched them go, then returned to the grave marker.

Caroline gazed at the rough wooden marker for a few
moments, then knelt beside it, resting one hand on top of it. She
spoke, not to the marker, but to the plot of grass that covered
the grave. "James," she began, surprised to hear herself speak
his name after such a long time, "there is something I need to
tell you." She paused, glanced toward the horizon, then continued. "You know how hard it has been for the children since we

lost you. And, of course, you know how terribly much I have missed you." Her lip quivered slightly, but she allowed no tears. "And I know for sure," she said, "that you want what is best for the children. You always did, and so do I."

She stopped talking for a few seconds, as images of her four children floated through her mind. Then she resumed the conversation. "I never thought I would have to come here and tell you this," she said, "but now I must." She wondered what his face would look like if he were really there with her, what his expression would be as he heard what she was about to tell him. She wrinkled her brow, and said, "This is harder than I expected. I don't know why. Guess I'd best just tell you now."

A breeze had come up from the south, gaining momentum as it moved up the hill. It kicked up a cloud of dust, which swept through the cemetery, stinging Caroline's skin and blowing her hair into her face. She drew the hair back from her face, using her fingers as a coarse comb. "James," she said, "I have agreed to marry Mr. Adamson. He lost his wife last year, about six months after you were gone. He has a fine house and an honorable reputation. He has met the children and will get on fine with them. He can provide the things they need. I think if you saw them together you would be pleased."

Caroline stopped, closed her eyes, and reflected on what she had just heard herself say. "No," she said to herself, "I don't think you said anything wrong. Just tell the truth." She opened her eyes and said aloud, "There is just one thing you may not like. Mr. Adamson knows I come here every Sunday, and he thinks it's a fine thing. But it bothers him to think that his wife would leave him alone on the Lord's day to spend time here with you. And I don't want to do anything that would hurt the man, or have him think me unfaithful. So I have agreed to stay with him on Sundays once we are married."

Caroline paused a bit to let the news sink in. "James," she said, "just so I am clear, this means I won't be coming to visit you anymore. The children may come if they wish, but I will keep my agreement with Mr. Adamson. I hope you understand." She took a deep breath and continued, "So, this will be our last visit." Caroline paused and gazed off into the distance. Then she returned her attention to the grave and continued, "Mr. Adamson and I will exchange vows during next Sunday's service. It will, of course, be a big day for the children. They will get a stepfather." She smiled slightly as she said, "And one more thing about next Sunday. I'll bet you forgot all about it. It will be my twenty-fifth birthday. Isn't that a coincidence?"

Caroline stopped talking. She looked down at the grass that covered the grave. She looked at the wooden headstone, and then at the lone tree in the center of the cemetery. She walked slowly through the gate, turned around and closed it tightly. She thought of her children and suddenly wanted very much to be with them. She walked quickly down the hill, reached the edge of town, and moved briskly toward her house. The sun had set, and she could see the glow of a kerosene lamp in the window. She smiled slightly and wiped away a single tear as she approached the house. She opened the door and stepped through it, into her children's arms.

16 THE STORM

The couple stood on the west side of the small log structure that was their home, peering intently toward the sky. Clouds streaked with grey were building in the west, blotting out the sun as they tumbled over each other, moving steadily toward the east. The man and woman pulled the collars of their coats up around their necks in a vain attempt to shield themselves from the cold. The wind had shifted from east to north, and then to the northwest, and was becoming stronger. The couple looked at each other, and without a word turned and walked around the cabin and toward the small barn that sat some fifty yards from the dwelling.

The man walked to the barn and opened the door that faced the cabin, while the woman walked around behind a small group of livestock grazing just beyond the barn. Then together they began to herd the animals into the barn. The building was just large enough to accommodate their team of horses, three cows, and two calves, plus a stall filled with barrels of water, sacks of oats, and assorted tools. The space between the barn's ceiling and its roof was filled with hay that had been stored there since the summer.

With the animals secured in their stalls, the woman left the barn and walked to the cabin. The sky gave every indication of an approaching storm, which on the prairie could be severe and lengthy. Although the couple kept their dwelling stocked with food, water, firewood, and other essentials, she would feel better having confirmed the adequacy of their provisions. She did not want to experience, as some other settlers had, running out of supplies when a storm lasted longer than anticipated. During a blizzard that kept them isolated for a week and a half, a nearby family had once misjudged the winter weather and survived on food normally sufficient for three or four days.

While the woman was ensuring that things inside the cabin were ready, the man tended to preparations outside. A light rope hung from a board just inside the barn door. He took the rope down, picked up a hammer and two large nails, and went outside. He pounded one of the nails into the jamb beside the barn door and tied the rope to the nail. He shut the barn door and double-checked the door latch to be certain it was securely closed. Then he walked to the cabin, uncoiling the rope as he walked. He pounded the second large nail into the jamb of the cabin door and tied the end of the rope to the nail. A severe winter storm could cause a "white out" in which swirling snow reduced visibility to mere inches. In such conditions, the rope would provide a secure link between the barn and the cabin. By following the rope, he could reach the barn to check on the livestock and return safely to the cabin. His tasks completed, the man joined his wife in the cabin. He closed the door tightly against the expected storm and turned his attention to building a fire in the potbellied stove that sat in the middle of the cabin.

It was not the first adverse weather the couple had faced together. In the six years Otto and Bertha Braun had been living on their homestead they had witnessed the full repertoire of storms generated by prairie weather systems. They had endured rainstorms, windstorms, hailstorms, flash floods, tornados, grass fires triggered by thunderstorms, and blizzards that lasted for days. They had survived these attacks of nature through a combination of constant attention to approaching weather, careful preparation, and plain good luck.

Like thousands of others, Otto and Bertha had been attracted by the vast amounts of nearly free land offered under the Homestead Acts passed by Congress. Stories of unlimited fertile lands and bountiful crops, propagated by railroad boosters and land speculators, spread rapidly eastward. When such tales reached Indiana, the Brauns were convinced it was time to seek their fortune further west. They sold their home and the few luxuries they had afforded themselves, loaded their remaining household goods, food stores, seed, and other basic provisions in a wagon drawn by a pair of oxen, and bid farewell to their neighbors. Filled with anticipation, they headed west to claim their share of the former Indian land opened to settlement by the government. The terms specified in the law - file a claim, build a dwelling, and reside on the land several years in succession - were undoubtedly generous. However, fulfilling them amid the harsh conditions of the Midwest prairie would prove to be a serious challenge.

Otto and Bertha trekked slowly across Iowa, which was already largely settled, and into southeastern Dakota Territory. They were surprised to find the bulk of that area already under claim, so continued west well beyond the Missouri River. Eventually, they crossed the White River by ferry, traveled due west for two and a half days, and staked their claim on the first parcel of ground not already occupied by a previous arrival. It was their good fortune that the piece of land they happened upon was near enough to a sizeable creek to ensure a supply of water until a well could be dug, yet far enough away to avoid the flash flooding that occurred during the summer months. Rainstorms here were more dramatic than in the East. On the western prairie, huge banks of dark clouds moved east from the horizon and unleashed their contents in torrents of rain, often preceded by dramatic displays of lightning and sometimes accompanied by pounding hail. The wide creek near the Braun's homestead also provided a natural barrier against wildfires. During the dry periods of summer or early fall, prairie fires would race across the vast grasslands, sending thick columns of smoke and flame into the air and consuming everything in their path. Only once had the Braun homestead been seriously threatened by a wildfire, but a change in wind direction had turned the fire and narrowly spared them from its fury.

Summer storms on the prairie were often frightening and could be destructive, but seldom caused significant loss of life. Livestock might be struck by lightning or drown in a flash flood, but such incidents were not common. Winter storms, however, were to be feared as potential killers of both livestock and humans. Blizzards could last for days. Howling winds drove sheets of snow horizontally across the prairie, and where the wind was broken the snow piled up in great drifts capable of completely engulfing a house or barn. Horses or cows caught out in such storms turned away from the wind and tried to survive by standing closely together. But the severity and duration of some storms were often too much for the animals. Settlers who failed to gather their stock in barns before the worst blizzards hit would, after the storms passed, find the animals dead from suffocation, their nostrils covered by thick coats of ice, or frozen solid, buried under frigid drifts of snow.

Only once had Otto and Bertha lost an animal to a snowstorm. A young calf, probably frightened by the howl of the wind and rattling of some loose boards on the side of the barn, had managed to force its way through an opening in the barn siding and wander out into the storm. It was later found completely frozen, having made its way less than a hundred yards from the shelter of the barn before succumbing to the ravages of the storm. Following the loss of the calf, Otto diligently maintained the barn in good repair. When winter storms hit, he and Bertha holed up in their cabin, carefully tending the fire that kept the inside temperature just above freezing. Periodically, Otto left the shelter of the cabin and braved the storm to make his way to the barn. After ensuring the animals were fed, watered and secure, he would again venture out into the storm to return to the cabin.

The unspoken prediction of a snowstorm that had prompted Otto and Bertha to sequester their livestock in the barn and themselves in their cabin was soon fulfilled. The first flakes of snow had begun to fall while the couple was moving the livestock into the barn. By the time Otto headed toward the cabin, the wind was strong and the tiny bits of snow stung his cheeks. Now, as he and Bertha felt the heat radiate from the wood-fueled stove, the storm hit with full fury. The wind howled so loudly the couple, had they felt the need to speak, would have had to raise their voices to be heard. Sheets of heavy snow pelted the cabin, and gale force winds drove the icy crystals into every crack and crevice. A small snowdrift began to accumulate at the base of the cabin door. The Brauns sat in silence, mindful of the severity of the storm, but also sensing the assurance of having survived serious blizzards in the past.

Some three or four hours after the storm commenced, Otto got up from his chair and pulled a sheepskin coat on over several other layers of clothing. He looked at Bertha, and said,

"Better go check." She nodded, stood up, and they walked the handful of steps to the door. He unlatched the door and opened it just enough to squeeze through to the outside. As he pushed his way into the snow, a blast of frigid air roared into the cabin. Steadying himself against the wind, Otto grasped the rope attached to the door jamb and set out for the barn. Bertha pushed hard on the door, and it reluctantly swung shut against the wind. She latched it tightly and returned to the stove, brushing snow from her clothing as she sat down. She thought about the winter storms she and Otto had endured since arriving on the western prairie. It seemed the storms had become more severe the last couple of years, but perhaps it was just her imagination. She opened the pot-bellied stove and stoked the fire. It flared up a bit; the warmth felt good. She settled back in her chair, thinking about Otto carefully tending to the animals in the barn. Her eyelids slowly closed and she drifted off to sleep.

Bertha awoke with a start. She was cold, and it was pitch dark. It had been daylight when she fell asleep. Now it was night, but she had no idea of the time. Her eyes darted around the cabin, though she could see nothing. Where was Otto? Was he resting on their bed? Or had he let her sleep while he was in the cabin, then gone to the barn again? She carefully made her way to the stove and opened it. All that remained of the fire were a few small embers. She felt for the poker and stirred them into a small flame. By the light of the tiny fire, she grasped some sticks and a small log and placed them carefully on the flame. Soon the fire grew and brightened, and Bertha began to feel new heat from the stove. She listened. All she heard was the howl of the wind and the snow hitting the roof and sides of the cabin. She found a candle, lit it from the now blazing fire, and placed it on the table. She could see the interior of the cabin plainly. Otto was not there.

Bertha tried to get some sense of the time. She looked out the tiny window of the cabin searching for the moon, then realized it was useless to do so during the raging storm. She walked to the door, looking for signs that it had been opened recently, but there were none. Otto must be in the barn, but how long had he been there? How long had she slept? How long must she wait until he came through the door, covered with snow and emitting frost with each breath? How long until the storm let up? Then a thought she did not want to acknowledge crept into her mind. What if she had slept for hours, and Otto had gotten lost out in the storm? What if he had lost his way to the cabin and called out to her but received no answer? What if he were lying in a snowdrift, slowly freezing to death? What if this storm was the one they would not survive?

Bertha moved quickly to the door and opened it. She was met by a stormy blast, as snow and sleet flew against her face, stinging her cheeks and forcing her to close her eyes. "Otto," she cried out, "Where are you?" But she could barely hear her own voice amid the howling wind. She stood facing the blizzard, snow swirling around her into the cabin. Then, forcing herself to do the only thing that made sense, she stepped back into the cabin and forced the door shut against the wind. She moved slowly toward the stove and let herself down onto her chair. "Oh, Otto," she sighed, "What have I done?" Bertha sat silently in front of the stove, her head in her hands, pondering the likelihood that Otto had become a victim of the storm. Aside from tending the fire, she sat stone-like in the chair the remainder of the night and all the following day. She did not eat or drink, and moved from her chair only to tend the fire.

Toward evening of the second day, the wind began to let up, but Bertha did not notice. She remained at her stove-side vigil, her face frozen in a vacant expression. Somewhere in the back of her mind she knew the storm would end, and she would have to go outside and look for Otto, where she would find him lying stiff under the snow. But she pushed that thought away, thinking instead of nothing in particular, waiting for something or someone to break through her state of mental oblivion. With Otto gone, she would have to make decisions about the homestead and the livestock, but she was in no condition to deal with such issues now. First, she must let the neighbors know about Otto. She would welcome their sympathy, as well as their offers of help. That was one good thing about life on the western prairie; everyone was willing to help a neighbor.

Bertha was roused from her rumination by a sound just outside the cabin door. She did not immediately realize what it was. It resembled the noise made by a dog thumping its tail against the floor, or perhaps a cow or horse pawing the ground with its hoof. Puzzled, she moved to the window and looked out. It was then that she realized the storm was nearly over. It was snowing only lightly and the wind had dropped. In the west, the sun was peeking through the clouds. She was so surprised she temporarily forgot about the noise outside the door. Then the sound came again, more distinctly this time. Something or someone was pounding on the outside of the door. She went to the door and opened the latch. The hinges creaked as the door swung open, and Bertha stood face to face with Otto.

"I thought you weren't going to let me in," Otto said, his slight grin almost totally hidden between his large fur hat and the upturned collar of his sheepskin coat. "I hope you have some food and coffee ready," he continued. "I haven't eaten for nearly two days, you know." Bertha did not reply, but turned away from the door and set about preparing hot food for the two of them. Otto carried the conversation without any assistance. "When the rope broke, I thought you might be worried I couldn't get back from the barn," he said. "Then I figured you'd open the door and see the rope was slack at this end, and know I had to stay in the barn until the storm let up." Bertha looked at Otto. Her eyes were slightly red. "I'm glad you didn't wander away from the barn without that rope and get lost in the storm," she said. Otto smiled at her. "Yah, me too," he said. Bertha set two plates on the table, poured two cups of coffee, and the couple sat down to eat.

17 THE LESSON

I f the residents of Plainview were asked to identify a local person they viewed as most successful, the consensus would probably settle on the name C.T. Barrett. Mr. Barrett lived not in Plainview but on a ranch north of town. He was seldom seen in town and did not own property there, yet he was a highly respected figure in the community. The name C.T. Barrett was synonymous with large-scale ranching and the cattle industry that flourished in the region beginning in the late 1860's. He was a wealthy, influential man of strong character and enviable reputation. Everyone around Plainview knew or knew of Mr. Barrett, and very few people had ever heard a bad word about him.

Like a number of other ranchers in the area, C.T. Barrett had come west after the Civil War when demand for beef was growing rapidly and land was available for the taking. He started with nothing, working long, hard days as a cowhand for meager wages. But he possessed both extraordinary ambition and natural business acumen. At the time, many ranch boundaries were vague or not legally recorded, and sizeable numbers of unbranded cattle grazed in areas of uncertain or disputed territory.

Barrett negotiated an agreement with his employer that allowed him to keep one of every five strays he brought in from these fringe areas and thus began building his own ranching enterprise. He lived frugally and used most of the money from the sale of his cattle to buy land. Within a decade C.T. Barrett was on his way to owning one of the largest ranching operations in the Southwest.

The ranch house in which C.T. lived, which he largely built with his own hands, provided a happy home for the Barrett family. He married a local girl several years his junior who over a period of half a dozen years gave birth to a daughter and three sons. Although C.T. and his wife were better off than most of their neighbors, they raised their children in an environment of hard work and few luxuries. In a time when it was common to seal a business deal with a handshake, C.T. insisted the deals he struck were documented by written contracts. And he never signed a document without first having his lawyer review the terminology to ensure it accurately reflected the terms that had been negotiated. His reputation as both a top-notch cattleman and a shrewd businessman grew along with the ranch, and as his holdings expanded C.T. became a wealthy man.

The Barretts' oldest child was twelve and the youngest six when their mother died. Like a number of others in the area, she had contracted a case of influenza. The doctor's best efforts, including moving her to town to better tend to her amid the heavy caseload of the local outbreak, proved unsuccessful. She expired three days before the couple's fourteenth anniversary. The disease had claimed several local victims in quick succession. Rather than conducting individual funerals, Rev. Rhodes suggested a joint service for the three adults and five children who had died. Their family members all agreed and C.T. offered to pay the funeral expenses for all eight victims. A couple families initially resisted this gesture but accepted the offer when Mr.

Barrett explained that he meant it not as charity, but as an act of remembrance to honor his late wife.

Some townspeople thought that Mrs. Barrett's death might lessen her husband's drive or his dedication to the family ranch, but they did not know C.T. He did not let up, and though the loss of his wife no doubt affected him he never let it show. He hired a housekeeper whom he charged with managing the operation of the ranch house and the children's daily activities. She also taught one of the hired hands basic cooking, so the men in the bunkhouse were relatively self-sufficient. C.T. was not an inattentive father, and concentrated his efforts on educating his offspring about ranching. He taught his children, including his daughter, about cattle, horses, grassland, livestock diseases and treatment, and finances. He poured into them his considerable knowledge of the ranching business, equipping them with all the skills needed to manage a cattle operation.

Those who knew the Barrett family naturally expected the children, or at least C.T.'s sons, to become ranchers like their father. But as the youngsters grew toward adulthood only the oldest son, Clyde, remained on the ranch. One of the other boys chose a military career, while the third went east to attend college in hopes of obtaining a law degree. Their sister, who in school had shown an impressive talent for writing, also left Plainview to pursue a career as a journalist. C.T. surprised his friends by accepting his children's decisions with magnanimity. When a fellow rancher hinted that the Barrett offspring might benefit from more fatherly guidance regarding career choices, C.T. simply said, "I'm not gonna rein 'em in. A good youngster is like a good horse. Give 'em their head and they'll find their own way."

While C.T. Barrett was teaching his offspring how to manage a ranching operation, a young lady close in age to the oldest Barrett child was preparing to become a teacher. Agnes Callihan, the daughter of a teacher, was just a young girl when she decided to follow in her mother's footsteps. After completing high school she enrolled in a "normal school" or teacher's college in Saint Louis and graduated two years later as a qualified secondary school teacher. She no doubt could have found a position in a high school in the area, but in addition to her desire to teach, Agnes had a strong urge to experience life in the West. Through correspondence with a cousin who had made the move to the frontier several years earlier, she learned of an opening for a teacher in the town of Plainview. She applied and the local school board, impressed with her credentials, offered her the position. Agnes accepted and soon boarded a train headed west, intending to teach there a year or two before returning to St. Louis.

Agnes Callihan soon learned that life in Plainview differed a great deal from life in St. Louis. During the school term, which lasted 110 days, she boarded with a succession of parents who volunteered a turn as the teacher's host. Although school was in session only from 9:00 am until 2:00 pm, in winter the teacher had to arrive early enough to build a fire in the pot-bellied stove and warm the building above freezing before the students arrived. Agnes was also responsible for emptying the stove ashes, cleaning the building, and giving monthly progress reports to the school board, some of whom had less than an eighth-grade education themselves.

Agnes's students, ranging in age from six to sixteen and ostensibly in grades one through eight, were together in a single room. Some of the older students were less advanced than some younger ones. The school's library consisted of the teacher's small collection of novellas, six copies of the Bible, ten copies of *McGuffey's Reader*, two mathematics texts, an English grammar manual, and single copies of *American Lion: An-*

drew Jackson in the White House, Narrative of a Journey Across the Rocky Mountains to the Columbia River, Jefferson's America, Gulliver's Travels, The Count of Monte Cristo, and Paradise Lost.

Although she was initially discouraged by the school's scant resources and the apparent inadequacy of the children's prior education, Agnes found comfort in her ready acceptance by the community. The women of the town included her in the occasional ladies tea or card party and parents were supportive of her efforts to help their children learn. Generally, the most respected positions in western towns were those of doctor, lawyer, preacher, and teacher, and Plainfield was no exception. When the school held a program to let students demonstrate their progress it seemed the entire community attended. Although her salary was minimal, Agnes felt rewarded in other ways and over time developed a feeling of loyalty toward the town and its residents. Her initial plan to return east after a year or two faded into the background, and eight years later she was still the schoolmistress of Plainview.

During her tenure at the one-room school in Plainview, Agnes Callihan's students included the Barrett children. They attended regularly and were bright and eager to learn. Despite their family's wealth, the daughter and sons of C.T. Barrett made a sincere effort to fit in with the other students. They purposely avoided wearing or using anything that would draw attention to the gap between their financial status and that of their fellow students. When he learned the parents of one of his classmates were facing particularly hard times, Clyde Barrett asked his father for permission to invite their children to the ranch for a weekend stay. When the children returned to their home on Sunday evening they were accompanied by a large basket of food from the Barretts' larder.

Agnes Callihan got to know Mr. Barrett through his children. Although he refused a nomination to the school board, C.T. was supportive of the school and its teacher and made it a point to attend school events. Because of the distance between town and the ranch the Barrett home was not one in which the teacher boarded during the school term. Instead, C.T. made an equivalent contribution by supplying beef to the families that hosted the schoolmistress. During the summer, he also permitted the children to invite their teacher to the ranch for an occasional picnic or a meal in the ranch house. He thought the teacher did a fine job and viewed her as an asset to the community.

The fall after his youngest left for college, C.T. decided to make some changes. With his children grown and his son Clyde the only other resident in the ranch house, he finally dismissed his housekeeper. She had not been needed for some time, but C.T. was hesitant to let her go until he was sure she could find work elsewhere. When a couple in Plainview needed help with their growing family C.T. recommended his housekeeper. She accepted the new position and left the ranch with a generous gift from C.T. and Clyde, an expression of gratitude for her faithful service. With just the two men in the house, life at the ranch continued much as it had been through the fall and winter and into the next spring. It was sometime early the next summer that the rumors started.

No one knew who first noticed, but it did not take long before virtually everyone in Plainview was aware. Agnes Callihan had rented a tiny one-bedroom house on the north edge of Plainview. She had tired of boarding with her students' families and despite the extra expense decided to try living alone for a time. The house was modest, as was the rent, and she enjoyed the solitude of evenings and weekends not shared with students and their families. However, by mid-summer there were reports that the teacher was not spending all her evenings alone. One evening a horse was seen tied to the post behind the teacher's little house. It was there well over an hour before a neighbor saw a man exit the rear door of the house, mount the horse and ride out of town.

The next week a horse was again tied behind Miss Callihan's house. This time the incident was witnessed by both Emily Sanders, the owner of the boarding house near the teacher's residence, and Emmet Walker, who was walking home after closing his café for the evening. By noon the following morning, the entire town knew about the secret visitor entertained by the schoolmistress. It was soon decided some effort should be made to determine who was spending evenings with the teacher, whose reputation was rapidly becoming suspect.

A short time later Emmet Walker acquired new information regarding Agnes Callihan. He had stopped to chat with Pete, the manager of the livery stable, and happened to mention the situation involving the local schoolmarm. Pete volunteered that the prior Sunday afternoon Miss Callihan had hired a horse and buggy from the livery and taken it for a drive north of town. She returned it early that evening without revealing where she had gone. Emmet was certain she had paid a visit to the mysterious stranger who had been seen at her house. Soon Agnes noticed an unusual amount of foot traffic passing her house about sundown each day. She could not imagine where they were going, as she lived on the very edge of town.

The following Sunday the teacher again appeared at the livery and hired a horse and buggy for the afternoon. Pete called her attention to clouds building in the west and advised her to keep watch for bad weather. Miss Callihan replied that she had an umbrella and would be fine. She climbed into the buggy and drove north out of town, with Pete watching carefully until she disappeared over the horizon. About an hour later it began to rain. The drops came down lightly at first but soon turned into a downpour. Pete thought the teacher might get caught in the storm, but he was not particularly concerned until darkness fell and the rented buggy had not returned. There was not much he could do, so he closed the livery and walked home in the rain.

The next morning, shortly after Pete opened the livery for the day, the rented horse and buggy appeared. Neither Miss Callihan nor the rented conveyance seemed to have suffered from the storm. Pete was too embarrassed to ask where she had found shelter for the night. When he hinted that she had somehow managed to stay dry despite the rainstorm, she made a nonchalant comment about the rain being good for prairie grass and vegetable gardens, bade him goodbye and walked home. When Pete shared this information with some other townspeople, their reaction was anything but nonchalant.

Sally Walker, Emmet's wife, took the lead in bringing the latest story about the town's schoolmistress to the attention of her fellow citizens. Although several expressed concern, there was no consensus as to where Miss Callihan spent the rainy night or the connection between her trips in the rented buggy and the unidentified visitor to her residence. "This much we know," Sally said, "Agnes Callihan, a single woman and a school teacher, is seeing a person or persons unknown at least one of whom is male. And she's not telling who it is." Emily Sanders looked questioningly at Sally, and said, "Has anybody asked her?" Sally Walker responded, "Of course not! But one way or another, we'd better find out." Emmet, Sally's husband, added, "Let's not forget, this is the woman to whom we are entrusting our children's education."

Rumors about Agnes Callihan continued to travel about Plainview. The mysterious man on horseback was seen coming and going from the teacher's house several more times. Finally one of the neighbors, carrying a lantern while pretending to go to their outhouse after dark, recognized the horseman. The man's identity came as a shock to the town's residents. The mysterious stranger secretly visiting Miss Callihan during summer evenings was none other than C.T. Barrett.

With the visitor's identity known, the townspeople turned their attention to determining the motive for the clandestine meetings between the schoolmarm and the rancher. Certainly there was a romantic aspect to the mystery. The citizens of Plainview understood why Mr. Barrett, having lost his wife years before, might be in search of a new bride. Having endured years of loneliness, he could be forgiven for secretly wanting to spend time with the young woman. But for the teacher, a person responsible for inculcating morals and honesty in the young people of the community, to engage in such behavior was far from acceptable. And why would a young woman take up with a man so much older than she? The answer, of course, was obvious. He was wealthy. If she could entice him into some immoral arrangement he would feel obligated to marry her, and she could trade her life of hard work and meager income for one of ease and comfort.

A small group of citizens agreed to bring the matter to the attention of the school board. Although the townspeople were generally satisfied with the education their children received under Miss Callihan, the current issue was not about ability to teach. It was about standards of morality. A teacher who entertained a single man in her home and had probably stayed overnight in that man's home could simply not be retained. It was unfortunate, but the school board must not renew her employment for the coming term.

It fell to Rev. Rhodes, as head of the school board, to deliver the news to Agnes Callihan. He thought through the situation prior to their meeting, trying to anticipate questions or objections the schoolmarm might raise. As he understood the situation, the community was not certain the teacher had stayed overnight at Mr. Barrett's ranch, but the two had been repeatedly seen together at the teacher's house. It occurred to the parson that C.T. Barrett might intend to marry Miss Callihan. However, since female teachers were required to be single, doing so would not change the board's position regarding her employment. The parson felt the whole thing was a shame. That a capable person like Agnes Callihan would risk her job and potentially her career as a teacher by secretly taking up with a wealthy older man was just plain foolish.

The conversation with Miss Callihan went better than Rev. Rhodes expected. They met alone at the church. When he first broached the subject of her dalliances with C.T. Barrett she acted surprised. But when he laid out the evidence that led to the school board's decision to terminate her employment, her reaction was muted. She sat in silence as he gave his explanation, occasionally nodding or shaking her head as if in disbelief. When he asked if she had any questions she simply said, "None that would make any difference now." He wanted to say something positive about what she accomplished with the students over her years in Plainview but realized doing so would be awkward at best. Finally, he said, "I do wish you well, whatever path your life takes." Agnes smiled weakly and left the church.

Several months later, in mid-December, Rev. Rhodes attended a program at the school. The new teacher had been well-received in Plainview and a fine audience was present for the children's Christmas program. Everyone enjoyed the children's songs and the brief pieces recited from memory. Afterwards, the attendees stayed for punch and cake furnished by Emmet and Sally Walker from the local café. The parson felt obligated as head of the school board to circulate among the townspeople and greet as many as possible. Eventually, as people drifted away from the gathering, Rev. Rhodes found himself next to Clyde Barrett, the son who had remained on the ranch with C.T. For the time being they were alone, and the parson took the opportunity to bring up something that had been on his mind for some time.

"Clyde," Rev. Rhodes began, "I want to ask you about something." Clyde looked mildly surprised but said, "Go ahead." The parson exhaled slowly and said, "It's not a very pleasant subject and forgive me for asking. But has your father ever said anything about Agnes Callihan leaving town?" Clyde Barrett took a sip of punch and said, "Only that he was disappointed she left so suddenly." The preacher nodded. "Well," he said, "it was probably for the best. There's little doubt her interest in your father had to do with money." Clyde looked confused. "Well, sure it did," he said, "That's why she did it. He paid her well and Lord knows she was not long on money." It was the parson's turn to look confused. "He paid her?" he asked, incredulously. "He paid her to spend time with him?" Clyde Barrow frowned deeply as he looked at the preacher. "I don't know what kind of man you think my father is," Clyde said, beginning to raise his voice, "but he's not the kind of person that would take advantage of a woman like Agnes Callihan. She was teaching him to read and he paid her for it fair and square." Clyde shook his head, set his glass of punch on the table, rose and left the building. Rev. Rhodes stared emptily after Clyde. "Oh my gosh," the parson whispered to himself. "Oh no, what have we done?"

18 THE HUNTER

Jesse was bored and he was definitely tired of riding on the
train. For what seemed like an interminable length of time
he had endured heat, dust, general discomfort and the absence on the train of anyone near his age. The windows of the
passenger car were open in an attempt to provide relief from the
intense summer air, and a fine coating of ash from the locomotive had drifted into the car and settled on every surface. Mile
after mile the passengers listened to the click-clack of the
wheels upon the rails as the steam engine pulled its entourage
across the seemingly endless prairie. Occasionally the tracks
ran close enough to a river to offer a view of the trees along its
banks. For most of the route there was little else of interest to
most of the passengers.

Jesse looked up at his mother, who was seated beside
him reading a thick book. Her hat and dress, like his clothes,
showed the effects of the day's exposure to the dust and ash
that came through the windows. Her glasses, perched midway
down her nose, were tinted by the airborne debris. She was
concentrating on her book, interrupting her reading only to turn

a page or briefly glance out the window at the barren country-side. Jesse wondered how she could be so interested in such a dull book. He had examined it during one of the train's stops and found that not only was the story about an ancient king and queen but the book was devoid of pictures. Jesse was not fond of reading, but when he did read he wanted stories of adventure and fighting.

The four passenger cars had been nearly full since the train's stop in North Platte, where a platoon of about forty soldiers headed west from Fort McPherson had boarded the train. As the wife of a military man, Jesse's mother felt comfortable around the soldiers. She was also grateful for the protection they might provide should the train encounter unfriendly Indians while traversing the lengthy expanses of open countryside between towns. She had never intended to become an army wife. Her husband, Jerome Manning, had enlisted in the Union Army during the war. He won a battlefield commission, reenlisted after the war and was stationed for two years at Madison Barracks, New York. It was there she fell in love with and married the handsome young officer. He subsequently served on the staff of West Point, where he rose to the rank of Major. Recently the army ordered Major Manning to take command of an army outpost in Wyoming Territory. In accord with normal practice, his family remained in the East until he was settled into his new assignment.

During the last station stop Jesse's mother had visited with one of the soldiers and learned they shared the same destination. She inquired about what to expect there, but he knew very little about Wyoming Territory or the army's presence there. When the soldier learned her husband was the ranking officer at Fort Bridger, he assured her that living conditions of officer's families were no doubt as superior in western forts as they were at other military sites. She replied that she did not expect the same level of comfort she had enjoyed at West Point, but hoped her new home would at least be acceptable. Like other military wives, she was accustomed to following her husband wherever the army sent him. Although it was not the type of life she had imagined when younger, she was proud of her status as an officer's wife and enjoyed socializing with other officers and their wives.

Despite his dissatisfaction with the lengthy train trip, Jesse was excited about this new chapter in his family's life. He looked forward to being reunited with his father, who had gone ahead to Fort Bridger several months ago. And he was eager to experience the West that had filled his imagination ever since he read a series of dime novels about frontier life. He had absorbed the contents of these brief books, which were known to embellish and exaggerate many aspects of the stories they told, and believed every detail. His father, in letters to the family from Fort Bridger, had described days filled with routine and rather mundane activities. Jesse thought his father must have omitted the more exciting and dangerous events in order to avoid frightening his mother.

Jesse and his mother remained on the train during its brief stop at the depot in Ogallala. A handful of new passengers boarded the already crowded conveyance and began to occupy the few remaining seats. Jesse noticed a tall, muscular man enter their car and walk down the aisle. The man was dressed in buckskin and carried a leather bag and a very large rifle. He paused in the aisle next to Jesse, placed his bag on the empty seat directly across from the boy and looked at the overhead rack on his side of the aisle. It was completely full. He turned toward the boy, noticed some open space on the rack above him, and tapped Jesse's mother on the shoulder. She reacted with a start and frowned at the man.

"Pardon me, ma'am," the man said, "hope you don't mind if I place this up there." As he spoke he nodded toward his rifle, then toward the overhead rack. "If need be go ahead," Jesse's mother replied as she smiled politely. The man reached over Jesse and carefully placed the rifle, which seemed taller than Jesse, on the rack. The man smiled at both of them and addressed Jesse's mother. "Frank Mayer, ma'am," he said loudly. She nodded and replied, "Violet Manning, and this is my son Jesse." The man said, "Gotta speak loud, please, I'm a bit hard of hearin'." Jesse's mother repeated their names. The man smiled again and sat down opposite Jesse.

For the next hour Jesse tried to get the man's attention. He was intrigued by the stranger's appearance and by the huge rifle in his possession. Was he a real frontiersman like those in the dime novels? Or maybe even a mountain man? And why did he have a gun so much bigger than the ones Jesse had seen his father's soldiers carry? Maybe he was going to hunt grizzly bear. "Yep, that's it," Jesse said to himself, "he's a grizzly bear hunter." Jesse's mind carried him to an imagined scene in which the man was firing his huge rifle at a grizzly bear. Then the gun jammed and the bear came at the man, who pulled a large knife from his boot and began attacking the bear with the knife.

Jesse's daydream was interrupted by the man across the aisle. "Where you headed?" he asked. At last, an opportunity to talk! "We're going to Fort Bridger," he said. "My father, Major Manning, he's already there." The man nodded but said nothing. Jesse pursued the conversation. "How about you?" he asked. "Cheyenne," the man replied, "meeting my crew there, then heading toward Laramie." Jesse's mother was now aware the two were talking. She turned toward Jesse and said, "Son, don't pester Mr. Mayer." Jesse frowned. The man said, "It's OK, ma'am, I don't mind and it's a long haul for a young fella his age." Jesse's mother smiled and went back to her book.

Jesse was glad the man was willing to talk. Dozens of questions were forming in his mind but his foremost interest was in the big rifle. "What kind of gun is that, Mr. Mayer?" he asked. "You call me Frank," the man said. "It's a forty-five caliber Sharps. Best gun there is." "Do you hunt grizzly bears?" Jesse asked. The man chuckled. "Nope, and I sure try to avoid places where they could hunt me. That there's for buffalo." Jesse brightened. "I've read about buffalo hunting," he said, "about crawling on the ground to get close to 'em and then shootin' 'em right between the eyes!" The man chuckled again. "Where did you get such malarkey?" he asked, shaking his head. Jesse was embarrassed. "I read books," he said, somewhat defensively. "Have you ever really shot one?" he asked. Frank Mayer laughed out loud. "I think so," he said. "Wanna know how it's really done?"

Jesse sat with rapt attention as Frank Mayer described in detail the realities of buffalo hunting. The man explained the behaviors of a buffalo herd, their grazing habits, the animals' willingness to follow the lead of an older cow and the unpredictable nature of stampedes. He talked about how strong and tough they were and the importance of placing a shot correctly to ensure a clean kill. "No shootin' like in them stories," he said, "hit 'em in the lungs and stay out at least three hundred yards so ya' don't spook the herd." Jesse wondered how far three hundred yards might be. He was surprised about where the hunter shot the buffalo. "So you don't git 'em between the eyes?" he asked. "Nope," the man replied, "their heads are so hard it'd just bounce off."

The hunter went on to describe how his crew dressed the buffaloes and transported them to the railroad for shipment. "I just shoot 'em," he said, "and other fellas do the rest." He explained to Jesse how skinners cut the animals from chin to rear, carefully removed the inner organs to prevent fouling the meat, and usually saved the heart and liver. "You all right hearin' this blood and guts stuff?" he asked. "Sure am!" exclaimed Jesse, "I want to know all about it." Frank nodded and smiled. "OK," he said, and went on to tell Jesse how the crew drained the carcass of blood, cut up various parts of the animal and packed the meat in sawdust to avoid spoilage in transport.

Mrs. Manning had taken a break from her reading and decided to listen in on her son's conversation with the buffalo hunter. She was intrigued but found the details disturbing. "Doesn't it bother you to kill those magnificent animals?" she asked. Frank Mayer looked at the woman. "Yes and no," he said, "we don't waste much, and if I don't shoot 'em somebody else will." "I see," said Jesse's mother, "and who do you sell the meat to?" "The meat goes to the army," he responded. "I expect you'll get plenty at Fort Bridger. The hides go east. Get made into robes and coats." "It does seem a ghastly business," she said, "but perhaps no more so than slaughtering cattle." The woman thought for a bit, then asked, "Can there possibly be enough buffalo to feed the army and the Indians?"

Frank Mayer was not surprised at the woman's question. Many easterners had the mistaken impression that a major function of government-employed hunters was to provide food to the Indian tribes. He decided not to tell the woman that the federal policy regarding buffalo hunting was to eliminate the buffalo as a food source for the Indians, thus forcing them toward compliance and reservation life. "There are enough to keep us hunters busy," he said. "And is it a suitable trade to generate an adequate income?" she asked. "Yes, ma'am," he replied. "Goin' rate is three cents a pound for meat and two dollars and a half per hide. Course I got expenses. Crew of four men, wagon, horses, cartridges." He paused, then added, "It ain't makin' me rich but I'm doin' all right."

Jesse listened intently to the conversation between his mother and the buffalo hunter. He hoped to see some buffalo either on the way to Fort Bridger or once there, on a horseback ride with his father. He could imagine the thrill of seeing one of the big animals brought down by a rifle shot or maybe by multiple shots. He wondered if they ever charged the hunters and if so how the hunters got away. There were many more questions in the boy's mind, but one was such a point of curiosity that he interrupted the adults' conversation to ask about it.

"Mr. Mayer," Jesse asked, "how many buffalo have you shot?" His mother's head tilted downward and she frowned at him. "Son," she said sternly, "that is not a polite question. You are asking Mr. Mayer to boast." The hunter smiled slightly. "He's just curious, ma'am," he said, "like any young fella would be. Okay if I tell him?" Mrs. Manning shrugged her shoulders. "To be honest," she said, "I'm a bit curious myself." The man looked at Jesse and said, "Fact is, I don't know." Jesse's face dropped. The hunter continued, "I usually shoot about twenty-five a day 'cause that's all my crew can handle. But I did once kill somewhat over a hundred and twenty in a couple of hours. Had to switch back and forth between two guns so the barrels wouldn't overheat."

Jesse was in awe. His mother was not. "Mr. Mayer," she said, "it is one thing to engage in exaggeration with an adult, but I do not appreciate your filling my son's head with such a ridiculous bit of nonsense. One hundred twenty an hour, indeed!" She glared at the man and put her arm around her son. For a moment Frank was speechless. The woman clearly thought him a liar, and he quickly realized he had no way to prove his veracity. Protesting or arguing would be futile. There was only one practical thing to do. He looked directly at Mrs. Manning and said, "Beg your pardon, ma'am." He turned and sat down, resuming his position across the aisle, and said no more. But as soon as

Jesse's mother turned her attention back toward her book he grinned and winked at Jesse. The boy instantly understood the man stood by what he said and simply wanted to avoid a pointless argument.

A couple hours after the unpleasant end of the conversation between his mother and the buffalo hunter, Jesse was gazing out the window of the train car when he noticed a large cloud hovering low on the horizon. He was not sure if it was a sign of impending rain or perhaps one of the prairie dust storms he had read about. His mother was absorbed in her reading and had not looked out the window for some time. Jesse glanced at the man across the aisle and realized the man was paying careful attention to the cloud. Jesse caught the man's eye and gave him a questioning look. Too softly for Jesse's mother to hear, the man said just one word, "Buffalo." The boy and the man stared out the window as the train moved steadily west, slowly closing the distance between it and the cloud. As the cloud drew nearer and larger Jesse realized it was an immense mound of dust kicked up by a herd of buffalo. Just then one of the officers aboard the train walked rapidly down the aisle and stopped in front of the buffalo hunter.

"Sir," the officer said, "are you Frank Mayer?" "That's me," the hunter replied. "Sir, I've spoken to the conductor and the engineer," the soldier said, "and have their agreement to stop the train when we're near the herd. If I can impose on you, sir, the army would appreciate your taking some of the animals to supplement the food supply of our men on the train. We'll handle the dressing and all if you will make the kill." The hunter did not reply audibly but nodded his agreement. He stood up, turned toward Jesse's mother and said, "Excuse me, ma'am." He reached over her head and gently retrieved his rifle from the overhead rack. He picked up the leather bag from the floor beneath his seat and walked toward the rear of the train. When he reached the door at the end of the car he turned around and looked at Jesse. "Well c'mon," he said. Without waiting for his mother to react Jesse jumped out of his seat and rushed to join the hunter.

Mrs. Manning resisted the urge to retrieve her son. He was in the company of an army officer, after all, and therefore no doubt safe. Although she did not like the idea of Jesse being in the company of a man she thought dishonest, perhaps this was an opportunity for him to witness the limits of the hunter's ability with the rifle. She had not told Frank Mayer, but she was not without experience as a hunter. In the eastern woods she had taken several deer and had once gone moose hunting in Maine with her husband. She knew full well nobody could shoot one hundred of any type of game in an hour. She just hoped Jesse would not be too disappointed when he learned the man had misrepresented his skill as a hunter.

A few minutes later the train slowly came to a halt. Mrs. Manning looked out the window expecting to see buffalo alongside her car. The herd was in clear view but was by her estimation at least a third of a mile from the train tracks. Since this was much too great a distance for shooting she expected to see horses unloaded from the freight cars and men riding off in the direction of the herd. She waited but no horses appeared. Perhaps the men decided the distance involved did not justify unloading the horses and chose to walk toward the herd instead. They could probably get within shooting range within ten to fifteen minutes. She would read a few more pages of her book and then check the men's progress.

Meanwhile, three people stood on the rear platform of the last train car. The army officer and Jesse stood nearest the door. Frank Mayer stood at the rear, gazing intently toward the buffalo herd. He had extracted from his leather bag a carefully measured charge of seventy grains of black powder and loaded it and a patch ball in the Sharps rifle. "Gotta find the lead cow," he said, squinting as his head moved slowly back and forth. After a moment or two he said, "Got 'er." He kneeled on the floor of the platform and carefully placed the barrel of the gun on the surrounding railing. He slowly brought the rifle to his shoulder. He took a breath, aimed the rifle and slowly exhaled. He squeezed the trigger.

Mrs. Manning and the other passengers jumped at the massive report of the buffalo gun. She was not expecting to hear a shot so soon and was certainly not prepared for a sound so deep and loud. It sounded nothing like the rifles she had shot. It was more like the roar of a small cannon. She wondered how she had missed the sight of the men moving to within range of the herd. She looked out the window, straining to make out individual animals within the distant buffalo herd. Then she heard another "boom!" as the Sharps was fired a second time. She heard a voice behind her and turned to face a soldier holding a pair of binoculars. He offered them to her and she accepted. She raised them to her eyes and adjusted the focus. Almost immediately she spotted a large buffalo cow lying on the ground, blood seeping from near its front leg. A short distance away was another cow, shot precisely in the same place, its life draining away as she watched.

As Mrs. Manning watched what she considered a most remarkable sight, Jesse returned to her side. He did not ask his mother for permission to accompany the soldiers going to dress the animals because the man who shot them remained aboard the train and Jesse wanted to be near him. Jesse's mother handed the binoculars back to the soldier and thanked him. "Well, ma'am," the soldier asked, "what do you think?" "I've never seen such a thing," she replied. "And you prob'ly won't again," said the soldier. "We're dang near a half mile from that herd. By the way, ma'am, you know who did the shooting, don't you?" "His name is Mayer," she replied. "Frank Mayer, ma'am," the soldier said. "You may have heard of him. Prob'ly the best buffalo hunter in the country. Once shot two hundred of 'em in forty minutes."

The hunter entered his car, walked up the aisle and stopped beside Jesse. He turned toward Mrs. Manning. "Excuse me, ma'am," he said, "just need to put this back up there." He motioned toward the overhead rack and carefully placed the weapon back where it had been stored earlier. He, or the gun, smelled strongly of burned powder. Jesse looked at the hunter, then at his mother. Mrs. Manning said, "Mr. Mayer, I think I owe you an apology." "Think nothin' of it," the man replied, "in fact, I might be the one that owes an apology to young Jesse here. His ears will prob'ly be ringin' for a few days." The boy turned to face the man. "Mr. Mayer ..." he began. The man cut him off. "Frank," he said. "Yes, okay, Mr. Frank," Jesse said, "when I grow up I want to be a buffalo hunter just like you." Mrs. Manning smiled. "That's going to be a while. You'd best ask if there will be enough of them left by then."

"Yeah," Jesse said, "you won't shoot all of 'em before I get a chance, will ya?" Frank smiled and chuckled. "That you don't gotta worry about," he said. "Wait until you been around this country a little more. That herd back there was nothin' compared to some. There are millions of 'em. When you're old enough you come see me and we'll go get 'em by the hundreds. That's one thing you can be certain of."

About an hour and a half later the conductor made his way slowly down the aisle of the passenger cars. "Sorry about the delay, folks," he said. "As you may know we agreed to a request by the military aboard to secure some additional meat for their use. It is now aboard and we will continue shortly. Thank you for your patience." Jesse heard the sound of steam escaping from the locomotive's drive cylinders. There was a lurch as the play between the cars was taken up and the train began to move. As he looked out the window at the now distant buffalo Jesse gave in to his imagination. He saw himself standing hundreds of yard from the herd, his Sharps rifle resting firmly in the crook of a tree branch. He aimed slowly and carefully and squeezed the trigger.

***Epilogue** - Though a reliable count of bison (Bison bison, or American bison, commonly called buffalo) in North America was not available until near the end of the 19th century, the best estimates place the population in the 1700s at roughly 30 million.*

Transcontinental railroads created a north and south herd division in the 1860s, and professional bison hunters began killing en masse on behalf of the railroads and the army, and later to meet the demand for buffalo robes, meat, and bones (ground into fertilizer). Approximately 2 million of the southern herd were killed in 1870; by 1872 thousands of hunters were able to kill up to 5,000 head per day. Huge auctions sometimes sold as many as 100,000 hides from the southern herd in a single day.

In 1875, reflecting an apparent consensus on the part of the federal government, General Philip Sheridan defended the hunters' wholesale slaughter of bison as a means of forcing Indians onto reservations: "For the sake of a lasting peace let them kill, skin, and sell until the buffalo are exterminated."

Decimation of the northern herd accelerated during the 1880s. A hunt conducted during September 1882 in Dakota Territory destroyed over 10,000 bison. By mid-1883 the northern herd was almost totally gone. A document from 1884 estimated the total remaining wild bison population at 325 head. The animals were saved from extinction only through the efforts of a small number of citizens dedicated to their preservation.

As of this writing, the American Bison population stands at approximately 500,000, the vast majority in private herds. Only four small herds remain whose genes are considered genetically pure; some cattle genes are present in the rest.

19 THE AVIATOR

The rules of the contest were few and plain but strictly enforced. The consortium of wealthy individuals sponsoring the affair agreed that a minimal number of restrictions was most likely to foster innovation and vigorous competition. They also agreed a substantial monetary reward was needed to attract the most capable and best-equipped participants. Thus, they jointly funded a first place prize of ten thousand dollars.

Contestants would be required to depart from Chicago within a designated three day time period following routes of their own choosing. The prize money would go to the aviator who arrived in San Francisco with the least total time elapsed between initial takeoff and final landing. The sponsors had considered prescribing a route for the flyers and requiring stops at intermediate checkpoints along the route. But after some discussion, they decided that public interest and press coverage would be greater if pilots were free to select their own routes and stopping points.

The promoters advertised the contest in major newspapers across the country, and promotional posters were sent by mail to each of the 134 airports and recognized landing strips listed on an official roster maintained by the U.S. Government. The ads and posters described the contest as "the event of the decade, sponsored by a group of public-spirited citizens willingly dedicating their personal fortunes to the advancement of air travel in the Western United States." The prize offered the winner was touted as "a stupendous sum of money that will guarantee the finest aviators in the world will join the contest." Interested parties were encouraged to apply by mail to an address in Highland Park, Illinois, to the attention of J.J. Wickersham, Attorney at Law, one of the event's sponsors.

Paul Bowman saw a poster promoting the contest at an airstrip in Lincoln, Nebraska. He had just finished his last flight of the day, having taken a local resident on her first airplane ride. The fifteen-minute adventure over the town and surrounding countryside commanded the standard fee of two dollars and fifty cents. His passenger was a retired school teacher well into her sixties and Paul admired her enthusiasm for flight. She had greatly enjoyed her time in the air, but no more than Paul did. Each time he flew he felt the same exhilarating sense of freedom he had felt during his first flight three years earlier. Paul loved flying and his acquaintances often heard him declare, "There is nothing like flying. Nothing at all." Paul wanted nothing in life so much as to fly. He woke up every morning with a single aim - to climb into the cockpit, hear the engine roar to life, head the biplane into the wind, open the throttle and lift off into the sky. Most mornings he got to do just that.

Paul Bowman did not own an airplane, although it was his dream to do so. Like most pilots, he flew a machine owned by someone else. Generally, there were two types of airplane owners. Some owners invested in aircraft as a business proposition, routing their planes and barnstorming pilots from town to town, offering rides for fees intended to cover expenses and provide a profit. Others, usually people of considerable wealth, funded airplanes and pilots simply because they wanted to be part of the great new adventure of powered flight. Rudy Caswell, the man who owned the biplane flown by Paul Bowman, was a blend of the two. He found the idea of airplanes fascinating and wanted to be part of advancing aviation. But he was also keen on getting a return on his investment in the plane he hired Paul to fly. Caswell was a widely known businessman and the principal investor in a chain of newspapers published in a group of Midwest cities. While scanning one of these papers, the *Independence Weekly*, Rudy Caswell noticed the ad announcing the Chicago to San Francisco flying contest.

Two days after he had seen the poster in Lincoln, Paul Bowman arose just before dawn, dressed and went downstairs to the dining room of the rooming house he stayed at when in Omaha. He knew breakfast would not be ready for another half hour, but he could not sleep when the sun came up and the day held the promise of flight. Another boarder soon entered the dining room and initiated a conversation. "So, where are you from?" asked the stranger. "Kansas City, until three years ago," replied Paul. The other man continued, "But a traveling man now, huh? What do you do?" "I fly," said Paul. The man raised his eyebrows and looked directly at Paul. "Really!" he exclaimed, "That's quite a way to make a living." "There's nothing like it," said Paul, "nothing at all." "Well," the man said, "I suppose it's all right if you don't mind risking your life in a bundle of sticks and wires." "It's not quite that bad," Paul said with a grin, "the new planes are put together with chewing gum and school glue." The other man chuckled. "Whatever you say," he replied. "It's your life."

Paul had just finished breakfast when the proprietor of the rooming house entered the dining room, walked directly to Paul and handed him an envelope. "For you," the man said, "a telegram." Paul opened the envelope and read, "Don't fly. Meet me Omaha Hotel tomorrow 4 p.m. Rudy." Paul was puzzled and not pleased. Not fly? Why? And what was he to do until the next afternoon? He did not like waiting, especially when he didn't know the purpose. It was a beautiful, clear morning and he should be flying, earning more dollars for Rudy Caswell. It wasn't like Rudy to squander an opportunity to make money. If Paul owned his own plane he could be in the air right now. Instead, he was stuck on the ground on Caswell's orders. There might be a good reason, but Paul would have to wait until his meeting with Caswell the next day to find out.

Within minutes of reading the advertisement for the flying contest, Rudy Caswell had not only decided to enter the competition but formulated a plan to win it. In his typically self-assured manner, he instructed his secretary to draft an entry letter and send it to the address listed in the ad, book train passage for himself to Omaha, and wire Paul Bowman to cease flying and await his arrival. The flying contest was exactly the type of event Caswell relished, and he looked forward to his biplane placing first in the competition. Competing in the contest would require significant expenditures beyond those normally required to operate the plane. But he was willing to spend the funds required to ensure his plane stood a good chance of beating the other contestants. Caswell liked to win, and in this case doing so was worth more than money to him.

Paul Bowman was waiting in the lobby of the Omaha Hotel when Rudy Caswell arrived. He offered only a cursory greeting to the prominent businessman and did not wait for Caswell to register or suggest a private location for their conversation. "Rudy," Paul began, "what's this all about? Why am I not in the air?" Caswell was a bit surprised by Paul's directness, but grinned as he replied, "Oh, you will be, and lots of people will know about it." "What's that supposed to mean?" asked

Paul. "I don't suppose you've heard about a flying contest from Chicago to San Francisco," Caswell said, "and I don't suppose you'd let me know about it if you did." He was baiting Paul, having a bit of fun with the intense younger man. "Why sure I would," Paul began. He stopped short, "You don't mean …." "Yes," Caswell interrupted, "we're entered and we're going to win." "Holy cow," Paul said, "you're serious aren't you?" Caswell nodded.

Paul Barrow had seen the poster advertising the flying contest the same day Rudy Caswell read the promoters' newspaper ad, but reacted very differently from his airplane's owner. Paul had no interest in any kind of flying contest. He enjoyed the independent life of a barnstormer, flying every day that weather permitted, moving from town to town and introducing people of all sorts to the wonders of powered flight. He had little contact with Rudy Caswell, other than an occasional request for money when income from the venture fell short of the expenses involved. But the man who owned the airplane was clearly determined to pursue victory in the upcoming flying contest. Paul knew there was no use arguing. He listened while Rudy Caswell outlined his plan to win the ten thousand dollar prize.

Despite the haste with which Caswell had developed the plan, Paul had to admit it sounded feasible. Caswell would send two top mechanics to Chicago to prepare the biplane for competition. A meteorologist and a surveyor well-traveled in the West were already mapping a proposed route for the flight. As soon as the route was laid out Caswell would use his connections in the newspaper business to contact local editors in the town along the route. In exchange for exclusive coverage of Paul's milestone flight, the editors could be counted on to assist in the project. They would do this by locating and marking landing sites, arranging supplies of fuel for the plane and lodging for the pilot, and painting arrows on rooftops to guide Paul toward the next town.

Paul wanted to fly the airplane to Chicago, a two-day trip, but Caswell was determined to ship it by rail. "You know how finicky that engine can be," he reminded Paul, "and I don't want to put any wear on it getting to the starting line. We'll put the plane on the train you travel on and you can look after it on the way, then make sure it's ready to go in Chicago." Caswell continued, "The departure day is one week from today. If you leave tomorrow you'll be in Chicago by late Monday. That leaves five days for the mechanics to work on the plane. I want absolutely everything gone over before you take off. I expect you'll get in the lead and stay there the whole trip." This type of optimism was not unusual for Rudy Caswell, who had gambled and won often enough to consider his highly confident attitude perfectly reasonable.

The men Caswell assigned to prepare the biplane for the contest were already in Chicago. They purchased and organized all the provisions deemed necessary, including a spare propeller, various lengths of cable and fasteners, several yards of wing and fuselage cloth and appropriate adhesives, maps of each state from Illinois to California, spare tubes for the tires, and an assortment of engine parts, including spark plugs, a carburetor kit, and a spare magneto. The men also designed, and were having made as quickly as possible, two modifications to the biplane. An extra fuel tank installed in the rear passenger cockpit would extend the flying time between refueling stops. Just behind the fuel tank, an ingenious water tank and tubing system would, when the pilot opened a valve in the cockpit, direct water to an engine cooling system. The plane's engine was air cooled, but the mechanics had modified it to increase its power and therefore the heat it generated, and a supplemental cooling system was deemed necessary. At Caswell's insistence, the supplies carried on the plane included a victory banner to be hung from the top wing after it landed in San Francisco ahead of the other contestants. If the airplane piloted by Paul Bowman failed to win the contest, it would not be due to insufficient planning or investment on the part of Rudy Caswell.

The departure point for the contest was a recently constructed airport west of the Chicago city limits. The airport was surrounded by open fields that provided ample room for the rapidly growing number of airplanes, tents, boxes of supplies, and fuel and freight wagons, as well as the dozens of pilots, mechanics, aircraft owners, newspapermen, and members of the general public who congregated to participate in or witness the start of the flying contest. Members of the press made themselves welcome in the airport's small office building, in the tents and other shelters used by the crews working on the planes, and in some instances in the cockpits of the airplanes. Detailed preparations were underway, all intended to enable the planes to endure the cross-country flight. Wire services carried daily stories about the men and machines who were about to embark on such a remarkable and challenging venture, and interest in the event was building across the entire country. Paul Bowman and the mechanics begrudgingly tolerated the interference of the newspaper reporters. However, Rudy Caswell willingly gave interviews predicting a close race in which the modified biplane he owned would, barring unforeseen circumstances, almost certainly win the contest.

The day before the contest was to begin, the organizers called a mandatory meeting of the owners and pilots during which the contestants learned that more planes had registered for the contest than the schedule could accommodate. Twenty-nine planes were registered for the event. To ensure adherence to the contest rules and safety of the aircraft, each airplane and pilot were to undergo a pre-takeoff inspection by event officials.

This process would require about thirty minutes per plane, which limited each day's takeoffs to twenty aircraft. In an attempt to fairly deal with the limited capacity, the names of each of the owners were to be placed in a hat and a drawing held. The order of takeoff would follow the order in which the owner's names were drawn, up to the limit of twenty planes per day. Nine aircraft would have to wait until the next day to begin the journey.

Rudy Caswell's name was the seventh drawn from the hat, which placed his aircraft's takeoff time at approximately ten o'clock in the morning of the first day. His pilot preferred an earlier departure time so his plane could get in a full day's flying. Rudy, however, was satisfied with the schedule. A mid-morning departure gave the mechanics time to do a final check of the plane and make any last-minute adjustments. Since the contest was based on total elapsed time from takeoff in Chicago to landing in San Francisco, the first planes to take off did not receive an unfair advantage. Seeing the initial direction taken by the first pilots might even help those with later takeoff times by giving an indication of the earlier pilots' routes.

The departure day dawned clear and bright with a moderate north wind. The runway ran north and south, and takeoffs would be north, into the wind. Pilots and mechanics were at their planes at daybreak even if no additional preparation was needed. Anticipation was high and a crowd of several hundred spectators and press assembled to watch the contestants depart. When the first plane roared down the grass runway and lifted off, some observers waved flags and a cheer came from the crowd. The onlookers followed the plane with their eyes until it became a small speck and finally disappeared against the western sky. A second plane followed, then a third, and a fourth, all on schedule and without incident.

When the organizers reached the seventh aircraft on their list, Paul Bowman listened impatiently to a repetition of the contest rules while he watched the men inspect the carefully prepared biplane. The two mechanics followed the inspectors around the plane and explained the modifications they had made. As expected, the plane passed inspection and one of the organizers gave a thumbs up signal to Rudy Caswell. Caswell turned to Paul and said, "It's up to you now. You know the plan. We'll make sure the folks on the ground are pointing the way for you. Send me a wire whenever you can. And good luck." Caswell was brimming with confidence as he shook Paul's hand, holding on to it long enough for a photographer to take their picture.

Paul climbed into the cockpit, pulled on his goggles and safety harness, and signaled a crewman to pull the propeller. The engine caught on the first pull, sputtered once, and came to life. Paul pushed the throttle ahead enough to get the plane moving and taxied to the south end of the runway. He turned the plane into the wind, gave the engine full throttle, and the sturdy biplane rolled across the grass, steadily gaining speed. He pulled the stick back and the plane's wheels left the earth. He was airborne. He smiled to himself, glad to be aloft again as he watched the crowd below shrink and slowly disappear. From force of habit, he turned his head to observe the reaction of the passenger behind him. But he was alone. Just him, the biplane and the sky. He gently banked the plane to the left and made a wide, sweeping turn until his compass read two hundred seventy degrees due west. He straightened the plane, checked the temperature and fuel gauges, and flew toward the horizon.

With the extra gasoline in the auxiliary fuel tank the biplane could, dependent on conditions, remain in the air between five and six hours. The careful planning done by Rudy Caswell's men included refueling points approximately five hours flying time apart. This meant the biplane could, under good conditions, complete a ten-hour day aloft while landing once to refuel. Most other airplanes in the competition would need to land at least twice per day to refuel, if not three times. This advantage, plus the care taken in mapping the route Paul Bowman was to follow, accounted for much of Caswell's belief that his airplane had a very good chance of winning the competition.

For the past three years Paul Bowman had been a barnstormer (though he objected to the term, stating, "I take people up into the sky, not into a barn"), giving short rides to people who wanted to experience powered flight, most for the first time. He was not accustomed to remaining in the air for hours at a time. At an altitude of twenty-five hundred feet he had a clear view of the roads, buildings, rivers, and fields below. The landscape seemed like a repeat of the same scene, over and over again. By the time he was two hours west of Chicago his usual delight in flying was tainted by the onset of boredom.

The route laid out by the meteorologist and surveyor hired by Rudy Caswell was easy to follow. The local newspaper editors Caswell had persuaded to help mark the route by painting arrows on rooftops of buildings had done so as promised. Paul simply followed the route outlined on the map clipped to the inside of the cockpit, going from town to town as if playing a giant connect the dots game from the sky. When he reached a town he adjusted his heading to align with the arrow plainly visible from the air and continued to the next reference point. Primarily to break the boredom, he sometimes dropped below five hundred feet so he could wave to the people below and they could see his plane more clearly.

As planned, Paul made his first refueling stop just outside Marshalltown, Iowa. He landed on a freshly mown grass strip marked by a large square of red cloth. The local newspaper editor was there to greet him, along with a small gathering of townspeople. Rudy Caswell had arranged for a wagon loaded with several barrels of gasoline to be waiting at the site. After refueling and a short visit with the editor, Paul taxied to the east end of the runway, turned the biplane around, and took off into the wind. He consulted his map, adjusted his heading, and settled in for more hours of steady flying.

The second leg of the journey was uneventful. After several hours in the air, Paul reached his second refueling location at Norfolk, Nebraska. He had no difficulty finding the town but had to make several passes over the area searching for a landing strip. He circled the town in ever-widening arcs until, unable to spot the strip, he decided to look for a smooth field in which to land. On the edge of town, he spied what looked like a recently cut alfalfa field, pulled the throttle back and glided down toward the patch of green. He touched down at low speed with only a small bounce but was barely able to stop the plane short of a fence at the end of the field. He turned the plane around and taxied toward a building at the other end of the field.

To Paul's surprise, a group of citizens, including the local newspaper editor, were standing beside the building awaiting his arrival. "Guess we could have marked the strip a bit better," said the editor. "It seemed you had a little trouble seeing it." Paul was tempted to tell them what he thought of the so-called landing strip but held his tongue. The editor indicated he had reserved a room for Paul at the local hotel and would cover the cost in exchange for an interview to be printed in the local paper. Though he was tired from the day's flying, Paul agreed to meet with the editor over an evening meal. The plane was refueled, the cockpit covered with a tarp, and the editor drove Paul to the hotel. The editor sensed that Paul had little energy remaining and kept the interview short. By nine o'clock Paul had retired for the night.

The next morning Paul arose at dawn. He ate a quick breakfast at the hotel, then walked to the telegraph office to check the weather. The forecast was for clear skies and brisk winds from the northwest. "Well," thought Paul, "better wind than rain." He walked to the edge of town, not stopping for conversation with the few others who were also out early. When he reached the biplane he walked slowly around it, carefully checking for any signs of future trouble but found none. He uncovered the cockpit, opened the fuel valve, set the magneto and throttle to the start position and pulled the propeller. The engine started quickly and Paul dodged the propeller as the plane slowly started forward. He ran around the end of the wing, jumped onto the single step on the side of the fuselage and pulled himself into the cockpit. It was a rather risky way to get underway, but Paul had no desire to wait for help, let alone be delayed by a group of local spectators. He gave the engine full power and, at the last possible moment, pulled back hard on the stick. He narrowly cleared the fence at the end of the field, eased off the stick to avoid a stall and began a slow climb. He banked the plane to adjust his heading and headed west across the wide expanses of the Nebraska prairie.

The men who laid out the route and prepared the maps on which Paul depended had been somewhat apologetic when they explained this portion of the route. The prescribed heading of due west was not directed toward a town, an airport, or a recognizable landing strip. In order to maximize the distance traveled on each leg of the flight and travel as directly as possible toward the end destination, the planners had to be creative. The next refueling stop was at a point some fifty miles north of the town of North Platte, far from any type of aviation support. The editor from North Platte was responsible for having things ready at the site, including a supply of fuel, food, and water. The editor was to select a level stretch of road, use large strips of red material to stake out an X on the roadway, and ensure no vehicles or people were on the road when the biplane approached.

Paul shook his head when he recalled the conversation explaining these arrangements. He began to wonder why he had even agreed to make a trip across such inhospitable country. But he knew the answer. He simply wanted to fly. And if that included navigating across sparsely populated country totally devoid of suitable facilities, so be it. He had no trouble following the route west, though more than once he caught himself on the edge of being lulled to sleep. The droning of the engine, the fresh air, the sunshine, all combined to make him drowsy. Mile after mile he fought sleep.

He crossed the Calamus River and headed toward Thomas County. A headwind put him slightly behind schedule but he saw little danger of running low on fuel. It was nearing mid-day when he passed over the tiny community of Brewster and began watching for a red X on a road. About ten minutes later the X appeared. Paul dropped to a height of about a hundred feet and saw several people standing beside what looked like tree stumps at the edge of the road. He banked to the right, lined the plane up with the roadway and guided it down for a smooth landing. He taxied toward the figures along the roadway, came to a stop and shut off the engine.

As planned, the editor from North Platte was on hand and had made all the arrangements requested of him. While Paul ate a sandwich and a slice of apple pie, washed down with a jar of fresh whole milk, the local citizens fueled his plane from the barrels that Paul had mistaken for tree stumps. He asked the editor about the weather to the west. "A fellow that came in on the train last night from Scottsbluff said there are storms out that way," the editor replied. "You might run into them before the day is out." Paul reflected on the significance of this bit of news compared to similar weather reports received when he was barnstorming. On the ride-for-hire circuit, a storm simply meant suspending flights until the bad weather passed. Now a storm might delay him long enough to destroy the possibility of winning the contest.

Although anxious to get underway, Paul felt obligated to answer the questions posed by the editor and his companions. They asked about the plane, the contest, and what it really felt like to be in control of a flying machine. Paul did his best to provide answers that newspaper readers would find satisfying. Then, mindful of the weather report and with an eye on the western horizon, he thanked the locals for their help, shook hands all around and climbed back into the cockpit. A volunteer pulled the propeller and the engine gave up its brief respite. Paul opened the throttle and a cloud of dust enveloped the people standing by the road. Despite being bombarded with dust and dirt, they did not move at all, but stood still and watched with wonder as the biplane bounced on the road once, then left the roadway and soared into the sky. Paul was genuinely appreciative of their efforts and hoped that Rudy Caswell would compensate them well for their help.

As the biplane flew farther into western Nebraska there were fewer towns to serve as refueling points or overnight stops. The buildings with arrows on their roofs were farther apart, and Paul had to carefully watch his headings to avoid getting off course. Once, having underestimated the speed of the headwinds, he miscalculated the distance he had traveled and thought he had somehow missed the next town. He was about to turn back in search of the missing community when he saw what appeared to be a grove of trees some distance to the northwest. He decided to investigate and took a detour in that direction. As he neared the trees he realized there were houses among them, and spotted a building with an arrow painted on its roof. The incident shook his confidence somewhat and made Paul even more attentive to the landmarks on his maps and meticulous about the accuracy of his headings.

About an hour past the refueling stop near North Platte clouds began to build in the west. The wind picked up, and as Paul flew toward the line of clouds he watched the weather carefully. By the time another half hour passed a long row of cumulous clouds stretched out across the prairie. Then, with surprising suddenness, the clouds expanded upward as they transformed into the cumulonimbus formations known as thunderheads. Flying into a thunderhead was something a good pilot avoided at all costs since such clouds werc usually filled with lightning and often contained dangerous downdrafts. Getting caught in a strong downdraft could cause structural failure, or the wind could totally overcome the plane's lift and slam it into the ground. Paul kept his eye on the brewing storm while he studied his map.

The storm appeared to be somewhat weaker to the north. Paul did some quick mental calculations, then banked the plane to the right. At a heading of three hundred twenty degrees he straightened the plane, pushed the throttle forward and began to climb. If he could fly over the top of the storm and avoid the thunderheads he might lose only twenty to thirty minutes. As the biplane moved closer to the storm front the temperature dropped rapidly and the plane was buffeted by gusts of wind. The cooler, denser air increased the output of the engine and Paul was sure he could climb over the cloud bank. The modifications made to the engines in preparation for the contest paid off as the plane maintained its heading and steadily gained altitude. It was burning extra fuel to do so, but the auxiliary tank would ensure an adequate supply to reach the next scheduled stop. When the plane reached an altitude of eighty-five hundred feet, Paul could see rays of sunshine streaming through a gap between the tops of the clouds directly ahead. He climbed another five hundred feet, then leveled off and banked the plane to the left in order to pass between the ominous thunderheads.

Paul had never before found it necessary or advisable to challenge a thunderstorm. He was concerned, but not worried, about this storm. He focused on keeping track of the deviation from his route so he would not miss the next town that had an arrow painted atop one of its buildings. He was unaware that the effect of thunderheads can extend well beyond the visible clouds themselves, creating invisible downdrafts. The biplane was more than halfway through the bank of storm clouds when, with no warning, it entered such a downdraft. The effect felt as if a huge, invisible hand had grasped the plane and was pushing it rapidly toward the ground. The altimeter recorded the plane's descent. The gauge flew past eight thousand feet, seventy-five hundred feet, seven thousand, sixty-five hundred, six thousand, fifty-five hundred, five thousand. Paul desperately tried to stem the fall. He pulled back hard on the stick and pushed the throttle fully forward, but neither action had any effect. As the plane plummeted it passed through rain, then hail, then more rain coupled with lightning. The sky lit up around the plane as great bolts of lightning flashed in all directions. It felt as though the plane would be torn apart by the wind. The engine roared, the wings shook and chattered, and Paul realized he and the plane were totally at the mercy of the storm.

At the bottom of the downdraft, about three thousand feet above the ground, the plane's violent descent ended as quickly as it had begun. To Paul, it felt as if the aircraft had slammed into the ground. The ends of the wings shot upward, then snapped back to their normal position. Paul unconsciously pushed the stick forward to compensate for the sudden change in direction but quickly realized his mistake and leveled the plane. It was a miracle that the wings were still attached and none of the lightning had struck the plane. Paul felt weak, the natural aftermath of an adrenaline rush, as he did the only thing he knew to do. He kept the plane on course and flew on through the storm to the other side of the clouds.

Ten minutes after the harrowing incident the biplane passed out of the clouds and into the sunshine. Paul estimated his position, compared it to the point on the route where he should have been, and turned the plane to a heading that would intersect the prescribed route. He examined as much as he could of the wings, the fuselage, and the struts and cables that had been subjected to the brutal punishment of the storm. Two of the lighter wires bracing the left wing had snapped but there were no broken struts. Amazingly, there were only some small tears in the wing fabric and very little damage to the fuselage. He would have to give the plane a thorough inspection at the next stop. But unless he found a problem not visible from the cockpit he was confident the damage could be repaired with supplies carried on board the plane.

After flying about twenty miles to the southwest Paul picked up the route when he flew over a town that had an arrow painted prominently on one of its larger buildings. He smiled to himself as he realized how thankful he was to see the arrow and know he was back on course. By carefully following the increasingly sparse arrows and watching for natural landmarks, Paul managed to arrive on target at Wheatland, Wyoming, just half an hour behind schedule. The landing strip was well-marked and the local welcoming committee treated him as if he were a celebrity. Paul was not accustomed to such attention but decided to let the townspeople have their fun. After carefully checking every inch of the biplane, patching the wounds it received at the hands of the thunderstorm, and refueling, he regaled the group of local citizens with tales of flying machines. He told them of his experience with the thunderstorm and found it unnecessary to add any exaggeration to hold his audience's attention. He closed his impromptu monologue by telling his audience, "There is nothing like flying. Nothing at all."

Paul stayed the night at the editor's house, where he was treated to a hearty meal cooked by the newspaperman's wife. During the meal the editor shared some news about the contest. "So," he asked Paul, "have you been keeping up on the other contestants?" Paul realized that not once during the many hours of solitary flight had he given any thought to the status of the other fliers. "I haven't heard much," he said. "Oh," the editor said, "then you don't know about the fellow who crashed yesterday in Kansas. Just dove right into a field. They said he must have fallen asleep. I don't know how you can do something as exciting as fly an airplane and fall asleep." "I'm sorry to hear it," Paul replied. "I hope the rest of the pilots are doing all right." He thought about his own battles with sleep and decided that if necessary he would land and take a nap rather than risk a similar fate.

Twenty-nine airplanes had been admitted to the competition, but three experienced mechanical problems or failed to pass the pre-flight inspection. Thus twenty-six aircraft had taken off from Chicago headed toward San Francisco. The majority of the pilots, intimidated by the thought of attempting to cross the Rocky Mountains, elected to head southwest. Their routes went around the southern end of the major portions of the Rockies, passed through New Mexico and Arizona, headed west into southern California, then turned north toward San Francisco. It was rumored one or two pilots were going to attempt to cross the Rockies by navigating along rivers and streams in hopes of finding mountain passes their planes could conquer. The rest of the pilots selected routes similar to the one Paul Bowman was following. Cross the plains to the west, then thread your way through the northern Rockies, passing over either Idaho Falls or

Salt Lake City before heading toward San Francisco. Either of these northern routes required finding a way around or through the Sierra Nevada range of mountains that ran along the eastern side of California.

Of the original twenty-six planes, two fell prey to mechanical difficulties before reaching the western border of Illinois. Five more broke down before completing a second full day of flying, one of which had a sudden engine failure while over the city of Des Moines, Iowa. The pilot was credited with preventing a possible disaster when he glided the plane toward a large park and landed, albeit roughly, without serious injury to himself or anyone in the park Three more aircraft suffered mechanical problems that were repaired, but left their pilots with such little hope of catching the leaders that the sponsors withdrew them from the competition. These incidents, plus the fatality in Kansas, left a field of fifteen planes three days into the contest. Most of the remaining pilots had heard little about their competitors' progress and assumed a full roster of planes remained in the event.

After a restful night in the editor's comfortable home, Paul Bowman arose the next morning at dawn. Despite the hospitality shown by the residents of Wheatland, he was anxious to get underway. As he walked toward the airstrip he found himself deep in thought. Having been reminded of the other pilots winging their way toward San Francisco, he felt a growing determination to arrive there ahead of the others. The news of the Kansas fatality gave Paul a different perspective on the contest. He concluded that the possibility of serious injury or death meant that participating in such an event could be justified only if one made every effort possible to win. Why else would he risk flying alone across the prairie, the edge of the Rockies, and eventually the Nevada desert and portions of the Sierra Nevada mountains? He certainly wasn't doing it for Rudy Caswell, who was safely at home reading reports about the contest in the newspapers he owned. It was Rudy who had gotten him into this thing and who would claim the glory if his airplane won the contest. But Rudy hadn't promised anything to Paul, not even a mention in the articles that would certainly appear in Caswell's newspapers. Paul knew he wanted badly to win the contest, and he wanted to win it for himself.

After the usual round of thank-yous and good-byes, Paul once again climbed into the cockpit of the biplane. He gave the signal to pull the propeller to a strapping young man who promptly did so, awakening the engine and causing the spectators to shield their faces from the debris kicked up by the prop wash. Paul opened the throttle and waited for the right time to pull back the stick. When he did, the plane responded as if it, too, had a desire to reach San Francisco ahead of the others. Paul felt an enthusiasm and desire to win that would keep him motivated for the rest of the trip. He adjusted his heading to two hundred sixty degrees, slightly south of due west, and barely noticed the chill in the air as he climbed to a height of six thousand feet. The sun was just above the horizon and its rays felt good on the back of his head and neck.

Paul remained at six thousand feet of elevation for twenty minutes, then pulled back slightly on the stick and began a gradual climb toward eight thousand feet. According to the maps supplied by Rudy Caswell's planners, the mountains west of Wheatland were no more than seven thousand feet in elevation, and the refueling stop of Rock Springs was nestled in the mountains at an elevation of just over sixty-seven hundred feet. However, because he was not certain of the accuracy of this information, Paul had decided to add a safety margin of an additional thousand feet. This meant an altitude of at least eight thousand feet was required to pass over the mountains en route to Rock Springs. This leg of the journey was one Caswell's mechanics had in mind when they boosted the power of the biplane's engine and added the auxiliary fuel tank. Climbing to eight thousand feet and remaining at that altitude required extra power and would burn additional fuel. The alternative was to follow the rivers that snaked through the lower portions of the mountains, adding many extra miles and an estimated extra half day of flying. The lower route would be easier and perhaps safer, but it was not the way to get to San Francisco first.

Paul kept a close eye on the altimeter. At higher elevations the thin air offered noticeably less lift and he had to reduce the rate of climb. Despite wearing several layers of clothing he began to feel the cold. The open cockpit exposed his upper body to a rush of cold air. He pulled his scarf up over his nose and mouth and slapped his hands together to warm them. The altimeter showed seven thousand feet and was inching upward. To be sure he crossed the ridge at the top of the pass with plenty of clearance, Paul needed another thousand feet of altitude. The ridge was enveloped in clouds and he could not avoid entering them. When he did he felt a fine drizzle. The moisture soaked his clothing and began to solidify on the biplane's wings. The plane was normally capable of climbing much higher but the buildup of ice quickly generated drag and seriously reduced the wings' lift. Paul knew he dared not descend and risk crashing into the ridge, which was hidden by the clouds. He could turn around and follow the slope of the mountain down, but going back was tantamount to giving up on the contest. He gritted his teeth, pushed on the already wide open throttle and held the stick in position to continue the climb.

Paul was wise not to depend on the figures the planners had used to lay out the route across the mountains between Wheatland and Rock Springs. The altimeter had just touched eight thousand feet when the aircraft reached the top of the mountain. Its engine roaring disapproval of being put to such a test, and laboring under an increasing layer of ice on its wings, the plane cleared the peak of the ridge by less than two hundred feet. By the time the plane reached the west of the ridge, so much ice had accumulated that it began to lose altitude even at full throttle. There was no way to dislodge the ice and Paul knew he had one chance to reach the landing strip at Rock Springs. As he searched the horizon for signs of civilization the altimeter dropped steadily to seventy-five hundred feet, then to seven thousand. He kept the throttle wide open but the altimeter continued a slow decline. Suddenly, through a break in the cloud cover, he spotted a town and thought he saw an open area in which to land. He pointed the plane in the direction of the landing site and watched the altimeter drop to sixty-eight hundred feet. As the plane fell below the clouds Paul had a clear view of an open area free of trees directly in front of him and only about fifty feet below. He pulled the throttle back and let the plane hit the ground hard. He was shivering from the cold and the tension, and as he shut the engine off and let the plane roll to a stop he held his head in his hands and felt the last ounce of reserve energy leave his body.

The men who met Paul at the edge of the clearing were amazed to see an airplane land in Rock Springs and treated him with a mixture of awe and uncertainty, as though he were superhuman, crazy, or perhaps both. They started a series of small wood fires under the wings to help melt the ice, which would melt much too slowly at the ambient temperature of forty degrees. They offered Paul some hot coffee, which he gladly accepted, and peppered him with questions about the plane and the flying contest. They also informed him that the area in which he landed had been cleared only because a businessman from back east, a Mr. Caswell, had promised a generous donation toward the town's plans to build a schoolhouse.

When the wings were clear and the fires had died down, the plane was refueled and turned into the wind for takeoff. Paul studied the route map, which showed a heading of due west over the Wasatch Range toward Salt Lake City. One of the men drew Paul aside and asked, "You really goin' straight west out of here?" "That's my route," Paul replied. "Well," said the man, "unless you want to die tryin' to win that contest, my advice is to follow the river south out of here. Go due south about eighty miles, then west along the river valley about another hundred miles and you'll reach Provo, Utah. You can go that way without any daredevil flyin'. That is if you're not too stubborn for your own good." "Thanks," Paul replied, "I'll think about it." "Don't think too long," the man admonished, "or it might be your last thought."

Paul climbed into the cockpit. He adjusted his goggles, pulled his scarf up over much of his face and gave the signal to pull the propeller. The engine started quickly in spite of the cold, and after a brief warm-up he pushed the throttle fully forward. The plane accelerated slower at this altitude and Paul was grateful the Rock Springs residents had cleared an area longer than the typical landing strip. At the right moment, he pulled back on the stick and the trusty biplane left the ground. Paul banked hard to the left, waved at the men on the ground and headed south along the river.

The flight to Provo, though off the planned route and totally lacking in buildings with arrows painted on their roofs or editors awaiting exclusive interviews with a daring pilot, was comparatively uneventful. Paul did his best to gauge the wind direction and speed, mentally calculated the difference between the plane's airspeed and ground speed, and kept careful track of the time. By doing so he knew when he was approaching the eighty-mile distance from Rock Springs. He turned west to follow the river valley, and as he threaded his way between the mountains he admired the beauty of the scene below. He reached Provo as expected and considered landing in a field there. However, he thought it best to get back to the planned route through Salt Lake City as soon as possible. He set a compass heading of three hundred and fifty degrees and in less than an hour arrived at the designated site in Salt Lake City. He identified the landing strip without difficulty and, after a low pass to alert anyone waiting for him, brought the plane in for a landing and taxied to a stop. He was grateful to be back on his route. He was met by a cordial newspaper editor who at first seemed disapproving of the flying contest but did not say why. The editor was also skeptical of Paul's account of his flight over the mountains to Rock Springs and was convinced of the reality of the story only when provided sufficient details of the surrounding area to suggest the experience was real. Once convinced of Paul's credibility, the editor was a gracious host. He brought Paul to his home, where the two men joined the editor's family for a hearty meal and a lively discussion about the future of flying, railroads, and automobiles. Paul was offered a comfortable room in the editor's house and enjoyed a night of very sound sleep.

The next morning Paul confessed to the editor that he had neglected to wire Rudy Caswell as to his whereabouts or any other details of the trip. The editor remarked that the lack of communication seemed to be two-way, since Caswell had apparently not kept Paul informed as to the status of the other contestants. The editor told Paul what he knew of the others, including the fact that the number of planes remaining in the contest had, as of the day before, dropped to a total of nine. The editor also told Paul that he and Caswell had known each other for many years and the two men had once jointly owned a newspaper in Missouri. The man offered to send a telegram to Caswell and assure him that Paul was alive and well and was at great personal risk diligently pursuing the prescribed route. The news of a reduced number of contestants bolstered Paul's hopes of being the first to reach San Francisco and he was anxious to resume his journey. The editor transported him to the landing strip, and after a brief inspection of the biplane the aviator was once again in the air.

As the men who planned the trip recognized, the next two legs of the biplane's cross country flight were the most difficult to navigate. Paul was about to strike out over the deserts of western Utah and eastern Nevada, an area with very few residents and almost no towns. The technique of hopping from town to town following arrows painted on the tops of buildings was useless here. Caswell had managed to reach an agreement with an individual in Elko, Nevada, to arrange a supply of fuel, food, and water. According to the contact in Elko, no landing strip would be marked or needed. In a wire to Caswell, he simply stated, "Land anywhere. All flat." The instructions for reaching Elko from Salt Lake City were uncomplicated: "Use compass heading 275 deg. for 200 mi., then N. around mountain, SW into valley & Elko." With no other information, Paul left Salt Lake City. He put the biplane in the air, set a heading of two hundred seventy-five degrees and kept careful track of ground and wind speed in order to determine when he had gone two hundred miles.

To describe the area Paul flew across as inhospitable falls short of expressing the desolation, rugged terrain and dearth of human presence he observed from the air. Had the biplane's engine quit or some other misfortune of flying occurred during this part of the journey, it is quite possible no trace of Paul or the airplane would have been found. Fortunately, the only mechanical issue that arose while crossing the hot, barren landscape was a rise in engine temperature, which was controlled by use of the supplemental water cooling mechanism devised by Rudy Caswell's mechanics. Although Paul was often uncertain of his exact location between Salt Lake City and Elko, he was not worried or discouraged. His recent experience in the mountains near Rock Springs made the navigational task of locating Elko seem relatively minor.

Paul followed the brief set of instructions precisely, and three and a half hours after leaving Salt Lake City reached the small range of mountains that formed the eastern boundary of the valley in which Elko was located. By flying an arc around the north edge of the mountains, then turning southwest, Paul approached Elko from the northeast. He aligned the plane with a flat, open field that appeared suitable as a landing area, pulled the throttle back and descended toward the field. Suddenly, the engine began to run unevenly and lose power, while making a noise that resembled popcorn popping. Paul guided the plane down onto the field and it rolled to a stop, to the amazement of workers in the neighboring fields.

Soon a large, deeply suntanned man arrived at the field and introduced himself as the owner of the property on which Paul had landed. Paul began to apologize, but when the man heard the reason for the biplane's presence on his property he dismissed the damage to the crop and offered his assistance. The individual who was in charge of local arrangements, Paul learned, had been taken seriously ill but had first managed to arrange for a supply of fuel. The requested food and water were lacking but the man who owned the field volunteered to supply both. When Paul described the engine noise he heard just prior to landing, the man said, "It's missing. Running on six of its seven cylinders. I can help you with that." Paul was astounded. "How do you know that?" he asked. "I know all about engines," the man replied, "used to build them in a factory in Ohio before I came out here." "What incredible luck!" Paul exclaimed, "Any chance you can help me fix it?" "Of course," said the man, "we'll start right away. But it might take the rest of the day."

Paul and the man who identified himself as Henry Waldron worked on the engine the rest of the afternoon. Henry's diagnosis was correct and the next step was determining whether the root of the problem was a lack of ignition, fuel, or compression. Through a process of trial and error the two men identified the ignition system as the culprit. Fortunately, the spare parts put on the plane by Caswell's men included several critical ignition parts. One at a time, Paul and Henry installed replacement parts, then tried the engine. Each time, the engine started but continued to miss. After replacing the third ignition part they tried the engine again. It started and ran smoothly. Paul shook Waldron's hand and offered his congratulations for a job well done. The man shrugged and said, "It's good to fool with this again. I sort of miss it." Then he changed the subject. "It's too late to go farther today," he said, "I'll find you a place to stay tonight and you can leave first thing in the morning." Paul hated the thought of a delay, worried that it might cost him the contest, but he realized his companion was right. He had to stay the night. Paul covered the cockpit of the biplane and the two men rode into town.

The next morning, as soon as there was sufficient light, Paul and the landowner fueled the biplane, refilled the water tank and discussed the next leg of the trip. After the experience in Rock Springs Paul was attentive to locals' input regarding routes to take and areas to avoid. Mr. Waldron recommended a route slightly north of a straight line from Elko to Reno, the mid-day refueling point. "You'll go over a bunch of mountains," he told Paul, "but they're not as high as what you flew over in Wyoming and you'll save some miles." Based on the man's advice, Paul altered the recommended compass settings and was confident he could arrive in Reno only slightly behind schedule. He climbed into the cockpit and turned to the man who had helped repair the plane. "If I win, I'll know I couldn't have done it without your help," he said. "My pleasure," the man replied. "You know I used to fly some in those days, too. I miss it." "I understand," Paul said, "There is nothing like flying. Nothing at all." Paul nodded and the man pulled the propeller, then moved to the edge of the field, where he stood motionless as he watched the biplane accelerate down the field, climb into the sky and turn toward the west.

The mountain ranges between Elko and Reno ran northeast to southwest. The topography allowed Paul to follow some of the depressions between the ranges rather than fly over the tops of each range. The peak elevation of the ranges he did have to cross directly over was between five and six thousand feet, an altitude maintained for only a short period of time before descending into the next valley. Following this pattern of alternating high and low altitude flying avoided any icing on the plane's wings, and the biplane survived this segment of the trip without any problems. Paul's only concern was his fuel supply. The distance from Elko to Reno was greater than most other legs of the journey, and the climbs past the five thousand foot level consumed fuel rapidly. Though he did not expect to run out fuel Paul remained alert for possible emergency landing spots.

It was nearly noon when the biplane approached the edge of Reno. Paul banked the plane and flew around the town in a large circle looking for a landing strip. At about the halfway point of the circle, he spotted a green length of property with a red X at one end. He pulled the throttle back and banked toward the strip. He landed smoothly, taxied to the end of the strip and flipped the magneto switch to "off." He was met by only one person, a woman who turned out to be the local editor's wife. She explained that a town picnic was in process and Paul was to be the guest of honor. Paul expressed his surprise at this development, then explained his priorities. "I'm grateful for the picnic idea, certainly," Paul said, "but this is only supposed to be a quick fuel stop and then I need to leave. Maybe no one told you but I'm in a cross-country race to San Francisco." The woman looked crushed. "Well, I wish I had known. Everyone will be so disappointed." "I'm sorry," Paul said, "but I thought your husband knew." "Oh, he probably did," she said, "in fact that probably explains the business with the gasoline." "Did you say gasoline?" Paul asked. "Yes," the woman replied, "there are barrels of it in that shed right over there. I suppose it's for you." After another apology from Paul and an expression of dismay from the woman, they parted company. The woman walked toward the center of town while Paul searched the shed for a bucket and began transferring fuel to the airplane. When he finished refueling and totaled the number of gallons used, Paul realized he had landed in Reno with less than two gallons of gasoline remaining.

With the plane refueled, Paul opened the fuel valve, partially opened the throttle and set the magneto to start. He used the same risky technique he had used before to start the engine himself. He pulled the propeller and the engine fired off immediately, He skirted the end of the wing and jumped into the cockpit just in time to turn the plane and avoid a collision between a wing tip and the shed from which the fuel had been secured. He pointed the plane straight down the strip, opened the throttle and was soon airborne. He stayed low, banked the plane to the right and buzzed the town, passing directly over the picnic site. He could see the confused look on the faces of the people at the picnic and even spotted the woman who had met him. She looked angry and was pointing her index finger at a man who was apparently on the receiving end of an unpleasant conversation. He presumed it was the editor, and Paul smiled as he wondered what the man would put in his paper about the day the flying contestant visited Reno.

Paul climbed steadily to two thousand feet and pointed the plane toward a compass heading of two hundred and twenty-five degrees. By air, San Francisco was just under two hundred miles away. The route was easy to follow, though it entailed some high elevation flying. Southwest to Truckee, then west over the forest, then directly southwest to San Francisco. The highest point on the route was six thousand feet, but the weather was clear, the humidity was low and the biplane performed as if it knew the end of the journey was near. Paul followed the route with care. This was no time to make a mistake, not this close to the end. If all went well, in three hours he would reach the finish line. He wondered about the other flyers. Were there still nine aircraft heading toward San Francisco? Was anyone closer than he was? What would he do if he came in second? Or third, or worse? The whole thing would only be worth it if he won. No, he was not going to think about that. He would not think about winning or losing, but simply concentrate on flying the plane. The engine droned smoothly on as the biplane left Nevada and crossed into California.

Although the contest was billed as Chicago to San Francisco, the contestants were actually racing toward a small airport in Oakland, on the east side of the bay. Paul had studied the map carefully and memorized the landmarks that would guide him to the finish line in Oakland. As he neared the Bay area he noticed what looked like low clouds ahead. "That's odd," he thought, "it's been clear all day and the sun is out in full force." Before he could think through the possible explanations for the clouds, he was in them. Then he realized he had arrived in Oakland on a foggy day. Fog could be deadly. If Paul continued on he could become disoriented. But if he turned back the delay might cost him the winning position. Without prompting, the words of the man from Rock Springs echoed in his head. "You can go that way without any daredevil flyin'. That is if you're not too stubborn for your own good." Paul debated with himself just a moment, then banked hard left, made a half circle and headed back toward the northeast.

Within a short time, the biplane emerged from the fog. Paul looked at the ground and quickly got his bearings. He was about ten miles northeast of Oakland, headed into the wind. What wind? There hadn't been any wind a short while ago. But now a stiff breeze was blowing toward the ocean, sufficient to slow the biplane so that its ground speed was ten miles per hour less than its airspeed. Paul thought for just a bit. Then he banked left, made another half circle and again headed southwest toward the fog.

By the time the biplane reached Oakland the wind was breaking up the fog and Paul could see the airport where he was to land. He pulled back on the throttle, aimed the plane toward the runway and began his approach. About a hundred yards from the end of the runway, at an altitude of fifty feet, the plane's engine malfunctioned for the second time. It made the same noises, the same vibration, and lost power just as it had in Elko. The nose of the plane dropped. Paul pulled back on the stick and pushed the throttle forward. He just cleared the end of the runway when the wheels touched down. With the engine loudly misfiring, he taxied toward the only building on the site. A crowd of people had gathered near the building. He saw some men in suits, presumably the race officials. Then he saw something he did not want to see. Just past the building, parked beside the runway, was another airplane. Paul recognized it from Chicago. Someone else was already here.

Paul reached forward to shut off the magneto and close the fuel valve, and the engine stopped its crackling noise and the propeller came to a standstill. He let out a deep breath, then slowly climbed out of the cockpit and began to walk toward the waiting crowd. As he did so, he heard the crowd erupt in cheers, whistles, yells, and every conceivable kind of noise. There must have been a thousand people there, come to celebrate the arrival of the first airplane. Now he had landed second and had to listen to the cheers intended for the man who had beat him. Well, he may as well find a place to send a telegram and let Mr. Caswell know. The plane's owner probably wouldn't even keep him as a barnstorming pilot now.

As Paul stood looking toward the building, wondering if he should go inside, one of the men in a suit approached him. The man extended his hand and said, "Congratulations. How does it feel to be the fastest man to fly from Chicago to San Francisco?" Paul was stunned. "But what about the other plane that ..." he began. The man cut him off mid-sentence. "Did you forget? The winner is determined by total time lapsed from Chicago to here. That plane was the first one to leave Chicago, and it's been here less than an hour. You left two and a half hours after he did. So you beat his time by nearly two hours." Paul just stared at the man. "Oh," the man continued, "I need to give you this." He handed Paul an envelope marked "Paul Bowman. Open only if you win." He didn't understand. He just stood there, envelope in hand. The man in the suit said, "Well, go on, open it."

Paul shook himself as if to clear his head. He opened the envelope. Inside was a handwritten note, on stationery bearing the imprint of The Independence Weekly. It read:

> *Paul, Congratulations! I did not tell you this in Chicago because I did not want you to take any unnecessary chances. The $10,000 will be divided as follows - $500 to each of the four men who helped us get ready,*

two mechanics, the meteorologist, and the surveyor. $1000 to ship the plane and you home, and repair the wear and tear you probably put her through. That leaves $7000, of which I'm going to keep $2000 for having the idea and putting up the money. The remaining $5000 is yours. Buy yourself an airplane, so you won't have to cool your heels at the Omaha Hotel waiting for me. All the best! (signed) Rudy Caswell.

Paul was overwhelmed. He wanted to sit down. He wanted to laugh. He wanted to cry. Instead, he turned to the crowd, which had grown silent and was waiting to hear from the new aviation hero. "Folks," he said, "Thanks for being here to welcome me. I appreciate it a lot. I really do. But I'm not much of a speech giver. I guess there is only one thing I want to say. And that is .... There really is nothing like flying. Nothing at all."

20 THE ADVENTURER

Two men sat facing each other on the front porch of the Eldridge House. Both appeared to be in their mid to late seventies. One had a head of wavy white hair some would say needed trimming, which flowed down the nape of his neck and touched his collar. He was of average height and rather rotund, with a ruddy complexion. He had not shaved for several days but was otherwise reasonably well-groomed. The other man, taller and thinner than his companion, was nearly bald. A thin remnant of gray hair circled his head just above his ears. His face bore deep wrinkles, with prominent crow's feet beside his squinty eyes. His natural expression made him appear worried. Neither man's clothing suggested wealth or professional appearance. Both wore eyeglasses. A half-smoked, unlit cigar was clamped in the white-haired man's teeth, while a cigarette hung from the lips of the bald man.

Between the two men sat a small oak table holding two coffee cups, an ashtray, and a checkerboard the two men used to carry out a daily ritual of competition. Fortunately, the two were evenly matched in checker playing ability, as an unbal-

anced record of wins and losses might have injured their friendship. As residents of one of Kansas City's older hotels, the duo
exhibited their genial rivalry in a public setting on a daily basis
and had done so for years. Weather permitting, they played on
the porch; otherwise they faced each other in the hotel lobby.
The constancy of the pair's checker games engendered an expectation on the part of the other residents and regular guests
of the hotel. On the few afternoons the two happened not to engage in their daily battle of wits, the other residents and guests
of the hotel felt as though something was seriously amiss.

"Your move," said the white-haired man. "I know," the
bald man replied, but he did not reach toward the checkerboard.
"Might as well take yer lickin'," the white-haired man said. The
bald man slowly leaned forward, picked up a red checker and
moved it forward. The white-haired man smiled, then reached
toward the board. He picked up a black checker, carried it
across a red checker and placed it on a square at the far end of
the board. "Gimme a king," said the white-haired man. The bald
man picked up a black checker from beside the board. He was
about to place it on top of the other man's piece when he noticed two people approaching the hotel. A woman who appeared to be in her thirties ascended the steps, followed by a
young boy. The woman paused just outside the door, near the
two men. "Now you wait here while I go inside," the woman told
the boy. "I might be a while."

The boy, left on the porch near the two checker players,
turned toward them and smiled. The white-haired man nodded
toward the boy and said, "Yer welcome to sit and watch if you
like." The man gestured toward an empty chair. The boy slid the
chair next to the table and sat down. "Thank you, sir," he said.
The white-haired man extended a hand to the boy and said
simply, "Samuel Anders." They shook hands, the boy's small
fingers enveloped in the man's fleshy palms. The boy turned

and looked quizzically at the thin bald man. The man nodded but did not offer his hand. "Hannigan," he said. "Garrett Hannigan. And yours?" "My mother told me not to tell my name to strangers," he replied.

Garrett Hannigan muttered, "Mmm hmmm," and returned to his game. He placed the black checker on top of the piece the other man had moved to the end of the board. "There's your king," he said. Then, to his opponent's astonishment, he picked up a red checker and quickly jumped over two black checkers, removing them from the board. The red checker was now on the end row nearest Samuel Anders. "And a king, if you don't mind," said Hannigan. Anders sputtered, "Dang, I didn't see that comin'!" He picked up a red checker from beside the board and placed it atop the other man's piece.

"Don't go gittin' proud now, the game ain't over yet," Anders said. Hannigan chuckled slightly. "No, mebbe not," he said, "but yer in trouble fer sure." Anders studied the board. The boy leaned forward as if to help the man analyze the situation. Samuel Anders turned toward the boy. "I been in a lot worse fixes than this, son," he said, " and I'm not talkin' about checkers, nether." The other man looked over the top of his eyeglasses and pursed his lips. "Now don't let's go down that trail again," he said. The boy frowned slightly and asked, "What trail?" Anders replied, "Well, it could be one of many trails. I rode lots of 'em in my time on the frontier." Hannigan exhaled loudly, shook his head from side to side, and said, "Once again, I'm ahead but I gotta feelin' this game ain't gonna be finished."

The boy's imagination had been captured by Anders' remark about the frontier. "Did you really ride a trail?" he asked. "Lots of 'em," said Anders. "Wanna hear about it?" "Oh, yes sir!" the boy said, grinning widely. "Well, son," said Anders with a smile, "you just pull your chair over beside mine and I'll tell you all about it." The boy stood up, moved his chair and sat down. Hannigan stood and said, "Guess I'll put this away." He reached under the table and brought up a box, gathered the checkers, folded the board and put everything in the box. Then he picked up the box, winked at the boy and walked into the hotel.

"What's it really like out west?" the boy asked. "Well," said Anders, "it depends. I been a lotta places and they ain't all the same." The boy looked up at the man as if sitting at the feet of a guru. "What's the most exciting place you've been, and the most exciting thing you've done?" he asked. Anders reached into his pocket and extracted a wooden match. He struck it on the tabletop and held it to his cigar. The tobacco responded and the man took a deep draw and slowly exhaled, blowing a ring of smoke toward the edge of the porch. "I'd have to say that mebbe the most dangerous, if that's what you mean by excitin', was Dodge City. That's in Kansas." The boy grinned again. "I know," he said, "everybody's heard of Dodge City. What did you do there?"

Samuel Anders leaned back in his chair and looked out across the street as if he could see something far away. "Darn near lost my life, for one thing, " he said. The boy was impressed. "How did you do that?" he asked. "Well, it was like this," said the man, launching into what was to become more than a brief anecdote. Anders began to describe a series of events that originated with his desire to experience the "real" West. He had joined a wagon train headed for California via the Sante Fe Trail, hoping to seek his fortune there. Most wagon trains took the relatively safe Mountain Route even though it was lengthy and required traversing mountains. "But we didn't take that route," Anders told the boy. "Oh no, we was in a hurry, so we took the Cimarron Cutoff. Went across the dry sandhills and through territory with them Injuns still runnin' around all over. We was south of Dodge when we was attacked by 'em. All was killed 'cept me and two others."

The boy's mouth was agape as his mind conjured up a mental image of hundreds of Indians riding around a group of circled wagons, whooping and yelling blood-curdling war cries. "What happened then?" he asked. Anders described in detail how he and his companions had escaped to the banks of the Cimarron River. "We broke off some reeds growin' near the shore, jumped into the river, and breathin' through the reeds floated downstream underwater," he recounted. Undetected by the pursuing Indians after an hour or more in the river, they swam ashore and hid in a grove of trees. There the three survivors remained two days and nights with nothing to eat and without a fire until they were certain the Indians had given up looking for them.

"Did you get to California then?" the boy asked. "Nope, we sure didn't," the storyteller replied. He explained that without provisions or means of transportation going on to California was impossible. "We had to turn tail back toward Dodge City," he explained, "bein' careful to avoid contact with them Injuns." The little group traveled at night and hid in the brush of creek beds or the hollows of sandhills during the day. They drank and filled their canteens from the few streams that crossed the area, and picked berries from sparse bushes that grew near the water. Although they were armed they dared not fire their weapons, so hunting was out of the question. "If them savages heard a gunshot," Anders said, "they'd a knowed where we was hidin' and we'd a been goners fer sure." Four days later they stumbled upon a sod house near Dodge City, where they were taken in and fed. "If it hadn't been for one of them other feller's sense a direction," Anders said, "I wouldn't be here to tell ya."

The man continued his story. He remained in Dodge City, which became a boomtown when a rail line was laid through the area. The town was filled with railroad workers, soldiers, buffalo hunters, and drifters. "They weren't 'xactly genteel folk," said Anders. "And there weren't no law in them days, neither. Fellers shot each other and the dead was hauled up to Boot Hill. That's just how it was." Anders told the boy about his encounters with ruffians in the town, as well as some of the well-known characters with whom he became acquainted. "Clay Allison, Big Nose Kate, Doc Holliday, Wyatt Earp, I knew 'em all," the man said. This statement heartily impressed the boy, who had apparently heard of some the individuals. "In fact," the man continued, "Doc and me was together in a gunfight one time." The boy was wide-eyed. "Really?" he asked. "Yep," said the man, "I'll tell ya about that too."

According to Anders, he had become acquainted with Doc Holliday at a saloon both men frequented. One evening the two men were both playing poker, but at separate tables, when a disgruntled loser accused Holliday of cheating. Tempers flared and guns were drawn but the other man was fast and got the drop on Holliday. Anders intruded, and by a skillful application of reason and an offer of whiskey convinced the other gambler to rescind his accusation. "Naturally, Doc Holliday was powerful grateful," Anders explained, "and that's how we become friends." According to Anders the two men frequently played cards and drank together. And when Holliday accepted a position in law enforcement the duo often patrolled the town together.

It was during one of the occasions when Doc Holliday and Anders were making their rounds in Dodge City that they ended up in a gunfight. A shipment of buffalo hides had recently left town by train, and the buffalo hunters were flush with cash from the sale of the hides. As they were prone to do, the hunters spent freely on whiskey. Late in the evening four of the cele-brants became excessively rowdy, even by Dodge City stand-ards. The saloonkeeper sent a messenger to summon Doc Holliday, who immediately asked Anders to come along. "Doc said to grab my gun and come a runnin'," Anders told his listen-er, "so I did." As the two approached the saloon one of the hunters recognized Holliday from a previous altercation. The hunters exited the saloon by a rear door, came around the side of the building and began firing on Holliday and his companion. "Wow," the boy said, "did you get shot?"

Samuel Anders smiled at the boy. "No, son, I didn't," he said. "If I'd a got hit by a slug from one of them buffalo rifles them fellas might have shipped my hide out along with the buf-falo." He went on to share in detail the lightning-fast shooting of Doc Holliday and his own lucky shot that disabled one of the hunters. Although Holliday had killed one of the hunters and wounded two others, he credited Anders' wounding of the fourth man as having saved him from possible death. After that, An-ders said, "We was tied to each other as if we was brothers."

"Tell me more," said the boy. "Tell me about the buffalo." Anders obliged the boy. He related the story of the bison, be-ginning with the massive herds that roamed the prairies before the arrival of the railroad and the buffalo hunters. At the time Anders resided there, Dodge City was the major terminus for shipment of hides and meat provided by the buffalo hunters. He described sights he had seen during the heyday of the hunts, including piles of hides numbering in the thousands and mounds of buffalo bones over thirty feet high and hundreds of yards long, awaiting shipment by rail. And he recounted how he apprenticed himself to one of the top buffalo hunters in order to develop his own expertise. "So you shot them too?" asked the boy. "By the hundreds, son," the man replied, "by the hundreds." "Then what?" the boy asked.

"Well, eventually them hunters killed so many buffalo there weren't none left to hunt," the man explained. "But right after that them big cattle drives comin' up out of Texas come to Dodge and them cowboys was jest about as ornery as them buffalo hunters." Anders told the boy about the herds of long-horn cattle roaming wild in Texas after the Civil War and the long drives that brought the beeves to railroad towns for shipment east. Initially, the drives went into Missouri, but fear of disease carried by the longhorns led the locals to outlaw drives to that state so the cowmen headed west. Dodge City became the leading destination for the cattle drives, just as it had been for buffalo shipments.

"Did you get to see the big herds of cattle, too?" the boy asked. "More than that, son," he replied. "I worked one of the biggest drives there ever was." The boy's attention did not waver. Anders continued, "Me and a pal of mine, feller named Tex, we joined up with a crew that drove a herd of three thousand longhorns from south Texas to Dodge. We was on the trail for four weeks. Worked day and night. Stampedes, lightning storms, Injun raids, bakin hot days and freezin' cold nights. We seen it all." The man went on to describe the daily routine of the cowhand, including the long hours of hot, dusty work herding the cattle. He talked about the ease with which a herd would spook, setting off a dangerous stampede. And he told the boy about the celebrating the men did when they reached Dodge City and were paid for the drive.

"Somethin' funny happened when we hit Dodge," Anders said. "We was all full of trail dirt and thirst, so when we was paid we all headed to the saloon. Well, me and the other boys got to drinkin' and I guess I kinda took the lead, 'cause it weren't long and I took a notion to do a little target practice inside the saloon." "You mean you shot your gun inside the saloon?" the boy asked incredulously. "Sure did," said the man, "and it didn't take long 'fore somebody sent for the law. So in a bit I hears this feller at the door of the saloon and he's tellin' me to put my gun down or he's gonna plug me. Well, I looks up and if it ain't my old buddy Doc Holliday!" The boy grasped the fortunate irony of the situation. "So the two of us goes to drinkin' together right there in the saloon, and the saloonkeeper he's so mad he could spit." Anders let out a long burst of laughter, and the boy joined in.

Meanwhile, the boy's mother concluded her business in the hotel. As she walked toward the main door she was approached by the bald man she had seen on the porch earlier. "Pardon me, ma'am," Garrett Hannigan said, "may I have just a word?" He motioned for her to step away from the door, far enough inside so the two people on the porch would not overhear. "That's my good friend out there with your son," he said. "Yes," the woman replied, a look of distrust on her face. "He's a fine feller," Hannigan said, "means well and all. It's jest that, well, he sometimes tells young'uns stories that ain't 'xactly true through and through." "I see," said the woman, "and do you think he's been telling such stories to my son?" "Most likely," Hannigan replied, "jest to keep him entertained a while." Hannigan looked embarrassed. "The thing is, ma'am," he continued, "if yer son tells you some wild tales about the frontier, or Indjuns, or gunfights or the like, jest sort of ignore 'em if you will." The woman looked directly at Hannigan. "So," she said, "you're saying your friend hasn't really had much experience with Indians, or gunfighters, or the like?" The man peered at her over the top of his eyeglasses. "Ma'am," he said, "he ain't never been west of the Missouri River."

<u>**To the Reader**</u>

Thank you for choosing to read these stories. I trust they have deepened your appreciation for the trials and triumphs of the common but uncommon people who carved out of the often desolate and inhospitable American West a place of opportunity and hope.

Mark Huenemann